The Moon Lake Legend

L.J. RUSSELL

PAGE PUBLISHING, INC.
Conneaut Lake, PA

First originally published by Page Publishing 2020

ISBN 978-1-64701-194-9 (pbk)
ISBN 978-1-64701-195-6 (digital)

Printed in the United States of America

To Nancy and Larry Russell
The greatest parents

PART 1

The Resort

1

May 10

There were a few limbs down across the front lawn that had areas of long green grass that needed serious mowing. The lake spread before him like a calm blue mirror with two loons slowly patrolling the water, occasionally speaking their mournful tones. The hills that surrounded the scene were really beginning to green up after the long cold winter that had seemed especially harsh that year. The gray skeletal limbs were disappearing behind their verdant summer coats. The entire vista sent an exhilarating warmth through him that matched the almost summerlike temperature that had descended on the Adirondacks. The change of the seasons truly felt like a rebirth, and he felt a sense of contentment that was palpable.

Thomas soaked in the beauty and breathed out a deep sigh. This place, the lake and the hills, was the place that he had called home for the past thirty-five summers with only two exceptions. That thought was astounding and somewhat depressing in an unexpected way. Although at that moment he couldn't think of anywhere else he would rather be, there were moments when he wondered where his life had slipped off to. Yeah, it had been thirty-five years earlier when he had only been a twenty-five-year-old, recently divorced bum who was offered a job by a friendly lakeside resort owner. The employment had saved his lost skin back then, but unintended, he had become tied to the lake and the summers by the water. That also meant that his life never expanded much beyond the central mountains. The million dollars that he had boasted about making to his teachers in high school never really materialized. In fact, that was a stupid dream of youth, which now seemed as distant as the Andromeda Galaxy that appeared as a bright speck in the night sky over the lake. His lake. Moon Lake.

"Crud," Thomas muttered as he bent over to pick up a rock from the grass that had somehow gotten lost. His knee popped, and there was no pain, which was a good sign. With a grunt, he let the stone fly toward the water and was pleased to see how far it traveled before landing close to where the dock would be once they got it into the water. Getting the dock in was a true sign that summer had arrived. Ripples spread out from the spot where the rock made contact with the water, and he was amazed by just how calm it was. Not a puff of wind spoiled the calm surface nor moved any air. It was actually getting hot in the sun, and he wanted to take off his long-sleeved thermal shirt that had been a daily part of his wardrobe since October. Thomas had thin gray hair and looked a little like a scarecrow because he was very bony. He felt healthy, and the mountain air only made him feel better. He decided to leave the shirt on. Spring came slowly to the Adirondacks, but when it showed up, it was magnificent. That was if you could avoid the black flies and mosquitoes.

That made him think of the screening on all the open areas of every building—porches, windows. They all needed to be checked for repair. He turned and looked back toward the lodge, which was the hub of the resort. During a visit to the property, when the snow had mostly melted, he had noticed that a screen on the main porch of the lodge had ripped as well as one on cottage 9. Those were just two of hundreds of jobs he would have to do to get the place in shape for opening day, which was luckily still a ways off. It was only mid-May.

Thomas walked across the leaf- and stick-strewn lawn toward the main building. The lodge was a classic Adirondack lodge, made of wood with a beautiful wraparound porch taking up two sides of the building. Inside were the offices, restaurant, and bar as well as four guest rooms. The main atrium was pleasant with couches and a large stone fireplace that was usually blazing in the early and late part of the season. He remembered the times he had spent in that building. He always thought that he should write a book about it, but who would want to hear his incoherent ramblings, anyway? In the woods to either side of the lodge were a good number of cabins, which housed the guests, and a large one for employees. The resort was fairly isolated, and the day staff was minimal. Generally, locals from the immediate area only made up a small percentage of the workforce. Mr. Riley had liked it that way. He wanted his employees to stay on the premises. It *promoted a family atmosphere*. Thomas chuckled at the memory of his boss. There had been an atmosphere, all right. Family? Well, some families had gotten too close to the employees but it had all been plenty of fun. He sighed and turned back toward the water, and he wondered. He wondered if it would ever be the same again.

One autumn night many decades before, Thomas and a couple of his buddies had somehow found their way to the Camp Wildwood Resort after a day of drinking and driving around aimlessly. They had been to at least a dozen bars before his old friend, Beezer, had suggested dropping by the bar at some camp he had been to with his family years before when he was only a kid. Somehow they had made their way through the roads, which were tightly crowded by the forests on either side. Thomas barely remembered passing the big wooden sign that bore the resort's name as they pulled up to the lodge with the September afternoon losing sunlight. The booze left him feeling no pain, even though he had just been served the divorce papers that would sever his marriage to Courtney. Thomas had not wanted the proceedings to go down, but in retrospect, he didn't blame her. He had been the exact opposite of a good husband. Sometimes you got what you deserved. The trio had made their way to the bar where only two other people were imbibing. They took the place over and laughed and drank and probably made fools of themselves. That was when Colin Riley walked in and sat down for a Manhattan. He always had a Manhattan. Before Thomas knew it, he was pouring out his story to the man. Jobs were hard to find. He had skipped from employment to unemployment and back many times until Courtney finally took off; now what his sorry ass going to do? Unbelievably, he actually broke down a little, for the first time truly understanding the pointlessness of his life. He was twenty-five years old and going backward in the great game of life.

"Call me late this winter. Maybe I can find you some work here next summer." Mr. Riley tossed back the remnants of his Manhattan and handed him a card with his phone number. Most times, Thomas would have tossed the card or simply forgotten the entire conversation when the next morning rolled around, but this time, for some reason, he held on to the card tightly. In February, after losing a job at a sketchy diner on Route 8, he called Mr. Riley and was given hope, which he greedily seized. Now Colin was gone, and that wasn't easy.

He was sitting on the steps that led from the patio by the lawn up to the front porch of the lodge. Although he still sat in the sun, the day had turned colder, and he shivered. Colin was gone, there was no doubt about it. The knowledge that he would not return to the resort was devastating. Meredith had called him the day after Halloween with the news. The information had hit him in the stomach like a Mike Tyson jab. Thomas had put down his phone and cried. He hadn't even done that when his mother passed, but in reality, Colin was more important to him than his mother had been. Meredith had said it had been suicide. That was shocking information, but Thomas didn't want to press the poor girl, having no idea what personal pain she must be in.

Suicide. Colin had only been back home down in Fort Lauderdale a couple weeks when he took his life. Thomas had just wished him a good winter, and they promised to see each other the next spring. He had watched Colin get into his Toyota and leave the resort for a long drive to South Florida. That had been only days earlier. Thomas was still having a hard time coming to grips with the whole situation. Decades earlier, Colin had been good to his word and given him a job washing dishes and working on the grounds crew. That first summer had stretched into consecutive seasons, and with this longevity came trust and the assignment as head of grounds. But perhaps the best part of the deal was the friendship he made with Colin. That had happened easily and became as important to him as any relationship that he had ever had. Thomas wasn't sure how he would handle the summer without him. It would be hard, especially with the question that nagged at his brain: why had he done it?

"Crud," he muttered again. He guessed he should be happy that there was going to be a summer at all. When Colin died, he was sure that the resort wouldn't open that summer or that the property would be sold off to some morons from Boston who would turn it into a massage spa complete with a wine bar. When Meredith called him and explained that she wished to continue on with Camp Wildwood, he was surprised, happy, and skeptical all at once. How could the resort be run without Colin?

He sighed and looked out at the water with the hills rising from around it. The place held him, and inertia kept him grounded right there at the resort. This was home, and he couldn't leave it. Therefore, life carried on, with or without his friend. With a groan, he lifted himself up and began the chore of cataloging what needed to be done. He would be busy getting the place ready for the summer.

2

May15

The music coming through the speakers of her car filled the space around her and yet went unheard no matter how loud it was being played. A Weezer album was playing from her iPod, but her mind was elsewhere, barely focusing on the road in front of her. In fact, she drove forward without much recollection of where she was. It came as a surprise when Lake George appeared, and she hardly remembered anything from when she drove past Albany. Her thoughts were raging through her head, totally out of control, and there was no way to stop it. Meredith was being haunted by memories and tormented by the uncertainty of the future. Only a few months previous, she would not have expected to be in this situation.

The mountains were obscured by low clouds, and a light drizzle fell from the sky, completing her gray emotional mood. Although they were wet, the roads were not slick, but she took her time, anyway. There was no huge hurry. As the green trees and occasional large boulder drifted past, her mind wandered, but she kept on driving. When she heard the shocking news of her father's death, she had been working at a bookshop near the campus of the University of North Carolina in Chapel Hill. It was a long-term temporary job while she tried to finish her master's degree in education, which had moved quietly to the slow lane. Her original enthusiasm for teaching had been sidetracked by the sudden anti-teacher feelings sweeping the country. Although teaching was fun, she wasn't sure if it was worth the enormous negative pressure being pushed on educators for such a small amount of income. How was a person supposed to teach a kid to read when their lives outside of school revolved around the Internet, video games, and marijuana? It was a losing equation. Working in a bookshop was a much mellower way to exist, especially since Michael had the completion of law school in sight.

Michael. That was just one more card thrown into the pile of issues racing through her mind. They had met one summer on the Outer Banks when Meredith was vacationing with some college friends while she worked at a prep school outside Baltimore. They had quickly become friends with some serious physical attraction that had led to increased contact and her decision to attend UNC to get her graduate degree. Of course, it was also to be near him. Things had been fun at first, but the thrill had slowly begun to bog down, and she began to question her decision to throw her eggs into the Michael basket. He had been a trooper when her dad passed away, standing by her every step of the way, but she couldn't help but get the vibe that he was doing this because he had to and not because he wanted to. That thought had added to her questioning the whole scenario that Chapel Hill offered.

One of the hardest things she had to do was to deal with her father's estate. The complexity and pain of the legal passing of her father's possessions had been very difficult. Michael came in handy when she needed a lawyer to deal with the proceedings, but he wasn't so great when it came to emotional support. The flare-up had occurred when the conversation turned to what to do with her father's holdings.

"The house in Florida?" she had asked aloud.

She had a clear memory of Michael reading the news on his laptop, probably the Fox News webpage. "I think it would be prudent to put that property on the market. It would be superb to have a retreat to go to in South Florida, but the land isn't really on the beach, you know?"

It wasn't.

"Camp Wildwood?" That was the real issue because it was a large piece of property with a resort on it. The value was high, but it had to be managed, which had been her father's job for most of his adult life. And it had been her summer home for many of her formative years.

"Sell," Michael said without looking away from the screen. "That would most likely garner a respectable price, and we would not have to be bothered with running the lodging. The overhead on that place must be brutal."

His brusque manner had surprised her and immediately made her defensive.

"But you've never even been there. Every time I go north, you have an excuse here at school or you just head for Kill Devil Hills."

Michael momentarily looked up from his laptop, and the look of condescension drilled her like a knife. "It's in the forest. I mean, come on. The Outer Banks rule, hon."

It had been the next day when she met with her lawyer to try and hammer out some of the outstanding issues of the estate, and when Camp Wildwood was brought up, Meredith surprised even herself when she said that she would keep it. Her lawyer gave her an interested look, and Meredith clarified that she would maintain the property for the interim and perhaps sell it later. That seemed logical, and her plan for the summer was already coming into focus. Leaving Michael might be good for both them.

For the first time in two years, she was out on her own without Michael, and the experience filled her with conflicting feelings. But that was nothing compared to the way she felt as her SUV moved closer to Wildwood.

The last time she had seen her father alive was at Camp Wildwood the autumn before, only a few weeks before he died. UNC had been on a long weekend break, and she had flown up to Albany and driven the rest of the way in a rental. It was early October and the leaves were already just past peak, but it was still astonishingly beautiful. The air was cool, but the sky was a deep blue for the two days she was there. There were still guests in the cottages, and the atmosphere was joyful yet somewhat sad at the end of the season. Her father had been happy, and that was what she tried to hold in her head ever since the day she heard the devastating news. She was going back to that place again, and the thought scared her to the core. With every rotation of her tires, her anxiety grew, and the chances to turn around and run back to Chapel Hill dissolved. She would be strong. This had to be done.

The low clouds did not magically part like in some sappy movie as she approached Wildwood. They hung tight like a dull gray blanket overhead that leaked small droplets of water. The nearest town to Wildwood was named Mayson, and there wasn't much to it. There was a gas station that sold extremely high-priced gasoline and had some cans of baked beans and Spam on the dusty shelves. She had been in the place the fall before and was shocked to see that they still had a wall where they rented VHS movies. Who still had VHS machines? Next to it was a building that apparently was a diner, but she knew that it also contained a bar. That was scary. There were a series of small homes ranging from relatively well kept to completely dilapidated. Some of the day workers at Wildwood came from Mayson, and that meant that the workforce from this crossroads was small and pretty scary. She thought of what Michael would think of Mayson and smiled for the first time in hours.

After having the forest open up a little as she drove through Mayson, the trees crowded the road again, and the scene was dark for that time of day. She drove the car through winding roads that were at times so narrow that she worried about cars coming up the other lane, although none ever did. If the day was clear, she knew that through gaps in the trees, she would have views of the mountains rolling off to the north with occasional glimpses of Mount Marcy, Whiteface, and Algonquin. It was beautiful but not on that day. Although many of the visual markers were obscured, Meredith still knew exactly where she was and could feel the senses homing in on her old summer home. Her stomach began to tingle with excitement and fear as she made the last couple of turns before she saw the sign set up in the trees. It didn't light up, and no neon blazed in brazen letters. Simple. Like the Adirondacks.

Camp Wildwood
An Adirondack Tradition

Her SUV was stopped in the middle of the road as she stared at the sign. It was simple natural wood backing with bright yellow and green lettering: "An Adirondack Tradition." That tradition was now hers to carry on. The thought of her father suddenly fell on her like an anvil, and she burst out weeping with her head on the steering wheel. The sobs racked from her chest, and there was no control over it. The emotions had to be released, and she let them go. Luckily, she was on a road in the middle of nowhere, and no cars approached. Slowly, she pulled herself together and turned into the sandy drive that led toward the lake. Meredith looked in the rearview mirror and saw her face. Instead of her fair, pretty face bordered by auburn hair with blue eyes, the image that gawked back looked tired and frazzled. She *was* tired, and the huge cry had only made matters worse. It was okay. No one would be at Wildwood except for good old Thomas and maybe Olga. They would understand and make her feel at home. She drove to the camp.

The lake was a gray mass bounded by deep green trees before they, too, became an indistinct gray farther up the slopes of the hills. The scene was not the sun-splashed homecoming she had dreamed of, but as she pulled her SUV into the gravel parking lot next to the lodge, a familiarity spread through her, and memories from her childhood swept her mental video screen. She had truly made it back, and it felt as if a weight had temporarily lifted from her. The decision to manage the resort this summer had not been simple or forthright. Michael had certainly been of little value as he argued tenaciously for her to abandon the idea and stay in North Carolina. Every time she convinced herself to go ahead with the plan, Michael would shoot it down. Meredith had spent many sleepless nights, many visited by her father in a dream state, and she would wake up even more confused and unclear. It had been a phone conversation with her father's sister, Aunt Helen, that had been the clincher.

"Your father totally loved that place on the water," Helen had said. "It became his life."

His love. His life. Meredith had considered the buildings in the mountains sitting abandoned over the summer, or perhaps worse, owned and run by someone who didn't share her father's love of the property. That night after the talk with her aunt, she had slept well without any crazy dreams. That was the moment of no return.

The car engine was still running as she sat looking at the side of the lodge with the windshield wipers intermittently swiping away the drizzle that formed droplets on the glass. That moment back in December seemed to reach back toward her from a different life. What had she been thinking about? A feeling of being overwhelmed threatened to send her crashing into a paralysis of her strength that might send her right back down the road toward Carolina. She thought of her father wanting her to carry on. Her head shook vigorously, and she gained a piece of determination, at least enough to shut off the engine and step from the car.

Cool air hit her. Two mornings earlier, she had left a humid, eighty-five-degree Southern morning. The air-conditioning had been ripping in her car, and this air was much cooler than that. She reached behind her driver's seat and grabbed a UNC sweatshirt that she had put there in case it was indeed cool in the mountains. Good call.

The gravel crunched underfoot as she made her way toward the front lawn that sloped down to the water. There was a poured concrete patio at the base of the stairs to the lodge that her father had put in ten years ago. It was a perfect place to sit and enjoy the sun or an evening cocktail. Patio furniture would be placed around the area, and in the evening, tiki torches blazed, burning citronella, to keep the bugs at bay. No furniture had been placed out yet and no tiki torches had been set up. Instead, the concrete was wet and seemed to radiate a coldness through the soles of her sneakers. Where was summer?

She heard a noise from the screened-in porch behind her, and she quickly turned. Standing in the doorway, holding the screen door open, was Thomas. He was wearing a plaid work shirt with the sleeves rolled up to expose the white thermal shirt that he always wore in cool weather. His hair was as gray as ever and even more wild.

Although she had seen him in October, he seemed to have visibly aged over the winter, although he still carried with him some hint of youthful energy. A smile was spread across his face.

"I was wondering what was keeping you," the man said.

"Long drive," she answered, matching his smile with her own. There was Thomas, a man who had been like an uncle to her. A few years older than her dad, Thomas had always watched out for little Meredith as she spent the summers running around the resort. He had become one of her father's closest friends. The memory of calling him last November to tell him the grim news struck her, and a tear welled in her eye. She opened her arms and headed for the steps, but he was already coming down to meet her with his arms wide open. They met and hugged, and she gave in to the tears. After a long moment, Thomas gently pushed her away and took a look at her.

"Just as beautiful as ever."

"Right," she responded. "I just drove nearly a thousand miles and I decided to cry every hundred miles or so. I must really look lovely."

Thomas laughed. "You must be tired, girl. Why don't we get inside out of this rain? Miserable weather for sure."

Meredith followed Thomas up the steps into the screened-in porch. It hadn't changed from October except that the furniture had yet to be placed out for the summer. They walked into the lodge where it was brightly lit against the gloomy day outside. Meredith could immediately smell a pungent odor that assaulted her nostrils but not in a negative way. She instantly placed the smell.

"Varnish?"

Thomas stopped and smiled. "I've been workin' on the main staircase, trying to refurbish it while the weather outside has been rough."

Meredith actually took a half step backward to take in the room, which held such a strong part of her memories of the resort. The main room was large with a high ceiling that went all the way up to the second floor. The staircase that Thomas had been working on was against the far wall and was an open ascension to the floor above. All the wood was the natural color of medium brown. Sofas, chairs, and tables were spread around the room. To the left was the main desk, and to the right was the true eye-catcher in the room—the huge stone fireplace that rose all the way to the ceiling and through to the outside. It was beautiful, and she knew at that moment that she had made the right decision to come north.

"Your father and I discussed doin' the staircase last fall, so I figured I would go ahead and do it."

"Good idea," she said. "It will look great."

"I'm also doin' as you said—maintaining the same schedule as I normally would. We're on schedule, although the weather has been cruddy."

Meredith smiled and looked around the room while considering what needed to get done before the guests arrived. Wow.

"Olga is here, and I'm sure she'll like to see you. I can go get your bags and you can look around."

"No, Thomas. I can manage my own bags. You finish up your chores, and we can go into the bar for a drink and maybe some food before I go to bed. A rum and Coke will probably put me in a coma!"

"I can help you."

"Nope," she commanded. "I'm the boss now."

"Crud," Thomas muttered and smiled. "Okay, boss. See you in a few."

Meredith smiled and walked back out into the drizzle, feeling secure and at home. Maybe it would all work out.

3

May 30

Josh drove through the mountains to an unknown destiny, and that wasn't making him happy. In fact, he was downright pissed off. This was not the way he was supposed to be spending one of the summers of his precious college years. And the reason for his exile to the mountains was so stupid and unfair. The judge hadn't even placed this sentence on him. It had been his own father, and that had hurt most of all. His dad had always been his number one fan, following him wherever and whatever he did. It was a betrayal and it was incredibly upsetting.

The road wound through woods that seemed to lead right smack-dab into the middle of nowhere. Every time Josh drove his truck around a bend in the endlessly curvy road, he hoped to see something. A large grassy field. A hotel. A freaking McDonald's. But there was nothing but more woods, and he began to wonder just where the hell his father was sending him. Nova Scotia? And what was he expecting to find when he got there? A summer camp? A grizzly bear? This was not right and bordered on cruel and unusual punishment.

The sun played through the leaves of the trees that bordered the road, casting bright spots on the macadam. Even though it was beautiful, he mentally scolded himself for taking any pleasure in the trip. This was supposed to be painful. Maybe if he hated the experience enough, his father might renege and allow him to return home. That was his hope, although he knew from his father's temperament that his chances for a reprieve were slim and none.

Josh Martin had been some kind of athletic wunderkind since he was very young. Always bigger than the other kids with solid athletic ability, he had been a natural at sports and had a decent enough head on his shoulders to receive above-average grades. Throw in his light brown hair and chiseled good looks and he was a leading figure in his high school. Of course, his father hadn't cared a bit about his grades or other school activities but only that he played varsity football as a freshman. He honestly wondered if his father would have even been concerned if he was scraping by with a sixty-five average as long as he could still play ball. Josh knew that his father's attitude was bullshit and against everything a good parent should do in an attempt to raise a functional child. But Josh honestly didn't care. Why would he when he got everything he ever asked for and his father often turned the other way when Josh did questionable things? Unfortunately, those questionable things seemed to be piling up.

His mother was gone, and sometimes he wondered what would have happened if she had been around to raise him. The circumstances of her downfall had never been articulated to him in any informative way. When he asked, he received vague answers that left more questions. All he really knew was that his mother had had a mental breakdown when he was very young and that *she had gone away for her own good*. Josh's parents had taken a vacation for a weekend, and when they had returned, his mother had slipped off the sanity wagon and had landed hard. Her parents had stepped in and whisked their daughter off to somewhere in New Mexico. Josh had heard the rumor that his maternal grandparents had never approved of their daughter marrying his father. Twice a year, he received a phone call from his mother and gifts at Christmas and his birthday. In all reality, she didn't exist to him.

Mr. Martin, known to some as David and simply Dad to Josh, was a rich man, and people didn't mess with him. By all accounts, Dave was extremely intelligent and had parlayed his abilities into the real estate market after he graduated from Quinnipiac College. Josh's father quickly became a mover. His first ventures were in simple housing developments, but he rapidly expanded into strip malls. The money poured in, and by the time he met Josh's mom, David Martin was worth a pretty penny. His parents were together for exactly four years, and in that brief time, Josh had arrived.

The fact was, Josh had been raised by his father's money. When he was young, David was often too busy to spend time with his son. As he accrued more wealth, he fell into all the trappings, which included chasing young women around and dabbling in drugs. There was always a nanny who was hired to look after young Josh. As a kid, Josh didn't mind, as he had a pretty cool nanny named Mazy, who became a surrogate mother to him. Then he grew up, and his focus changed from having fun after school in his neighborhood to sports and girls and all the hijinks that came along with being the big man on campus. By the time he was in the seventh grade, he had lost his virginity to a ninth-grade girl who professed love for him but in reality was more interested in hanging out in his father's house, especially the pool. One day not much later, he had been walking from the middle school to the locker room for football practice and had seen the girl sucking face with another guy. The image had been shocking, and even more appalling had been the girl's denial of the entire event. Wow. How could a person lie so blatantly? Josh had been devastated as only a thirteen-year-old kid can be when he felt his first love and the inevitable broken heart. The event would have an impact on him in ways that he never fathomed but was brought out by a court-ordered psychologist. The psychologist determined that he did not trust women.

Many freshmen in high school spend a large portion of the experience feeling alienated and scared. Being in a school with seniors was a huge leap from being around middle school kids. For Josh, the jump to high school had been nothing more than blissful. He was larger than most kids his age, larger than many seniors for that matter, and he felt no physical fear. He was the first freshman to play varsity football in fifteen years at his school, and he reached a kind of cult status for it. College coaches began to show interest, and his legend began to grow. And his father was one of the richest men in Western Massachusetts. The upper class boys invited him to hang out, and the girls all fell in line to date him. It was insane, and Josh grew up too quickly.

By the time Josh was entering his senior year in high school, everything was lining up. Boston College had offered him a full scholarship to play football as well as some other colleges that he wasn't as interested in. Even better, his father had allowed their home to become the team's party central. The entire downstairs of the seven-thousand-square-foot home was Josh's, and it included a pool table and refrigerator constantly stocked with beer. His father made sure this happened. As long as the players didn't drive, it was all right with David. He even enjoyed coming down on occasion and partaking with the guys, especially if there were girls involved. The whole scene was unbelievable, and Josh lived it like it was the experience of a normal seventeen-year-old high school kid. When he finally understood how abnormal his experience truly was, it changed his outlook on life.

The girl's name was Rebecca, and she was a piece of work. She was only a freshman and she was already strikingly beautiful at that young age. Half Mexican and half Irish, the girl was a live wire, and she quickly gravitated to one of Josh's Saturday night parties at the house. They were invitation only, but Rebecca had potential and was on the guest list quickly. It was common knowledge among the guys that this girl might be Josh's new conquest. Rebecca had come to the party in a playful, fun mood and had a few beers with Josh and his friends. There was no doubt that she was happy to be there, and she quickly came on to him. He had a hard time remembering how the situation had turned so quickly, and it wasn't because he had been drunk but because it had been stunning. Josh had applied his moves that were devastatingly effective, and Rebecca had been as receptive as most girls. As they moved to a dark back room, Josh felt the rush of expectation rise and take control. That was when the girl punched him in the chest and pushed him away. Josh could bench-press 290 pounds five times, so the blow had no physical effect on him, but he was shocked by her outburst. He actually took a step backward and found himself on the defensive for one of the first times of his life. The girl began to scream profanities at him and continued to strike out at him. Josh was pushed up against the wall by the unexpected and violent outburst. The girl opened the door to the room they had slipped into and ran out crying and cursing. In only a moment, she had left and taken his perfect future with him.

The next day, he was arrested for sexual assault. The reality of that accusation was like the weight of Mount Everest falling on him. It was especially tough since he hadn't done anything. The girl accused him of throwing her onto a couch and attempting to rip her clothes from her body while he lay on top of her. She had departed so quickly, none of the partygoers could say for sure if her clothes had been ripped or not. He knew they hadn't been, but it had suddenly become her word versus his. His lawyer had brought up the Duke rape case where three lacrosse players had been charged with raping an African American stripper in 2006. In the events that revolved around the case, his lawyer explained a feeling that some people had against "helmet" sports—lacrosse, hockey, and football. They claimed a certain aggressive personality that the players of these sports possessed. This aggression was often taken out on women off the playing field. Bullshit. Even though the Duke case had been thrown out because of a lack of evidence, and even with the arrest of the accuser for murdering her boyfriend, there were still people in Durham who considered the kids guilty. This was the mentality that Josh was facing, and it was hostile. His father and their lawyer settled out of court, even though they knew that the girl had probably orchestrated the whole thing for money. In fact, by Christmas of that year, Rebecca had transferred out to a different district. That was good because Josh felt an anger that was close to overpowering every time he saw her. Out of sight, out of mind.

The whole event had been an eye-opener, and Josh had gotten the hint. His coach had put a kibosh on the parties, and even his father had pulled the strings a little tighter around the guests who were allowed into his home. Unfortunately, Boston College found out about the "attempted rape," and as easily as taking a deep breath, they pulled his scholarship. Josh was devastated. The senior year, which was supposed to be a sweet moment of his life, was collapsing like an ancient ruin.

Josh made his way through the rest of the year without any joy or excitement. He just wanted to get out of high school and move on to college. After BC pulled his scholarship, he was able to get into Mount Union College, which was a great small college football program, and their coach was thrilled to have him. It wasn't division one, and there was no scholarship. Every day he felt a loss of what could have been. All of this because of a stupid moment in which had had really done nothing wrong. He had changed and was now very cognizant of what he was doing because of the long-term implications. And he didn't trust women.

His freshman year at Mount Union went exceptionally well. He started at middle linebacker, and the team went to the national championship game. More importantly, his grades were good, and he stayed clean. Sure, he had fun but he tried to tone it down. Playing football was too important, and as his coach often said, playing was a privilege and not a right. Don't screw it up. Then he went on spring break.

It was something that was so moronic. He had been so stupid to be involved. He and four of his teammates had gone to Florida over their March break. Why had he gone? Because that's what a college kid was supposed to do. They rented a room in a crappy beachside motel in Fort Lauderdale and went south with all the intentions of getting some sun and finding some girls. They accomplished those goals but also found trouble.

One of Josh's teammates met a girl on the beach who invited them to her house. She was a local girl home on her college break and was having a party, which was cool because they were too young to get into the bars. When they arrived at the girl's house, Josh was surprised to find a full-scale party happening at a pool in the back of the house. Music was playing, and kids, mostly his age, were milling around the pool drinking beer. It seemed like a perfect situation to enjoy the night. But nothing in the world was perfect.

Josh and his friends tried to fit in, but it seemed that they were at a party full of local friends and they stuck out like a pink umbrella on the surface of the moon. And to make it worse, the males at the party seemed to find offense to these interlopers at their local party. The taunts started, and one foolish kid came up to one of Josh's friends and began to give him crap about being a northerner. That kid quickly ended up in the pool. That was when the foolishness broke out. Bodies were thrown around as well as pool furniture and a stereo system that had been on a shelf near the pool. The actual fight had been pretty mellow without any blood being shed. It was mostly people just being pushed around, but that didn't stop the police from arresting the football players when they arrived after a complaint about a violent party. They were labeled goons, and again Josh had to call his father for help. In this case, there was no out-of-court settlement, but the judge had simply fined the boys $1,000 each plus damages. This was simple chump change to Josh's dad, but Josh could tell that some strap that was holding together his father's restraint for his son had snapped.

When Josh told him he was going to stay in Ohio for the summer to train with his teammates, his father had ordered him home, and if Josh refused, his tuition would be cut off. What choice did he have? Mount Union gave no athletic scholarships, and he certainly didn't qualify for financial aid with a father that made upper six figures annually. Josh expected to spend the summer at home under his father's watchful eye but was surprised to hear that his father had other plans for him. He was sending his boy to work at a resort. At first, this sounded awesome until the truth came out that the resort was on a little lake in the middle of nowhere in the Adirondack Mountains. It was not on the Jersey Shore or on Martha's Vineyard. The Adirondacks? The only thing he knew about those mountains was that there were a lot of bugs. His father handed him a brochure, and it stated that staying at the resort was like going back to summer camp. Great. He hadn't even been to summer camp when he was a kid. Stuck in the mountains without anyone he knew. The entire proposal was unacceptable, but his father made it clear—Camp Wildwood or no tuition to college. Josh protested and carried on, but it was clear that his father had made up his mind. For Josh, the decision was a no-brainer. He had to go.

The GPS unit on the dashboard told him to take a left in five hundred feet. Josh didn't see much ahead of him that would indicate a major intersection. No sign or stoplight. Hell, he hadn't seen a stoplight in hours. The little town he had just passed through had been downright scary-looking, and the GPS said he was only three miles from his destination. If that was the closest town, then he was going to miss out on a lot of modern conveniences this summer. He hadn't seen a fast food place since somewhere back near Lake George. He really didn't think that the sparsely spaced homes he passed had digital cable with all the ESPN networks. ESPN was a staple that couldn't be denied, but it looked like he would have to deal with withdrawal.

Following the GPS guidance, Josh turned onto a road that was even narrower than the last and followed it through the woods. He kept expecting to see a bear or a freaking sasquatch jump out in front of his vehicle. But the road was mostly quiet except for a pickup truck that moved past in the other lane, looking like the rust holding it together might crumble at any moment. Then he came upon the sign that announced that he had arrived at Camp Wildwood. It was less than impressive, and whatever mental equilibrium that he had arrived at on the drive into the mountains rapidly tilted toward turning around and running back home. Screw college. He didn't need football. He could become a professional wrestler. Hell, that occupation was now considered training to become an actor or politician in today's world. But he made the left-hand turn and drove down the dirt road until he saw a lake shimmering a brilliant blue through the green trees. He stopped the car and stared ahead, surprised that the beauty in front of him could affect him in such a way. It was like a postcard, and although he was nervous to be moving into an unknown situation, he could feel the water pulling him forward like a magnet. The summer would be a transformation that he would never have imagined only a month before.

4

May 31

"Finally," he exhaled as he stood on the porch overlooking the lake. The water was blown up with small waves as a west wind sent a coolness through the air that made him remember that it was still spring in the Adirondacks. Although the waves weren't very big—they never were—there was enough chop to rile up the waters. Still, to Davey, it was the prettiest sight he had seen in months.

"How's the place look?" came the voice of his wife from behind him. Jeanne was the ultimate trooper, following him up onto the wooden porch. "Is everything all right? It better goddamn be. I'm too old to help you cut up downed trees."

"Jeanne, watch your fucking foul mouth." He looked at her, and a smile spread across her face, although he could see that the journey had taken a lot out of her. Getting to the camp was not an easy experience, and every year it was getting harder. Jeanne's face was red, accented by her gray hair that was disheveled around her head. Sweat was dripping from her forehead.

She stood up straight. "That was a bigger pain in the ass than last year," she wheezed.

He walked to her and gave her a hug. "Well, honey, we are getting older. It is part of life, you know."

She was right. It had been harder than the past years, and he would never admit it to her, or to himself for that matter. Age was a bitch, and whatever youth he had been desperately clutching to was beginning to slip away faster than ever. To get to the cabin was no small feat. Unlike the resort across the lake, to get to the Cramer cabin was not as simple as driving a car right up to the front door. Davey was forced to park down on a dirt road that had been originally used for logging but had been leveled over time and now serviced a number of secluded properties. They had to park in a hidden turnoff and hike up a trail that was not much wider than a golf cart path on a Florida golf course. In a shed next to the cabin, Davey kept a four-wheeler that they used for travel up and down the path all summer. The problem was always the first time when they had to hike up just to get to the machine. When Jeanne's brother had visited ten years earlier, he had suggested that they widen and pave the path. Davey had let him have it with both barrels. This was the Adirondacks, and roughing it was an accepted part of the experience. Unlike those fools across the lake at Camp Wildass, Davey and Jeanne had the real Adirondack experience. This year, the hike from the car to the cabin had seemed longer. Luckily, the battery on the four-wheeler was still charged, and the machine started right up. He still had a number of trips to make back and forth from the car, and he would use the four-wheeler to avoid a massive heart attack. It had been a pain, but he was at the lake. Finally.

"I'm scared to see the inside," Jeanne moaned. "Some Mickey Mouse impersonator probably set up shop this winter in the center of my favorite pillow. Mouse shit heaven."

"I'm just happy that a bear didn't decide to hibernate in the living room."

Davey unlocked the front door, which he was pleased to see had stayed locked since August. If his camp had been almost anywhere else, he wouldn't have been concerned, but with Camp Wildass across the lake, he couldn't be too confident. A secluded lake across from Resort Wildass. Damn.

A musty smell wafted from the opening. Many city folk would cringe at the smell and run for the nearest Ritz Carlton or Motel 6, but to Davey, the smell was the opening of summer at the lake. Perfect.

"Yep," Jeanne said, nodding sarcastically. "The old musk du cabin."

Davey walked into his summer house and couldn't help but smile and feel a thrill sweep him. The place was simple with a main room with natural wood siding and a stone hearth fireplace. The porch furniture was pilled inside, and he would have to lug it back outside. Simple birch wood furniture circled the area in front of the fireplace with special attention paid to the seating facing the picture window that faced the water. A couple of throw rugs with brown and green treelike shapes covered areas of the wooden floor. To the right was an attached kitchen that was simple but functional. He walked over to the electric panel next to one of the cupboards and placed the fuses back in, and the electricity was back on. Years before, a logging company had come up from the dirt road to clear a few old growth trees. Davey had had the power company come up and wire the camp, and he also had a septic system put in. The forest had long ago reclaimed most of that scar on the land, and the outhouse was gone, which had made everyone happy.

"We have power!"

Jeanne nodded. "How about water? It's been too long since I've drained the bladder."

"Go outside like the old days." When he had bought the cabin in 1985, there had been a simple outhouse, and the lights were lit by propane. This was luxury. "I'll go and try and get it going."

Davey took a look around the room and noticed a few pictures were cockeyed. Lucky that was all that had happened, or at least that was his hope. He walked out onto the porch and left Jeanne to walk around the cabin and find everything that had happened over the winter, including every single piece of rat shit. He stopped to look at the water through a couple of birch trees. The frame was bookended by pines. Glorious. It was better than any image that some imaginative painter could create. Real life was better than art, and that was how he lived his life.

For the second time, he wandered into the large shed behind the cabin. The interior was full of stuff that he needed to maintain the cabin and the grounds. If he desperately needed something, a quick run to the hardware store was a two-hour ordeal. So Davey stocked up.

In the corner was the blue water pump right where he had stored it when last summer ended. With a grunt, he bent over and lifted the metal piece that was awkward to carry with two pipes extending from either side. Although pushing sixty, Davey was still a big, strong man who prided himself on being able to do things himself. He hauled the pump to a small cubicle on the side of the cabin. He put down the pump and lifted the box to reveal a cement slab. Near the surface was an electric setup and two pipes, one from the lake and the other going into the house. Perfect.

Then he noticed the crack in the cement that he had repaired a few years earlier. It still seemed to be holding. His memory flooded back nearly thirty years when he and his buddy, Boogie, had laid the concrete slab for the pump. They had done a great job, and it had been perfect for decades. A crack had formed in their perfect foundation, and he knew what had caused it.

"Shitballs," he muttered, hoping that it was over. Every so often, some bad shit went down at Moon Lake that was the stuff of legends. If it was all true, then he didn't want Jeanne or himself around if it occurred again. He looked over at Wildass and saw the activity as they prepared for the season. Obviously it was not affecting them. Good stuff.

After a few minutes of sweating, cussing, and banging his hands on the metal pipes, Davey had the pump hooked up and primed. This was the actual moment of truth. If this didn't work, his dear bride would be shitting in the woods.

"Please," he moaned as he plugged the pump's cord into the electrical socket. The pump's engine came to life, and he could hear water pumping into the ten-gallon holding tank he had attached to the side. That was good. Davey stood and watched the pressure gauge rise until the pump shut off, which meant it was pressured up and that his wife could now enjoy a modicum of luxury. That was a relief.

"There's water flying out of the kitchen sink!" Jeanne yelled from inside. The pump kicked back on. After all the years, he thought she would remember the drill.

"Run around the camp and turn off all the faucets." There were only four, so it wasn't a big deal. They had been left open when he drained the system. Didn't want any water hanging out in the pipes in twenty-below weather. Now he had to hope that no pipes froze over the winter. He would know quickly because there would be a geyser in the kitchen or bathroom in an abnormal place. He heard her footfalls as she moved from one room to another. Silence and that was good. Screaming would have been bad. Davey believed he had water. He walked around to the front porch again and wiped some sweat from his brow. Luckily the wind was blowing, or it would be a very warm day. Jeanne was on the porch smiling for the first time.

"Forgot how beautiful it is."

He laughed. "You've spent too much time in Florida. Although it's scenic there, nothing matches this."

"Right," she said. "This place is heaven in January."

January. She was right. He had only ventured up here a couple of times in the winter, and it was rough. Syracuse was very bad, but the Adirondacks were a different level altogether.

Dave Cramer was an American Lit professor at Syracuse University and had been there for thirty years. He was getting on in years, but no one mentioned retirement to Dr. Cramer, who had published seven novels that many felt rivaled Ernest Hemingway. When Davey heard that crap, he laughed, often in the face of an adoring student. Hemingway he was not. He liked to compare himself more as a cross of Stephen King and Maya Angelou. The novels had been good, but they were nothing that he thought some college class would be talking about in fifty years. They did make him money. Enough money to comfortably retire on and buy a vacation mansion somewhere far from Moon Lake. But he still loved analyzing some of the great American novels with young kids who somehow kept him feeling youthful. And he loved this piece of water.

That was the truth behind his lack of desire to retire—the kids. And he liked SU. Jeanne and he lived in Jamesville near the university, and it had been everything they could have wanted. Two of their children had gone through the local public school system and were off doing fantastically on their own. He didn't even mind the numbing ten feet of snow that began to fall in November and lasted until April. But Jeanne had long since lost her thrill of knee-deep snow, slush, and roads covered with salt all winter. They had vacationed in the Florida Keys every winter, and Jeanne finally decided that they needed to move. Davey loved the Keys, too, but he needed to continue working and throw the occasional snowball. They purchased a nice, quaint place on Big Pine Key, and Jeanne had spent the last two winters there while he stayed in Syracuse. With some creative scheduling, he was able to fly to Key West every other weekend, but it wasn't enough. He missed his wife, and that was why the summers were so special. Retirement had become a more attractive option recently, although he needed the snow.

"It's beautiful here in January."

Jeanne smiled, and he knew when she was reading through his bullshit. "Right. We have to get the rest of the stuff from the car."

Davey nodded. "We'll drive down in a minute. Look at the water."

She came up to him, and he put his arm around her. It felt very fine. The moment would be etched in time.

"The pictures were crooked."

Davey wondered if she had noticed. There had been an earthquake in early October that had been small comparatively but enough to rumble the lake, and that was a bad thing.

"Think things are all right?"

He nodded. "I do. It's nothing to worry about."

It was an honest statement because he had not heard any negative stories. In fact, he had called Thomas over at Wildass in mid-October just to make sure. Nothing had happened, and luckily this wasn't San Francisco. The earth moved rarely here.

"I'll fire up the four-wheeler and get the supplies," he said, breaking away from her embrace.

"Be careful going down the path."

Always.

June 1

Meredith looked at the white dry erase board next to her desk and sighed. Listed on the board was a series of projects that needed to be done that had been categorized from pressing to urgent. The urgent projects were at the top and were written in red marker. Opening day was only two weeks away, and Meredith could feel the stress, and it was making her tense.

"I think I've got that one beat," Thomas said, standing in the doorway. He was referring to a water issue in cabin 6. "I believe we might have had a pipe freeze up last fall before we drained the system and never knew it. We had some damn cold nights before we closed, and six wasn't used at all after September. That led to the flood in the kitchenette."

Meredith breathed out. "Can we salvage the rug?"

Thomas smiled. "When it dries out, it'll be better than new. And it didn't do no damage to the wood floors or anything. It's okay."

"I know, I know. It just seems overwhelming sometimes. Every time something gets finished, it seems another project arises."

"Well," Thomas said, shifting his weight from his right foot to his left. "We kind of got off lucky this winter. Wasn't much damage. No trees down or roofs ripped off. We are right on our normal schedule. The Martin kid seems to be working out all right. I wasn't sure at first, but he's a pretty good worker. I have him paintin' the banisters on the cabin porches as we speak."

"Yes. Are we getting more help? When is Pete showing up?"

Pete was quite the character. Most people around the resort referred to him as Slip. Slippery Pete. During the days, he spent his time as the lifeguard, boat pilot, and general recreation director. At four every day, he put on a golf shirt and headed into the bar and served as the lodge's bartender. Pete was tall, thin, and in his early thirties. By mid-July, he would have a deep tan. And he never stopped acting like a kid, which suited his real job as a math teacher in a Vermont prep school.

"I'm expecting Pete in a few days. His school year ended just yesterday, and he *needs* to take off for the ocean for a couple of days. He'll be here."

Meredith nodded. "We'll need the help. I know the season starts slow, but I want to get off on the right foot. You and Josh are going to begin building the new picnic benches for the water area?"

Thomas nodded and walked out of the office. This allowed Meredith to lean back and have a moment to herself while she tried to avoid a panic attack. The job of running the resort was more than she had planned, and it was getting at her. She was simply amazed that Thomas was so incredibly nonchalant and calm. Of course, he had been through this process many times before and he was probably correct in his take that this was all routine. But she needed it to be perfect, and that was what was driving her nuts.

It was even tough sitting at his desk. When she had entered the office for the first time, it was still her father's. It had actually been left exactly as it had been when he walked out that day back in October. It was the day he departed from his lake for the last time. There was a plastic bottle of diet Mountain Dew with about two swigs still left in the container sitting on the desk. This was a physical artifact that was a direct link to her father, and that was tough. It had been very difficult going through his personal belongings in his condo in Florida, but this was somehow much worse. The office was his private space, and she felt like an intruder going through his personal effects. She didn't want to throw anything out, or even disturb, any papers left lying on the oak desk. It took her a full day before she could actually sit in his chair and recycle the Mountain Dew bottle. But she had and was slowly coming to terms with the idea that this was now her office.

For the office of the owner of the resort, the view was less than perfect. Instead of a view of the water and the hills beyond, the only window in the room looked back away from the lake into the woods of pine and birch, which was cool in its own way. Her father had always believed that the good views were for the guests. The room wasn't very large, only about fifteen by eighteen feet, but there was a lived-in, mountain feel to it. On the wall to her right was an aerial picture of the lake that one of her father's friends had taken one day as his plane did a flyby. The day had been sunny, and the blue water was striking against the thick green all around it. The buildings of the resort seemed small and insignificant against such a backdrop. It was a magnificent photo. There were a couple of filing cabinets and two chairs in front of her desk for any meetings she might need to have. Much of her father's clutter had been removed from the desk, and the surface now had her laptop and a picture of her dad. She brought a picture of Michael with her, but she didn't feel the need to put it out.

Michael had actually called her once since she had been at the lake. Surprisingly, she had honestly not even thought of him. To add to her negative feelings, she couldn't help but glean from his tone that he was expecting her to run back to North Carolina at any moment, tail between her legs, probably just because she heard his voice. Ass. She wasn't going anywhere. Maybe she was moving away from him for good.

Meredith sighed and tried to think a positive thought. Two weeks until the opening of the resort. They were on track to be prepared. The weather had been super, and the mountains were devastatingly beautiful. She thought of the view of the water from her bedroom window where she could hear the lapping of the water on the shore on the nights when it was warm enough to have the windows open. The atmosphere of the area was so incredibly peaceful, and it pissed her off that she wasn't enjoying it. Instead, she couldn't break the negative ideas that constantly flew through her head. The cause of the thoughts were obvious when she thought it all through. This opening had to be perfect because she did not want to disappoint her father and needed to keep his dreams alive. The burden was heavy.

She looked at a filing cabinet across the room that was full of her father's papers and records. She needed to go through the files, but the thought of the task was just too depressing.

"Enough," she muttered and stood and moved to the door. She needed to get outside in the sunshine before she went nuts. Maybe she could lend some help to Thomas and the kid they had hired. Anything would be better than the four walls confining her in her father's space. It had to get better when the guests arrived. It had to.

Being outside had helped Meredith, and her mental well-being was better. Actually, working on some of the projects had a therapeutic effect, and she could honestly believe that they were indeed on the right track. The kid they had hired, Josh, seemed like a decent person, although he was oddly quiet. He did do what he was told, which seemed atypical for the kids of the current generation. Olga had a girl on staff whom Meredith had briefly met, and they were thoroughly cleaning all the rooms and the main lodge. The place was really sprucing up, and her confidence slowly began to build. And one afternoon, while she, Josh, and Thomas were getting the furniture from storage and arranging it on the patio, a shiny black sports car pulled into the parking lot with music cranked inside the rolled-up windows. Thomas smiled and laughed. Meredith even found that she was looking forward to having him back, although she was hoping things wouldn't be awkward. The driver's side door swung open, and Pete rose from the car.

"Why isn't the dock in yet?" he said from behind dark sunglasses. Pete was tall and fairly skinny with hair that was now brown but would be nearly blond by Labor Day. He actually bronzed in the sun, and Meredith was sure he would get skin cancer one day. "Come on, guys. Summer is here."

Thomas chuckled. "You should've been here yesterday morning. We had frost!"

Pete came around his car and walked across the grassy lawn and onto the patio where he met Thomas, and they hugged. Then he turned to Meredith. She was unsure how this reunion might go down. Her memory of Pete was strong, and she had an idea he might have difficulty working for her.

"Well, Meredith, it is nice to see you."

She smiled. "You too. How was the ocean?"

"Ah," he said with a beaming smile. "We went to Provincetown out on the Cape. Interesting place for sure."

"We?" Thomas asked.

Pete nodded. "Some friends."

Pete stole a quick glance at her that she did not imagine. What in the world did that mean?

Pete was a staple at Wildwood for the past nine summers and had gotten a reputation as a bit of a womanizer. In fact, Meredith knew that her father had had to sit him down a number of times and clarify the fact that the guests were off limits to employees. He also found his way around some of the younger female staff members, which was also frowned upon, especially since he was a much older schoolteacher. He liked to flirt with the younger girls, and that was exactly how she had become interested in him. It was hard to avoid.

Thomas held his hands up. "Are you ever gonna settle down and get hitched? You know you have to someday?"

Pete smiled. "Why?"

"Why?" Thomas echoed with a surprised look on his face. "A man needs someone to grow old with."

Again, he glanced at her, and a wave of electricity rushed through her.

"Slip settle down?" she interjected awkwardly. "I believe that'll be the day hell freezes over."

"Wow," Pete answered with a smile. He took a step toward her and abruptly stopped. Yeah, it was going to be uncomfortable.

In the midst of their personal oddness, Meredith noticed Pete looking in the direction of Josh and abruptly felt bad that introductions had not been made. Luckily, Thomas caught the same vibe and stepped in.

"Pete, I'd like you to meet one of the newest members of the staff, Josh Martin. Josh, this is Pete Anthony, also known as Slip. He is our lifeguard, water supervisor, and bartender in the evening."

The two men shook hands, and Pete looked down slightly at Josh, although Josh had to have had one hundred pounds on him.

"Nice to meet you, Josh," Pete said. "You're a big feller. You play football?"

Josh spoke for the first time in his quiet voice that Meredith found so interesting for such a big kid.

"I play at a school in Ohio."

"Ohio State?"

Josh shook his head, and Meredith saw sadness wash across the kid's eyes. "Mount Union."

Pete nodded. "Good ball at that school. I'm impressed."

They all stood for a moment in the sunshine soaking up the warmth. A light southwest wind was blowing across the lake, and it was indeed very much like a typical summer day. Although it was already four in the afternoon, the day was still brilliant and warm. Later she would remember how perfect the moment was. Nothing lasts forever.

"Well," Meredith said, "why don't you unload your car and we'll finish here. I think it's proper to kick off the season with a couple of drinks in the bar so Slip can get his feet back under him behind the bar."

There seemed to be general agreement among the gathered. Pete turned and went toward his car to begin unloading. Josh moved off to finish with the patio furniture. Meredith stood for a moment with Thomas, and they looked toward the water. The breeze was mellow and warm, and it was really beginning to feel like summer, even up here in the mountains where spring tended to linger toward mid-June. The smell that reached her nostrils told the story, bringing with it the images of grass, trees, and clear water.

"Beautiful today," she said.

There was silence for a moment before Thomas spoke.

"Are you sure you're okay with Slip here?"

Meredith chuckled. "Yeah. It was a long time ago, and it was mostly overreaction on my part."

"Your dad didn't think so."

"He was being too protective."

Meredith remembered the summer. She was sixteen and had matured quickly. At that age, she was frankly proud of the attention she collected from boys and she promoted the interest. That summer, she left her hometown near Albany when school let out to join her father at her summer home in the Adirondacks. That was always a special moment. For most of May and June, she had been forced to live with her aunt and uncle while her father left to prepare Camp Wildwood for another season. Man, it was at moments like those that she really missed her mother.

The situation had occurred just after the Fourth of July, and to her, it was a pretty stupid event, although her father differed in opinion. There had been a fire on the beach as there was every Fourth, and Pete had made a move on her. It was Pete's first year, and he was twenty-four, not that much older than she was honestly, but it was still wrong. He had put his arm around her and kissed her passionately. Meredith hadn't thought it a big deal, but her dad had found out and flipped his brain. Pete had received a dressing down, and it was amazing that he had remained employed. Meredith was sent back home for a week, while her dad cooled off and reanalyzed her presence at Wildwood.

Over the next few years, Pete had always been very cool around her until she went off to college and spent much less time at Wildwood. The past had been forgotten until last summer when she spent two weeks at the resort. Things had happened, and it had been nice except for the guilt she felt about Michael. With Michael in the picture, nothing could happen with Slip. God, her father didn't even know about that, and he would have exploded. Still, through the marvels of e-mail, texting, and Twitter, she and Slip had stayed in touch over the winter. Now she was his boss, and that might be weird.

"No, Thomas, it's no big deal. I'm a big girl now, and I can deal with Pete."

"Crud," he muttered. "Your dad is rolling over right now."

Meredith chuckled again. "He was cremated. Impossible."

"What?" Thomas said, showing some surprise. "I didn't know that. What did you do with his...ashes?"

She smiled. "I have them. I figured some nice, calm night after we get the boat in, you and I can go out and put him where he always wanted to end up."

Thomas had turned his head toward the lake, and he slowly nodded his head. The sun had been moving toward the west, and that shoreline was falling into the shadows of the hills and trees. The sun was still brilliant over most of the water. It was beautiful.

6

June 5

It was actually very warm and humid, which made the prospect of the project easier to take. Josh stood in his bathing suit and nothing else on the dense sand of the beach area. The beach was nothing like the beaches in New Jersey or Lauderdale. This was densely packed sand that felt slightly mucky. The sun beat on his shoulders, and he could feel it, hoping he wouldn't get a burn. He had put some sunscreen on the areas he could reach but felt weird about asking one of the guys or Ms. Riley to lather up his back. His comfort level with the group wasn't at that point yet. Josh knew he was the new guy, and he also knew that his size could lead people to make judgments about him. He had seen it in Pete's face when they first met, although that hadn't lasted long. Pete seemed goofy for a thirty-something-year-old teacher, but he also seemed honestly friendly, which was a nice development.

"Okay," Thomas said. "This is a chore every year, but if we take our time and do it right, it'll be easy."

It seemed that everyone who was working at Wildwood was on the beach, including the kitchen and room staff. Oddly, they didn't seem to be present to help but to watch. Maybe this was a seminal moment to every summer.

"Sure you want to do this?" Pete asked him. "I mean, Thomas and I should be able to handle this without getting wet."

"I wish we had a bigger wetsuit," Meredith added.

Josh smiled. "I'll be okay. If it gets too bad, I'll just come out quick."

He turned to the water. Lined up on the sand were the sections of the dock and two swim floats. Today was dock day, and it took some muscle to get the sections into the water aligned and bolted together. He had heard that the water was only fifty-eight degrees. That was cold. Not too cold to dunk in, but standing in it for a period of time might get a little numbing. But he could do it because he wanted to help out, which was a much different mentality than just working for a paycheck.

When his father had sent him to Wildwood, Josh had considered it a death sentence. There was no way that he would enjoy the summer. The wilderness was a far cry from the thrills and girls of the Jersey shore, which was where he had expected to be all summer. And to make matters worse, he wouldn't be training with his teammates, which would put him at a serious disadvantage when camp opened in August. There was nothing positive about Wildwood, and he tried to envisage as many scenarios as he could that would send him home.

But he had actually found the mountains amazing and cathartic. Yes, he was far away from the clubs and beaches of Jersey, but he discovered that sitting on the beach as the dazzling stars above the Adirondacks shone made him more peaceful than he could have imagined. Josh was finding an inner peace that he wasn't sure existed in him before. Snookie could have Jersey.

Besides hanging around the lake at night, he took to a daily routine of running on the roads in the vicinity of the resort. Rarely did a car pass him as he jogged through stands of trees where he saw all types of wildlife. At times, he would stop and just listen to the woods where no human-made sounds could be heard, not even a distant airplane. On some days, he took to the path that circumnavigated the lake, which wasn't long but was breathtaking. The lake's circumference was just over three miles, but the jog was challenging, more like a cross-country run. One day, he decided to follow a path he had seen on an earlier run that climbed the hill and angled away from the lake. The trail wound through spruce and birch trees until it increased in pitch and became covered with granite outcroppings. Josh concentrated on his footing and moved farther upward until he came to an opening near the top where it appeared people occasionally came to camp out. He turned and the lake was below him, gleaming blue in a sea of green. It was that moment when he had the *aha* moment. The lake was shaped like a gibbous moon, hence the name. Actually, it looked more like a kidney bean, but that would have been an awful name. Kidney Lake. No thanks. The hill he was on wasn't that high, but it still gave a magnificent view of the area that he was calling home this summer. The resort was on the circular side of the moon shape, and there were two bays on the other side. Whatever the name, the lake was an inviting jewel.

On the far shore, the trees were thinner and cleared near the main lodge. It was Wildwood Resort, and Josh felt a connection that surprised him. There were no hot women. There was no ESPN. There was no modern workout room with free weights and mirrors to watch the muscles bulge. He only had an occasional beer that Pete let him sneak out of the bar. But he was happy.

"Okay," Thomas said, "let's do this."

Josh watched him walk into the water, and there was a rapid opening of his eyes as the cold water swept up his legs. He knew that the lake water had slipped into his wetsuit and that it would take a few seconds for his body to warm it. Thomas and Pete each had wetsuits on, including booties for their feet. There was only one other wetsuit on the premises, and there was no way that Josh was getting his large form into the neoprene suit. The boots didn't even fit. He would have to suck it up.

"What do I do?" he asked Pete as he also stepped into the water.

"Why don't you lift from shore," Thomas said authoritatively. "You'll have to get wet but not as much."

After some quick discussion, Thomas and Pete grabbed the lakeside part of a section of the dock. It was made of steel with plastic floats in the middle and was close to four feet wide, which made it pretty heavy. It was designed to give the guests the greatest possible vacation. Josh was learning that it was all about the guests.

"Why do you take it out?" he asked as he grunted and lifted the land end by himself. It was heavy.

Thomas let out a breath as he and Pete muscled their end into the water.

"Okay," Thomas breathed through lungs that seemed too old to be doing this. "Put it down. Josh, there should be two metal stakes in the sand. Try and place the dock on those to secure it."

Josh quickly saw them and dropped his end so that the stakes were inside the steel frame. They all stood up and took a few breaths. So far, Josh hadn't gotten wet.

"To answer your question, the lake freezes, and if conditions are right, the ice can move and take whatever is frozen with it. Also, it doesn't get as beat up on the shore. Less maintenance."

Good answer. The next section was lifted, and Pete and Thomas moved out into the lake until their thighs were submerged. Josh had to walk up to mid-calf, and the coldness of the water was tangible. After only a few moments, it felt as if little knives were stabbing his feet. It was cold, but he gritted his teeth and stayed in. Once the dock was aligned, Thomas came back and threw bolts into the two holes that connected the sections. Josh handed him a socket wrench that he was carrying for the purpose. He watched Thomas work and didn't need to head for shore as his legs became accustomed to the cold.

"You know," Pete said when Thomas finished with the bolts. "You won't be able to help carry the next section into the deeper water and get back to put the bolts in. I can't carry the dock out there by myself."

Thomas looked from Pete to the dock, taking in the situation. Josh knew Pete was right. The water at the end of the dock had to be chest level, and that meant chin level for Thomas, who was shorter than the other two. Josh got a quick image of Thomas standing in the water, trying to lift the dock over his head, and didn't like the vision.

"I'll go out and help Slip hold it up."

Pete chuckled and Thomas looked at him.

"It's mighty cold out there," Thomas warned, although Josh was pretty sure he was thrilled to not have to go out and lift the heavy dock.

"I'm getting used to it."

"Okay," Thomas said, "youth might have the muscles, but us old folk are smart enough to know when to accept a gift."

"Are you sure, Josh?" Meredith said from the shore.

He nodded and moved to the next section of dock next to Pete. With a grunt, they lifted the section and dragged it into the water. This time he went in above thigh level, and the cool liquid wrapped around his private parts, which was a shocking moment. Pete looked at him and laughed, but they kept moving out until the water was up to mid-chest. Thomas was struggling to get the other end of the section aligned with the piece they had already attached. Josh couldn't help him because he and Pete were holding the outer edge up. If they dropped it, the dock might tip and capsize. Thomas let out a quick yell of accomplishment, and the dock was secure. Josh headed for the shore a little quicker than he wanted, but he did want to get back in the warm air and sunshine.

"Are you okay?" Meredith asked.

He nodded and tried to look as tough as possible, although his feet felt numb.

They were able to maneuver the last section out, which crossed the end of the dock to make a T shape. Wood decking was then laid over the top of the dock, and Josh was told that he would have the job of screwing the decking down once he warmed up. That was fine because it would be in the sun. But as he stood in the water that was up to his knees, a wild urge swept him as he looked out over the water. With a quick yelp, Josh turned and ran into the water, splashing through until he leapt forward and dove in, totally submerging himself. The water was shocking, and he came to the surface with a shout and a smile. It was freaking cold but wonderful. He looked at the people on shore who were applauding. He felt like a million bucks, but that wasn't enough to keep him in the water. He quickly exited and stood on the beach, feeling emboldened and somehow accepted.

"Nice job," Meredith said. "First full swim of the year."

Pete walked up to him and put a neoprene-clad arm around his shoulder. "That was insane, but it earns you a reward. It's boat time!"

Thomas backed the boat trailer across the beach from the parking lot like he had done this a thousand times, which might very well have been possible. The boat on the trailer was not anything to get overly excited about. It appeared to be a seventeen-foot Boston Whaler with a center console and an open deck. Last summer, he had spent some time off Cape Cod on his father's sixty-foot Sea Ray that included a stateroom and two televisions on board. His dad kept it moored at a place in Buzzard's Bay and tried to spend as much time as possible on it from Memorial Day until Labor Day. This boat could fit on the deck of his father's yacht, and yet Josh found himself eager as the trailer neared the water's edge.

"Keep coming, Tom," Pete said, waving the truck backward. Pete seemed the only person that called Thomas anything but Thomas. Even Meredith referred to him as Thomas. The driver didn't seem to mind and continued to slowly move the boat toward the water. Josh decided that he wasn't yet ready to call Thomas by anything other than that. Maybe by August.

"Wheels wet yet, Slip?" Thomas asked with his head leaning out the driver's side window.

"Just now. Things are perfect. Keep her coming."

The truck continued smoothly as the trailer now began to submerge into the lake until water was lapping the waxed hull of the boat. Josh found that he wanted to help in some way instead of just standing like an idiot watching this ritual transpire.

"Is the plug in?" Josh wondered aloud. This was a common mistake many boat owners made every spring. When they pulled their boats out in the fall for winter storage, most people pulled the plug at the very back of the stern to drain any excess water from the craft. Unfortunately, many also forgot to replace the plug the next spring and received a surprise when the hull sat in the water for the first time. Instead of thanking Josh for his forethought, Pete laughed.

"This is a Whaler, man. Unsinkable. Haven't you ever seen the ad? This baby doesn't need a plug, and she self-bails. The perfect boat."

Josh had never thought of this, even though he had heard the legendary tales of the Boston Whaler's ability to float. He had tried to be helpful and decided to just let the two pros finish the job. Quickly, the water level rose, and the stern end of the boat bobbed a little bit, indicating that she was floating. Pete, who had removed his wetsuit and was shirtless, had waded out behind the boat and flipped a catch, and the black Mercury outboard engine hissed down into a running position.

"Josh," Pete said to him, "come over here and grab the gunwale and we'll see if we can pull the boat off the trailer."

Josh moved through water to the side of the boat. Although the boat had been floating a little on the water, it was still firmly on the trailer.

"A foot more, Tom!" Pete yelled toward the truck. "Step back for a second, Josh."

The truck's brake lights went out, and the whole apparatus rolled backward a few feet before Thomas reapplied the brake. Now the boat was deeper in the water and was mostly floating. He and Pete both gently pulled, and the Whaler slid from the trailer and into the water. Pete came around with the water now up to their waists.

"I've got this stern line. Go up front and grab a bowline and we'll tie her to the dock."

"Gotcha," Josh said and slowly walked to the front end of the boat. Within a minute, they had the boat tied to the dock and were headed out of the chilly water where Thomas was standing. The truck and trailer had been pulled from the lake.

"How's she floating, Slip?" Thomas asked.

Pete nodded. "Perfect. Now we'll see if the engine starts."

"Why do you doubt?"

"Ah yes," Pete responded with a tinge of sarcasm. "The eternal optimist. I'm still nervous that we might have an ethanol problem from last summer. Remember?"

"Taken care of," Thomas said confidently. "Carbs rebuilt and the lower unit oil changed. She'll purr for you."

Pete gave him an odd look, jumped up on the dock, and then jumped back down smoothly, this time into the hull of the boat. He sat on the captain's seat behind the center console and looked at Thomas, this time without the look of mischief.

"I hope this works."

Josh saw Thomas nod just before Pete turned the key. There was a brief cranking sound before the engine roared into life with water bubbling behind it and the sweet smell of gas and water. Thomas smiled, never doubting that the boat would run.

"Take her out and warm her up."

Pete was smiling ear to ear as he revved up the boat's engine. Smoke bubbled up from the water at the base of the lower unit. He let the throttle back down, and the engine fell into a mellow murmur.

"Josh," Pete said to him, "go grab that cooler and jump aboard."

Josh saw a small plastic cooler and quickly snatched it and climbed down into the boat. He swiftly looked around and sat on a small bench in the back of the boat. Slip watched him sit, nodded, and pulled the boat from the dock. Josh looked back on shore and saw Thomas standing next to Meredith, his face full of pride. The boat moved away from shore into the sunshine that was warming Josh's body in the bright afternoon sun.

There wasn't much to the lake, so the grand tour lasted only minutes and not hours. Still, Josh sat on the bench in the stern of the boat gazing at a beautiful shoreline. Birch, maples, and evergreens grew all the way down to the water, concealing the forest that grew behind them. Occasionally, Josh could detect the trail that he ran and could recognize a certain tree or rock along the path. Boulders were strewn along the shore in between small sandy beaches where no one sat on the early summer evening. The hills rose around the lake, and he could look up at the one that he had climbed, remembering the tight path to its summit. The entire world seemed dominated by only two colors—green and blue. The boat cruised along the far shore of the lake from the resort into small bays and around points that marred the kidney shape of the body of water. There was a small cabin up in the woods, and Josh noticed some movement.

"Who's place is that?"

Pete looked where Josh was pointing, although he didn't need to. There weren't many options.

"That is Davey Cramer's summer cabin."

"Pretty isolated."

Pete was looking closely at the cabin, and Josh did likewise. It looked as if the place was lived in. The door to the porch was open, and there were glasses on a table.

"He showed up," Slip said softly. "He's still kicking.'"

"Who?"

Pete looked at him. "Oh, Davey. Have you ever read *The Evergreen Life?*"

Josh shook his head. "I think one of my teammates did for an English class."

"Davey's the author. Quite the character. He's lived on this lake for the past thirty summers or something ridiculous. He'll drop by the bar some night."

"Is he the only other cabin on the water?"

"There's one other place, but I'm not sure if anyone will be there. It went uninhabited most of the last couple summers."

Josh was watching the cabin and saw movement. A man was walking down toward the beach, and his intentions were unclear. Josh kind of felt like a voyeur checking out someone's living room through a window. Instead of turning the boat away, Pete turned and headed toward shore and shut the engine off.

"You made it through another winter," Pete yelled at the man. The guy wasn't tall but was broad-shouldered. He had gray hair that Josh could see was streaked with some long overtaken color. Older. Maybe sixty.

The man smiled. "You married yet?"

"Fuck no," Pete answered with a crazy smile. "Good to see you, Davey."

"Likewise, Slip. Looks like the lake held up over the winter."

"I think so. Scary for a moment, but it's all okay."

The man nodded and looked down at the sand. "I'll be over before too long."

Pete nodded and pulled the boat away from the shore and farther into the lake. The two had just had a moment that Josh desperately wished he could have been a part of. Two people who were friends who hadn't seen each other in a while. It was as if they were speaking a foreign language that only they understood. It was awesome and it was old. There were relationships that developed on places like this that were strong and seasonal. It just happened that Pete's pal was a best-selling author.

Pete took the boat out to the middle of the lake and slowed down. They sat in silence for a minute, soaking in the sun and the solitude. The water made a mellow lapping sound on the hull, and Josh began to sweat in the sunshine. It was nice. Pete finally moved and raised his beer can, and Josh tapped it with his.

"This is pretty sweet," Pete said as he took a sip from his can of beer. He had given Josh one as well, explaining that he deserved one after all the work he did but to keep the knowledge on the down low. Josh agreed and savored the beer and drank it slowly. "I think about this all year when I'm sitting in my classroom. Pissed at the world and looking out at a realm of cold white. This is what gets me through the winter."

"What do you teach?" Josh asked, warming up to Pete, who seemed to be a truly nice, fun-loving guy.

"I teach math to a bunch of overprivileged kids who don't know the concept of working for anything. It's pretty depressing why I have to explain every day that the seventy-five-percent grade they have is what they earned and not some arbitrary number I put by their name. Something for nothing. It's become the American credo!"

Josh thought of many of his friends and had to agree that there might be something to that. Hell, he was like that throughout his entire high school career and his freshman year at MU. He found the thought depressing and was somewhat worried when Pete asked the inevitable question.

"How about you? You're a big, young, good-looking guy. Why are you hanging out this summer up here in the wilderness and not along the shore somewhere?"

"There's plenty of shore right here."

Pete smiled. "Funny guy. You know I'm talking about the Cape or the Vineyard and not northern nowhere."

Josh had thought this out because what people thought of him was important. He wasn't thrilled with the thought of people thinking of him as an assaulter, criminal, or lush that got into tight spaces when he drank. That persona he wanted to leave behind and not revisit. But that was why he *was* here after all.

"Well, I go to college, and my dad thought this place might help me out. I don't think he wanted me hanging around with my friends cutting up all summer."

"Why here?"

"He and my mom spent some time here, I guess. It was a long time ago. He liked it and hooked me up."

Pete drank from his beer, and Josh followed suit. The boat was cruising at walking speed along the south shore of the lake. A bay seemed to curve to the right and inward ahead before the shoreline jutted back to the left as the east side of the lake approached.

"What college do you go to again?"

"Mount Union in Ohio. I play on the football team."

Slip raised his eyebrows. "That's right. Good ball. What position?"

"Linebacker."

"Good stuff," Pete asked no more questions and handed Josh a fresh beer as the boat rounded a boulder outcropping and pulled into a sunny, calm cove. The air was very still here, and the water was glass. The whole area was about the size of two football field. The forest was thick around it.

"Nice spot."

Slip nodded in agreement. "This place is the quietest spot around and can't be seen well from the resort. It's not kosher to take the boat out without guests, but sometimes I do sneak over here. The bass fishing is awesome. You know how to drive a boat?"

Josh considered telling him that he had often driven his father's cabin cruiser but thought better of it. Didn't want to sound *overprivileged*.

"I do."

"Good," he responded enthusiastically. "You can help me out if we get too busy."

Pete idled back on the throttle, and the boat slowed to nothing right in the middle of the calm bay. The hills rose quick and steep from the water's edge, and there was a large bird, maybe an eagle, soaring above the trees. The peace was astounding.

"The summers up here can get hectic at times, but there is always peace nearby." Pete turned and looked at Josh. "Are you good with people?"

"I try to be."

Pete laughed. "You'll get better. Just wait until the guests arrive. It will be good to develop thick skin."

Josh took that in, even though he had realized this before he had entered the world of Camp Wildwood. His world would change when the people arrived. No longer would he be able to go off and do projects by himself. No longer would he have the beach to himself at night. He had grown to love this, and yet he found that he was excited to have the people arrive. He was ready to meet new people.

7

June 12

Meredith was way more nervous than she would have ever thought possible. It was Thursday morning, and the first guests of the season were scheduled to arrive later in the afternoon. Preparation was over, and it was time to let it happen. Two cabins were booked for the night, and six were reserved for the weekend. They would actually have three cabins booked for the entire upcoming week, which was a good sign. The long-term guests tended to be more reliable. Although she could financially afford a relatively slow summer, she needed to be successful for psychological reasons. The nagging doubt kept surfacing in her head, and it was weakening her resolve. Should she have followed Michael's advice and just sold the property? The doubt was like poison ivy that couldn't be ignored and was annoying as hell. But after spending a month in the mountains, her determination to keep the resort only grew stronger.

Through the wonder of modern technology, they had Wi-Fi across the area, which many of the guests had demanded. It wasn't the best or fastest connection, but slow was better than nothing. She knew that guests would bitch about the snail's pace service, but she tried. The great thing for her was that she was able to update the resort's web page and add a chat room. The hope was that the word of mouth would help draw people to the lake, and in the modern world, information spread on the Internet. Although no one had been to the resort that summer, many people had already weighed in their opinions. Most people who posted comments had previously been to the resort and sang praises about their stays. Some people were disappointed that the place hadn't opened Memorial Day weekend. The thought had crossed her mind, but her father had been dead set against it, as there was often frost well into June. In fact, once he claimed there were still drifts of snow in the woods in late May. That was hard to believe, but frost was definitely a possibility. The patrons could wait until June.

The lodge was quiet as she entered the front door. She breathed in, and it smelled wonderfully clean and woodsy. There was no fire in the fireplace, although a morning like this would normally deserve one. It was only thirty-nine degrees outside with a low fog hanging tough over the lake and up the mountainside. She knew from experience that the fog would burn off and a southwest wind was supposed to develop, which along with the sunshine would push the temperature to near seventy. If it was this cold tomorrow morning, Thomas would definitely light a fire.

Kristin was sitting at the small table behind the large wooden front desk that served as a check-in and general information area. She was busy typing at a computer when she looked up and saw Meredith walking up.

"Good morning, boss," Kristin said with a smile. Kristin was a pretty young woman who was in her second year at Camp Wildwood and was very good at organizing the front desk. She was a graduate of the hotel management school at Cornell and was looking for a full-time job in a big city or a Caribbean island. Meredith's father had convinced her to gain some experience at Wildwood, and Kristin had enjoyed it enough to return for another summer.

"Morning, Kristin," Meredith said with a smile as she walked around the large front desk and through a side entrance into the office. "Anything new?"

"The Connors called and said they wouldn't be in until between eight and nine tonight. I said it wouldn't be a problem. Also, we have a couple more online reservations, including next weekend, and two more for the Fourth of July week. That means we are almost booked that entire week. Good news."

"Sounds pretty good," Meredith responded, hoping that this all meant things were going well. It reminded her to examine her father's books on the past year's guest list to get an idea of this year's business compared to past years. "Thomas and Olga should be in soon. Let me know when they show up and we'll meet in the bar."

Kristin nodded and watched Meredith as she walked past and down the narrow hallway toward her office. The hallway was not long and had an old matted carpet on the floor. Few people saw this hallway, as the guests were not allowed and most employees only saw this place if Meredith had to have a serious talk with them. Using her key, Meredith unlocked the office door and wandered in to her space on her first opening day. With a quick look out the window at the misty woods, Meredith found her chair and sat down heavily. She shivered and wished she had put on more than a sweatshirt. Leaning over, she turned on the small portable heater under her desk that came in handy on these cool mornings. She opened the small refrigerator next to the desk and grabbed a Diet Pepsi. Most mornings she drank a couple of cups of coffee, but she was hoping that the fizz would calm her stomach. She opened the bottle and took a long swig, and her stomach did feel better whether it was the soda or just a mental cure. Okay, she could deal with this day.

Meredith had found the computer files from the last five years, and that was a huge help in understanding the clients that had stayed at the resort. Names. Addresses. Sometimes even ages and the names of all the family members. The data was incomplete, but it did provide the information she wanted—when they stayed. Meredith had actually been able to gauge an idea of when to expect the most people, and it seemed to be middle July until early August. It would be key to have the place booked during that time if a profit was to be made. There were few, if any, computer files dating before this five-year period, and she wondered if her father even had a computer then or whether he just threw out the files when he junked an older model computer. He had always maintained that Wildwood was not the Ritz Carlton and that staying here meant an Adirondack experience without modern frills. If someone wanted that, then they could stay in Lake Placid. Meredith wouldn't be surprised if her father didn't have a computer until recently.

Her nerves were still bouncing as she waited for her morning meeting, and she couldn't stand still. Across the room was an old wooden filing cabinet that she had looked through briefly while searching for the files dealing with old clients. She decided it was a good a time as any to look through the documents within.

The upper drawer did contain some files that dealt with customers, but most of it was billing, dating from 1978 to 2009. She opened the file in front—1978. Inside were the names of customers and the prices that the resort charged, including a brochure that was sent out to homes and travel agencies across New York and New England. Cabin 5, the nicest cabin on the property, rented for $45 a night. Today it was $250. Ah, wasn't inflation dandy. She chuckled and returned the file. The second drawer opened, and there was a variety of notebooks stacked inside. She remembered looking at this earlier and recalled these notebooks listed projects that were done on the grounds from painting to installation of windows. This was also useful for a timetable for the renovations that were constant at Wildwood.

Below these were notebooks that had a different cover. She inspected them, and unlike the others, there was no writing on the front indicating the contents. Curious, she opened the top book and was shocked to see her father's handwriting. It appeared that she had stumbled upon some kind of personal journal that her father had kept. There were paragraphs on the page, and every few were headed by a date: May 2, 1985. 1985. Wow. She had yet to be conceived.

May 2, 1985

> 54 degrees and cloudy. Still some snow in the hills and woods and small amount of ice on lake. Met with Josiah and Thomas. Josiah knows the place and Thomas seems to be a good enough guy. Talked about replacing the shingles on half the cabins. Needs to be done but it's my damn money. I guess if they say it needs to be done, then it needs to be done. Set opening date: June 10th. I'll have to move up here before Memorial Day and Mary will be pissed. But we need to make money. Hopefully season will be good.

As she read these words, she felt her breath catch in her throat. It was like looking into her father's mind, and that was almost too much to take. And he mentioned her mother. Mary. Oh, it had been a long time since she had heard that name. Meredith wanted to read on, but she knew that the process would be tough, and she wasn't willing to tackle that mountain at the moment.

"Meredith?" she heard Kristin's voice from down the hall. "Olga and Thomas are here."

She quickly shut the notebook as if hiding a secret.

"Okay. I'll be there in a minute."

Meredith returned the journal to the cabinet and vowed to read through it over the summer. But now, she needed to make sure the resort was ready to go.

*****

"Every room is prepared," Olga said in a defensive tone. Olga had a European accent that she claimed was Swiss, but Thomas wasn't so sure. There were plenty of times when he thought she was just full of piss and was really from Plattsburgh with an accent she developed while working in a Red Roof Inn. It cracked him up that she got so defensive about her dang job.

"I was just making sure that all is in order for our guests," Meredith said, trying to not sound confrontational. Thomas just shook his head.

"My staff has all the rooms prepared. The guests will be happy."

"Well, good. Are you fully staffed?"

Olga shifted in her seat and never smiled. "I have three girls working in the rooms and another to clean the lodge. The last girl just arrived, and she is a local girl."

Meredith smiled at her and quickly moved on. Olga was hard to deal with, and Thomas knew it well. He had worked with her for twenty years. Colin had put up with her because she was very good at her job and as dependable as the sunrise. There were plenty of times when Thomas was lonely at the resort and any female companionship would have been appreciated. Olga never crossed his mind.

Meredith looked at him and he nodded.

"The grounds are in great shape. Best in years. Heat is ready in all. The stoves in the cabins that have them are all checked and ready to go. The beach is set. Josh, Pete, and I pulled out all the kayaks and canoes. The swimming buoys are out. We're ready to go."

They were. Meredith had actually pushed them a little harder than Colin had, and they were almost too ready. The Josh kid had worked out great, and Pete was always reliable help. Of course, from now on, it would be the unexpected problems. Clogged toilets. Blown-down limbs. Broken furniture. There was a bunch of things that just failed over the course of the summer. Inevitable.

Meredith turned to Pete, who was reclining in a chair and looking very bored. On most workdays, he didn't hit the beach until ten, so the 8:00 a.m. meetings were early for him.

"Is the bar ready?"

Pete leaned forward. "We have the firewater, and the place is cleaner than a NASA lab. Bring on the boozers."

Thomas chuckled. He liked Slip, even though he seemed to be a cocky party boy from time to time. The guy had a sense of humor, and it was the perfect contrast to Olga. Every place needed a cutup, and most summers, Pete fit the bill.

Meredith finished the meeting with Jack. Jack was a guy from Newcomb, a small town in the Adirondacks who went to Paul Smith's College and never wanted to leave the mountains. Jack could cook with the best of them. The restaurant was the only place around where a person could get decent food for literally miles, and it was good. One of the finest days every spring was when Jack showed up and Thomas no longer had to cook for himself. Hot dogs and baked beans got old pretty quick.

"Okay," Meredith said with an energetic sigh, "we're ready to go. Does everyone have their walkie-talkie?"

Thomas briefly touched the radio that he now had on his belt. Colin had never needed a radio. If he needed something, he just went to where the person usually was and spoke face-to-face. Meredith demanded the radios for fastest possible communication. Thomas didn't care if he had the radio that much, although it seemed like overkill.

When everyone nodded, Meredith nodded too.

"Okay. Let's make this a good day."

Thomas stood from the chair he had been in, suddenly wanting to be outside, although that would be delayed. Meredith walked toward him. He could tell that she was wicked nervous, and he figured it was normal. Her father would have been laid-back, but he had been doing it for thirty-five years.

"We're okay," he said.

"Really?"

"Really," Thomas answered, hoping to calm her mind. "Go out and go for a walk. The guests are still hours away, and there's nothing you can do."

She smiled and nodded. He placed his hand on her shoulder in reassurance and then walked out. Her tension was making him nervous.

Pete wasn't around, but Josh was. The sun was just beginning to make some progress through the fog, and the water was changing from gray to blue. The temperature was climbing, and the chill was rapidly dissipating. The weather was going to cooperate beautifully with the opening day. A puff of breeze blowing from the lake hit him, and that was also a good sign. A south wind bringing warm air was generally good for business. By noon, the beach would be a great place to be.

Thomas watched Josh raking the sand along the shore. It was important that the beach looked as good as possible. When guests came to Camp Wildwood, the amenities were pretty much provided by the resort. There was no town to dine in or movie theater to escape to. There was no shopping or water park. Sure, people could drive to Placid or Old Forge for some entertainment, but within twenty miles or so, there wasn't much to drive to in the neighborhood. So Wildwood had to provide the experience, and Thomas had to make it look good every day. It was easy if the weather cooperated and if he had good help.

Josh had a long sand rake that Thomas had purchased from a golf course equipment catalogue. Josh was dragging it along the sand, leaving long parallel tracks. It looked good, and Thomas said so.

"Thanks. It's not exactly rocket science, though."

Thomas chuckled. "No, it's definitely not, but if it was, there'd be a bunch of dorks with pocket protectors on this beach."

Josh laughed, and Thomas smiled and looked at the sky where blue was now more dominant than the gray. He sighed.

"This is tough for you, isn't it?"

Thomas looked at the kid, surprised by his accurate observation. "Tough?"

"Sorry," Josh muttered with his head down.

"No," Thomas said quietly. "You're right. Come over for a second and take a load off."

Thomas moved over to one of the beach chairs and sat without worrying about the dew that had gathered. Josh followed and sat down quietly, waiting for Thomas to speak. He looked at the water and gathered his thoughts.

"This is my thirty-fifth opening day. Kinda hard to wrap the brain around that idea. Most folks like me have retired and moved off to Florida to live out their days looking at a canal or golf course they will never use. I guess I've seen it all. Rain, sun, hot, cold. Even some snow in the fall. Good folks and the bad. Great times and… horrible times. But the constant was Colin Riley. He was a great man and he ran a tight ship. The customers loved him, and we all depended on him."

He stopped and looked back at the lake, an image of Colin standing at the end of the dock with his fly-casting rod in motion. Ten to two. It was a hard image to see.

"Colin was a great man, and he believed in me a long time ago when no one else did. I loved the man. It's just…tough this year."

Thomas felt his voice choking up and stopped. This was much harder than he imagined it would be. Crud but he didn't want to show weakness. He was just a washed-up sixty-something-year-old man.

Josh put a hand on his shoulder.

"I appreciate all you've done for me, Mr. O'Brien. You've been a big help."

Thomas looked at the kid who could have picked him up and thrown him twenty yards into the lake. The kid was all right.

"Thanks, kid. We'll have a good summer."

The water was just starting to ripple with the growing breeze. The image of Colin standing over the water was still on his mind. The lake had secrets, and Colin knew them. Unfortunately, Thomas knew too.

8

June 17

The evening had come, and he couldn't find a logical reason to turn down Jeanne's needs. They had been at the lake for over two weeks, and with the exception of a few trips to the market in Newcomb and a day trip to Old Forge, the Cramers hadn't left the area directly around the cabin. Davey knew that the resort across the water had recently opened and that Jeanne was looking for a night out. The weather was perfect—clear and relatively warm with a waxing gibbous moon to help light the way. There was no wind whatsoever, so the excuses were hard to come by.

Davey didn't mind the occasional trip to have dinner and a few drinks. In fact, he rather liked the resort itself, and the lodge especially. What bothered him was the entire resort as a whole, which he sardonically called Camp Wildass. For the majority of the time that he and Jeanne spent on the lake during the summers, the resort didn't bother them. It was when the kayakers found their way into his cove and decided to pull up and hang out on his beach or when hikers deviated from the path around the lake and decided to investigate his property. One day, he had been on the toilet dropping a present when three young vacationers came around his house and had the balls to walk up on his porch to admire the view. He had run out and vocally admonished them to get the hell off his property. It had screwed up his intestines for days. Nothing worse than being cut off at that critical moment. Generally he liked people, but there were boundaries.

And Colin Riley was no help, which only seeded their relationship. Davey had known Colin for nearly thirty years, and for the early portion of that time, they had been friends. But as the resort grew and Davey became older and less likely to drink at Wildass, the relationship soured, especially when the guests took liberties on Davey's property. Jeanne always said he was being childish, but even she became annoyed when a group of guests set up a few boats in the cove with some beer and stayed for a noisy couple hours. Davey and Colin had had a few epic encounters that had only soured the blood further.

"How much longer until the queen is ready to leave?" Davey inquired to his wife, who was putting makeup on, which was indeed a rare occurrence at the lake.

"Do you have the boat ready?" she quickly shot back as she leaned forward toward the mirror while applying eyelash makeup.

Davey gritted his teeth. "Yes, darling. And I have limbered up and am ready to row your high-society butt across the lake."

He smiled because she had the opportunity to really act like a wealthy snob but didn't. Davey had more than a comfortable financial situation and was getting royalties every day from his novels and the movie that was created from *An Evergreen Life*. Both the book and the movie had done surprisingly well to his complete amazement. If most of his readers knew that he lived in a tiny Adirondack cabin with very few modern luxuries, they would call him a nutty author. Well, that would probably boost his sales even more.

Watching her get ready was like watching grass grow, so he walked out onto the porch and down to the water for the fifth time to make sure he had everything—two floatation cushions, a waterproof flashlight, and extra jackets. Going out in the rowboat at night was nothing unusual for Davey. He had done some of the best writing on the water, originally on yellow legal paper and more recently on his laptop. The bugs were a problem at night around the lit computer screen, but when he zoned into his work, he didn't even notice them. One of the nicest things that Colin had done recently was installing Wi-Fi for the resort. The signal at the cabin was too weak, but when he rowed into the middle of the lake, the connection was all right. Colin had used a password, but cracking it was child's play since it was designed for use by the guests. His last novel had actually been delivered to his publisher in New York by e-mail sent from the center of Moon Lake.

He heard the scuff of a shoe behind him and turned to see his wife walking down the path to their small sandy beach.

"It's an exquisite evening."

Davey nodded and looked across the water. The sun was still fairly high in the sky, and the water was glass. He helped Jeanne to the rowboat, which he had already pushed close to the water. She was a pro at boarding the twelve-foot aluminum craft, but with age, the limbs didn't bend the way they used to. Jeanne sat down on the bench seat with a relieved sigh, and Davey told her to hang on tightly as he shoved the boat into the water. He waded in the water before hopping in. That was why he preferred shorts on occasions like this. Davey settled into his seat, gripped the oars, and began pulling. The trip would take a good twenty minutes, although the distance was less than half a mile. He could do it much faster alone but he wasn't complaining. Jeanne leaned back as the sun struck her face, and he felt a warmth in his chest that hadn't cooled since he had married her so many years ago. The trip across the lake was perfect.

Davey led the way through the front entrance of the lodge and strolled to the back where the entrance to the bar and dining room opened under an arched entry. His head was on a constant swivel looking for Colin, not sure what his reaction would be when he laid eyes on him. The encounters had been decidedly cool the year before, and Davey would avoid Wildass altogether if it wasn't for the fact that Jeanne wanted to go "out." The room was quiet, which was logical since the heart of the season was still weeks away, and he thought it was a Wednesday night. The days of the week had little significance during his summers.

A young industrial-looking waitress served them, and they enjoyed a peaceful dinner, which was a bit disappointing. He was expecting Colin to come in and deliver some of his usual crap. When they finished, it had grown dark outside, but they didn't head for the boat but instead went into the bar and took two stools. The bartender had his back to them, making change for the only other customers—a younger couple at the end of the bar. When he turned, there was not even a brief second of mental processing. The bartender looked at Davey as he handed the other patrons their change.

"I was wondering when you'd row your lazy ass over here."

"Getting tough to do as the years pile up."

"Buy a freakin' motor. With your salary, you could buy a yacht."

Jeanne spoke for the first time. "That's what I tell him all the time."

Pete smiled and held his hand out. Davey smiled as widely and took the offered hand.

"Mr. Cramer, it's really great to see you." Pete turned to Jeanne. "And you too, Mrs. Cramer."

"It's Jeanne, Pete. We go over this every year."

The bartender nodded. "I know. Sorry. You guys want the usual?"

It was simply amazing that Pete remembered what they both drank. Gin and tonic for Jeanne and a Captain and Coke for Davey. The drinks were quickly served, and Davey put a twenty on the bar that Pete refused.

"First drink of the summer is on me."

"Thanks," Jeanne said.

Davey looked around at the bar that he had spent so much time in over the years. The lighting at night was perfect against the wood-lined walls. The place oozed comfort, and sometimes it was hard to leave, and many times even more difficult to row back across the water. Those were the moments that he did wish he had an engine on the boat.

"Quiet this early in the season," Davey said.

Pete nodded. "Always slow this early. So how have you guys been? I saw *An Evergreen Life* last Christmas in a mall theater complex. It didn't come close to doing justice to the book."

Davey shrugged. "They tried." It was something he expected. There were but a handful of movies that he had seen in his life that ever surpassed the book they were based on.

"And you, Jeanne, you look younger every year."

Jeanne chuckled. "It's the Florida sun and being away from the cold and snow all winter."

Pete and Davey laughed, and that was fine. For some reason, Davey felt a strong feeling of being home again at the bar. It wasn't an unpleasant feeling.

"Where's Colin hiding? Did he know I was coming and went off to hide?"

Pete stopped and gave him the oddest look with his head cocked to the side. Davey suddenly felt nervous as if something horrible like a tarantula was lurking over his head.

"You don't know?"

The dread was blooming in his head, and he knew it was about to explode. He understood before Pete spoke.

"Colin didn't make it."

"What?" he heard Jeanne say next to him, but his brain had slipped into the fog that only comes with shock. He had no idea how long the mist hung in his head, and he had trouble speaking.

"What...happened?"

Pete had a dishrag in his hand and was wiping the bar without looking up.

"Suicide. In Florida after he and Thomas closed the resort up for the winter."

Suicide? That was ridiculous. Davey didn't consider Colin a best friend, but they went back a ways, and he was a man who would have been sickened by the idea of taking his own life.

"Why?"

Pete chuckled and looked up for the first time, and Davey noticed that his eyes were wet. "Who knows? Things here were going great. Makes no sense."

"Who's running the place?" Davey asked, still trying to process the numbness.

"Meredith. His daughter."

Jeanne spoke up quickly. "Little Meredith?"

Pete chuckled. "She's not so little anymore, Jeanne. She's doing a great job in a tough situation."

"Wow," Davey said. "This is some..."

As suddenly as a lightning bolt, sudden knowledge struck him, and it was nearly paralyzing.

"When did you say it happened?"

"Well," Pete muttered, "it was very close to Halloween. Late October."

Davey suddenly knew and he didn't want to accept the knowledge. The earthquake had been in mid-October. The twentieth. He had remembered seeing the report on the Internet. Oh, Jesus.

"Are you okay, Mr. Cramer?"

Jeanne's arms were rapidly around his shoulders, and he realized that he must look shocked. Well, that made sense because he was shaken. But he didn't want to let on to his knowledge, at least not yet because it was something that shouldn't be talked about in the bar at Camp Wildwood.

"I'm fine. Just a little taken back by the news. I think we should go."

Davey stood from his stool, aware that Pete was looking at him with serious concern.

"You want me to take you over in the Whaler? You can leave your rowboat on the beach."

"Thanks," Davey said, meaning it. He was feeling better by the second, and the open waters would be a huge relief. "The row will help me deal with this, I guess."

He threw the twenty on the bar, promised to be back soon, and led Jeanne out the front doors. The night was bright as the moon was just to the west of overhead. The water sparkled like a diamond. Old Moonie Lake. Damn.

"Are you really all right?" Jeanne asked.

"Yeah. Let's get in the boat."

He began rowing out toward the other side and their cabin. Jeanne hadn't caught on yet, and when she did, he knew she would have a tough time sleeping. He decided to not tell her and allow her the opportunity to enjoy the moon. They would talk about the earthquake tomorrow in the light of day.

9

June 20

Liza wasn't sure about anything, and that was about as depressing as things could possibly get. Only the day before, she had walked out of her high school for the last time, and at this point, she wasn't sure that she would even attend the graduation ceremony held in the athletic field behind the school. The building faded behind her as she drove away, and she came to a comprehension of just how important that school had been to her. It had been her rock and her stability against awful times. Now the cord that had allowed her to find refuge away from her crappy life was being cut. Instead of feeling joy at the end of her high school career, Liza felt pain and apprehension unlike any she had known. Her future was now unclear, and the reality of where she was headed was thoroughly depressing because it appeared to be nowhere.

Liza Grant had grown up in the Adirondacks with the peaks surrounding her home. This setting would be awe-inspiring in many instances, but for her, it brought pain and claustrophobia. The Adirondacks were not the wealthiest part of America. In fact, poverty was common in many of the towns scattered around the wilderness. Unless a town was a tourist destination, Adirondack State Park held few opportunities for the inhabitants. Mayson held nothing for Liza.

To say that her life had been rough was an understatement. Her parents had divorced when she was only four years old, and her father was really nothing more than a bum who spent way more time back in the woods than with his family. Occasionally Liza saw him in town or at the store in Newcomb, but he was mostly out of her life.

In the divorce, her mother had gotten the double-wide trailer that was their home and the acre of mostly scrub land surrounding it. The family—her mother, Liza, and her little brother, Ashton—survived in the dwelling. Her mother had a job working at the diner in Mayson and made almost enough money to exist. Liza did not have cable television or the Internet but did have food, although rarely anything that wasn't fried or left over from the diner.

When Liza was eleven, a man moved in with the family named Burt. Burt worked for some logging company, and he and Liza's mom had quickly begun to cohabitate. The new situation was a breath of fresh air as Burt seemed to really care about her and Ashton. He was able to rip apart a scrubby section of the property and coax some corn, squash, and pumpkins out of the rocky ground. The tall grass that had made up the backyard was mowed down, and for a while, the house actually felt like a home. Liza had the happiest days of her childhood. Then Burt cheated on her mother and he was gone forever. The garden grew thick with weeds, and the scrub began to grow back. For Liza, the happiness ended with the end of summer.

Her mother also began to change. She began to spend more nights away from the house, drinking at the nasty little bar out on Route 28. There were some nights when she never came home, leaving Liza to take care of her brother. Those were some scary nights, but in some sense, they were better than the nights when she came home. That was because she often came home with company and not of the sweetest variety. Those nights were the worst. Her drunk mother stumbled through the door with a guy equally as drunk, and they retired to the master bedroom for a night of loud sex. Liza got little sleep on those nights, and the men that her mother brought home were mostly scumbags. A few extended their stays and moved in for brief periods of time, and those moments were the worst. Most had violent tendencies, and although they never touched Liza, she was still afraid to be around these men.

That was when school truly became her sanctuary. The school was clean. The food was warm and nutritious. And the adults were civilized and genuinely seemed to care for her well-being. Liza excelled in her studies and shot to the top of her classes. She joined the band where she used a school-issued clarinet. If there was a the-atric performance, Liza signed up, and she even tried playing soccer, which would carry her through the autumns. The biggest obstacle was transportation to and from school, as the buses only ran before and just after school. Her mother sure wasn't driving out to pick her up at six o'clock, and it was a long walk home. Thank god for Matt Trendle.

She met Matt when she entered eighth grade at band practice, and they quickly bonded. The two had similar classes, which increased the amount of time they spent together. It also helped that she had a crush on him, and that boosted her need to be around him. Matt was from a solid middle-class family that lived closer to Newcomb and not in the stick lands around Mayson. His father owned an outdoors shop that catered to fishermen, hunters, kayakers, and most other activities in mountains. Tourists cruising through miles of wilderness caught sight of a sign of civility and stopped in droves at his shop. The family lived in a nice modern home on a few well-sculpted acres along the side of a forested hill. Liza began to spend a lot of time at the Trendle home. When she stayed late at school, it was usually Mrs. or Mr. Trendle that gave her a ride home. It was an oasis that got her through some tough times.

But here she was. They were about to graduate, and that sig-naled the end of that scenario. She guessed it could be a new begin-ning or the end of a sad road. Although they had slowly grown fur-ther apart in high school, she and Matt had remained best friends, even when one or the other had a "special" friend. Matt was off to the College of Environmental Science and Forestry at Syracuse, and Liza was going…

Nowhere. And that was the root of her anguish. At least, she was leaving Mayson for a while. She drove her beat-up Toyota Camry down a dirt road toward her summer job.

The parking lot was dry, and rocks crunched under her sneak-ers. It was hot and it felt as though summer had truly arrived. Being done with school only intensified the sensation. During most sum-mers, she helped out at the diner or made some money babysitting the kids in the neighborhood—all twelve families. The fact was that she tried to spend most of her time at the Trendle home or on a day trip with that family. Those days were over, and she had to move on. She hoped this job would be acceptable. She needed money because she didn't plan on living in Mayson for much longer.

After deciding to leave her bags in the car, Liza moved around the building she had parked behind. She passed a couple SUVs and a Mercedes sedan. A Mercedes. That was pretty awesome, but a sliver of doubt clouded her mind. *Do I fit in here?* This was the issue that preyed on her ever since she decided to take the job at Camp Wildwood. Everyone in Mayson knew of the resort, and there tended to be a negative vibe about the clientele. Rich people from out of state. Conceited. Taking advantage of good mountain folk. The couple of Mayson residents who worked at Wildwood were ostracized all summer and had to work their way back into society all winter. It had been her counselor at school, Mr. Wethers, who had pushed her toward Camp Wildwood for something to do over the summer. He was devastated that she was not attending college, and that only made her feel worse. She wished she was headed off in September as well, but shit happens.

The situation was both frustrating and completely disheartening. Her grades were not the highest in her graduating class, but they were still excellent by most student standards. Liza was finishing third in a class of one hundred and one. Not too shabby and with the extracurricular activities, she was a solid candidate for college. Unfortunately, her mother refused to pay the application fees for the schools she was interested in. Mr. Wethers stepped up and helped her pay for two applications to SUNY Albany and St. Lawrence University. Liza was accepted at both, but the money was not there. Although she would easily qualify for financial aid, her mother failed to fill out the needed forms. Her reasoning revolved around a general idea that college was a waste of money and time. It was better to just get a job and start earning money. That had been bad. Liza had considered packing up her meager belongings and hitting the road, making space between herself, her mother, and Mayson. But it had been school that had kept her home. The school's spring musical was about to be performed, and she had a lead role and couldn't leave the crew in the lurch.

The current plan was nebulous. She hoped that this job panned out, and when fall came, maybe she could decide where to move off to with some money in her pocket. Maybe in a few years she could earn enough money to seriously consider college.

Walking past a first-floor window set in the main building, she saw her reflection perfectly in the glass. Her shoulder-length brown hair was straight as always and brushed out to perfection. She was wearing her best polo shirt, which she had gotten while in the jazz band. Her blue eyes stared back at her. The overall image was that of a pretty young woman. It was as impressive as she could present herself. Although she had already interviewed and gotten the job, her first appearance was still of the highest importance. To the amazement of most, especially her mother, he had been prom queen. Looking at her reflection, that thought still seemed alien. She was just a redneck from the mountains.

She sighed. This job had to work.

The day she had interviewed for the position had been a gray, rainy Sunday. This day was the polar opposite. When Liza turned the corner of the lodge, the lake appeared before her. Its blue water was devastating, and she stopped in her tracks. Although only nine in the morning, a group of people, probably a family, was already setting up an area on the beach for a day of sunbathing. There was a dock, a boat, and a raft for swimmers. It was a resort. A man wearing a golf shirt, khakis, and flip-flops strode past her with a pleasant "Good morning." He wandered off toward a cabin set back in the trees. It was an overload of alien conditions. She didn't belong. Her brain willed her body to turn and walk back to the car. Within an hour, she could be back in her bed, waiting until afternoon to go to a pregraduation party. The summer could progress along like all the others in her life. But...

Liza attempted to control her breathing and forced her feet to step onto the sidewalk and walk around to the front door. This had to happen. This had to be the beginning of her future, or all was lost.

*****

Meredith was sitting at her desk looking at the bills that had arrived in the mail. They were adding up, but finally, cash flow was coming in. The first week had gone exceedingly well, as all guests seemed to enjoy their stay and the only early season glitches were minor. A few light bulbs blew out. The flue in cabin 4 was not opened all the way open when a couple started a fire on a cool night and ended up with a smoky cabin. On the opening Saturday, an eleven-year-old boy fell off the dock, and Pete quickly moved in to pull him out of the lake before it got more serious. Normal opening pains according to Thomas. Nothing to worry about, which was a huge relief.

"Mrs. Riley?"

Meredith recognized Olga's voice at the door. Olga had total control of the cleaning service for the interior of all the buildings, which was a great help, but Meredith was also learning that she could be a huge pain in the ass. Common sense was lacking in the woman, and Meredith wished she could just make a decision on her own. The woman should be able to pick a brand of glass cleaner without approval from the owner.

"Olga," she responded toward the door. Olga could not actually be seen, but she was there in the hallway. "Come on in."

Olga stepped into view and then into the room with an odd carriage of authority while a younger woman followed behind her.

"Mrs. Riley, this is the new girl that we have been expecting. She can begin work today."

Meredith nodded. "Thank you, Olga." There was an odd silence before she spoke again. "What's your name?"

The young woman looked at her with eyes that were meek.

"Liza Grant."

Meredith smiled, hoping to get a similar response from the girl. "How old are you?"

"Eighteen, ma'am. Just graduating from high school."

A slight smile touched the corner of the girl's mouth.

"Okay. Olga will show you the ropes, and if you ever need to talk, my door is open."

"Thank you, ma'am."

Olga turned, and the girl quickly did the same and followed. The new girl was quite attractive, but she seemed extremely nervous and uneasy. Meredith hoped she would fit in because they needed the help. One of the women they hired to clean rooms had already quit, leaving them shorthanded.

She turned to the computer and hit the saved tab for the National Weather Service site. One thing she learned was that the local radar wasn't all that accurate in the mountains. It made sense with all the interference from the hills. The seven-day forecast popped up, and it was mostly sunny with a few days that had small chances of showers or thunderstorms. Highs were near eighty most days. Summer was finally settling in and sticking around. The Fourth was coming up in just over two weeks. She hoped for great weather because they were now mostly booked for July and most of August.

The money would be rolling in.

10

June 21

The woods were dark around him as he sat on a boulder looking out over the lake. Opposed to the shadowy woods, sunshine brilliantly beat onto the calm blue water in front of him, making it almost hard to look at from the shade. The sun was at its highest and brightest point of the year. Josh had discovered this spot just on the edge of the Camp Wildwood property and slipped away to it whenever he needed a break from the tensions at the resort. As he sat, he sometimes wondered what this view was like on the other side of the seasons. What was this spot like in January? It was a chilling thought even on a hot day. Looking back toward the lodge, cabin 9's roof could just be made out over a tangle of brush at ground level and the boughs of a pine that rose above the building. No one was in cabin 9 at the moment, but he was sure that it wouldn't have mattered because he was almost invisible on his rock.

Across the calm water, he could see most of the beach, the dock, and the lawn leading up to the lodge. There were a few groups on the sand, mostly families, that were migrating to the resort now that most schools were done for the summer. He could see kids frolicking in the water and an adult lying out on the swim raft absorbing some sun. Slip was sitting in his chair above the beach, keeping his watchful eye on it all. The boat was tied to the dock, and Josh knew that Slip was dying to go out for a spin, but that could only happen later and only if a guest requested it. Surprisingly, a few did. He knew that if he was staying at a place like this, he would be all over a cruise around the lake.

The sounds of any summer beach carried clearly across the water to Josh's spot, and the sound gave him mixed emotions. The sound of people having fun at the resort was exciting. There was some symbiotic relationship that he fed off when the guests enjoyed their vacations with such fervor. It was almost like he was on vacation too. But at the same time, he relished the moments when he was alone near the water when the lake surrendered to the quiet of the forest. The time was pure relaxation. Bliss. That was why he was sitting on his rock.

When he had time off, he found it awkward to hang around the guests, and the employee dormitory offered little comfort, so he headed for the woods. Some days he retired to the trees to eat his lunch. At times, the guests just got on his nerves a little too much, so he needed a peaceful break. Today Josh was on the rock because of his mother.

The times when he spoke with his mother were few and extremely uncomfortable. He had never really known her, and when they talked, the conversation was usually forced by two people who felt obliged to speak but had absolutely nothing to talk about. Therefore, the moments of communication were rare. That was why she had shocked him just an hour earlier with a phone call. The strange conversation kept playing over in his head.

He looked at the phone and saw his mother's number in New Mexico. He quickly did some math and realized that it was eight in the morning there, way earlier than she had ever called him before. To make it odder still, it wasn't a birthday, Christmas, or any other pivotal day that a mother and son needed to talk. Maybe Hallmark had invented a new day. Son Day or Offspring Day or Stupid Bullshit Day. Either way, it was very unusual to be getting a call from her at this time. He was busy sweeping the lodge patio and debated allowing the call to forward to voice mail but finally decided to answer.

"Mom?"

"Josh?" she asked, sounding very far away. "Josh, are you there?"

"Yeah, Mom, I'm here. How are you?"

There was a brief hesitation. "Are you there, Josh? Are you all right?"

Frustration began to build in him. Talking with his mother was often worse than talking to a six-year-old.

"I'm fine, Mom. How are you?"

"I...I just had a horrible dream. You were...not safe."

Okay. This was a new one. His mother was having weird dreams about him. Great.

"I'm fine, Mom. What was the dream?"

Silence greeted this question, and Josh actually thought for a second that she had hung up on him until she finally spoke.

"Where are you?"

"I'm at my summer job. Dad set it up for me in the mountains."

"Mountains?"

"Yes. Dad hooked me up with a job at a resort up in the Adirondacks."

Josh was almost convinced that he heard his mother gasp before another prolonged silence set in. He waited, now rather intrigued by the whole conversation. His mother's response took him back a step.

"Camp Wildwood?"

"What? Well, yeah. Camp Wildwood. Did Dad tell you?"

Josh knew damn well that his mother had not spoken with his father. That hadn't occurred in years. Then how did she know? Again there was silence.

"Mom?"

"Josh, be careful."

"Come on, Mom. How did you know I was here?

Silence.

"Mom?" Josh asked, becoming agitated.

"It was in the dream. Please, Josh, be careful."

This time, the silence that followed was total, and after a few seconds, Josh realized his mother had hung up. He stood still on the patio, feeling something akin to a goose walking over one's grave.

The water was like a mirage that he was being sucked into. Staring at it was similar to staring at a fire. Hypnotic. It allowed the mind to roam, and his had been rambling ever since he arrived at his spot of seclusion. After his strange talk with his mother, he texted his father and asked if they had ever been to Camp Wildwood before. His father had texted back a simple answer:

your mother &i did yrs ago. why?

They had been here before, and Josh had not been along for the ride. Was that before he was born? An image of his mom and dad as a younger couple on a romantic premarital excursion seemed plausible. He could imagine them staying in cabin 9 on a cool fall weekend with a fire going in the stove. But what if the trip had occurred after he was born? What if it had been the fateful vacation that his mother had never truly returned from?

Josh, be careful.

The words stuck in his head. He wanted to call her back but knew that a call would yield nothing at the moment. She might not even remember the conversation or the peculiar dream.

The water was beautiful, and he could hear kids squealing in the distance. He needed to get back to help Slip in case someone wanted to use a kayak or the Whaler. He found that he really had come to love this place, but was it all that it appeared to be? A chill swept him as he headed back through the cool woods toward the hot sun.

Slip was standing on the dock talking with some guests when Josh returned to the beach. The guests were a young couple from New York City, and they were here to have a couple of days of raucous fun. Slip had said that they shut the bar down the night before at midnight, which was like 6:00 a.m. for this place. Why hadn't they decided to vacation in Lake George where the bars *were* open until 4:00 a.m.? Camp Wildwood was the antithesis of rowdy Lake George.

"C'mon, Pete?" the young man was saying with exaggerated hand motions. "You are the man and can make this happen."

"Just wait an hour until the beach quiets down," Pete answered calmly.

"She might be drunk in an hour!"

Slip saw Josh walk up, and the relief on his face was obvious. Slip waved quickly with his hands, calling Josh out onto the dock. The guy whom Slip was talking to was skinny with a deep tan and black shocks of hair. His girlfriend, fiancée actually, was a looker with light brown hair and a killer body. There was a very small pastel green bikini covering a tiny part of her body, and she was holding a plastic cup, which probably held an alcoholic mixed drink. At Wildwood, the guests could drink anywhere on the premises as long as it wasn't in glass containers. Slip had said that it was like Key West, but Josh had never been there. The guy was being persistent, but Josh didn't detect any ill feelings.

"Josh!" Slip yelled with a big smile as Josh stepped onto the wooden deck of the dock. "Come on over here."

The guest turned and looked at Josh, and there was a big half-drunk smile on the guy's face. This couple was enjoying Camp Wildwood to its fullest.

"Vic, this is Josh Martin, one of our best employees. He can help make this happen."

"All right!" the guy cheered.

"Josh, this here is Vic Silverman. Vic wants to teach his fiancée, Julie, how to waterski. The issue is the number of hands available. We need someone to drive the boat, spot in the boat, and someone to help this young lady in the water. This is in addition to the eyes needed to watch the rest of the guests on the beach."

Josh looked at Julie and smiled at her. She was very pretty in the green bikini and she also looked very scared. That bikini was going to have a tough time staying in place if she really tried to ski. He was hoping that she would give it a shot. Unfortunately, Julie didn't seem to be completely on board with the whole proceedings that were carrying on around her.

"I can help out."

"Great," Vic said with a big smile and a clap of his hands. "Honey, you're going to ski!"

"Super," was the subdued reply with a slight slur.

"Aw, come on. Do this and then Pete promised us a booze cruise later."

Slip looked at Josh with a huge smile and pointed his finger at him while mouthing the word *you*. Slip would be working in the bar in an hour and a half, which meant Josh would be driving the boat. Booze cruise captain.

After a quick lesson, Slip and Vic dove into the Whaler while Julie slipped into the water, visibly shaking.

"You're doing great, honey." Vic was waving his two thumbs in the air. Julie didn't respond.

"Lie back and let the ski vest float you," Josh said. He had skied millions of times and was actually getting a kick out of teaching someone, especially when the student was extraordinarily attractive. "See if you can get the skis on your feet."

Julie was trying to slide the ski onto her right foot, but the effort was rotating her body as if she was weightless. That was why NASA astronauts trained for spacewalks in huge tanks of water. Josh reached out and grabbed the shoulders of the life vest, trying to keep her steady. The girl was grunting and straining and somehow managed to successfully get the skis on.

"You good?" Josh asked the girl whose lips had gone over to a deep purple color. They were luscious, and he felt something stirring in him despite the cool water. He tried to shake off the arousal and concentrate on his job.

Julie nodded, and that was a positive. Josh remembered his first time skiing, and yeah, he had been scared too. The fear and cool water led to shaking. He recalled wondering why he was sitting in the water behind a boat and wanted nothing more than to get out of the water and back into the warm sun. When the boat did pull him out, the adrenaline and sheer joy made him quickly forget his coldness. He hoped Julie would soon have the same sensation.

Josh nodded to Slip, who was standing over the stern gunwale with the tow rope in his hands. Vic was behind him with a camera taking pictures of his poor fiancée in distress. It was actually pretty funny. Slip brought his right arm back and then flung the colorful ski rope far above his head and out toward Josh. The heavier handle splashed about a foot from his head, and he gave Slip a good-natured glare.

"Okay," Josh said, trying to sound positive. "Here's the rope. Grip it with two hands. When the boat starts out, let it pull you up, don't yank back. The boat will drag you right out of the water."

"T-t-that's all I...I do?"

"That's it," he answered with a smile. Keep your tips up as high as you can and don't pull back on the rope."

He handed her the well-gripped handle and took a couple of steps back before he asked if she was ready. There was no response, and he was pretty sure that she was incapable of talking at that point. Shivering paralysis. Josh looked up at Slip, who had taken his spot at the captain's chair and waved him to go ahead. Slip smiled and put the throttle gently down. The result was not what Josh had expected. Just as the boat began to move, Julie lost her floating balance, and her ski tips dipped below the surface. A bad sign. The boat moved her forward but only her upper body. She ended up doing a Superman with her arms outstretched, getting a face-ful of water. He began to yell at her to let go of the rope, which she finally did. She had only been dragged a few feet, but when he got to her, it sounded as if she was dying from ingestion of Moon Lake water. Coughing spasms wracked her body as the boat did a circle and came back toward the dock.

"You okay?"

Although coughing, Julie nodded, and he instantly gained some respect for the girl. She was tough. The shivering had stopped, but the water in the lungs might be a more serious problem.

"Do you want to try again?"

That was when the boat came in close, and Vic yelled out after putting down his camera.

"That was great, honey, but let go of the rope sooner. You'll get it this time."

Slip was recoiling the rope, and Josh knew he was thinking something similar to what he was—there was no way this girl was going to try again. Surprisingly, she nodded, grabbed her skis, and began to prepare for another attempt. Again, Josh was awestruck by the girl.

"All right, this time we'll get it."

Josh knew an old trick that this cousin had used to get him to ski the first time. On this attempt, when the boat began to pull the towline taut, Josh lifted Julie from the bottom of her life vest. The effect stabilized her and lifted her. When the boat took off, Josh used his strength to push her into an upright position, which meant she was already skiing. As he did this, his hands slipped, and he found himself pushing her up by her firm buttocks. It was a cheap thrill, and he felt it through his entire body. Oh, that was bad. Hopefully she wouldn't notice his grope and he could keep his job security. Damn, but she had a nice ass.

To his amazement, Julie stood, and as the boat accelerated, she skied off into the lake. It was wobbly, but she was skiing. The event lasted for about five hundred yards before she pulled back on the rope and almost did a full gainer into the water. Her day was done.

Josh stood in the water up to his chest with the sun beating down as it slowly moved to the west. If every day was like this, then he was going to have a super summer. Perhaps due in part to the image of Julie in her bikini, he had completely forgotten the talk with his mother.

11

June 29

The graduation ceremony had been a jumble of emotions for Liza. Being with all of her classmates one final time was stirring. Before they walked onto the school football field with "Pomp and Circumstance" playing repetitively, they gathered in the gym. All one hundred of them packed onto the hardwood floor with the thrill of the moment ripe in the air. Liza had looked around the room and saw some close friends, along with simple acquaintances and a few people she cared not to recognize. The Newcomb district was small, and everyone knew their classmates. Like any group, there were nice folks and ass-holes. She had dealt with plenty of the latter over her school career and didn't want to deal with them again. Surrounding her was a group of her closest friends, including Matt and her best girlfriend, Alison. They tried to talk over the din, but Liza stopped trying. She wanted to savor this brief moment and then be done with it.

Eventually they marched to the football field and sat through a number of speeches and a piece played by the jazz band. Finally, they all walked across the stage to gather their diplomas. When Liza stepped onto the stage, there were no shouts or whistles as some students received but some subdued and polite clapping. She didn't have raucous friends or family members that screamed her name like she had just won the freaking Super Bowl. Her mother and brother were out there, or at least her mom said they would be. She looked down from the stage and saw her favorite teacher, Mr. Palmento, smiling at her with his thumbs sticking up vertically. That was nice, and a smile spread on her face as she focused on the principal's hand and the diploma he held out to her. Liza smiled, moved her tassel from one side of her mortar board to the other, and walked off the stage. That was it. In the blink of an eye, she was officially done with high school, and as she settled back into her seat, the reality started to crush her.

After the ceremony, everyone milled around the school parking lot as kids smiled and parents cried. Her mom had come up and congratulated her and then taken her brother back to her car to drive back to Mayson. She was alone and felt as if she had crossed a monumental threshold only to be deserted. No longer a child, Liza was ready to move on, and she knew at that instant that she would never return to her school. It reminded her of the Steely Dan song that Burt used to play. The great thing was that she was okay with the realization. A kid next to her said that this was the greatest moment of his life. God, she hoped that wasn't true. It was just freaking high school. She wanted to move on something grander, but she wondered if that something existed for her.

Liza was now looking across the bowling alley, recalling the sense of transition she had had after graduation. The after-graduation party was actually hopping with loud music, lots of lights, and people that had a family member graduate that evening. On most occasions, the bowling hall was a dump, but it almost looked nice tonight. She had come along to the party with Matt and Alison, although she wasn't sure why. She had no desire to attend the party, but where else did she have to go?

That was the question that plagued her thoughts. Where was she going? Matt was leaving for Syracuse. Alison was going to SUNY Albany. Many of her classmates would be nowhere near the old high school come September, and Liza feared that she would still be in the vicinity, and that scenario was unacceptable. The depression that accompanied the thought was overwhelming, and the weight of her failed life pressed down like a lead sky. Hopelessness. That was all she felt, and being in the exultant atmosphere of the bowling alley wasn't helping.

"Come on," Matt said next to her. "Let's go bowl a game."

Liza couldn't imagine mustering the enthusiasm for that at the moment.

"I'm just going to stand here."

Matt cocked his head and looked at her funny. "You okay?"

No. Tears began to well in her eyes, and her throat choked up. No, she wasn't okay but she wasn't the type that wanted to make a scene. She managed to smile, nod, and wave Matt off to bowl. He gave her an odd glance and walked off, leaving her alone. She found that she desperately wanted him to stay and listen to her. Maybe they could have gone outside where she could have cried a good one on his shoulder. She needed to vent and have someone tell her that everything would be all right.

"Liza!"

She turned to her right to see the person who had called her name and found herself looking at Mr. McDonald. Mr. McDonald was the school's only foreign language teacher. He somehow taught sections of French, Spanish, and even tried to teach a Latin class. Although a decent teacher and nice guy, he had the creepy personality of trying to be involved in the students' lives a little too much. Facebook. Social groups. It was common knowledge that he often came close to crossing the student-teacher line. There were plenty of rumors about Mr. McDonald around the school, and Liza tried to ignore them. He was one of the only teachers at this student party, however.

"Hi, Mr. McDonald."

"Everything all right? You have a long face."

Liza tried to smile. "It's the only face I have."

"Ha!" Mr. McDonald exclaimed. "There's your spunk. Ah, such a nice night. Beautiful ceremony. You all look so excited headed out on your future adventures."

"Yep," Liza responded, simply hoping that Mr. McDonald would wander away. His presence was making her uncomfortable.

"You staying here long?"

Liza looked out and saw Alison high-five Matt after getting a spare. They were enjoying the moment, solid in the knowledge that this was just the beginning steps in an exciting voyage. Instead, she was standing next to a teacher who was straddling a thin line. True, she was no longer a student technically, but he better not be propositioning her. The stories she had heard about Mr. McDonald and students flooded her head but didn't blur her thoughts.

"Nope," she replied quickly. "I have to get back to work."

And with that simple statement, she stepped forward and away from high school forever. Camp Wildwood would be her home for a few months. She wasn't going to her mom's or to Matt's. She would go back to her single room in the dorm building at Wildwood. That realization was surprising but also made her feel surprisingly pleasant. She wanted to see the water under the starlight.

"Work?" he asked. "Tonight? Where do you work?"

Liza suddenly wanted to leave, but she couldn't be rude.

"Camp Wildwood out past Mayson."

Mr. McDonald's eyes widened suddenly. "Camp Wildwood? On Ghost Lake?"

"Moon Lake," she corrected.

Mr. McDonald was looking at her funny. "Lots of people call it Ghost Lake."

"I've never heard that."

He nodded slowly. "Indian legend says it's haunted."

"What?" Liza said in a high-pitched voice.

Mr. McDonald stepped away from her and smiled a small weird grin. "Probably a stupid old wives' tale. Have a nice summer, Liza."

He turned and walked back into the party where kids and parents laughed, all probably slightly intoxicated on booze or weed. One kid, Efram Johnson, tilted his head back in wild laughter that reminded her of a hyena. Oh yeah. It was time to blow. She looked down at Matt and Alison and saw the joy they were sharing. It wasn't fair for her to bring them down, and it also wasn't healthy for her to stand there and suffer. As a strobe light flashed on the lanes, she turned and quickly exited through the door. A Taylor Swift song was blasting as she left, and she would always remember that moment when she heard the tune. It was only nine-thirty, and there was still light in the western sky, although only a little. She needed to leave once and for all. She started her car and peeled out of the parking lot, leaving her youth behind.

*****

The stars were as bright as they were every night, forcing a person's eyes upward to gaze upon them. He had never seen the night sky as brilliant as it was in the Adirondacks, even when he had been to the Caribbean with his family. This was impressive, and it was hypnotizing.

Josh was making this his nightly routine. When the dinner crowd began to thin out in the lodge, Slip would smuggle a six-pack of beer to Josh through the kitchen. Slip said it was a tip for helping him during the day, and Josh was appreciative. It was actually funny considering a six-pack would hardly give him a buzz at school. A case was more on the order for a night of drinking in college. But as odd as it was, the six-pack was perfect for what Josh did at night.

He had one of the cans of beer on the dock next to him as he dangled his feet in the lake water. Although the water temperature was still only in the sixties and far from hot tub level, it felt wonderful as the nighttime air temperature dropped even lower toward the fifties. He slowly moved his feet back and forth in the water, and the massage was amazing. The whole experience was outstanding. Never had he been able to achieve such a relaxed state. The lake and hills were completely tranquil, and the effect was as calming as any therapy. This shit should be in the resort brochure. "Come to Camp Wildwood where relaxation is free! Just grab a beer and shove your feet in the water!" This crap should be bottled and sent to New Jersey and Boston and NYC. Those crazy-ass people could use a dose of Moon Lake water.

This time represented his daily healing. Sitting in paradise with a slow beer just thinking. Back in high school or at Mount Union, it would have been painful to sit alone on a Friday night. During football season, he could deal because there was always a game on Saturday, but out of season, the parties called. It was an expectation to go out. To a frat party or a house. To a bar or a club. He went where the girls were. There was always something going on, even if he was underage. Only losers stayed in on Friday nights, and he was definitely not a loser. To be stuck in on a Friday sucked more than just about anything. The thought that the right girl might be at a party that he wasn't attending was frustrating, but here in the mountains, it was all right and, in fact, perfect to be alone. To hear a loon make its haunting cry or a big bass smack the water after leaping after a fly was simply amazing. Josh enjoyed the dock more than anything at Camp Wildwood. He smiled, thinking that he was having a bunch of John Denver moments.

A car's headlights briefly swept over the beach. The lights of cars in the parking lot were weak on the dock, but in the complete darkness, it was noticeable. He could hear a television with what sounded like the Red Sox game from one of the cabins, and there were a few people drinking and talking on the porch of cabin 4. Occasionally a gust of laughter floated down, and instead of ruining the solitude, it only added to the experience of the resort at night. It was perfect.

He liked most of the guests, but just like in the real world, for every awesome person, there was at least one asshole. They occasionally showed up at Camp Wildwood, but Slip said he hadn't seen anything yet this year. The Fourth was coming up, and that threatened to be hectic. He said the holidays brought out the assholes. *Bring it on*, he thought and drank from his beer. He had only had two cans, which was a minimum record of sorts. Crazy.

A light flashed on the dock for a brief instant and went away. That was something different, and Josh turned to see a wobbling light on the lawn between the dock and the lodge. It was clear that it was a flashlight that someone was holding on the way to the water. He didn't like the idea of his solitude being broken. In fact, only a few nights earlier, Slip had come down after closing the bar, and they had had a good time drinking and shooting the shit on the dock. But he felt very awkward being found sitting alone with his feet in the water. Not very cool and maybe a little weird. As the light bobbed, it centered on the dock, and Josh realized that the person was headed for his general area. Instead of moving, he sat still, hoping that the person would miss him, but it was clearer every second that the flashlight holder was headed for the dock. The light finally settled on him, and the person stopped dead in their tracks with the beam shining in his eyes.

"Howdy," he said, trying to sound unobtrusive but feeling suddenly exposed and uncomfortable. The flashlight lowered.

"Hi," a soft female voice answered. He had no idea whom the voice belonged to, but he was positive that he had heard it before.

"Um," he stuttered, suddenly wondering if it was Julie the cute skier. He certainly hoped it was Julie. Ever since the skiing episode she and her green bikini had washed in and out of his mind. Maybe her boyfriend got wasted and she had decided to come down to be with a real man. "What's up?"

There was a silence that made him momentarily uncomfortable until she spoke again.

"I'm sorry. I didn't mean to bother you."

The light briefly bobbed up, and he caught a quick view of light brown hair and a pretty face that he recognized as one of the new housekeepers. He had passed her a number of times in the lodge and the dorm, and she was pretty, even wearing her work clothes.

"You aren't bothering me. Care to sit down and have a beer?"

The moment was frozen, and Josh wouldn't forget it. It was as if time had decided to take a break for a second to get a cup of coffee. When time came back, the girl moved forward and turned off the flashlight. The night once again fell into darkness, even more so now that his eyes had adjusted to the glow of the electric torch. The girl mumbled and sat down, crossing her legs and not dangling them in the lake. Josh grabbed a lukewarm beer, opened it, and handed it to her. He could see her white teeth as she smiled.

"Thanks," she said. "I'm not much of a drinker."

"Tonight I'm not either."

Silence fell over them again, and the lake made its own noises, as did the people on the porch of cabin 4. The girl took a sip from her can, and that was about it. Josh caught a glimpse of her. She was very pretty and she was just staring out over the water. Then she spoke out of the blue and bluntly.

"I graduated from high school tonight."

"Congratulations. Locally?"

She nodded. "Yeah. An hour from here. There aren't many high schools in this neck of the woods."

"That's great. What are your plans for next year?"

Josh could sense the girl's sudden tension and realized that he had stepped in some mud that he shouldn't have. He was actually surprised that she had taken control of his space and the conversation. The girl had a certain power that was transfixing.

"I left my after-graduation party to come here. I wanted to see the water. Isn't that weird?"

"No," Josh answered. "I totally understand."

She looked at him, and Josh found himself looking into eyes that many called bedroom eyes. Soft and mellow. She turned back to the water and just looked out.

"I needed to see this lake."

"Do you like working here?" Josh asked, knowing he sounded stupid but not knowing where else to take this conversation.

The girl nodded. "Yes, I do. I wasn't sure at first if I'd like it, but it's a great spot. It's almost like home now." She stopped and chuckled. "I've only been working here six days. Home. That's crazy."

"But," Josh said slowly, "what about your real home?"

The girl drank from the beer and said nothing. Josh tried to get a take on her and was surprised to realize that she was crying. She was silent, but he noticed distinct hitching in her shoulders. Okay, this was peculiar, but even odder was a feeling that invaded his consciousness. He felt an intense need to reach out to her. And it wasn't a need to smash his lips on hers and feel up her crotch. He wanted to comfort her.

"Are you all right?"

The girl didn't answer and continued to silently let whatever was ailing her out. Although he wanted to help, he decided to let her go and wait until she was ready. He awkwardly sat next to her with his beer, focusing on the water. Someone raised their voice at cabin 4, and gales of laughter followed. A punch line. The noise seemed far away and inconsequential. This girl had just graduated from high school? Tonight? Why wasn't she with her friends? He thought back a year before to his graduation and remembered a night that had been epic. Man, this didn't add up.

"Sorry," the girl said quietly, pulling Josh from his own memories of graduation that felt like a decade and not just a year earlier. "I..."

"It's okay," he said. "If something is eating you up inside, this is the perfect place to deal with it."

"Yeah." She spoke softly. "I guess so. It's why I came back here. Pretty weird."

"What's your name?" Josh asked, trying to help out the best he could.

The girl straightened her legs and readjusted her sitting position. "Liza. Yours?"

"Josh. I work grounds and down by the lake in the afternoons."

He was somewhat surprised that she began to stand. This wasn't what he expected at all. He wanted to know what was eating at her. He wanted to help the damsel in distress. She was cute, and that was somewhat rare around old Camp Wildwood, especially within the staff. Meredith was the only decent-looking woman, and she was definitely off limits.

"Nice to meet you, Josh, and thanks for the beer."

Liza smiled at him, and in the starlight, he could see the beauty and he felt something stir inside his chest.

"Umm…yeah," he managed, trying to get up quickly but deciding that he wouldn't be able to without falling into the lake. "I hope you feel better." God, that sounded lame. This girl had him tongue-tied.

"Yeah," she said before she turned on the dock and toward the buildings. "I do feel a little better. See you around, Josh."

He watched her walk away and saw the silhouette of her body as she crossed in front of the lights still blazing from cabin 4. He had noticed her before but hadn't given the sightings much attention until now. She was beautiful, and he knew that she would be on his mind for days to come. Wow, had the man-killer Josh Martin just been hit with a cross to the jaw by a local Adirondack girl? He smiled and drank from his beer. The lake was the same as it had been before she had wandered down the dock. The occasional loon cried. A bass flopped. And someone said something hilarious at cabin 4. But the night was different, and the experience of Camp Wildwood would not be the same. She was dragging him down a new road, and he hoped it would end awesomely.

12

July 2

Fourth of July week was upon them, and the resort had filled up overnight. Having the Fourth on a Wednesday created a unique dilemma for most vacationers. On what weekend did a family celebrate the holiday? Did they vacation the weekend before that started in late June just as most kids were released from school? Or did they take off the midweek and extend the vacation until the post-Fourth weekend? This might sound moot and insignificant, but when a person ran a resort, it was nice to have groups move out on Sunday to accommodate a new influx of guests. At Camp Wildwood, it seemed most people were coming in to spend the whole week and the place was full.

Meredith had just finished giving Kristen a hand inputting data into the computer behind the main desk, and she was already sick of some of the guests, especially Bernie Winsor. Freakin' Bernie Winsor. Bernie was actually a Bernella, a name that no normal human being would ever name their child since the 1830s, but here she was at Camp Wildwood. Bernella Winsor, better known as Bernie. The Winsor clan included a husband, Andy, and two very loud, annoying children named something stupid. They had pulled in Sunday afternoon for their stay. Meredith remembered when Kristen had taken the call from a family who wanted a two-week stay at the resort in cabin 11, one of the most expensive available. The amount of money they would spend in two weeks would be significant, and the thought of renting out the cabin for a full block was attractive but strange. Because of the remoteness of the resort, few guests stayed on for more than a week, especially the ones with children. The lake and the grounds only offered so much entertainment, and in foul weather…it could get ugly. Yet the Winsors had been enthusiastic saying that they were going to spend a night or two in Lake George but would still pay for the room at Wildwood while they were gone. It was almost too good to be true from a financial standpoint. Unfortunately, reality was often a much different story.

Bernie Winsor was one of the biggest pains in the ass that Meredith had ever met, and the woman had been on site for less than twenty-four hours.

"I'm going back into my office for a bit," she told Kristen, who had to leave early for a doctor's appointment.

"Thanks for helping me get through this crap," Kristen replied. "Busy, huh?"

Meredith nodded tiredly and wandered down the short hall to her office where she just wanted to sit alone for a long moment. Sunday afternoon had seen a constant flow of guests arriving, and all the cabins and rooms had been filled by eight in the evening. They were busy, and that was an expected issue, but she hadn't planned on Hurricane Bernie.

Her father's old padded swivel chair behind the desk accepted her form, and she sighed, feeling her weight slip into the cushioning. She reached down into the little refrigerator and pulled out a Diet Pepsi because she needed some caffeine. After a long swig, she leaned back and shut her eyes. Wow, how did people like Bernie Winsor exist in our society?

The Winsors had arrived at around four o'clock on Sunday, which was a cloudy and cool day. They weren't the only group that showed up at roughly the same time, and there was a small wait at check-in. It very quickly became clear that Bernie was not going to wait. She actually pushed a couple out of the way as she barged to the counter, complaining that she needed her room immediately because her son needed to make a bowel movement. That had elicited a chuckle from the couple who had been knocked out of the way by snowplow Bernie, and she had apparently given them a stare that would have stopped a charging rhino. Somehow, her incredibly rude behavior had worked, and Bernie was able to quickly get into her cabin so her son could blow up the septic system. If that had been the only event, then it would have quietly passed and been joked about, but there was nothing quiet about Bernie.

The dining room had been as crowded as it had been all season that night, and it was the first real test for the new crew. Bernie and her clan had stormed in with kids whining loudly about being bored with nothing to do. They were escorted to a spot as far away from other human beings as possible, but Neptune wasn't distant enough. When her oldest son ordered a shrimp cocktail only to be told that Camp Wildwood didn't serve shrimp cocktail, the kid blew a fit that was only made worse when Bernie ranted that the dining room was second rate. The kid had finally settled for a peanut butter-and-jelly sandwich. The waitress who had worked the table received a generous tip from Mr. Winsor, but she was still near tears and talking about quitting when the Winsors stormed out into the evening.

When the night settled in and the guests retired to their accommodations for a peaceful slumber, the office got an emergency call from cabin 11. Pete had been closing the bar at the moment the call came in, so he ran across the grounds to the cabin. As he approached, he heard screaming from within, and the neighboring cabins all had their lights on with guests on the porches looking toward the ruckus. Bernie was frantic and ushered Pete into the cabin where one of her sons was screaming uncontrollably. From what Meredith gleaned, the kid was flipping out over a moth that was fluttering around the room. Pete had laughed at the kid, and Bernie had ripped into him. After removing the bug, Pete had explained that they were vacationing in the Adirondacks and not on Park Avenue and there was certain wildlife that lived in the woods. Bernie had called the office to complain about Pete, and that woke Meredith up from a deep sleep. She would actually be surprised if Pete showed up for work today after the lashing Bernie gave him.

She sighed and took another drink from the bottle. It was ten in the morning, and she knew that she should wander out and check up on operations, but she was actually kind of scared. What a mess, and the Fourth was only a couple days away. It would get nuttier. Her gaze fell on the cabinet in the corner, which held her father's log that she had been meaning to read. At this point, it might be a nice release from the chaos.

"How'd you deal with people like this, Dad?" she asked the ceiling above her and was startled to hear a response.

"He came in here and I think had a nip of Southern Comfort."

Meredith's gaze quickly dropped to the door, and she saw Thomas standing there in his white long-sleeved thermal shirt with a large smile.

"That would explain the half-empty bottle of the stuff that I found in his desk."

Thomas kept the smile as he came forward and sat in the chair in front of her desk. "It does get hectic at times. The key is to grin and deal with it, or it'll get the better of you."

"Does this mean I'm going to end up drinking whiskey at ten in the morning?"

Thomas just smiled. "It can be tough, and that woman is something else. One of the worst I've seen. Probably a good acquaintance of Satan himself."

She looked at him. "How's Slip?"

Thomas nodded. "Fine. He probably had ten beers afterward and laughed about it. You know him. It takes way more'n an obnoxious woman to bring him down, but I'm not sure about Olga."

"Olga?" Meredith asked, surprised. "What happened to Olga?"

Thomas chuckled. "Mrs. Winsor confronted her this morning about the moth and the *shabby* housekeeping. Olga was pissed."

"What the hell? She's going to ruin the entire summer in a couple of days. She's booked for two weeks! Can we kick her out?"

Thomas looked at her and shrugged. "Your dad had a way with people. I don't know how he did it, but he was amazing."

Meredith looked at the cabinet and realized that she had to read his journal.

"I haven't even been outside. What's the weather like?"

"Luckily," Thomas said, "It's beautiful. I don't want to imagine that woman and her kids if it rains."

Meredith stood and sighed knowing how true Thomas was. The weather better hold.

*****

He hadn't seen so many people on the beach and in the water before, and it was as close to utter chaos as he figured Camp Wildwood could get. Josh had not been able to mow any grass as he had assumed he would because he had been recruited to help with the kayaks and beach chairs while Slip watched all the people swimming. He had heard that the resort could accommodate just over one hundred guests, and he figured that they were all near the water. It was sunny, hot, and really a perfect beach day. The positive aspect was that all the guests seemed to be enjoying themselves, even Mrs. Winsor.

Josh hadn't been privy to her antics the night before, but Slip had filled him in and gave him a stern warning. Watch out for her. Slip explained that she was the perfect example of a guest that wouldn't think twice about having an employee fired over stupid, trivial matters. So far, except for some general unpleasantness, she was just a typical, generally unhappy tourist. The funny thing was that although he tried to ignore her, it was nearly impossible. The woman was like a mother bear with her two cubs. In fact, she kind of resembled a bear wearing a tight bathing suit that was completely unflattering. People her size should not go out in public showing the skin she was.

Certainly one of the oddest members of the Winsor family was her husband. Where Bernie was pushing two hundred pounds, her spouse couldn't weigh more than one-twenty. He was wearing a long bathing suit past his skinny knees and a blue T-shirt with Scranton on it. He wore glasses and seemed to be extremely timid, especially when his wife turned her wrath on him. His two sons were fat little monsters, running around the beach, bothering everyone else. The father sat in a chair in complete oblivion of his children's behavior as if sedated. Josh figured that the life the man had found himself in had finally pushed him to a point of a blissful waking coma.

Josh saw a young woman struggling to pull a kayak up on the beach, and he jogged down to help.

"Thanks," the girl said and turned to run up the beach to where her family was huddled together.

He wandered over to the lifeguard chair where Slip sat at attention, soaking up more sun.

"Lots of folks out here."

Slip nodded without taking his eyes off the water. "It's a zoo. How's my sweetheart doing?"

Josh looked over his shoulder at Bernie, who was yelling at one of her offspring.

"Bitching at her kid."

Slip smiled. "I might kill that woman before they leave. Might come down to her or me. Bad woman."

Josh agreed and figured that a response would be redundant, so he just looked around at the guests while waiting for Slip to speak again. There was splashing in the water, and a few kayakers had paddled out toward the middle of the lake. The Whaler sat at the dock. There were way too many people around to offer ski lessons or a cruise. Too bad.

"Any talent out here? I saw you help that girl with the kayak. She's pretty hot."

"Yeah, I guess." The girl had been very attractive, and Josh realized he hadn't noticed. He looked back toward the lodge involuntarily as he had done a thousand times over the last few days, hoping to get a glimpse of Liza. He had laid eyes on her a couple of times and had even said hello, but there had been little conversation beyond that. The hope was that she would return some night to the dock and they could renew their conversation. But unfortunately, the night before, a few guests had been out there ruining his routine, and that had been frustrating. It was completely shocking what she was doing to him.

"I guess? That girl is rocking. Man, you are twenty years old and single. Get on that shit."

"Why don't you?"

Slip laughed. "I'm almost ninety! Way too old for high school girls."

"Right," Josh responded sarcastically. "I have a feeling that age doesn't stop you."

Slip snorted. "I teach girls that age."

Josh shook his head, and his gaze went to the girl he had helped with the kayak. She was very attractive and…

There was a vibration in his khaki pants pocket that actually startled him. He grabbed his cell phone and was surprised to be getting a call and not a text. He was completely floored to see "Mother" appear as the caller. He had just spoken to her a couple days earlier, which had been totally unusual. This was just unprecedented. Josh quickly stepped away from the lifeguard chair and put the phone to his ear.

"Mom?"

"Josh? Josh? Is that you?"

"Yeah, Mom. It's me. I'm working."

There was a moment of silence. "You're at Moon Lake?"

Moon Lake? How did she remember that? She couldn't remember to brush her teeth in the morning.

"Yeah, I am, Mom."

There was a moment of silence before his mother spoke, and the tone of voice was flat-out spooky.

"It was the earthquake, Josh. The earthquake."

"The earthquake, Mom? What does that mean? Mom?"

He looked at his phone and saw that the call had ended. His mother was off the line, leaving him standing like an idiot, completely confused. What the hell was she talking about? Earthquake? He looked at the lodge and saw Liza walking down the steps in her housekeeping green polo shirt and khaki pants. She looked at him and waved, but he couldn't wave back.

*****

Meredith was sitting on the patio with a drink in her hand, which was a comfort after a harrowing day. The tiki torches were lit, even though there was still plenty of daylight left in the sky above and the sun was just striking the tops of the highest mountains for the last time that day. Citronella scent filled the air and kept most of the mosquitos at bay. There were a couple of groups of people on the patio around her, but the majority were still in the dining room, hopefully enjoying their dinners. She could hear the general din from the windows behind the patio.

She sighed and drank from her glass, which had a potent rum and Coke in it. Pete had hit the rum hard, and she hadn't complained. Meredith had never been much of a drinker, but the moment seemed right. A calmness settled inside her as the booze began to make an impact.

"Nice night," Thomas said. He was sitting in the chair next to her holding a beer bottle. It *was* a nice night, and she didn't respond to him because she had no intentions of spoiling the moment. The water was calm, and there were two kayaks out on the water. *Tranquil* was too vague a word. Some Coldplay song was mellowly playing in the bar. She sighed again, trying to completely clear her mind of the problems that kept popping into her thoughts. Unfortunately, most of them that evening were because of Michael.

When she left North Carolina, she left Michael behind both physically and more importantly mentally. Camp Wildwood had absorbed her, and she had forgotten Michael and her old home down South. Being busy was a wonderful way to cure the soul, and she had certainly been preoccupied. And there was Pete. Although she hated to admit it, she had had a crush on good old Slip even with the problems that had occurred when she was younger. Her father had overreacted then, and his presence had kept a wedge between the two of them. Well, that block was gone, and she could feel gravity pulling the two of them together as though it was destined to be. Meredith found that she was willing to be pulled and was enjoying Pete's company.

Michael had called at about four o'clock, and that had shocked her. She had gotten numerous text messages from him after she had headed north, but this was the first call in over two weeks. And even more surprising, Michael informed her that he was going to *make her summer dreams come true* and come up to visit for a week. He was going to show up on July ninth and make her day. Meredith wasn't prepared for the idea of Michael invading the space that she had adopted from her childhood. Moon Lake and Michael didn't make sense. It was like two cultures clashing. And what would she do about

Pete? She didn't want to spoil that budding relationship because dick-weed wanted to visit. But what was she to say? No? That couldn't happen, especially after all he had done for her.

"How am I doing?" she finally said aloud, trying to drive the thoughts into the recesses of her brain.

Thomas drank from his beer and smiled. "Fair."

She cocked her head and looked at him. "Fair?"

His smile faltered slightly. "You know I miss your father, and it's not exactly the same."

Meredith nodded and knew that it was the truth. It had to be weird for many of the employees who had been here for years.

"I'm sure it's odd."

Thomas smiled. "I wasn't sure if you could pull it off, but here we are and it's going very well. You're definitely your daddy's girl."

"Thanks," she replied and meant it. She had respected her father, and to fill his shoes successfully by even a fraction was a huge relief, and she felt a sudden closeness to him. Her eyes started to tear up from the emotion that unexpectedly swelled in her. *No, don't cry. You are tougher than that.* This much she learned when she left Michael, and she didn't want to regress to that old person. She could stand up for herself and be strong. That was why she wasn't sure about Michael coming to visit.

The kayakers were coming into the beach, and she was kind of surprised to see the shape of Josh moving out to help them.

"What's Josh doing down there still? Isn't it late for him to work?"

"I had him go down and rake the beach," Thomas responded. "He'll do it again in the morning. Lots of traffic today."

Meredith liked the kid but was holding out complete acceptance for a while longer. He seemed like a solid worker, but she knew the entire situation revolving around his employment. His father had pleaded with her to hire him for the summer and had made a nice financial donation to the resort. This place was not a rehab center, and she didn't want some troubled kid working her first summer. But he had turned out to be a great worker and a nice kid.

"I think Pete's sliding him beer at night." She was surprised that she stated it so matter-of-factly, but the knowledge had been bothering her.

The kid was here because he had gotten in trouble drinking, and now the bartender was giving him alcohol. And he was underage to boot.

Thomas nodded. "Yup, I'm sure he is. But before you go off and yell at the boy, he is very discreet about it, and a few beers isn't gonna do much. That boy works hard and he's basically here without anyone his age. He's changed."

"Changed? How?"

"Well," Thomas answered. "He seems to be truly happy here and he sure as crud didn't come in the driveway the first day with that mentality. I think he's becoming a mountain boy."

"Okay," she responded. "I think you're right, but remind him to be cool. Okay?"

Thomas nodded and drank from his beer. Meredith reminded herself to relax. Thomas knew how to take care of his staff, and she should step back. She had other things to worry about, like the guests. As if on perfect cue, the unmistakable voice of Mrs. Winsor was getting louder as she came through the main door with her brood following. She was complaining about the humid air. She was unbelievable.

"What's the weather tomorrow?" Meredith asked Thomas.

"Cloudy with a chance of showers. Maybe a storm tonight."

They both knew that that wasn't good news.

*****

Josh was happy that things had worked out and he had the dock alone. A period of quiet time was essential because things were sliding toward the chaotic. His feet were in the water, and he had a can of beer, and it tasted particularly good as he tried to relax. There were moments this evening that made him believe that this relaxation by the water would never happen.

The day had been bedlam for the most part. People everywhere and every one of them seemed to want something from him. He and Slip were pretty much left to deal with them by themselves, although Meredith and Thomas had wandered down to the beach occasionally to lend a hand. Josh had been on the beach until well past eight o'clock pulling in kayaks and canoes and raking the sand. However, as the people began to disperse toward their cabins for drinks, naps, or whatever they did, he began to settle in and enjoy the water again without the mob.

A serious cause of stress that kept him from focusing on his job was the call from his mother about an earthquake. That had been really weird. Earthquake. What the hell had that meant? Was there one in New Mexico that morning? Was she talking about here at Camp Wildwood? It was bizarre but it was also stuck in his head. As he struggled with the strange comment, he had decided that he should call his father, and that had been even stranger still.

First, he had to wait to make the call until after six o'clock when the beach finally calmed down, and that meant cocktail time wherever his dad was. It happened that he was on Martha's Vineyard. Or at least on his boat in Edgartown harbor. When Josh brought up the conversation with his mother and the mention of an earthquake, it had taken his father three chances to even come close to understanding what Josh was talking about. He must have been hitting the vodka and tonic hard.

"What the hell is she talking about?"

Josh explained that he didn't have any idea and that was why he had called.

"She called *you*?"

Again, Josh elucidated that yes, his mother had called him. It was getting to a point where he was about to end the call and just try and forget that he had even spoken to her. He reminded his father about the earthquake.

"Earthquake? What the hell is she talking about…oh yeah. I think there was a little trembler when we were up there at the resort. So what? What's gotten into her ass all of a sudden?"

Josh cut to the chase and asked if anything had happened when they had visited the resort decades before.

"No. Nothing happened and just forget about it. We just grew away from each other."

With that, his father had lovingly told him that he needed to go and refresh his drink and cut the call off. The conversation hadn't clarified a thing. Actually, Josh was now sure that something damaging had gone down when his parents had been to Camp Wildwood, especially since it was only a few weeks later that his mother left for good. Something had happened.

With the thoughts of the conversations he had just had with his parents swimming through his head, Josh helped the last guests with their watercraft and raked the beach. He stumbled up to the employee dorm where he threw on some deodorant, changed his shirt, and headed for the lodge where he could get his employee meal, which was something that his rumbling stomach really needed. The employee dorm was a long two-story building that resembled a small barn and was set back in the woods a decent distance from the lake and the prime real estate. They had divided the building up into small single rooms that numbered ten or twelve and housed most of the summer employees. Josh knew exactly which room was Liza's because he had noticed her enter a couple of times. Yes, he had watched for her and knew that he was bordering on becoming a stalker. Big deal. As he walked by her room down the central hallway, he considered knocking on her door but wasn't yet sure enough to make that move. He wasn't sure he would ever get there. With that depressing thought, he left the dorm and went for his meal.

The lodge had still been packed, and the bar where he often took his meals was hopping with guests enjoying their vacations. Out the window, he could see that there were a good amount of folks on the patio as well. That did not bode well. It seemed that Slip was too busy to get him his six-pack and there would definitely be guests on the dock. His mood collapsed, and for the first time since he had been at Camp Wildwood, Josh felt a little lost and wondered if he was in the right place after all.

Karma had fulfilled its promise, and after a hard day, things began to fall in place. Slip did in fact slide him the beer, and as of the moment, no guests had intruded on the end of the dock.

The water had warmed under the hot July sun. The wind hadn't really blown either to mix the cooler, deep waters to the surface. Behind him, the resort was as loud as he had heard it. People enjoyed the night on the patio and on their cabin porches. At one point, he was positive he heard the distinctive voice of Bernie Winsor screaming out for everyone to *shut the fuck up*. Man, what a classy broad. Over the mountain to the south was a dim flash. Lightning somewhere far off. It might rain at some point overnight. Super. The fine summer weather had so far held, and it was actually pretty dry. A little rain would be good, but what would the guests do on a soggy day?

That wasn't his worry. His parents' strange story was, and he was coming to two conclusions: either some family history was being withheld from him or his mother was getting loopier every day. Either way, it wasn't something that made him pleased. The water moved silently below him. It was the perfect situation to have a beer and think.

*****

She had been kept busy. Only two girls were on duty today, and all the guest rooms had to be cleaned. There was not one vacancy at Camp Wildwood, and that meant a full schedule. Luckily, they were all deserted because the sun and beach had called and the guests had all responded. It had taken five hours to get every room and cabin cleaned, and on top of that, she helped out in the kitchen for dinner preparation. It was nonstop but it was awesome. Liza loved the job. It kept her busy and kept her mind off the problems that had seemed to haunt her head for the last year. What she would do in the fall seemed distant as she focused on the job at hand. The pay wasn't great, but the occasional big tip made up for it. The best element was that all the cash was going directly into the bank. She figured that she might put enough money away for a change of scenery in September after all. Maybe she could still attend Adirondack Community College. It wasn't St. Lawrence, but any college was better than Mayson.

She had retired to her room and was reading a Carl Hiaasen book on her bed when she had an abrupt attack of the moves. She couldn't sit in the room again as she had the last couple nights. The walls were pressing in. At first, a little isolation and self-reflection was fine, but she was human and craved some human contact. Unfortunately, the girls she worked with were nice enough but not exactly the people to sit with and have a deep discussion. She knew whom she could talk to, but she was terrified to approach him. He was attractive, but she didn't want a romance, at least not yet. She just wanted to sit with her feet in the water and talk about life with someone her age while she gazed up to watch Jupiter rise in the eastern sky. She just hoped that he would be receptive.

This time she didn't have her flashlight and had to stop for a moment to let her eyes adjust to the darkness. The dock was there, a slightly brighter finger sticking out into the black waters of the lake. There were still people on the patio drinking and talking loudly. She slipped past them and the mellow glow of the tiki torches, hoping that no one noticed the cleaning girl sliding off for the beach. As she moved away from the lights of the lodge, the darkness enveloped her, and her eyes began to see more, including a dark form the end of the dock. Liza walked across the sand silently and stepped onto the dock without a sound. The shape at the end of the dock didn't move. That was when she heard a voice and stopped. He was talking, and it took her a moment to realize that he was talking to himself. A smile crept onto her face as she debated which way to advance. She contemplated sneaking up and surprising him, but that might knock him into the lake. The polite way would be to make a noise and announce her presence. The simple fact that she was doing this was so unlike her normal personality that she decided to take the safe route. She cleared her throat loudly, and the voice at the end of the dock stopped.

"Hi?" Josh's voice asked.

"Mind if I come out? It's Liza."

"Nope." His voice carried across the water, and she tried to determine if he was excited or put off by her presence. The voice sounded small for his bulk, and she thought that odd.

She walked out to the end of the dock and maneuvered herself down to the deck. The wood was cool on her rear end, and she shivered. Before she could even settle in, Josh handed her a can of beer.

"Thanks," she said and opened the can. She wasn't really too interested in the beer but she wanted to be polite. The liquid wasn't very cold, which made it even less appealing, but she appreciated the offer. She sighed a breath of relief and looked out at the lake. The water was mostly calm, but an occasional impulse of breeze rippled the surface and blew her hair around her head. The breeze was pleasant as the night was still very warm. "Another beautiful night."

Next to her, Josh nodded and took a drink from his beer. "It's amazing. After all the craziness today, this is a perfect end of the day."

He was certainly correct on that score. Liza sat, still not talking, just soaking in the night. The noises from the resort behind them was louder than the previous night she had been down on the dock with Josh, but the sounds still seemed distant and disconnected. She wondered what it must be like to be on vacation like the families and folks in the cabins and rooms. Her family had never really taken a vacation. One weekend when she was younger, her mother and Burt had taken the kids to Darien Lake, a theme park near Buffalo. They had camped out in a tent and spent a whole day on the rides and in the waterpark. At the time, it had seemed the greatest vacation anyone could have, but now she realized just how redneck-ish it had been. Yet another example of missing out on a normal upbringing. She had only left New York three times in her life. It made her mad but also satisfied her as well with the knowledge that she was planning to step away from that life forever.

"What do you think of Bernie Winsor?" Josh suddenly asked, breaking her thoughts.

"You mean Mrs. Obnoxious? To be honest, I don't really care for her."

Josh chuckled. "I feel bad for her husband. Dude is a saint. Or maybe just plain insane."

"I grew up in a small hick town, and people were pretty much all the same. We categorized each other by satellite television service. The haves and the have-nots. Working here, I'm seeing a whole different hierarchy. There are guests with money and those who are just making enough to stay here. There are guests with bad manners and guests who seem to be the nicest people on the planet. It takes all types, I guess."

They sat for a moment with their own thoughts. It was Josh who asked the surprising question.

"Where do you rank Meredith? Good manners or bad?"

"Ms. Riley?" Liza saw the head honcho's face in her mind and tried to get a fix on what Josh had asked. She hadn't really had much time to hang out with Ms. Riley and had only talked with her that one time in her office. Her immediate boss was Olga, and she was stern but fair, and that was okay with Liza. Ms. Riley didn't seem to consort much with the room cleaners. "I don't really know."

"Weak answer," Josh responded.

"I haven't talked with her or been around her much. I eat in my room, and she doesn't check up on the housekeeping staff, which is good, I guess. She seems serious, but that would make sense since she owns the place."

"This is her first year," Josh added. "Her father owned the place but died after the season last fall. Suicide."

Liza was surprised. "That's horrible. No wonder she seems so driven."

Josh chuckled and drank from his beer. The water was rippled up, and a white flash strobed over the hills. Thunderstorm to the southwest. It could graze the lake from the looks of it, but it was a ways off. She had seen many in her years in the mountains. The breeze blowing across the water was warm and delightful, and she realized it was probably keeping some of the resort noise from reaching them. Her thoughts drifted to the guy she was sitting next to. He was good-looking in an athletic way, the kind of kid that was rare at her high school but common on most stupid MTV shows. She found herself drawn to him but not in any kind of absolute way. But there was something about the guy that was a little off, and she couldn't put her finger on it. Liza was a cautious girl, and although Josh seemed nice enough, her subconsciousness screamed caution when dealing with the budding relationship. It was inevitable that they would at least talk because they were close in age in a place where there were few others in their phase of life, but that didn't mean that it was cool.

"So," she asked with the subtlety of a hammer to the head, "why are you up here?"

"Huh?" he said, obviously surprised. "I'm here to work."

"No. I mean, I'm from a crappy town just down the road, and obviously you are not. Where are you from? What brought you to Moon Lake?"

Josh drank from his beer and looked at the water.

"I'm from Western Massachusetts. A little town just west of Springfield."

Liza nodded with the tidbit of information he had given her and was surprised that he didn't open up more. This guy was different, and she couldn't tell if he was weird or just quietly private.

"Okay, but why did you end up here and not someplace with a stoplight within fifty miles?"

"Well," he answered slowly, "my dad kind of made me come here. I got in a little trouble, and he sent me here to get away from it all."

Now Liza was interested because this trouble could make or break her relationship with this guy, even if it was only friendship. Perhaps her second sense was correct and the guy had some issues. She didn't really want to spend her summer befriending a rapist, serial killer, or crack ball dealer. If she had to, how quickly could she whip her feet from the water, stand, and sprint down the dock?

"What kind of trouble?"

He sighed and she could tell that he wasn't comfortable telling the tale, yet he did.

"I attend Mount Union College in Ohio. I play football. A few of my buddies and I got arrested in Florida over spring break because of a fight. It was stupid, and we honestly didn't start it. But my dad thought it would be best for me to be removed from that lifestyle for a while, so he sent me here to work."

"Bummer."

Josh drank from his beer and laughed. "Actually, I love this place. I've never been in such a relaxing, calming place in my life. I wish I could bottle this up and take it to Ohio with me."

A white flash lit the southern sky way more impressively, and Liza knew that the storm was making ground. There was a very low but audible rumble from over the hills. She loved thunderstorms as they slammed across the mountains.

"The mountains are beautiful, even in the winter. But away from the tourist towns and ski hills, it can be brutal."

Josh was looking at the dark hills. "What's it like in the winter?"

"Cold," she answered quickly. "Really cold and awfully lonely."

They sat quietly for a while as a few more flashes lit the sky and the distant rumble of thunder could now be heard above the ripples the fresh wind was blowing up on the water. She had to agree with

Josh on the point that the area was outstandingly gorgeous, especially when a warm breeze struck her face from across the picturesque body of water with a thunderstorm marching in. The scene was hypnotic and altogether engrossing as time wandered on. Eventually, a lightning bolt could actually be seen for the first time toward the southwest, and the following thunder had power behind it. It was time to head for the dorm because she had no intention of getting soaked or electrocuted.

"Well," she said as she stood, "I guess it's time to head in."

Josh looked at her. "I'm gonna hang for a few more but…never mind."

"What?"

"I was just wondering if you might want to hang out, you know. Maybe go for a hike or something sometime if we get the chance."

Liza smiled, glad that he had asked. "Sure—that is, if we can ever find some downtime."

They both laughed, and that was a good feeling.

"Oh," Josh muttered as his laugher came to a sudden stop. "Can I ask you something, Liza?"

Her wall of protection was rapidly creeping up, but she knew that she had to say yes and did. She was not expecting the question.

"Do you get earthquakes around here?"

"What? Earthquakes?"

Lightning flashed, and the wind picked up in her face.

"Um," she muttered, "occasionally, I guess. Had one that shook pretty good last fall."

Josh looked away. "Thanks. I heard that they were kinda common here."

"Well," she declared, not sure how to end this strange twist to their goodbyes. "Don't stay out here too long. Lightning kills fifty people per year in the United States."

Josh laughed. "I'll come running when it gets close. See you tomorrow." A stroke of lightning illuminated the evergreens on the hill to the west of the lake. Josh seemed nice but troubled. However, it seemed like she would find out more about the guy as the summer unfolded. It was only early July after all. The thunder rumbled behind her as she made her way to her bed.

13

July 3

Every man has a point at which he has to step away and take a deep breath before something tragic happens. Andy Winsor had reached that point, and he was bright enough to create some space. Even though the rain continued outside, he grabbed his light water-resistant jacket and stepped out into the gray day. He paused on the porch of the cabin and turned his back on the cacophony from within and steeled his determination to get wet. He needed to escape for a while, or something bad might happen.

The air outside was cool but far from cold. He knew that once he began moving, a sweat would develop but the jacket would still be needed due to a steady drizzle that had continued all morning. It followed the storm that had raked across the night before. Humid as all heck. The crushed stone walkway was wet and in some points totally saturated by the heavy overnight rain. It had come down in torrents. Across the scrub grass and sparsely separated pine trees was the beach. A low, gossamer fog hung over the lake, and there was not a soul on the beach, which was dramatically different from the day before when the area was packed. What was everyone doing? He knew what was happening in his cabin, and it was chaos.

Andy Winsor was not a wild man. In fact, most people who knew him would best describe him as serious and sedate. A computer network executive, he spent most of his time in the cyber world and actually had little human contact. Much of his work could be done outside a traditional workspace; nevertheless, he spent most of his day in his office. As a child, his mother had always called him an introvert, and he had few friends, but that didn't bother him because he never needed human companionship. He read books, played video games, and eventually immersed himself inside the digital world where he didn't need friends. Andy eventually went to college and excelled, graduating with a 3.9 GPA. He had what he wanted with the omission of one key component to a satisfying life: sex.

With very few exceptions, he was a love dud. By the time he graduated from college, he had only made it to second base, and that had been once with a drunken fellow computer geek. Andy found that he liked the feel of a woman but realized that it was painfully difficult for him to feel comfortable communicating with them. So he entered his post-college career with a solid, well-paying job but with virtually no social life. This continued on for almost ten years as his bank account grew and his social experiences stagnated.

Down the block from his apartment in Scranton was a small diner that served a meat loaf and mashed potatoes special that he loved to indulge in every Wednesday evening. The meal was better than his standard dinner from a bag that cooked in a skillet. It was one October Wednesday when Andy walked into the diner for his weekly loaf of meat and his life changed forever. That was when Bernella Campbell walked to his table wearing an apron and a bright smile. Andy was not taken by her looks. She was a big woman with a round face but a friendly grin. The smile was certainly screwed on for her employment and not her normal personality.

"What can I get you, hon?" she had asked, acting the part of the pleasant diner waitress.

"Um, I get the special on Wednesday."

Bernella smiled and wrote on a pad. "Anything to drink? You look thirsty."

"Water."

With that order, his future wife walked away, and his initial thought about her was a little more than a positive image of her use of the word *hon*. What he really wanted at that moment was the meat loaf. This routine lasted for over two months to the point where he walked in and Bernella had the meat loaf already ordered and waiting for his arrival. Then she dropped the bomb and asked him to go bowling. Andy had quickly responded *no* and spent the following week regretting his response. No woman had ever asked him out. As he sat in front of his television eating cooked carrots and a piece of grilled chicken on Friday night, Andy began to wonder if this was his lot for the rest of his life. For one of the first times in his lackluster life, Andy felt depressed about staying in on a Friday night.

Andy had been pleasantly surprised when Bernella had again asked him out on the next meat loaf night. This time he accepted and...

"I hate you," one of the kids yelled at the other. It sounded younger, so it was probably Marty. The kids on his soccer team called him Farty Marty. That was super. Geez, they were going to be a pain in the butt being locked up all day. Without another thought, Andy walked down the path toward the lodge. But instead of turning to the main building, he turned to his right, and the less travelled path that he had been told circumnavigated the lake. With the exception of two private homes where the path bent away from the water and up the hillside, it trekked very close to the water—or so he was told.

"What the hell," he muttered to himself, and instead of walking toward the lodge, he turned to his right and down the narrow wet path. The branches of trees and bushes were lowered by the extra weight of the rainwater, and many brushed him as he walked along, getting his jacket and pants wet. Andy didn't care. It was a small sacrifice to pay to get away from Bernie and the kids. And as he progressed further down the path, he began to feel as though he were on a mission. This particular adventure was to circumnavigate the lake. He walked often at home in Scranton, but that was mostly on asphalt or concrete in the evening after dinner. This was altogether unique for him and became clear when his sneakered foot slipped out to his right when he stepped on a slick, exposed root. *Geez, be careful,* he thought. He could probably lie out here with a broken ankle for hours before Bernie even thought to be concerned. Andy decided to watch every step he took while taking in the amazing forest that surrounded him. It was awesome.

The trail composed of dirt and pine needles with the occasional rock outcrop or root. It made him marvel at the difference from where they had spent the previous summer. Bernie had decided that it was time to let their children experience the fantasy of all American youngsters. She had decided that it was time to make the pilgrimage to the fiefdom of the mouse. They had booked ten days in a hotel that was accessible to the Magic Kingdom by monorail. Ten long days at Disneyworld. Andy had spent ten totally miserable days walking pavement and paying out ridiculous amounts of money only to feel dumber by the end of each day.

Orlando was ludicrous. It was as if the entire area around the park for miles was of some alien geological formation where the primary mineral was asphalt. The trees and plants that grew seemed fake and contrived as if each had been placed where it grew to serve some aesthetic purpose. But it didn't work. Nothing was random and nothing was natural. Everything was paved. It was outrageous, especially for Orlando in the summer. The daily temperatures hovered in the low nineties, and the pavement only soaked up the sun's heat and transferred it into the soles of the moronic mouse follower's shoes. Why people went there in the summer was mind-boggling. He had to remind himself constantly of the reason he was there. The kids.

The heat had been bad, but the actual park was painful. Disneyworld had been fun for about two hours, but that was about it. They had spent five days wandering the park while the kids whined about getting on certain rides and the length of the lines for those rides. The other days were spent at Epcot and the other satellite attractions and those he did find semi-interesting. The problem was that everything that he showed a curiosity in, the rest of the family had vetoed and moved on. Andy found himself with all the other shmucks looking at Disney propaganda to support its empire that did such a marvelous job of brainwashing America. It was terrible.

Somehow he had convinced Bernie and the boys that a trip to a quiet resort in the mountains would be an awesome experience. Unfortunately, there was no such thing as a quiet resort when the Winsor clan wandered in.

The trail twisted along the lake following changes in the shoreline and meandering around large rocks and the particularly large tree. Andy stopped short when he suddenly realized that he was not alone. Ahead on the trail, a white-tailed deer stood looking at him with an odd look of curiosity. The animal was large, probably a buck, with light brown fur that was short and looked very soft. The animal made eye contact with Andy's, snorted, and smoothly bounded off away from the lake into the trees. He watched as the white tail bobbed as the deer ran and hopped through the trees away from him. Andy just stood paralyzed as the animal disappeared into the forest. He had stopped breathing and shook off the moment when he inhaled. That was awesome. No deer in Disneyworld. At least, no actual live deer in a natural state.

For the second time, the trail deviated from the shoreline and moved up the hill away from the water. The same thing had happened a few hundred yards behind him, and he realized that a home was down the hill in the woods as he moved past. There seemed to be absolutely no sign of human life at the first cottage. Now there appeared to be another home, and this one was tucked into a cove on the water. Instead of heading up the trail around the cabin, Andy decided to sit on a large rock that actually touched the water. It was a big granite rock, probably as large as a Smart car. He climbed up aboard to take a rest before he walked up the hill and then around the far side of the lake and back to the resort.

As he sat, he sighed and felt the pressure fall from the bottoms of his feet. When a person wasn't accustomed to forest hiking, it took some getting comfortable to. The water still had a low fog just above the surface, but the atmosphere in general wasn't as foggy. The low gray clouds still held over the lake, which made the day darker than normal. The sunshine was trying to burn off the moisture, but Andy found this scene just as beautiful as full sunshine. It was tranquil beyond belief, and he felt like he could just sit on that rock all day and be happy as heck. Bernie and the kids were over a mile away, and he was pleased to find that he couldn't hear them. In fact, their noxious noises had even cleared out of his head, which never happened, even at work. This rock was magic.

Eventually, he felt moisture from the rock's surface soak through his jeans and into his boxer shorts. That would be hard to explain to Bernie, but he didn't care. He had found his spot of solitude and planned on returning soon. But he had to get back.

Andy sighed and slid off the rock. It was still a good hike back, and unfortunately, with every step, he was getting closer to his family.

*****

Josh thought that rainy days would be quiet, but he hadn't really thought that one out. When he had been in high school, he and his father had gone to Killington for an early season ski holiday. During many seasons, the Vermont ski season would be cranking up by Thanksgiving, thanks to the magic of modern snowmaking. But that year, the temperatures were in the fifties, and it rained. Not even the technology of producing man-made snow could overcome those climatic obstacles. So the skiing sucked, and most of the holiday skiers, mostly from places like New Jersey and Philadelphia, stayed off the slopes. So they were in a ski town with no skiing…what was there to do? They drank. When a large group of celebrants begin drinking early when they expected to be skiing, the outcome is usually negative. His father took the teenaged Josh to a bar on the access road, and Josh had witnessed firsthand what boredom and booze can lead to. Something approaching chaos.

His growing fear was that something like this might occur at Wildwood as the drizzle fell and kept the guests from the beach. He knew that a couple of groups had left for a day trip to Lake Placid, which was a fine idea. However, there were others that had gotten Slip to open the bar early, and that had been fine with him because there was no beach sitting today. Unfortunately, it was far too early for boozing, and that might lead to some unhappiness later.

"I just hope they don't overdo it," Meredith said next to him. They were standing on the front porch, which was under an overhang of the lodge. It could actually be enclosed with screens if the bugs got too bad. The rain, although not heavy, was still coming down.

"It'll be fine," Thomas responded optimistically. "We get days like this every year, and some folks'll act up but most are just tryin' to get through the day."

They had gathered on the porch because they didn't have much to do either, so standing watching the rain together seemed logical.

Josh kind of wished he was over at cabin 2 with the two couples who seemed to be having a great time drinking the rainy day away under the awning on their porch. Those days were classic. An image of his friends sitting there drinking a couple of cases and telling stories played nostalgically in his head. He smiled.

"Geez," Meredith moaned. "I can hear Bernie bitching at her kids from here. That is one mean woman."

Thomas looked at her with a smile. "I don't know if it's appropriate for you to speak that way of our guests, even the...tougher ones."

"I agree with Meredith," Josh chipped in. "She's mean as hell."

The three of them laughed, which was a release of some pent-up energy. Sometimes they had to make fun of the guests to keep a sense of sanity. That was when Olga walked up all flustered.

"Ma'am," she said as she approached Meredith. Olga had hair that might have at one time been blond but was now mostly gray. She had a wide body, which seemed to fit her name perfectly. "We have a problem."

Josh was looking at the woman, and a bunch of thoughts went through his head. Plumbing? Squirrels? It had to be serious.

"What is it, Olga?'

Olga looked around and waited a moment, obviously uncomfortable speaking in front of Thomas and Josh. "Well, frankly, the girls are having a tough time cleaning the rooms. The people won't leave!"

Thomas snickered, and Olga shot him a hot glance that forced him to turn away, still smiling.

"Did the girls ask the people if they wanted their rooms cleaned?" Meredith asked evenly.

Olga hesitated, and Josh thought of Liza. "Well, no, but they have to be cleaned."

"How about this," Meredith suggested. "Why don't the girls ask the patrons if they want their rooms cleaned. If they say yes, then the guests can come here and play gin rummy while the room is being cleaned. If they say no...well then, everything is cool."

Olga gave Meredith a cold look. "All right, ma'am. The rooms will go uncleaned." Olga turned and stormed back into the lodge.

"Wow," Meredith exclaimed. "Where the hell is the common sense?"

"You handled that like the President." Thomas smiled. Meredith shook her head and looked up at the sky.

"Thomas, you nailed the storm last night. What's the weather looking like now? Please say it will clear up. Tomorrow's the Fourth."

Thomas looked out over the yard and the lake where ripples were just appearing from a breeze that was coming up.

"It'll clear out by sunset, and tomorrow will be a beaut."

Meredith sighed. "It better be. We have nearly five thousand dollars' worth of fireworks for tomorrow night. I'm going to my office. Come by if you have a problem or need a shot of bourbon."

Josh smiled as he watched the owner of the resort walk through the doors into the lodge. He felt a sense of arrival, knowing that he had been involved in such a frank conversation with the owner. With Meredith gone, it left just Thomas and himself on the porch, and Thomas didn't seem too motivated to leave, and that fit Josh's plans perfectly. He wanted to ask Thomas a question.

"Hell of a storm last night," Josh said to make conversation. It had been with plenty of lightning, a heavy downpour but luckily no strong winds.

Thomas nodded. "Certainly was. Summer is here solid now, and it's storm season. Just hope none of 'em knock out the power. That's always a pain in the butt."

"Yeah," Josh added, not sure how to broach the subject but decided that he should just get it over with because his curiosity was commanding his thoughts. "Thomas, what's up with earthquakes here?"

Thomas's head snapped around, and he looked directly into Josh's eyes.

"What?"

Josh literally took a step backward. He hadn't expected that reaction from such a seemingly simple question. As quickly as he had asked it, Josh wished he could take it back. The sudden accusatory look in Thomas's eyes quickly mellowed, but the impact was still felt.

"Um…," Josh stumbled, "I was just wondering if there were ever earthquakes up here?"

Thomas smiled. "Well yeah, we get them occasionally. No big deal, though. Mostly little stuff."

"Oh," Josh said, listening to Thomas's minimal answer but remembering the look on his boss' face. "I was just curious. We're in the mountains and all. Mountains get earthquakes."

"They're rare."

With that, Thomas turned away and walked into the lodge, leaving Josh even more confused and…

Scared.

*****

It was a bizarre day, and that was no understatement. Liza was in her room, lying on her bed with a book, and it was only four o'clock. Normally, she would still be cleaning a cabin or a room in the lodge, but most of the guests had waved the housekeeping staff off for the day. That was fine because in essence, it meant a day where she didn't have to put in eight hours. It was a nice break.

The day was gray, and the whole mood of the resort had done an about-face from the day before when everyone was water-bound and enjoying the sun. Today some people just left, while others languished in a drizzle-induced stupor. But there were the few guests who decided to not waste the positive flow and decided to drink the day away. When Liza had approached cabin 2, instead of being asked to change the linen, she was asked to do a shot of what she guessed was whiskey. After declining and then being harassed for being a lightweight, Liza retreated to another cabin where the couple within were a few of sips away from being ploughed. Liza didn't even bother with that cabin. She was already worried about cleaning puke in the morning.

The four walls of her semi-Spartan room were beginning to close in on her. She looked out the window, and the day looked a little brighter, or maybe she just imagined it was. Her cell phone showed that it was only 4:06 p.m., which meant nearly two hours before she could wander over to the lodge for her dinner. She was bored with nothing to do, and like a line to a drowning sailor, there was a knock on her door. Even before she answered, she knew who the visitor was, and she found that it excited her. When she opened the door, Josh was standing in the hallway.

A smile spread on his face, and white teeth offset his tanned visage. Liza would look back and realize that this was the moment when she almost fell for him.

"Nice day, huh?" he said sarcastically.

Liza felt a smile spread on her face. "If you like London."

"Have you ever been to London?"

Liza laughed. "No."

"I have," Josh said. "The weather does suck, and they eat a lot of fish. What are you up to?"

Liza looked behind her into the empty space. "Just reading. I've gotten a lot of reading in."

Josh nodded. "I'm so freaking bored that the pinochle game in the lodge looks pretty good right now."

"You play pinochle?"

Josh smiled. "Don't have a clue. Want to go for a walk? I figure we could try the trail around the lake."

"Sure," Liza answered quickly. Not only was she thrilled to be getting out of her room but she would finally get out into the woods. With a good-looking guy no less. It was a no-brainer. "I'll meet you out front after I change."

As quickly as she could, Liza threw on a pair of socks and put on her sneakers. She looked out the small window that overlooked the woods and debated a sweatshirt but instead settled on a light jacket. She quickly slipped out the door and walked down the center hallway of the small dorm building where only eleven employees lived. She could see Josh waiting outside, and a thrill swept her that she concentrated on sending back. Enjoy the moment and don't get geeked up by it.

Josh was looking out over the lake and turned when she came out the door.

"Looks like the weather is trying to break. The mist has lifted from the water, and the sun is really trying to break through."

Liza looked to the sky and could perceive a lightening in the clouds. The air was still cool and humidity hung tight, making it feel damp. The woods had a musty smell that drifted toward the lodge.

"Ready?" he asked.

Liza nodded and Josh headed out, leading the way. She noticed that he walked forcefully and didn't try and play "women go first" games, which was actually refreshing. In fact, she got the impression that he wasn't the least bit interested in her, which was at the same time deflating and relieving. It was nice to have a friend, much like Matt. But Josh was no Matt either.

They walked across the wet grass toward cabin 9, and it was when they had come to the long grassy edge of the property that Josh led her onto the trail that went around the lake. The grassy lawn transformed into a narrow path that was only a couple feet wide and had pine needles and mud as the surface. Birch, spruce, and pine grew close to the trail, and occasionally a wet branch brushed her jacket.

"Watch for this branch," Josh warned as he pushed a spruce bough out of the way. The branch came back, and Liza had to move it again to get by. To her left, the lake glimmered without a ripple to break the surface. The woods were alive with the sound of dripping water as gravity pulled droplets to the ground. It was the only sound besides the noises they made and the occasional chipmunk scurrying for its hole. They walked without talking, and Liza absorbed the quiet of the forest around her.

After ten minutes, Josh stopped and looked backward across the water, and Liza followed suit. She could see that they had made it around the west side of the lake and were kitty-corner across from the resort. The day had indeed brightened, and it appeared that two guys were actually strolling onto the dock. Maybe it was part of the all-day drinking group. They seemed distant but not far enough away to be just random forms. The lodge rose behind the scene like some man-made hill that stood above all else. She had never realized how big the building was until it was contrasted against all the others. She recognized the cabins and was surprised at how small they looked, although she knew that cleaning each took half an hour. A small spot of sunshine hit the trees behind the lodge, suddenly changing the whole aspect of the scene. The place looked brighter and some-how more inviting, as if it was truly a resort and not just a scattering of rain-drenched buildings in the woods. The clouds still hung low, obscuring the mountain views behind the lodge. She understood this weather better than most at the resort and knew it would clear out and tomorrow would be sunny. It would be a pleasant Fourth.

"The place looks different from over here," Josh said. "It's like it's better understood."

Liza nodded and surprisingly knew exactly what he was talking about. "Yep. It's smaller than you'd think."

Josh smiled. "I think it's clearing out. See the sunshine?"

Liza nodded and decided not to speak.

"Meredith is planning a bonfire tonight to get the holiday rolling. I hope it's not too wet."

"Yep," was all she added as Josh began to blaze the way along the south side of Moon Lake. The going was pretty much the same, although there was the occasional large boulder that the path had to wind around. Also, the hillside rose abruptly to their right as they meandered along the shoreline. From across the lake, this hill didn't seem very impressive, but as Liza turned and looked up the wooded hillside, there was a lot more elevation there than she thought. While she was gazing at the slope, the toe of her right sneaker found an exposed root, and did not quite have the clearance. She stubbed her foot against the root and stumbled forward. To save herself, she tried to shoot her left foot forward as quickly as possible to compensate so she wouldn't land on her face. Unfortunately, her left foot got hung up on her right just long enough to delay the balanced help of that foot. Inertia took over, and her upper body kept moving forward without any support underneath. As she reflexively tried to get her hands out in front of herself, she had an image of a fool about to eat Adirondack soil.

The impact didn't hurt, and she tried to jump up as quickly as possible, but the damage was done. Josh had turned and made a quick step toward her with his hand outstretched. She had already gotten up, but he still grabbed her arm. She saw a smile creep onto his face.

"Are you okay?" he asked, stopping when he saw that she was standing and unhurt.

"Define okay," she answered, rubbing dirt from her knees and her forearms. Although she didn't totally block the blow, her forearms had prevented the full face plant. "I don't seem to be bleeding, but my pride is in tatters."

Josh laughed. "Gotta watch your footing. Thought you lived around here?"

Liza snarled. "I do. I'm just a klutz."

"Well," Josh smiled, "when I fall, I'll probably break my fucking nose. You sure you're okay?"

Liza nodded and Josh continued up the trail, and she took extra caution to place every step onto a safe location. God, what a brilliant way to impress a guy. Although, she felt embarrassment engulf her, Josh didn't really seem to care about her trip. *Just watch where you're going.*

Suddenly, Josh stopped short in the middle of the trail, and she nearly bumped into him. She was about to speak out and say something witty and probably inappropriate when she saw the guy standing near a deadfall with an axe in his hands and his back to them. His T-shirt was soaked through with sweat. There was very little chopping going on, and the man was singing. She was listening to a very bad rendition of a Bob Seger song that she couldn't name. The guy was belting it out and had no idea they were standing on the trail watching him. He had gray hair that was straight but wild around his head. He was wearing an orange T-shirt with "IT STARTS NOW" printed on it in blue letters. Liza guessed that he was between fifty-five and sixty-five years old and loved some classic rock 'n' roll. Liza did not want to startle the man, and she felt that Josh had the same feeling. She decided to be subtle and cleared her throat as loudly as she could without sounding ridiculous.

The man's head jerked up, and an immediate look of confusion was replaced by wariness. He checked the two of them out, and no one moved. Then a broad smile spread on his face, and the movement was electric. He had a smile that could chill out a rampaging Bigfoot.

"You two surprised me," he muttered, taking a couple of deep breaths.

Liza stepped forward. "Sorry about that. We were just wandering on the trail and well…"

"No problem," the man responded apologetically. "I should be more cognizant when I'm out near the trail. I can get carried away with a chore and get lost inside my own thoughts."

"And singing," Josh added. Josh was standing back, not as forward as Liza was.

The man smiled. "I used to love Bob Seger. *And those Hollywood nights, in those Hollywood hills…* My voice was much better a few decades ago. I'm Davey Cramer, local denizen of the south shore of Moon Lake."

"Nice to meet you. I'm Liza Grant, and this is Josh…" With a sense of horror, she floundered with Josh's last name. He had said it before, but it was hiding somewhere in her head where it would not illuminate.

"Martin. Josh Martin. It's nice to meet you."

Liza looked at Josh again, feeling mortified by her error, but Josh seemed unfazed. Instead, he was focused on their new acquaintance.

"Are you two vacationing over at Camp Wildwood?" Davey asked in a friendly manner.

Liza began. "We're actually employees…"

"Davey Cramer? Are you the Davey Cramer?"

Davey looked at Josh with in an odd gaze. Liza was looking at him like he was nuts. She had always taken Josh as a levelheaded guy, but he was now standing with his mouth halfway open, freaking out in front of this new guy they had run into in the woods. Liza looked at Josh and then to Davey as a peculiar moment of silence fell over the forest. Davey was just staring with a half-smile on his face.

Josh was beginning to smile. "*An Evergreen Life*. Yeah, I had to read that in my modern fiction class. English 117. My professor was all into the book."

"Did you like it?" Davey asked.

Josh smiled. "Man, I'm an ecology major and I had to take the English class to fulfill a liberal arts requirement, but yeah, I did actually read all of the book. It was pretty sick."

Davey smiled. "Well, thank you, I guess. I appreciate it."

"What did I miss here?" Liza asked. "You guys know each other?"

"Mr. Cramer," Josh answered, "is one of the best authors around today. Ever heard of the movie *An Evergreen Life*?"

Liza nodded. She and Matt had seen it at his house through an Internet-based movie rental company. She had liked the movie, and images of it flooded her mind. As she remembered the flick, a connection was made, and she stood somewhat astounded.

"You wrote that book?"

Davey nodded. "Yes, I did…among a bunch of other stuff that no one ever talks about."

Josh walked the twenty yards down the trail and shook Davey's hand.

"You look just like the picture on the back cover of the book I have. It really is great to meet you."

"Well," Davey answered, "it's a little shocking running into a fan out here in the middle of my woods. I'll tell you, I'm dying of thirst. Do you two want to wander down to my cabin?"

Josh stepped forward immediately, and Liza honestly didn't care. It would actually be nice to sit down. She followed Josh and Davey off the main trail and toward the lake where she noticed for the first time a cabin by the water.

*****

Davey walked toward his cabin knowing that he had just broken one of his golden rules. The regulation was to keep a wall between the resort and his private property. But here he was leading two kids to his home, and they didn't even seem to be of the legal drinking age. The boy had said he was in college, but the girl looked like she might still be in high school. He was cursing himself for being a moron with each step he took. The boy had seemed genuinely thrilled to meet him, but the girl was different. She had a look of intense innocence. It was as if an aura was blazing from her that only he could see. Davey understood that the girl was a special breed, and he immediately liked her. And although he hated to admit it, he and Jeanne were a little lonely for one of the first summers since they had been coming here. The pull across the lake in the rowboat was becoming harder every year, which meant their social forays to Camp Wildass had been cut down quite a bit.

Jeanne was sitting on a red Adirondack chair when Davey led the two hikers onto the porch. She turned with a broad smile designed for him, and the look of surprise that replaced the smirk was humorous. They rarely—*never*—had guests.

"Honey," he said with a humongous grin knowing that Jeanne was taken back. He turned to the couple. "Meet these two young Americans I met out on the trail. Josh and Liza. This is my beautiful wife of nearly thirty years, Jeanne."

With the grace of a Greek goddess, Jeanne stood and gained the composure that she so desperately valued. Her smile was warm, and he felt his love for her burn like a fire, even after so many years had washed away between them.

"Nice to meet both of you." She spoke with genuine warmth as she moved to take Liza's hand. "Are you two at the resort? Honeymoon maybe?"

Davey saw the girl take a shocked half step backward, and he laughed out loud. Oh, Jeanne. You have the talent to cut right to the quick.

"Honey, they are employees across the lake. I'm guessing it was a slow day because of the rain?"

Josh spoke up. "Actually, it's a little crazy. A lot of folks headed out to tour the mountains, but many are just hanging around the place. Lots of drinking. It could get ugly."

Davey laughed again, imagining a group of twenty-something people trapped in tiny cabins without anything to do. Booze was often the tonic, and a day of drinking often equated to trouble.

"Well, the day has cleared out some, I guess," Jeanne added. "Anyone want something to drink? I have lemonade and iced tea."

The two kids both asked for iced tea, and Jeanne slipped into the cabin. Davey grinned, again extremely impressed by his wife. He now had a better look at both kids, and the girl was definitely well below the legal age to buy a good old beer in New York State. And even if they had been of age, Davey probably wouldn't have begun drinking with them until he got to know them better.

"Here," he spoke up, "why don't you two have a seat on my deck. I have to admit that I really enjoy sitting here gazing out over the water."

The two picked seats next to each other, and Davey smiled. Was he watching young love bud at the summer resort? Jeanne quickly returned and handed drinks out to the guests, and Davey took one as well.

"Pardon the lack of choices, but it's tough to lug provisions up from our parking area."

Liza took a sip of her drink and looked at Jeanne. "Where do you park?"

"Down on the old lumber trail. What's it called, honey?"

Davey smiled. "I always call it Pain in the Ass Drive. I think its official title is Access Road 18. It doesn't get much use, and we park a good half mile from here."

"Wow," Josh chimed in. "How do you get your stuff up here?"

Davey pointed to the shed. "I have a four-wheeler. It actually isn't that bad. The worst duty is getting to the grocery store. We usually drive to Newcomb or farther. Once a week, we try and drive to Old Forge to stock up. Mayson scares us."

"I'm from Mayson," Liza said matter-of-factly, and Davey immediately kicked himself for stating such a harsh proclamation to someone he didn't know who and might very well have been from the area. Remove foot from mouth. At moments like these, he sometimes felt blessed to live alone in the mountains with only his loyal wife to hear his blunders.

"Um, sorry, Liza. No offense."

He was relieved to see her smile. "None taken. I mean, I grew up here and can't wait to get out. Newcomb *is* like the city compared to this place."

Davey looked at this girl, and he was yet again intrigued. He felt drawn as he had when they had been standing in the woods only moments before, and the feeling had just intensified. He was semi-shocked by it, and he shook his head to shake the images from his head. The girl was very pretty, but that wasn't an unusual situation for him. He was almost old enough to be her grandfather, and he saw plenty of attractive girls in his classes at Syracuse. Her beauty only added to the something else that charmed him. Whether it was her attitude or some subliminal quality that the normal senses could not perceive, Liza was like a magnet, and he felt himself slipping nearer to her. He actually found that he had begun to sweat. It was a hot day but…

"Do you mind me asking how old you are, honey?" Jeanne asked.

Liza shrugged. "No, ma'am. I'm eighteen."

"She just graduated from high school a week ago," Josh chimed in. Davey looked at Josh and didn't get anything close to the electric feeling he got from Liza. His initial impression of the kid was that he was a large cocky kid. He looked very athletic, handsome, and probably left broken hearts wherever he trod. Although Josh had been nothing but polite and respectful, Davey didn't care for him. Perhaps it was some weird male compulsion to dislike the guy with the pretty girl. If it existed, he was way too old to feel that crap. But there was something more.

"High school?" Jeanne said happily. "Congratulations. What are your plans?"

Liza looked down at the decking of the platform, and Davey immediately felt that a wound had been ripped open. He could feel her sadness wash past him in waves.

"I'm not really sure," she answered quietly. "Maybe community college."

Jeanne smiled, and Davey hoped that she wasn't just thinking that this girl was merely a simple mountain girl. Davey knew that was a gross underestimation.

"How were your grades?" he inquired, hoping that he guessed correctly and didn't overstep his bounds.

Liza turned to him, and he felt energy hit him like a gusty wind. "They were pretty good, I guess. I finished third in my class of one hundred."

"Did you apply to any four-year schools?"

"Yeah, and I got in, but the cash is very thin."

Davey felt emotions hit him that he wasn't expecting. There was something extraordinary about this girl who grew up in Mayson, New York, where the average yearly per capita income couldn't be much greater than $17,000.

Jeanne stepped in. "Davey is a professor at Syracuse University. Maybe he could pull some strings."

"I can look into it, but it's too late now for the fall semester." He desperately wanted to move from this awkward moment, so he dragged his attention from Liza's gravitational pull and looked at Josh. "How about you, Josh?"

The kid smiled. "I'm going to be a sophomore at Mount Union College."

"Do you play football?" Jeanne asked. Davey smiled, knowing that they were again riding the same wavelength. Josh's face lit up like a jack-o'-lantern.

"Yup. I play linebacker."

A question burst into Davey's mind, and he blurted it out. "Then why are you here? Don't you have summer workouts?"

The smile faltered on the kid's face, and Davey almost felt bad for asking the question. Why did he feel a distance from this kid? He knew, and it was unsettling.

"Well," Josh tried, "I ran into some problems last year, and my dad suggested I come here for the summer. It's pretty awesome, though."

Jeanne asked what positions the two had over at the resort, and Davey could have guessed. Josh was working with Thomas, and Liza was in housekeeping. He had thought that she might be a waitress, but he wasn't sure if that fit. They sat for another twenty minutes talking about Meredith, the resort, and the lake. The time went by quickly, and Davey truly enjoyed the conversation, although he found that Liza still had him enchanted, and that was incredibly inexplicable. The clouds had lifted further, and the day suddenly grew brighter as the sun burned through a blue hole in the gray. The conversation among the foursome dwindled, and they all looked out over the water that was again taking on a shade of blue and gray. The moment was glorious after a morning of dreariness. Davy knew that it would clear for the evening, and tomorrow, the Fourth, would be clear and beautiful. Then Josh dropped the bomb.

"Mr. Cramer? What do you know about earthquakes around here?"

Davey hadn't been moving much, but whatever motion he had froze with the words. He certainly had not been expecting the question. With the upbeat moment of sunshine and the energy from Liza, Josh's question was like a towering, threatening thundercloud on a perfect summer day. Where had this kid come up with this topic? Was he a geology student? Rocks for jocks.

Davey managed to respond. "Why do you ask?"

Josh shrugged and looked extremely uncomfortable, which only made Davey feel more uneasy.

"I heard that occasionally earthquakes occur up here in the mountains."

"They're rare."

Josh sucked in a breath and looked out over the water, which convinced Davey that there was more to this than just some geology question. The kid knew something. He also looked like he had ants in his pants.

"I mean, do they ever happen here? At Moon Lake?"

Davey stood up from the railing he had been comfortably leaning against, enjoying the conversation. The positivity of the conversation had turned in the blink of an eye.

"Yes, occasionally the lake gets rocked by a trembler, but they are never very bad. Had one last fall. But we only average one decent shaker every three years or so, so we're probably safe for a couple of years."

Josh looked at him and slowly nodded, but Davey got the distinct sense that his answer had not been satisfactory. The kid knew. Whether he had any idea about the truth was another story, and Davey felt that with some time, he might want to sit with the kid and discuss what his understandings were. However, this was not the time nor place for many reasons. In fact, Davey's pleasure with the conversation had quickly evaporated, and he wanted the guests to mosey back down the trail toward Wildass. He was frankly a little freaked out. Luckily, it seemed that the moment had passed for Liza as well. She stood and stretched her legs.

"Amazing how my legs stiffened. You ready to continue our journey, Josh?"

Josh also stood and smiled, but Davey could see a weakness there. It was clear that he was searching for something, and Davey had not provided the answer. Maybe he would someday.

"Listen, Josh," Davey added to try and help ease the kid. "There's the Adirondack Museum over in Blue Mountain Lake that might have some information that you are searching for. Tupper Lake also has a geology museum of some sort, but I've never been there. Hopefully that helps."

Josh smiled and said thank you. He led the way to the stairs that led off the deck, and Liza followed.

"It was wonderful to meet both of you," Jeanne said. "Perhaps we'll see you again at the resort."

They waved goodbye and walked past the shed back toward the trail, and Davey knew that they would encounter those two again.

14

July 4

The sun was already up and shining through the large windows in the front of the lodge, dust motes drifting in the shafts of light. The lake was like a mirror, and the morning sun rays bounced off the surface, making the reflection ripple. With the sun came the heat, especially since the humidity never really cleared out with the rain. She knew that it would be a warm day and just perfect for the holiday. The day before had been trying as the guests had mulled around the lodge and the grounds bored out of their minds. Keeping the clients happy had become a tedious affair. Today would be simple. The beach would be crowded, and the guests would be occupied.

Meredith had hung around the dining room as the breakfast crowd wandered in and then left to enjoy the day. The flow was thin, maybe because many of the people were sick of being in the lodge. It was now nine-thirty, and she found herself sitting behind her desk, taking a deep breath. The Fourth of July. Amazing. The holiday had always been special to her, almost as important as Christmas or Thanksgiving. Whether she was actually spending the summer at Camp Wildwood or somewhere far off, she always came back to spent the Fourth by Moon Lake. As she sat, she thought back on the memories from childhood, and she couldn't help but smile, especially when she thought of her father. This was the first Fourth without him, and a weight settled on her chest. At this moment, he was missed, and her eyes teared up. She looked across the room and saw the cabinet. That was when she remembered her father's logbooks and felt motivation to open them up again. After walking over and retrieving the notebooks her father had written his thoughts in, she closed the door to her office, which she never did. This moment of reflection with her father deserved solitude.

She randomly opened a book and found herself gazing at an entry her father had written on August 29, 2001. The date struck her, and she realized that her father had scribed these words only a couple of weeks before the World Trade Center attacks. She drifted and remembered that time herself. She had been a junior in high school and had been shocked to the point of tears. The funny thing was, she could not remember anything that was occurring before the attacks, but as she read, it was clear that her father had something on his mind.

> August 29, 2001—Summer of the Shark. Is that how pathetic our world has become that this is the only noteworthy item that is reported on the evening news? Every time I consult CNN or any other news network, all I hear about it this damn shark thing. So a couple of people got attacked. That shit happens! The world has become so boring that they have to manufacture monsters to terrorize the public. Bullshit! But I was thinking, maybe it will be good for business. If they keep scaring the shit out of the tourists, maybe they will avoid the ocean resorts and head to the less threatening shores of freshwater lakes, much like this here one. I can see the new brochure next spring: Camp Wildwood Resort! Fifty years shark-free! Not bad stuff.

The smile beamed on her face as she read the words. It was completely her father. The words reverberated in her ears, making noise even though nothing was spoken. She could hear him like he was sitting across the desk. There was a vague memory of a bunch of attention paid to sharks that summer. There was one vivid recollection of a helicopter taking video of long dark shapes in the shallow waters off Florida that were the dreaded Great Whites that terrorized the coasts.

The funny thing was, after the attacks on 9/11, the sharks all seemed to disappear, at least from the attention of the American media establishment. Meredith turned ahead to the entry for September 11, but there wasn't one. Instead, she read the following day's entry.

> September 12, 2001—Sorry about no entry yesterday, but I frankly was not in the mood. Terrorists used planes to attack NYC and DC, and another plane crashed in PA. Many dead. Yesterday was a gorgeous fall day with deep blue skies. No one here was even aware that anything had happened until Byron, the cook, heard something about it on the little radio in the kitchen. All of us, guests and employees alike, sat in the bar watching the coverage all day. This sucks! Goddamn terrorists. I hope Bush does the right thing and nukes the bastards today. Although this all seems very far from the lake, I have a feeling the world has just changed forever. I went out and sat on the dock today and tried to enjoy a peaceful afternoon. Weirdest thing to see, no contrails from airplanes plying across the blue sky.

If this was supposed to cheer her mood, she was picking the wrong dates to read. Those were tough days for all people, and she vaguely recalled calling her father from home. She needed something more uplifting to get her in the proper mood. Meredith began to flip through the book and read only Fourth of July passages that were all pretty similar. The variations were the weather. The similarities were fireworks and an odd wobbliness to her father's handwriting, no doubt caused by more than his usual alcohol intake either that night or the morning after. One particular entry in a different book was written the year of her birth. She slowly read the words her father had written, explaining his deep love and affection for the wife that was almost ready to give birth to their first child. The words were the most passionate that Meredith could have ever imagined her father writing about her mother. A breath caught in her throat as she imagined the passions her father felt toward her mother.

She sighed deeply, trying to avoid being overcome. Wow, she hadn't expected this when she opened the book. Her father truly loved her mother, which was something that Meredith would never get to see. Never once would she see her mother and father together on a birthday, Christmas, or a wedding anniversary. In fact, she would never see her mother.

Without thinking about the consequences, Meredith quickly turned a few pages to find no entry for October 1, 1982, the day of her birth. There was no entry on that devastating day when she was born and her father lost his greatest love forever. In fact, that was the last entry in this particular notebook. Her father had gained a daughter that day and suffered through the loss of his wife during childbirth. Meredith read the last entry two days earlier when her father drove his wife out of the mountains for the birth of their child. The entry was short.

September 29, 1982—An earthquake. We are leaving NOW. Lord, help my family.

Meredith read the words three times before quickly shutting the notebook. She shivered, and it was a while before she could stand on her feet to put the notebooks away.

*****

Thomas sighed and relaxed for the first time all day. It was dark, and the bonfire still burned on the beach. The air was filled with the familiar smell of the fire that was slowly replacing the pungent, sulfuric smell of the fireworks. There was still a group of people around the blaze, some standing and some sitting, although the majority of the revelers had retired to their rooms. The folks remaining were laughing and having a good time, so nothing was wrong. The night had been a success.

Thomas was not a part of their party, and that was fine with him. He stood alone on the edge between the night's darkness and the warm glow from the fire. He lifted his right hand that held a Pabst beer can. Thomas wasn't much of a drinker anymore, not for any moral reason but because it just plain made him feel cruddy the next morning. But from time to time, he tipped a few cold ones back, and the Fourth of July was as good a time as any to enjoy a few beers. This one he lifted to the starry sky above.

"To you, Colin."

He lifted his beer higher, toasting the former owner of Camp Wildwood. This Fourth had been very odd without his old boss, but he had to admit that with Meredith at the controls, things had gone smoothly. The day on the water had been fabulous— sunny and warm with good times in general. Except for a brief misunderstanding about the use of the Whaler, the guests had been happy. As per tradition, they had a barbecue on the patio instead of the normal dinners. Yeah, they had to cook the regular meals for the few pains in the ass who refused to lower themselves to eat a grilled Hoffman's hot dog or hamburger. Sometimes he wondered if some folks knew how to actually have fun and celebrate a holiday. But the majority of the guests and employees had gathered on the pleasantly warm, calm patio to mingle and have an old-fashioned cookout. Even the Winsors, kids and all, seemed to be enjoying the evening without screaming at each other. As dusk slipped toward darkness, Thomas and Josh set up and lit the fireworks on the east end of the property. They had a series of rockets and boxes of fire-works that always provided for a good show. The display always impressed him, and he enjoyed lighting the pyrotechnics to give the patrons a thrill.

The water was as calm as it could get with the glow from the fire reflecting off the surface out past the dock. In fact, he could see a couple out on the dock illuminated weakly by the firelight. Josh had said that he was going to sit out there and perhaps the housekeeping girl was out there with him. She was certainly a cutie, especially for someone from Mayson. Mayson made North Creek, where Thomas lived all winter, look like Aspen. Again, Thomas thought about how thankful he was that Josh had signed up to work. The kid had turned into a pretty good worker.

Thomas had one concern, and that was the question the kid had made about earthquakes. He didn't know why the kid had been so intent on asking about them, but there had to be some reason. It was Camp Wildwood's dirty little secret. But there was no controlling the shaking that occasionally moved the wild country. The hope was that if it did happen, no one was around. There was no concrete evidence linking earthquakes to odd occurrences, but Thomas knew as well as others that the oddities were tied to the tremors. It could be bad, and no one wanted to deal with the horror. Thomas knew. He knew too damn well. So did Colin. When the shock of the news of Colin's suicide wore off, he knew what had happened. There had been an earthquake only days before. That was a tough pill to swallow, and it was best if the lake was unpopulated when a quake happened.

He looked out across the water and saw one single light burning in the far side darkness. Davey Cramer. Davey knew about the lake as well, maybe more than any other person. He was a good guy, even after his disagreements with Colin.

Thomas drained his beer and looked back at the fire where already fewer guests stood. It had been a long day that ushered in the heart of the summer season. They were in for a busy few weeks, and he just hoped that it passed without a hitch. He turned to head for his room, knowing that Josh would take care of the fire before going to bed. It had been a good day.

*****

The fire was almost burned down, and Meredith was feeling no pain. She had been stressing big-time over the last few days with the Fourth looming. To a summer resort, the Fourth was like Christmas, and it had gone off without a hitch. She would have to put a little something extra in the staff paychecks this week. That was a good idea, especially through the alcohol fog that had begun to cloud her head. She had been drinking since dinner, more than she had since being at Wildwood, and why not? It was the Fourth and it was a great night to celebrate. Not that the end was near, but she felt that she had cleared a hurdle in her first summer at the reins.

Thomas was standing on the edge of the darkness, and she watched as he turned and headed for the lodge and his quarters. The man was amazing, and he guided her through the season as no one else could. She realized that somehow he had become a surrogate father for her, and that was okay. Her father would have liked it that way. Her father. The thought of him brought a hitch to her chest, and she raised the plastic cup that held her rum and Coke into the sky.

"To you, Pops," she muttered quietly, not knowing that someone had come up beside her.

"He was a great man," the familiar voice said next to her. She quickly turned in surprise and found herself face-to-face with Pete. His sudden presence brought a fuzzy feeling to her heart that alcohol could never create.

"Jesus," she mumbled. "You scared the shit out of me."

Pete smiled broadly, obviously happy about his stealth. "Sorry about that, boss. He was a great guy, though."

Meredith had to agree and was pleased that Pete had come over. Things were weird between them, seemingly changing by the hour. She had always liked Pete, even when her father kept them apart. He had a swagger about him, but it was good-natured and he made people happy. There had been an attraction growing between them from the day he showed up for the season.

"He was great, and I miss him."

"We all do. In fact, I wasn't sure I was going to come back this season," Pete admitted as he looked out at the water. "When I heard that your father died, a lot of thoughts flew through my head. Who would buy the resort? Would it even open? I began to send feelers out to other places in New England and around Martha's Vineyard. I thought it might be a time for a change, anyway."

Meredith looked at him. "I didn't know that. Why did you come back?"

"You."

"What?" She laughed. "What are you talking about?"

In the firelight, she could see him looking at his shoes. "When I heard you were taking over, I wanted to be here to help so the place wouldn't fail. I figured you would need experienced help, and it was what your father would have wanted."

"Okaaay," she drew out, suddenly feeling like Pete had just slapped her ego.

"But," he continued, "the number one reason I came back was to see you."

"What?"

He quickly looked at her and then back at his feet. She couldn't help but get the image of a fourteen-year-old talking to a girl. "You have to know I kind of like you. Yeah, when you were young, you were like a cute little kid, but you grew up…well. Last summer when you were here, I was surprised by my feelings."

Meredith stood stock-still, probably with her mouth hanging open like a fool who was lucky it wasn't raining because she would have drowned. The cool thing was that she had the same exact feelings for him. They had been growing closer as if the pure inertia between them was unstoppable. But she really was surprised that he was laying everything out on the line. Pete looked at her quickly and then turned his head toward the lake.

"I kind of wanted to tell you that. If you want me to leave, I'll be gone tomorrow."

She couldn't help it. It just boiled out of her chest, and she let loose with a gust of laughter. The emotion just poured out of her as if a dam had broken. It was clear that Pete didn't appreciate the reaction to his confession, and she tried to control herself.

"No, no," she managed. "I don't want you to go and I'm not laughing at you. It's just…odd. Unexpected. But oddly enough, I've been trying to get the guts up to approach you with the same rap."

Pete smiled and it was good. "I'm glad, I guess."

"Didn't I hear you talking about a girlfriend from Boston?"

A devilish smile bloomed on his face. "That wasn't going to survive this summer one way or another."

With feelings of relief, recklessness, and something else closer to her heart, she moved to him.

"No one can know about this," she whispered.

She hoped he agreed.

15

July 6

The computer screen in front of her told a positive story that buoyed her spirits. The resort was 95 percent booked for the next three weeks. That allowed only a minimal amount of space available for the persons who were looking for a place to stay on short notice. The lack of openings sucked for those vacationers looking for vacant rooms but was sweet, monetary music to Meredith. After all her misgivings and fears of following in her father's footsteps, it appeared that things were moving along nicely. It filled her with a pride that she had never felt before. The Fourth had been a landmark moment that had passed without a glitch, and she honestly believed that the guests had a wonderful time. Besides trying to provide a great experience for them this year, she hoped things would be so magnificent that they would become return business the following summer. That's what the business was all about.

Meredith closed the tab and connected to the Internet to see what was happening in the outside world. It was amazing how isolated she felt living at the mountain resort. Events continued to roll on in the world, but it seemed to have little or no effect on the lake. There were national debt and economic issues, political haggling, a big baseball fight in Chicago, and, believe it or not, a shark attack off the New Jersey coast. The issues, although current, seemed the same as always and were quite frankly boring and distant.

There was a noise in the hallway, and Meredith heard footsteps approaching from the main desk. In a moment, Kristen was standing in the doorway to the office. Kristen, who was normally a pretty laid-back person, had a sour look on her face as if she was about to spew some poisonous news. That was the logical progression after Meredith had just had a moment of contentment.

Meredith sighed. "What's up?"

"Um, it looks like we might have a problem with our favorite guest."

"Oh, shit. What now?"

Kristen took a breath. "I'll tell you, Meredith. This woman is going to drive some good people to get their guns and stick them in their mouths. Her husband should be delivered immediately to the Vatican to receive his sainthood."

Meredith rolled her hands in a circle, signaling Kristen to continue.

"Okay, I guess she is ragingly pissed off at one of our house-keepers. Seems she claims the girl was stealing from her."

"Who's the employee?"

"Liza Grant. Olga has taken the front line on this one and will be in to see you soon," Kristen added.

"Good job, Olga," Meredith complimented. "When Olga shows up, send her in so I can get to the bottom of this. And make sure she has Liza with her."

Kristen turned to head back to the front desk. "They should be here very soon. Want me to just send them back?"

Meredith nodded, and Kristen disappeared. She reached into the college refrigerator on the floor next to her desk and grabbed a Diet Pepsi. This moment was inevitable, and she had been wait-ing for it. Bernie Winsor was a royal ass ache who expected five-star service when she was only a two-star guest. Except for a few minor blowups over food and general service, she had been quiet. But like a volcano, it was an inevitability that she would one day erupt. It appears that that moment was upon them.

True to Kristen's words, footsteps were heard on the carpeted floor, and it appeared that Olga had arrived. Meredith was looking at the door when Olga stepped into the doorway looking forlorn. Behind her was the young woman that Meredith had met a few times, the girl whom Bernie had accused of stealing from her. Liza looked distraught and had red eyes and puffy cheeks. It was clear that she had been doing a lot of crying. She hoped that this wasn't about to get ugly.

"What's up, Olga?" Meredith spoke, surprising herself with the lightness of her words. She really didn't want to deal with any conflict today.

Olga stepped into the room. "Well, Ms. Riley, it seems we have a situation."

Meredith held up her hand toward the woman, who was fifteen years her senior. "Olga, for the fiftieth time, it's Meredith. Now I understand that Mrs. Winsor is upset about something."

"Yes," she followed, obviously deciding to not use any name to address Meredith. "She claims Liza stole from her."

"Did you talk with her?"

"Why, yes. It seemed she can't find her cell phone and assumes Liza took it."

"Did Liza clean her room today?" Meredith looked at the girl behind Olga, who was paying close attention to the conversation about her but remained quiet and still, although her eyes screamed anguish. Olga nodded at the question. "Has the cell phone been found?"

Olga looked toward the window, and Meredith could tell she wished she was outside in the sunshine.

"No, ma'am, it has not. But we are looking for it."

Meredith raised an eyebrow. "Looking for it? Do you mean in Liza's room?"

The girl's eyes widened and then slowly dropped toward the floor. Her discomfort was obvious, but stealing from the guests was a serious offense that would mean immediate dismissal, and maybe even the need for law enforcement.

"No," Olga answered, shaking her head. "In the garbage. Thomas is in the dumpster."

"Garbage? The dumpster? Why?"

Olga almost grinned. "One of their children mentioned that his brother put the cell phone in the room's garbage can. Liza emptied it into a large bag of refuse. The woman is still blaming Liza for

141

intentionally removing it and wants her fired. Her screaming was something awful. Profane. Words that I can only imagine are spoken in the Mayson Diner."

What the hell was wrong with that woman?

"Okay, I think I got it. Olga, could you leave me alone with Liza for a moment?"

Something that resembled relief spread on Olga's face as she turned to leave, handing the Bernie problem over to Meredith. Olga slid past Liza, who still stood in the doorway. The girl looked simply miserable. Meredith waved Liza in and pointed at a chair on the other side of the desk. The girl slunk into the seat.

"Would you like something to drink?" The girl shook her head. "I have soda and water. No booze for you, though."

A small hint of a smile touched the corner of the girl's mouth.

"I'd love a water if you don't mind."

Meredith reached down and grabbed a bottle of water from the fridge, handed it to Liza, and sat back in her chair, looking at the girl. Liza took a hefty swig, and Meredith thought that the liquid saved her from dehydration due to the tears that had coursed from her eyes. They were puffy and red. Obviously this situation affected the girl deeply. Meredith had read somewhere that in order to keep the upper hand, use silence. So she waited for a long moment before speaking.

"Liza," she spoke softly, "what happened?"

The girl sighed and spun the bottle around in her hands.

"Honestly, Ms. Riley, I don't think I did...anything...wrong." The last few words took effort to get out as her chin trembled, and she fought back a wave of new tears.

Meredith pushed a box of tissues toward the girl, but she took none and looked forward with eyes full of moisture.

"Okay. Olga said she accused you of stealing her cell phone. Did you take it?"

"No," Liza answered with conviction, her eyes swimming but looking right at Meredith. At that moment, Meredith knew she wasn't guilty of anything. Call it women's intuition or just plain clarity. It was obvious that this girl was taking the brunt for Bernie's problem with her own family. "I cleaned their room. That was it, like

I do every day. I was cleaning a cabin twenty minutes later when I was told that I was being accused of stealing. This is ridiculous. I love this job. I *need* this job. Why would I jeopardize it?"

Meredith nodded, understanding the circumstances. "Did Olga search for the phone on your person?"

Liza nodded. "Searched me and my room. I don't have the phone. I guess the only thing I'm guilty of is dumping the garbage. But Mrs. Winsor said she's going to leave if I'm...not fired."

The walkie-talkie that she kept on the desk squawked, and she heard Thomas's voice asking for her. Meredith looked at Liza and decided to let her stay. The call was probably about her, anyway.

"Thomas, what have you got?"

The voice coming out of the speaker was surprisingly clear but too loud. Meredith tried to turn the volume down but was scared she might turn the damn thing off.

"I spoke with Andy Winsor."

"What did he have to report."

"Says his son put the cell phone in the trash. The girl didn't steal it."

"Thanks, Thomas."

"No problem. Out."

"I'll talk with her," Meredith responded. Oh yeah, she would. If the Winsors decided to leave, then so be it. It was bullshit having guests intimidate the staff, especially when they were obnoxious and wrong. "This won't affect your job here."

Meredith saw relief in the girl's eyes, but it wasn't a joyous, total relief. There was something more bothering this girl.

"Thank you, Ms. Riley."

She took a swig from her Pepsi and looked at Liza. If Meredith recalled, the girl had just graduated from high school, and she saw her hanging around Josh on the Fourth. She realized that other than that, she knew little about her. Liza was quiet, a good worker, and flew under the radar.

"Are you enjoying the job here this summer, Liza?"

The girl cracked a smile. "Yes, ma'am. I really like it here. The job is kind of stupid and gross at times, but it could be worse."

Meredith chuckled. She could only imagine how gross it could be, thinking about some of the guests that stayed a few days. She knew she wouldn't want the job. It was bad enough cleaning her own bathtub, let alone other people's toilets after a long night of food and booze.

"You just graduated from high school, right?"

Liza nodded.

"From around here?"

"I grew up in Mayson and went to the consolidated high school. I guess it's nice to be done with that."

Meredith smiled. "I imagine. What are your plans?"

The glimmer of happiness that was creeping into the girl's eyes rapidly faded. It was clear that this kid was not cruising down a happy road.

"I really don't have plans. It kind of sucks."

"Were your grades any good?'

Liza sighed. "Yes. I finished third in my class. That's not the issue, and it's kind of hard to talk about."

Meredith drank from her soda and thought about Liza. She seemed like a very sweet, smart person who should be happy about moving on to the next stage of her life. But she was tormented inside, and here at Wildwood, there weren't exactly a lot of people to release to.

"If you don't mind my intrusion, what's the issue? I promise that what we discuss won't go past the walls of this office. Of course, you don't have to say anything to me, and I'll completely understand."

Liza was looking out the window, and Meredith sensed more than ever her desire to speak to someone.

"It's not easy, Ms. Riley. I mean, I see all these people coming here to vacation, and sometimes it hurts, you know. My family… well, we have nothing. I mean nothing. My father is nonexistent. I've only hung out with him a handful of times in my entire life. My mom likes to party. She is self-centered and worries more about having a good time than her kids. There has been a parade of boyfriends that have lived with us, and some were…rude. I felt more uncomfortable in my own home than I did at any time in school. It wasn't a happy place. Being here, away from Mayson and my family, is like a vacation for me. I try and enjoy every day because it will end and I will be stuck at a crossroads. I don't want to return to Mayson."

Wow, Meredith thought. This was heavier than she thought it would be. This situation that she thought needed nothing more than an emotional Band-Aid had morphed into a grave psychological discussion with a hurting kid.

"Are you going to college?"

Liza sighed heavily and quickly gazed out the window. "I got into St. Lawrence and a couple other schools. There's no money. My mom won't even apply for financial aid. I might go to community college, but…I'm kind of lost. I feel like I'm on the verge of wasting…my…life."

The tears began to flow again, and Meredith felt the tug at her heart again. For a second, she thought she might actually begin bawling, too, until she took a deep breath to gain some control. This girl seemed like a pretty decent kid who was obviously intelligent, but the circumstances of her life created a ceiling over her advancement. At UNC, she and Michael and their friends had often gotten into debates about entitlement and individualism. Although she felt that the country's welfare system pretty much sucked, she felt that there were people who had situations that were so horrible they honestly needed help. Of course, Michael was a firm believer of "pulling yourself up by your bootstraps" and that everyone had an equal shot at life. This was coming from a person who was born into a household that made middle six-figure incomes annually and had no conception of want. He had the privilege of the best prep schools and college paid for by his father. How easy it was for him to ridicule the poor or needy. Meredith was looking at an example of an individual who did all the right things and still could not advance. That sucked, and this kid was being ripped apart because of it.

Meredith got up and went around the desk to Liza. She wasn't sure if giving her hug would be appropriate, so she just stood close and put her hand on Liza's shoulder. The words weren't easy, and she just hoped that she didn't sound like an asshole.

"Listen, Liza. I'm not going to pretend that I know what you are going through. But I do know that you seem like a very bright kid and you have been shit on so far in your life." Liza turned her head from the window and looked at Meredith as she continued. "Hopefully you're putting some cash away, at least for community college. Listen, if you need help, please come to me and know my door is always open. And if I can do anything to help you out as far as school, let me know. Maybe we could set up a bonus for you if you make through the summer."

Liza looked at her with swollen eyes and a look of pleased surprise.

"Thank you, Ms. Riley. I appreciate it." She still looked serious. "Am I being fired?"

Meredith laughed out loud. "No. No, Liza. Keep doing the good job that you're doing. And don't worry about Mrs. Winsor. I'll talk with her and make sure you don't have to clean her cabin anymore."

Liza stood, and her relief was clear. "Thank you, Ms. Riley. I appreciate your help."

She nodded and walked out the door and down the hallway, leaving Meredith standing thinking about the whole situation. What a mess. She grabbed her Diet Pepsi and walked toward the front desk. How was she going to broach this with Mrs. Winsor?

*****

Liza finished her cleaning duties in a zombie-like daze. The entire episode with Mrs. Winsor and Ms. Riley had drained her of energy and had knocked her off-balance. No matter how hard she tried, she couldn't drive the events out of her head. At around two thirty, she finished cleaning her last room and wouldn't be able to recall the details of the job if she had wanted. Autopilot. When she returned to her room, she found the four walls pushing in on her, and she realized that she couldn't sit on the bed by herself and read. Not now. Without much deliberation, she threw on a pair of shorts, sneakers, and a T-shirt. As she went out the door, she also grabbed a sweatshirt because the day was cool, even with the bright sunshine. Typical summer day in the mountains when clear air pushed down from Canada.

Her original thought was to walk the path around the lake, hoping that the tranquility would calm her racing mind. The last thing she wanted was to have someone join her. She needed to examine her thoughts solo. Josh would be outside and he might want to join her, and that could not happen.

The sun was bright, and she slid her sunglasses over her eyes. A breeze blew in from the trees that wasn't strong but had just a nip of coolness to it. It would get cold tonight. Maybe even into the mid-forties. The thought of fall crept into her mind, and she forcefully pushed it aside. The coming autumn was inevitable, and with it came the most uncertainty that she had ever faced in her life. She turned the corner around the lodge and hit the grassy lawn next to the patio. There were way more people on the furniture on the patio because it was out of the wind and the sun was hot here. Down on the beach, a few groups braved the chilly temperatures and sat in the glorious sun. Josh was there, leaning against the lifeguard tower, talking to Pete. Instead of walking toward the trail, Liza headed for the beach. It was time to try out something new.

Josh turned and noticed her when she was ten feet from the lifeguard stand. A wary smile spread on his face.

"Hey. How're you doing?"

Liza nodded and tried to smile. "Okay. It was all a little crazy this morning."

"Woman's fucking crazy." Liza looked up and saw Pete leaning over the armrest of his lifeguard chair. He was wearing a UMass sweatshirt and sunglasses. "She needs to have her ass kicked. Just let me know and I'll happily do it for you."

Liza felt a genuine smile grow on her face and shook her head. "No. It's cool. I'm just going to stay away from her. Ass kicking is not warranted."

"Whatever," Pete feigned displeasure and leaned back in the lifeguard chair.

"What're you up to?" Josh asked, and Liza got the hint that he wanted to help somehow, although she really didn't want it. It was a semi-awkward moment, but she had the perfect solution.

"Well," she started, suddenly feeling nervous, "I'm thinking that I might want to try out one of these kayaks."

Josh nodded, probably as a reflex to not hearing what he expected. She was certain that he was expecting to walk with her around the lake.

"Have you ever been in one?"

"Yes," she lied but figured it couldn't be that hard. She personally witnessed sixty-year-old overweight women successfully use one. Even five-year-old kids got the hang of it in a few minutes. "I just want to take one for a spin if that's cool."

Josh smiled. "No problem. I don't think you'll be taking an opportunity away from the guests today. Better take a PFD, though. I don't think you need to wear it, but keep it in the boat."

Liza grabbed the life jacket and heeded his advice, even though she was a pretty good swimmer. Josh led her to a yellow plastic boat that looked like a torpedo. It had a small opening in the top that she was going to have to get down and slide into. This could be an awkward moment, and it would be awesome if she could climb in without anyone watching, but that wasn't going to happen. Josh would be standing right there watching every move.

"You can use this one. Need help?"

She quickly looked at the kayak and then at Josh.

"Thanks. I can handle it."

He handed her a two-bladed paddle and walked back to the lifeguard chair, although she knew he was inspecting her every move. Pete was also in his perch, watching the show that was the only act on the beach.

Fearing a humiliating flop onto the dark sand, she pushed the kayak toward the water and self-consciously lowered herself into the boat. To her surprise, once she was aligned, her body slipped into the space like a foot in a sock. The boat rocked back and forth slightly, but Liza didn't mind, mostly because she avoided a sandy face-plant. While adjusting her rear end to find the most comfortable position, she used the paddle to move the boat out into the lake. Nothing happened and it became clear to her that she was still stuck to the shore. Well, this was wonderful. Now she would have to get out of the boat and do it all over. Then the boat moved forward, and she turned around to see Josh standing right behind her.

"You needed a push," he said and smiled. "Be careful because they can be tippy, and there's a little chop out there."

Liza flashed a big smile at him and began to use a two-handed motion to paddle the boat. Unlike a rowboat, there is only one paddle on a kayak, and the operator had to alternate ends of it to propel the craft. It took Liza a few seconds to get the right rhythm, but it was actually much easier than she had feared. She was gliding out into the middle of the lake, feeling free and alone. It surprised her that the day's events had been pushed into the back of her mind, which was what she hoped the kayak ride would accomplish. But as she moved into the middle of the lake, the morning came back and she allowed it.

The issue that continued to arise actually had little to do with Mrs. Winsor. Liza had heard through the grapevine that after their conversation, Ms. Riley had indeed had a stern discussion with the woman and had actually threatened to end their stay at Camp Wildwood if anything similar happened again. Of course, this was not the first time Ms. Winsor had raised a stink over something during her stay, but asking for the termination of an employee when that person was completely innocent was serious. There had also been discussions with Mr. Winsor who promised to have a conversation with his wife. As long as Liza didn't have to clean her cabin, she felt confident that the episode with Mrs. Winsor was behind both of them.

But what was bothering Liza was what the situation had illuminated in her personal life. Where the hell was she going? Yes, this job at Wildwood was amazing, and it had the direct importance of releasing her from Mayson and her mother. That was why the episode was so scary. If she had been fired, what was she going to do? There was no way she was going back to that crappy house with her mom. She did miss her brother and worried about him every day, but there was little she could do about that. She needed to save herself, and that was why she was here. But if she had to leave, where would she go? The options she had were scarce, and none of them appeared very realistic. She had little money and a limited number of friends outside the mountains that could help her get her feet underneath her.

And of course, fall would eventually arrive. The air would become crisp and frosty. The leaves would start to go over to their brilliant autumnal colors. The people would begin to drift from the resort and the mountains to other places. Homes, jobs, school—that was where Josh would be headed, and she felt a pang of jealousy when she considered his life. It wasn't fair. And where would Liza be going? There was no plan for that eventuality. The thought was bringing her down and had been the true cause of most of her tears all day.

There was more wind in the middle of the lake, and Josh had been right about the chop. It still wasn't much to worry about, though. The breeze was cool for July, and the sky above was a deep blue without any humidity-induced haze. To add to her issues, the day was acting like early September, constantly reminding her of fall. Great.

The far side of the lake was much closer, and she marveled at the forested hillside and the occasional boulder-strewn natural beaches. She took solace in the beauty around her. No matter how screwed up her life had been in Mayson, the mountains had always been inspiring. Ahead she saw the cabin that she and Josh had been invited to. Dave Cramer. He seemed like a nice enough guy and seemed to have the rat race beaten. A professor and a best-selling author. That was it. Maybe she could write a book too.

Liza laughed at herself and turned the boat to head back to the only stability in her life and that had tottered on the brink of catastrophe only a few hours earlier. She hoped that it would all be okay.

16

July 8

Michael Slater hated leaving North Carolina, but he had to over-come that sensitivity because he missed Meredith. He was frankly surprised, and the feelings spoke volumes about his state of mind regarding their relationship. When her father passed away, Michael had just assumed that she would liquidate his property, especially the "resort" in New York. He knew that the place was important to her because it was her true family home, but it was in the wilds of the northern mountains, and what was she going to do with it, anyway? They could sell the property and begin looking for vacation homes near the ocean and the beach. There was nowhere better than the coast, and he assumed that she felt the same way. That's where they had met. A bar next to a sand dune next to the Carolina oceanfront. That was their spot. It had shocked him when Meredith had decided to keep the resort, and then she totally blew him away when she made up her mind to leave Carolina to run the place. Not only did it seem illogical for financial and entertainment reasons, but it also spoke toward the status of their relationship. The relationship was suddenly headed nowhere, and that bothered Michael.

Truth be told, when Meredith left for New York, Michael didn't really care. His job as a researcher for a local law firm in Chapel Hill was going very well as he approached the completion of his law degree and employment at the same firm. He was staring a solid six-figure annual income in the face, and that wasn't shabby. He was young and good-looking, and the future was rosy. There were a number of young coeds at UNC who were more than happy to spend time with him, and on more than one occasion, Michael allowed them the opportunity. He was never sure if Meredith had caught on, but he was positive that she was no longer thrilled with his behavior. When she left, it was like a weight had been lifted from his shoulders as he was able to troll for the young ladies unencumbered. What shocked him was the loneliness that set into the vacuum she left behind. That had been an unexpected outcome. Hunting the girls was always an exciting challenge, but when it was all over, there was nothing but emptiness. Meredith had filled a space that was now vacant.

So he had fought his desires to hit the Outer Banks and instead drove north into the unknown and an area that he had no desire to go visit. He was on the Skyline Drive of Virginia, moving above the fields of the Shenandoah Valley far below. His plan was to get on Interstate 81 and head to Binghamton where he would spend the night with an old fraternity brother. Monday morning, he could get an early, fresh start and make it to Meredith's resort by noon.

As he drove out of Chapel Hill, it really took willpower to fight the inertia trying to hold him in North Carolina. As the miles passed and he got farther from his home, the force that held him only slightly faded. He tried to think of Meredith and his need to see her. That was all that he had to motivate him.

It was approaching one o'clock in the afternoon, and he had not put many miles between Chapel Hill and his current locale due to a slow start. Although unplanned, Michael had stayed out later than he had intended the night before. He had gone out with a couple of guys from the firm and had ended up staying out until two, basically chasing a waitress around who ended up leaving without him, anyway. Michael was thirty years old, and his body didn't recover as it had when he was twenty. Back then, when he was an undergrad, he was able to stay out until four in the morning and rally the next morning for the UNC football games at noon. That was impossible today. So he got a late start and he was now starving. He pulled into a friendly-looking diner that reminded him of the days when he and his family had made family road trips. His father had hated the interstates and had always tried to travel the back roads as much as possible to experience what was left of Americana. To his father, McDonald's, Hardy's, and Waffle House were blasphemous places.

The diner was covered with natural wood siding and had a newspaper box next to the entrance. Behind it, the hills fell away, and the vista was pretty amazing. It was as if the road was on top of the world. A family came out of the door led by a boy who was yanking on his sister's ponytail while the girl screamed. The mother, wearing a halter top that was too small for her hefty frame, yelled at the boy to stop. She was followed by a heavyset man wearing a Virginia Tech hat and picking at his teeth with a toothpick. Michael nodded at the man.

"Great day," the man said.

Michael forced a smile that he didn't feel. "Yes, it is."

The man smiled. "Best damn pork roll in the state. Yessir. Ain't none better."

Michael felt his smile falter, but somehow he managed to keep it hanging on his face. He just nodded in return, hoping that the man would not respond. He didn't, and Michael slipped in the door.

The diner was on the immediate right as he strode in and seemed pleasant enough with wood paneling and booths against the wall. The lunch crowd was thinning, and there were plenty of empty seats. Before he moved toward a seat, he wandered to his left where there was a gift shop for the tourists that stopped by the diner who bought silly knickknacks. He wandered through displays with wood carved bears and deer. There was maple syrup and rock candy. And there was a rack of shirts with the "Virginia Is for Lovers" motto emblazoned across the front of each. How sad. The state that gave the United States four of the first five presidents. Patrick Henry's real motto, "Give me liberty or give me death," had faded into obscurity to be replaced by such a stupid slogan. Might as just as well say "Virginia is for getting laid!" Virginia sucked. He debated buying a cheesy shirt for Meredith but ultimately decided against it. Their relationship was seriously on the rocks, and it wasn't time for jokes. He needed to bring his A game if he really wanted to win Meredith back. But did he?

A very cute waitress wearing a very short skirt came up to him and asked if he wanted a table. She had brown hair but eyes that drove an electric current through his heart. She looked to be six-teen or seventeen. He made himself stop thinking the thoughts that were racing through his head and followed her to a booth where he sat alone. *Just have a sandwich and hit the road.* In less than twen-ty-four hours, he hoped to be at Meredith's resort. Then he hoped to straighten up the mess that their relationship had become.

17

July 9

The scuba divers showed up early in the afternoon and were waiting to move into cabin 2. Dan and Margo Milakaus were a young couple with boatloads of enthusiasm and a positive karma. They were graduate students at the University of New Hampshire majoring in marine biosystems and seemed to have a zest for life. They had taken the summer off from their studies and decided to tour waterways in the northern tier of the United States with the hope of using some of the data and experiences they collected for upcoming research papers. They had come in from the Finger Lake region where they had dived in Seneca Lake where the waters were rumored to be bottomless. They weren't diving Moon Lake but relaxing on the beach in the warm sun that had returned pleasantly to the mountains.

Josh stood on the grass just on the edge of the beach, watching the guests dig in and move the sand that he had carefully raked to perfection only a few hours earlier. The routine was becoming redundant, although he was still enjoying his opportunity at the resort. He woke every morning at six and went for a run through the roads that cut through the thick forests. There weren't many options, but he was finding some interesting logging roads and trails that made his jog more of a cross-country run. He didn't mind. It kept his mind sharp and focused on the path he needed to take. He showered and then went around the grounds picking up garbage, raking the beach, and doing any odd jobs that Thomas wanted done before the guests really got moving. On most days after breakfast, Josh got an hour or two to relax and do what he wanted. Most days he lay on his bed reading a book because the rest of the day would be spent outside on the grounds or the beach dealing with the vacationing masses. Unless there was a storm or some other emergency, the days were all pretty much the same.

He looked toward cabin 2 where he knew Liza was pushing hard to finish cleaning the mess left by a family that had spent the last three days. The Milakaus didn't seem in any hurry to move from the beach. He thought he heard a vacuum from that direction, but that was impossible over the noise from the water and sand. The damned Winsor kids screamed in decibel levels that had to approach a 747 engine winding up for takeoff. They were still at the resort, and Josh was frankly tired of them and their bullshit. What that woman had done to Liza was just plain wrong, and Liza had become somewhat sullen afterward. The blame for that had to fall on that obnoxious woman.

Over the holiday, it had seemed that things were progressing nicely with Liza, but he had hardly spoken to her the last couple of days. The silver lining appeared earlier when she asked if he would be on the dock later for some stargazing. Although he hadn't been planning on it, the dock is where he would be, and he was growing excited for the night.

Out of nowhere, Slip slid up next to him, leaving his lifeguard chair for what he called a walkabout.

"Do you think there is some species of fish in the lake that might like the taste of Bernie Winsor flesh?"

Josh laughed. "Largemouth?"

Slip shook his head. "Nah. She would turn and eat the damn bass. She is one foul woman."

Josh turned and observed Bernie yelling at her kids and then immediately turned to berate her husband. Josh had met Andy Winsor and was impressed by his intelligence and positive demeanor. The poor guy didn't deserve the Tasmanian devil.

"Have you talked with the scuba divers?"

"No," Josh responded. "Well, I said *hi* and all but I haven't really talked to them."

Slip nodded. "They seem pretty cool and they mentioned a tour of the lake. I was wondering if you could take them for a spin in the Whaler later."

"Sure." Driving the boat around the lake was far from a hardship. He also knew that Slip would make sure that the cooler had a few beers on ice as well.

"How're things with the girl? Liza?"

Slip knew her name and was just trying to push his buttons. Over the last couple weeks, Josh had confided with Slip about his attraction, and the advice that he received seemed endless. Josh wasn't sure if he was taking advice from some bullshit artist because he had yet to meet his girlfriend that he often talked about. Josh didn't believe she existed and wouldn't until he saw her with his own two eyes.

"She's been pretty quiet ever since the Bernie incident."

Slip turned and stared at Bernie, who was now reading a romance novel and semi-peacefully spending part of the forty daily minutes when she wasn't bitching about something.

"Evil," Slip muttered and then slapped Josh on the back. "Liza will get over it. She needs a friend here, and that, my friend, is you."

Sure, Josh thought as Slip walked back to the lifeguard chair. Maybe tonight he would make a breakthrough with her.

*****

She put the cell phone down and smiled. Michael, the manly man who was so independent and intelligent, had failed to use a GPS or even write down directions. So he was now rambling along route 8 near Speculator, nowhere near where he needed to be. Meredith had explained to him the right path, and she wasn't sure that he would make it without becoming lost again. It was okay. She was sitting at the desk in her office with no plans on leaving the space anytime soon. Her father's logbooks were strewn across her desk. She had been haunted the last couple of days, especially the nights as she lay in bed. The cause of her discomfort was the entry her father had made about the period just before her birth. Earthquake. Her father had seemed terrified that there had been a quake and had rushed his pregnant wife out of the mountains to give birth. It didn't seem to matter because she had died in childbirth. Meredith had never gotten to know many details about the tragedy, and that had always been acceptable to her, but suddenly she wished to know more.

Sometimes trying to read her father's handwriting was difficult, but luckily she wasn't reading word for word but only skimming for one term: *earthquake*. She didn't know why, but for some reason, she knew that the significance was extremely important. The day after she had read the account in her father's journal, she had asked Thomas about that time at Moon Lake that her father had written. Not unexpectedly, Thomas claimed to know little about the death of her mother. If he knew more, he wasn't saying. Then she mentioned earthquakes and a side of Thomas she had never seen rose and set her back a step. His face reddened, and he told her not to worry about it, quickly turning away. He said earthquakes meant nothing.

That had been strange and only intrigued her more. Back in her office, she had searched the web for information on the geology of the Adirondacks and found some interesting information. For one, the Adirondacks were not part of the Appalachian Mountain chain that ran from Georgia to Maine. The Appalachians were old and at one time as tall as, if not taller than, the Rockies and the Alps. But millions of years of erosion had ground the peaks down to the rounded mountains that people see today. The Appalachians are exceptionally close to the Adirondacks. Skiers at Whiteface and Gore can easily see the Green Mountains in Vermont, so she always assumed that the mountains were part of the same range. Not true.

The Adirondacks were young and growing. The rocks of the Adirondacks were some of the oldest on earth, part of the vast and ancient Canadian Shield. But something was pushing the Adirondacks up like a giant bubble. In fact, if looking at a map of the Adirondacks, the mountains almost look like a large circle. The lift is occurring at approximately the rate a fingernail grows, which may seem slow but is active on a geologic scale. And that was the key. The mountains were active and often had very minor tremors, but on occasion, the hills shook with more vigor. Sometimes the epicenter wasn't even in the mountains but in Canada or the Hudson River Valley. Some had been strong enough to buckle asphalt roads.

This information was all very interesting but was far from adequate in understanding the mystery of her father's words. The Internet had numerous stories of the oddities in the Adirondacks, but none opened the door to understanding.

Meredith found one entry in her father's journal that dealt with the earthquake topic, and it only added to the mystery.

> May 2, 1999—high: 54 low: 29 cool, sunshine first day and it's great to be back at wildwood. Snow in spots. The grounds are in good shape with exception of normal winter damage. Thomas was here cleaning up sticks and limbs that had come down. He mentioned that there had been an earthquake in November before the freeze-up. He had taken snowshoes weeks later and looked for any victims. Mostly dead deer but he saw a startling sight. A bear had been roused from hibernation and had been broken and ripped apart. Said it looked like its guts had been eaten out. Scary. I wonder what happened. Luckily, no people were around. Going to help Thomas tomorrow and head back south on Sunday. Plan on opening June 1.

That had been interesting, to say the least. *Luckily, no people were around.* Apparently, there had been a wildlife kill. What had caused it? Radiation? Gas? This was strange, and the Internet had no stories dealing with the connection of earthquakes and dead wildlife.

Her cell phone beeped, and she looked at the message. It was from Michael. He was in the parking lot. She glanced at the clock, and it read 1:56 p.m. She had just breezed through an hour of her life mostly consumed by her own thoughts. She shook her head, trying to shake the afterimages of earthquakes, mountains, and a dead bear from her mind. She needed to shift gears and prepare for Michael and the mess that their relationship had become.

She passed Kristen at the desk and quickly explained to her the situation and that she would be busy for a while. Kristen smiled, most likely imagining a quick hello and then a quicker retirement to Meredith's suite for a reacquaintance. Honestly, Meredith wasn't sure what to expect when she saw Michael. It was possible that the flames of excitement might be rekindled when she saw his tall, handsome visage, but she knew that that scenario was unlikely. Things had moved on, and there was Pete. How was the Pete situation going to play out in this mess?

Michael was standing on the porch, just above the patio. He was a tall man with wavy dark hair. He was wearing a red polo shirt, pressed khaki shorts, and loafers. If she was expecting a moment of love or lust to engulf her when she laid eyes on him, then she was sadly disappointed. It was just Michael, the same guy that she had said goodbye to a couple of months earlier and had no regrets as she turned her car north. The feeling was gone like the thrills of summer when they closed the resort every October.

When the porch door slapped back against the frame, Michael turned and saw her. A wide smile unfolded on his face. He threw his arms open wide, and Meredith moved into them, feeling no warmth. When she was released, she looked toward the beach and saw Pete, who was looking over his shoulder at them from his perch on the lifeguard chair. To say she had conflicting feelings was a wild understatement.

"Well," Michael said, standing back and waving his long arms around, "rustic."

Meredith forced a smile. "That's how we like it."

"Is this the hotel?"

She laughed out loud. "Michael, this is a mountain place. *Resort* has to be applied with candor. No, not a hotel. This is the lodge."

"The lodge," he repeated. "Nice."

Meredith watched him turn his head across the grounds and could read his eyes searching for a pool, hot tub, or fitness center. Out of luck, buddy. This wasn't going to be easy.

*****

He turned the key, and the engine roared to life. He rotated and helped Margo Milakaus onto the gunwale and then onto the deck of the Whaler. Dan Milakaus jumped in easily after his wife and looked happy as shit.

"Want to throw off the stern line?" Josh asked as he moved up to get the bowline. It was nice to have help, and he realized that Dan and Margo probably knew more about piloting a boat than he did. He chuckled. He was in a good mood. It was hard not to be in the fantastic weather and being on a boat.

Josh slowly pulled the boat from the dock. There were only two people in the water and alike number on the beach. Most folks had pulled back to get ready for dinner. It was five and happy hour had started. The sun was still blazing over the water, and it was a perfect time for a cruise. Once clear of the dock and swimming area, Josh gave the engine some throttle, and the boat moved off a little faster toward the middle of the lake. It didn't take long to get there, and as they approached the far shore, he idled back and let the boat drift.

"This is beautiful," Margo said, looking around her in 360 degrees of mountains and trees.

Dan nodded. "Breathtaking."

"Where're you guys from?" Josh asked, playing the role of tour guide but honestly interested. This couple was only a few years older than he was, and they had already found Slip's beer stash.

"I'm from Pennsylvania," Dan replied. "Margo is from New Hampshire."

"We met at the University of New Hampshire," Margo added. "We got married last fall and are working on the same graduate degree. We live in Portsmouth now."

Josh nodded, unfamiliar with New Hampshire. "You two are marine biologists?"

Dan nodded again. "Technically biosystems. We are basically interested in aquatic biospheres. This summer we are looking at freshwater lakes and rivers. Later this week, we're headed to Lake Champlain. We're trying to hit points of interest, not just from a biology standpoint but from a rumor one as well."

Josh was pretty sure that his face crunched up in a funny way as he quickly tried to grasp what Dan had said. "Rumors?"

"Yeah," Margo said. "This is really a tangent for us. We are investigating strange stories and rumors about some bodies of water. If we can find a biological story, then that's excellent, and we can use it in our research. If not, maybe we can make a cheesy television series on the Discovery Network. If people can make money investigating aliens or hunting Bigfoot, then there has to be plenty of other ways to dupe fools out of their time and money."

"Wow," Josh answered, impressed. If nothing else, their summer seemed interesting. "Where are you guys diving?"

"We were just in Seneca Lake," Dan answered. "Stayed in a place called Geneva. The rumor is that no one has ever found the bottom of the lake."

Josh nodded. "That deep?"

"Maybe seven hundred feet. The depth isn't the interesting part, though."

Margo stepped in and picked up the dialogue. Josh could see the common bond and interest between the couple. "There is a Navy presence on the lake. They have a barge in the middle that no one is allowed near under threat of the US government. Back during the Cold War, our paranoia revolved around the fear that the Soviets could take out our missiles before we could launch them. They tested some of the first American nuclear submarines in the lake, and to make it stranger, the rumors are that there are nuclear missiles at the bottom of the lake. The Soviets couldn't destroy missiles under five hundred feet of water."

"That's nuts," Josh stated. "Did you guys dive down there and see?"

Margo looked at Dan, and they smiled. "We can't dive much deeper than one hundred feet at the max. Usually we are only in thirty feet or so. The deeper you go down, the more nitrogen builds in the blood, and it messes up your head like you were drunk. Don't want to feel that way one hundred feet down. Then you have to come up slowly to wash the nitrogen out. If not, you get pretty fucked up. Bad shit."

Josh knew next to nothing about scuba diving, although he was aware of the "bends" or something. It sounded dangerous but cool.

"Did you get any answers?"

"Not really," Dan responded. "I'm betting they have something down there, though. There used to be an Army supply depot near the lake, and they denied that nukes were stored there. When the Soviets succumbed, they openly removed the nukes from the depot. Pretty wild. Next weekend we are going diving in Lake Champlain in search of Champy."

"Champy?" Josh muttered. Margo had reached into Slip's cooler and retrieved three beers, although Josh had only had a couple sips of the one he still had in his hand. This was the most interesting conversation he had had in quite some time. What the hell was a Champy?

Margo handed him a can of beer and opened hers. "Champy is an animal that some locals claim to have seen in Lake Champlain. The creature is very similar to the Loch Ness Monster. We're going to dive in areas of the lake to see what the conditions are like. We want to see if such a creature could exist in the lake."

"I heard the visibility sucks, but we'll give it a shot," Dan added.

The sunshine was still warm as the day slipped toward the dining hour. There was no immediate desire to return to the resort, so Josh allowed the boat to drift in the water. A question popped into Josh's head all of a sudden that seemed abruptly mysterious.

"Okay," he said. "But then why are you here at Moon Lake? I thought you were looking for strange stories?"

Dan chuckled. "We are."

Josh felt his eyes open wider. "What's strange about Moon Lake?"

"It's supposedly haunted," Dan answered.

"Wha…?" was all Josh could get out.

Margo smiled. "We found some random story on the Internet while we were doing research for our summer dives. It appears that there is some old story of this place being haunted. That occasionally weird things happen. Supposedly it goes back to the Mohawks and other local Indian groups that lived in and around the mountains. It's not a popular story because we found very little about it, but what the hell. We needed a break, anyway, and the place looked quiet. This is more of a relaxation visit than work."

Haunted? Yeah, right. Josh looked at the blue water around him with the deep green reflection of the forests ringing the lake. There were a lot of trees out there, and he had actually wondered while running the trail how far the wilds went and what might be out there. Bears? Moose? Who knew. But haunted? Crazy.

Josh heard a whistle and turned toward the south shore where they had drifted. There was a man standing on a small beach waving at the boat in a friendly manner. Of course, this had to be Davey Cramer, the only inhabitant outside the resort on the lake. *What the hell?* he thought and moved the boat slowly toward the shore. Whether Davey really wanted to or not, he was about to meet the Milakaus. His waving stopped, and he moved toward the water. The Cramer property had no dock, but about three or four feet of dark sandy beach and if Josh had to, he could pull the bow up onto the soft soil. Josh slowed the Whaler down to a slight drift, lifted the engine, and cut the power. Without the engine noise, Davey could be heard.

"Good evening," he was saying with a sociable smile. "Nice time for a cruise."

Josh agreed. "Mr. Cramer, this is Dana and Margo Milakaus. They are guests at the resort."

Greetings and pleasantries were exchanged, and the Milakaus gave a quick summary of their educational situation at UNH.

"Really?" Davey responded with a smile of his own. "Great school. I'm a professor at Syracuse."

Again, there were friendly exchanges and quick statements about the merit of both institutions. Josh did not bring up *An Evergreen Life*, leaving that up to Davey if he wished. Although unplanned, this meeting did open the door for more intelligence from a longtime resident of the lake.

"They are here because they heard the lake is haunted."

Josh watched Davey's eyes, and they betrayed little.

"Haunted, huh?" the older man answered, a small smile touching the corners of his mouth. "Where did you hear that?"

"Internet," Dan stated quickly. "Found a reference on some site that also had the Lake Champlain monster and a couple other upstate New York oddities."

"Ah, the Internet. The new bastion of all that's fit to know. Completely based in facts and truths. Haunted, huh?"

Josh looked at Dan and Margo. "Davey has been here for a few years and knows more than most about this area."

"Cool," Dan said. "So what's the deal?"

"The deal? You want the deal. Is Moon Lake haunted? Well, you are partly correct. I have heard stories and even done some research on the topic. I haven't heard haunted. Cursed maybe but never haunted. What's the difference between cursed and haunted, anyway? A local group attached to the Mohawks had a legend about this lake. They called it *Crazy Lake*."

"Crazy Lake?" Margo asked. "Why?"

"Supposedly, long exposure here could cause a person to lose their minds." Davey came forward as the Whaler beached in the sand, and he leaned against the bow gunwale. "I have heard a story that local Indians repeated about this vicinity. They say the water is poisoned. The legend states that some gods came from the sky and placed a stone unlike any other earthly stone by the shores of the lake or in the mountains nearby. When brave men came near the stone, they were turned into crying weaklings. Others who came near the stone dropped dead with their insides ripped out or went after their best friends with nasty intent. The power of the stone was dark, and the Indians knew it was wicked. Four young men displayed the courage of warriors and put the stone in a canoe and dumped it in the lake. Three of the men would die soon after, and the fourth would be an idiot for the rest of his life. However, the power of the stone seemed muted by the water, but the people had seen enough. They moved from the shore of the lake and never returned, warning all to stay away from Crazy Lake."

Davey finished, and no one spoke for a few moments. Josh looked around the lake, trying to understand the myth. Crazy Lake. Sounded like a crazy story. Dan and Margo were riveted on Davey, and it was clear why his books were such great sellers. The guy knew how to create suspense.

Dan was the first to speak. "Is that the basis of the haunting rumor? I mean, nothing like that has happened recently."

Davey regarded Dan for a long time, keeping eye contact and saying nothing. The moment hung between them, and Josh got the distinct impression that Davey was mentally in a tug-of-war with his own thoughts and what he should say.

"Some people still believe the cursed stone is in the water. They think it lies dormant until disturbed and then…well, bad and wicked things happen."

"Like what?" Dan asked with a look of excitement in his eyes. "Do you know where the stone is?"

Davey smiled and looked at the blue water. "Ah, just stupid rumors. I've heard the stone is in this very cove, but no one has ever seen it."

Josh saw the look that Dan and Margo exchanged, and he knew he or Pete would be bringing them to the cove for a dive, probably tomorrow.

"Pete working tonight?" Davey asked Josh, and he nodded affirmatively. "Jeanne wants to go out, so maybe we'll row over. Might see you later."

They waved goodbye to Davey, and Josh started the engine, giving it a little extra juice to pull from the sand. In a moment, they were motoring back across the water toward Camp Wildwood. Dan and Margo were animatedly talking about diving the next day. Josh was staring ahead, thinking about a stone and his mother's warning. Maybe the puzzle was coming together, and he wasn't sure he wanted to understand the picture it revealed.

*****

When she had seen him standing on the porch, an old wave of emotion swept her, and for an instant, she remembered the Michael that she had truly fallen in love with. The courtship had been rapid, and before she had time to rationalize her situation, she was moving in with him. The day at Kill Devil Hills came back to her like it had occurred only a week earlier instead of three years. She was sitting in one of those low folding chairs where a person's ass was only inches above the ground. They were meant for just the purpose of sitting in the sand. It had been a warm and glorious day with just enough wind to keep the real heat at bay. She was staying at her friend Tripper's house. Her whole group taught at a prep school and were celebrating the end of school with sand, water, and plenty of booze. Tripper and Benji were playing catch with their lacrosse sticks, and she, Theresa, and Megan were sitting back when Michael came up to them. He had been playing Frisbee and came over to retrieve the disk. Michael was tall and thin in a muscular way. He had tried to walk on to the UNC basketball team but had failed miserably. His love was basketball and baseball, two sports that Meredith had never gotten into but would end up in futility, trying to enjoy with him. Michael bled Tar Heel blue, and she came to understand that his passion for it might have surpassed his love for her. He had flashed his white-toothed smile that had profound effects on her. He was attractive, and at that stage, that was all that really mattered. Later that day, they met again in a beach bar, and the rest was history.

The man she had met on the beach was on the porch—tall, tan, and handsome. But first looks were always just a superficial taste of the actual being. Her Aunt Helen had once told her that she would never meet the man she would marry in a bar during a weekend of partying. Well, Aunt Helen, you can add the beach to that. Michael was intelligent, but he used that strength as an opportunity to look down at most people. She was positive that he would end up being a successful trial lawyer; there was little doubt of that. But he truly sucked as a person to simply have a discussion with about what to plant in the flowerbeds the next spring.

It had taken ten minutes for her to regret the moment she had said it was okay for him to visit. They were not officially broken up. That terminating conversation had been left hanging when she had bolted for the north, but most of her possessions were still in the house that they were presumably still renting together, waiting for her return. Good luck with that.

Her patience was running thin, and it was only made worse because of Pete. She hadn't expected that to happen at all. The same

Pete that her father had worried over and kept away from her was now in the picture. Pete was also attractive but different from Michael. Slip was fun and carefree. Unlike Michael, he sincerely enjoyed talking to people, and she was completely impressed by the way he handled himself with the guests. And yes, she was lonely. And yes, she was anxious. And yes, she was in an odd state being at her father's resort. She was vulnerable, but that didn't seem to be Pete's purpose of attack. He just seemed honestly interested in her, and that made everything extremely natural and…easy. It was completely unlike the exertion it took to remain with Michael. Now they were both in the same room together, and it was the most awkward she had felt since leaving North Carolina.

She had taken Michael into the bar, knowing that it would be tense but without any contrary options. It was clear that Michael had been itching for a drink, and the bar was the place to get one. Michael went into the room with his typical swagger, and Meredith could tell that he impressed some of the guests and staff. It was also hard to miss the forced smile on Pete's face and the eye he kept on Michael's every movement. It was not good.

The drinks did flow easily, especially for Michael, who Meredith could tell was trying to enjoy Wildwood, although she knew he wasn't. Michael had never wanted to come north, and that made his visit even more curious. The idea dawned on her that he might really love her, but she honestly didn't believe that possible. The problems began when they sat for dinner. Meredith thought it positive business sense to eat in the dining room to show a sense of community and family for the guests. She could also tell that Michael was not thrilled with the quaint Adirondack feel of the room nor the guests seated around them. A girl named Ashley came over to wait on them, and he immediately ordered another gin and tonic. She could no longer see Pete and wondered if he had the balls to slip some arsenic into the drink.

Then the devil entered with her brood and sat down at the table right next to them. Meredith knew a potential bad scene when it surfaced, and this was threat level midnight. The Winsors had arrived for dinner, and they came in like a thunderstorm downpour. The kids slid into their chairs and immediately began to fidget and yell at each other. Meredith looked at poor Ashley and could see on her face that she didn't want anything to do with that table. Bernie waved her hand in the air and beckoned the poor girl over.

"We would like to eat as quickly as possible," Bernie exclaimed. "The boys want to hunt fireflies before going to bed."

Ashley nodded and handed them menus, which Bernie pushed back.

"We know the menu. For god's sake, it never changes. My husband will have the chicken parm, the boys will have hamburgers and fries, and I want the sirloin with extra sour cream on the potato."

The waitress tried to smile. "How would you like it prepared, ma'am?"

Bernie sighed deeply and threw a penetrating stare at the girl. "Medium rare, just like every night."

Ashley hurried away with an obvious look of relief as if she had just hand-fed a tiger. The woman was unbelievable and was unaware that Meredith sat right behind her. Her husband knew, and a conspiratorial grin appeared on his face. Then Michael spoke.

"My word," he said with his Carolina drawl, where the vowels were held onto for way too long. "That was extraordinarily rude."

Bernie's head whipped around, and the look of red-faced anger quickly melted to confusion when she came face-to-face with Meredith. It was funny, but Meredith could also see below the red-cheeked surface to the potential storm that was about to unleash its fury.

"I…," was all she got out of her mouth, but Meredith saw her surprise melt to anger again.

"This young waitress is just doing her job and deserves, at least, some respect," Michael added, gaining some respect from Meredith. Ah, Southern chivalry. She contemplated that maybe Michael thought Ashley pretty. Great.

Bernie's face blossomed into a blaze of crimson. The next move was anyone's guess, but Meredith assumed it would be bad.

Bernie turned and looked Michael straight in the face. "I am a paying guest at this rat hole, and my family is hungry. No skinny-assed, fucked-up talking beanpole is gonna talk to me that way. No one talks to me that way!"

Michael looked as if he had been slapped. He leaned backward, perhaps because he actually feared a physical blow. Bernie was now standing, and Andy was reaching pointlessly out to restrain her arm.

"Are you apologizing?" Bernie demanded.

Michael had backed away, but his pride and ego had not.

"Well, I refuse to apologize to such a vile creature as yourself. You, lady, are a piece of shit."

Meredith cringed as she saw Bernie's face go white hot in nanoseconds. Michael had just thrown a gallon of gasoline on a raging fire. Dangerously explosive. To make it worse, Michael was now standing to face Bernie down. The situation could be tragic because Bernie probably outweighed the much taller, muscular man.

Pete suddenly slid between the two antagonists, which immediately diffused the situation.

"Relax, folks. This isn't the place for an ultimate fighting experience."

Andy had stood up as well and had wrestled Bernie back a few steps. The woman still looked capable of spitting nails.

"I...want...an...apology," she managed to get out through gasping breaths.

"After you," Michael responded, and Meredith wanted to kick him in the balls. What the hell was he thinking about? Just step down. This was her resort, and he didn't need to sabotage all she worked for.

"Come on," Pete said, grabbing Michael and pulling him away. "You and Meredith can eat in the bar."

Luckily, Michael allowed himself to be led from the dining room into the adjacent bar area. Meredith was left at the table to deal with Bernie, and she was about at the end of her rope. The only problem was that Michael had acted like an asshole, too, so her hands were tied.

"I demand an apology," Bernie commanded. Oh, that wasn't going to happen. Instead, Meredith looked right at Andy Winsor.

"We have discussed this behavior. My friend definitely acted inappropriately, but your wife has pushed my staff for too long.

I warned you before. You had best treat Ashley with the ultimate respect. Understood?"

Andy nodded, not letting his wife speak. "Understood, Ms. Riley. I promise that if there is one more issue, we will leave."

"Thank you, Andy," she said honestly. Sane people. That poor man.

Meredith did not look at the woman as she walked past her into the bar. Two assholes at once. Damn.

Pete had just made drinks for the Cramers, who had arrived in their rowboat and were sitting at the bar. That was when it had sounded as if a gang war had broken out in the dining room. He quickly excused himself and ran from behind the bar to investigate. There was no shock when he saw that the conflict involved Bernie Winsor, but he was surprised to see Meredith's boyfriend facing the woman down. It seriously looked like the two were about to brawl right there in the Camp Wildwood dining room. He could see it in next year's brochure: "Camp Wildwood! An Adirondack Tradition. Boating, Bears, Brawls!"

He looked at Meredith and saw a look of horror on her face and reacted without thinking. He stepped in between the two like he had done many times during his previous life as a bouncer and ski bum centuries before at Killington. It was stupid because any punches would likely hit him upside the head. But it worked, and he dragged Meredith's boyfriend into the bar.

"Let me go," Michael demanded, although Pete could tell that he was happy to be away from that psycho woman. "That is one rude bitch, and I'm not done with her."

Pete nodded and released him. "Yes, she is rude as hell, but it's not worth being arrested over. New York state frowns on guys belting females. Not a good idea."

After a moment, Meredith came into the room and flashed him a look that struck his heart. It was for him and him only and was the deepest thank-you that he had ever seen. It was at that moment that he realized that he was falling for Ms. Riley. Now that was a shocker that he hadn't planned on when he drove up here. He had actually been dating someone, but she stayed on the Vineyard, and he was more than willing to cut the bonds. Call it what you wanted, but being at Camp Wildwood was more important to him. This was home and his true love. Many of his friends thought he was nuts, but they didn't understand what it was like to wake up and watch the sun burn the mist off a mountain lake every morning. It was bliss.

The Meredith thing was unexpected. She had always been a cute kid, and no matter what Colin feared, he wasn't going to chase after a juvenile. He was a teacher for god's sake. He got along with kids easily, but that that didn't mean that he wanted to sleep with them. But things did change as Meredith progressed through college, every summer visiting and looking more and more beautiful. But she was taboo, and he had always respected that.

So why now? Pete shook his head every time he thought of the Fourth of July and his crazy admission to her. Things had worked out perfectly, but still it was bizarre. She could have been totally weirded out and sent him packing, which would have sucked on many levels. But things had taken an encouraging path, and he was blown away. He thought of her every moment—from the instant he woke up until the deep night as he desperately tried to fall asleep. The feeling was amazing, natural, and meant to be.

Then she dropped the Michael bomb on him. Only days after they had come together, she explained that her boyfriend was visiting from North Carolina. Boyfriend? He knew she had left someone behind when she came north, but he assumed that she had cut the cord like he had. She had actually clarified that she had broken it off when she departed North Carolina but that it wasn't official. Pete had a hard time grasping that concept and was completely disturbed by the idea of this guy coming to the resort. He would be sleeping in Meredith's bed—the very grounds that were sacred to him. He had dreaded the guy's arrival, although Meredith had tried to convince him not to worry. Didn't work. Frankly, as he moved back behind the bar, he felt some relief and felt the best he had in a couple of days. The guy was a total douchebag.

"What's up?" Davey Cramer asked.

Pete looked at Meredith, who was just about to sit on a stool at a tall bar table where Michael had already planted himself. She looked at him and gave him a quick smile that was electric. "Nothing. We have an ornery guest who got into it with some staff."

"Camp Wildass." Davey chuckled.

Jeanne smiled. "It takes all sorts of people. It amazes me that some folks just can't be happy. I see it in Florida all the time. People come down on vacation and do nothing but bitch."

"So true," Pete answered as he wiped the bar down with a rag. He watched Meredith, who was still trying to calm her friend down. She looked completely miserable. Pete thought of sleeping on his tiny twin cot in his room. The thought of the two of them sharing a bed caused a flare of pain right in the middle of his chest. Torture.

Davey spoke and dragged Pete away from the scene across the bar room. "Do you know the guy who works here named Josh?"

Pete nodded. "Sure. Work with him every day. Hopefully the kid's out on the dock right now with his summer romance."

"Liza?" Jeanne asked, and Pete showed his surprise.

"You know Josh and Liza? How?"

Davey explained how they had stumbled upon him one day on the trail.

"And earlier today, Josh came over in the boat with a young couple. Scuba divers, I believe."

"Sounds right," Pete responded, wondering if this was going somewhere. It wasn't like Davey to just mindlessly chatter.

Davey took a deep drink from his glass and slid it forward for a refill. Pete mixed the drink and returned it to the wet spot in front of the author.

"He asked about the lake."

Pete cocked his head. "The lake?"

Davey nodded. "Its history. I screwed up and told them about the stone story. I think the scuba couple might go diving to look for it tomorrow."

Pete stopped wiping the bar and looked straight at Davey.

"How did Josh find out about that?"

"The couple found something on the Internet about the lake being haunted," Davey answered with a shrug.

Pete sighed.

"And," Davey added, "Josh asked about earthquakes."

The dishrag in Pete's hand dropped to the bar. He stole a glance at Meredith, who was sitting on her stool, staring out the window into the darkness where the lake would be in the light. A shiver slipped down his spine.

"He *knows*?" Pete questioned. "But how?"

Davey shook his head. "He didn't say, but he is certainly inquisitive about it."

"Are you sure he was talking about earthquakes? Earthquakes dealing with Moon Lake?"

Davey slowly nodded his head. "Slip, somehow he knows."

Silence fell over the three, leaving each with their own thoughts. They all knew the lake's secrets. Thomas knew as well. Pete again looked at Meredith across the room. She had no idea, and he thought it best that it stay that way.

"Thanks," Jeanne said as she and Davey stood from their stools. "Long row back."

"I can give you a lift in the Whaler. It would take three minutes."

Davey shook his head. "The row is good for me, although my back will be stiff in the morning. Getting ancient. Thank god for ibuprofen. Later, Slip."

Pete smiled. "'Til next time, Mr. and Mrs. Cramer."

Jeanne smiled and waved. Davey moved close to the bar before following his wife into the main atrium and the front door. He leaned in close to speak.

"I think those scuba guys are going to dive and try to locate the stone," Davey whispered conspiratorially.

Pete took this in. "Do you think it's actually out there?"

Davey shrugged. "Don't know. But if it is, I don't want anyone disturbing it, that's for damn sure. Be good."

And with that, Davey walked out the bar, leaving Pete to mull over about a thousand issues in his mind.

*****

Liza heard about the ruckus in the lodge that involved Bernie Winsor from Callie, the other full-time housekeeper who had been in the kitchen when the situation had blown up. Bernie Winsor was a horrible human being, and there was no surprise when the news broke. But Liza was certainly shocked that the row had included Meredith's boyfriend. Crazy. Liza had gotten a good look at him after he arrived. He was tall and definitely handsome with a smooth and kind of sexy Southern drawl. But there was a vibe associated around the guy that turned her off immediately. *Cockiness* was the best word for it. He seemed like the type of guy who was wealthy and knew it but had done little to accumulate it except to leave his mother's womb. Family money. What was she born into? Family poverty? Family redneck? Whatever it was, she had grown up in a polar opposite world from Meredith's man. The guy was arrogant, and Liza wondered what Meredith saw in him.

As she walked toward the dock and crossed the sandy beach, she could just see in the dim light a rowboat moving away into the dark night. The creaking of oars and some conversation drifted across the water. It was probably the Cramers heading home. Boy, they had a cool deal, and Liza respected them so much. When she and Josh had visited their home, the love that the two shared between each other was plain, and she was envious. She wished them a safe journey across the water.

The dark hulking image at the end of the dock had to be Josh sitting alone with his six-pack. The feelings that struck her when she saw him brought the mixture of emotions that she had been struggling with over the past couple of days. They had been getting close very quickly, and that seemed perfectly natural. She welcomed the relationship. A nighttime rendezvous became the expected norm and not just a chance encounter. Then the Bernie situation dropped and knocked Liza for an introspective loop. Although she didn't want to admit it, the encounter had been profound and had given her a new perspective on where she was in her life. She had come a whisker away from having to pack her bags and exiting Camp Wildwood, and that had scared the fear of reality into her. This wasn't a summer vacation or a fun fling. This job was incredibly important to her. She needed to make money so she could have the opportunity to attend a community college where tuition was only part of her expense because she could not commute. Money would be needed for an apartment and every other expense that came along with living on one's own. Her teachers in school had often tried to express the importance of getting a real job by showing the costly expense of living a marginal lifestyle. It was freaking scary.

The other fear, which is of being fired from the resort, revolved around the emptiness of her life. This was all she had. If she could no longer work, spend time in her little room, and hang around the grounds, then she would have to go home, and that was a black hole of despair for her. She had come to the stage where that prospect was completely unacceptable. Mentally, Liza had already divorced herself from Mayson, and to go back would be the equivalent of an abused wife running away and then returning to the violent husband. It was depressing beyond words, and that was one of the reasons that she had soured on Josh.

Yes, there were more than physical reasons. On the night of the Fourth, they had hooked up for the first time, and although Josh had been fairly gentlemanly, he had tried to push their physical experience further than she wanted to go. When she had shut him down, he had not seemed disappointed, which was a relief. The thought that she was currently wrestling with had little to do with the carnal aspect but was much more complicated and deal with the differences in their lives. As she got to know Josh, she came to realize that she had met a guy who was indeed a privileged kid. Wealthy. Athlete. When he fucked up, Daddy threw money at the problem. Josh seemed to be honestly grounded unlike that rich jock stereotype, but she couldn't shake the idea that if he got fired, he would fall into an open safety net. In fact, he would probably be thrilled if he was fired so he could return to his college or his father's luxury boat. Things would be fine for him. That thought drove nails into her brain.

As she walked down the dock with her flip-flops slapping her bare feet, these thoughts raced through her mind. They were creatures from different worlds and yes, she was resentful. Why had she decided to come out here tonight? Damn Bernie Winsor.

"Hi," Josh said to her as he twisted his body around to watch her approach. His words slipped to her across the night, and she realized she did not feel the excitement from the previous encounters. A change had occurred that was perhaps impossible to overcome.

Liza moved up and sat on the dock next to him. "How are you?"

Josh handed her a beer, which had become the nightly custom. The can would be mostly full when they walked off the dock. She could see his broad smile even in the relative darkness. He seemed very glad to see her, which made her feel even worse.

"I'm doing great. Another beautiful night."

She slipped her feet into the water, and the surprisingly warm liquid enveloped her feet. Unlike the expected cold shock, the water was tepid and somewhat soothing. It had been a remarkable summer with warm days and lots of sunshine. To the benefit of the resort, there had been just enough rain to keep everything green and only a couple of total washouts. In previous summers, she hadn't really cared one way or the other if it had rained, but now she was cognizant because of the resort. If it rained, the whole atmosphere of the place changed. Things ran smoother when the people had nice weather to enjoy. Again the stars were brilliant, and she could make out a lone light across the lake, guiding the Cramers home. Another perfect night.

A sigh escaped her throat, mostly because it seemed a shame to be as uncomfortable as she felt while being surrounded by such serenity. She understood that it was confusion that was dominating her emotions and thoughts. Throw in the fear of the uncertain future and it was reasonable why she was a bundle of anxiety. To make it worse, she could tell that Josh was anxious, too, but she assumed that his revolved around the cooling of their fledgling relationship.

"How have you been?" he asked, and Liza had the feeling that he had been dying to ask the question.

Liza took a breath, knowing that she was going down a road that might become difficult.

"Doing all right. Tough couple days."

"I heard," Josh continued. "That Winsor woman is one mean character. Are you okay?"

Liza nodded but really didn't have much desire to rehash the entire episode.

"It happened and I hope it's resolved," she answered. She took a sip of beer and decided that she had to open up and spill her thoughts. "You know, the whole thing kind of freaked me out. Josh, I'm terrified of losing this job. And why? Because I have nothing else. I mean *nothing*. My mom is a self-absorbed drunk, and my poor brother… I don't have school to go to or a serious job. This is my retreat and my gold mine. I need this job, and when I got called into Meredith's office, I thought…"

Josh reached out and put his hand on her shoulder, and she recoiled slightly. His hand didn't move, which probably meant that he hadn't noticed her adverse reaction.

"It's okay. You kept your job."

Liza exhaled and looked at Josh, realizing for the first time that he was really just an overgrown kid. He had the depth of a kiddie pool. "It's more than that, Josh. I mean, you're working here before you go off to your college to play football with all your friends. Even if you didn't, you could escape to one of your father's homes. Pete has his teaching position to go to. Meredith will slide back down to North Carolina when the season is over. I have *nothing*. This job is everything to me. I can't lose it, and even when it's over, I'm staying here without any future. My only hope of any opportunity is to keep my head to the grindstone and make as much money as I can. Then maybe I can get an apartment in Glens Falls. So I can't lose this job."

Josh's hand began to rub her shoulder, and although it felt nice, the movement was contradictory to what she needed. The feeling actually became annoying, and she pulled away. She needed to be alone without any entanglements.

"Well, you still have your job, and from what I've heard, the blame has all been with Bernie Winsor."

"Josh," she said bluntly, realizing that he wasn't cluing in and that she needed to just say what was bothering her. "What I'm trying to say is this. I like you. You seem like a really cool guy, and I have completely enjoyed the time we've spent together. But we are from completely different galaxies that are rushing away from each other at the speed of light. There is way too much at stake in this game for me, and I can't lose focus because I like you. I'm aware that this must seem selfish, sudden, and particularly harsh, but I have to do what's right for me."

His jaw had crashed open, and his mouth was gaping, collecting dew that was forming in the cool air. Liza felt bad. Josh had come off as a big dumb jock, but she had unearthed a rational, emotional person within and she knew he was pining for her. She had just suddenly slammed the door shut in his face. The idea that he might abruptly blow a main circuit and freak out on her crossed her mind. That would be a sensational headline: "Mayson Girl disappears in lake. Slim lead to fellow employee. Happy Hour at the Mayson Diner at 4:00! ¢10 wings!" Would anyone even care if she disappeared?

"But...I thought we were getting along?"

Liza groaned as she stood from her sitting position. Her wet feet were quickly cold in the cool night air.

"I have to go."

Josh stood, and Liza felt a twinge of fear bite her. Josh was way bigger than she was, and she abruptly considered that maybe she had misinterpreted him after all. He took a step toward her, and she moved backward.

"What the hell, Liza?" he said louder than she desired. Sound traveled well over the water, and it was a quiet night with little wind. "I thought we were hitting it off?"

Liza was still stepping backward, now worried about stepping off the dock in the darkness. "It's not you, Josh. I'm just not right for you. Don't get mixed up with a poor mountain girl."

"Liza, stop moving away!"

The tone of his voice had become harsh, and she realized that she had to escape more than ever.

"Josh, I'm sorry," she said and turned her back to him. She half-expected at any moment to feel his hands fall on her shoulders, stopping her escape, but when she neared the shore, she turned back and could see his form in the darkness, and she was sure that his head was sagged down. He was not following. For a brief instant, she considered going back into his arms and explaining that she was sorry, but the rational part of her brain won out, and she stepped out across the beach. Although she felt ripped apart, she knew she had done the right thing.

PART 2

The Legend

18

July 10, 6:45 a.m.

The morning dawned like so many others during a mountain summer. In early July, the sun rose at just after five thirty, preceded by the early light that began filtering into the dark, the light slowly dissolving the black night away. The sun rose slightly later at Moon Lake because it had to ascend to a point above Bear Path Mountain to the east. The first golden rays first touched the tops of the tall spruce that rose on the west side of the lake and worked down toward the water. When the sunshine reached the water, it burned through mist that hung over the lake. The amount of mist varied from day to day. On this morning, the air temperature was cool, cold by many people's standards, so there was a good amount of steam rising from the warm waters. The mist would be gone by seven thirty, and most people at Camp Wildwood wouldn't even notice it.

The humans were slow to rise around the grounds on most mornings and tended to miss the glorious return of our star. Many of the animals that inhabited the woods around the lake were present but rapidly moved deeper into the trees due to centuries of learned instinct that it was best to avoid people in the daylight. Thomas was usually one of the earliest risers. By habit, he was awake at five and typically out and about by five thirty. For decades, he had taken a morning stroll across the grounds before the guests were up to take stock on the shape of affairs. On many mornings, he would find limbs down or notice some job that needed attention. Many mornings he found garbage left behind by some inconsiderate guests, and it was mostly beer cans and plastic cups from the previous evening revelers. It was a fine time to be outside by a mountain lake.

Across the water, Davey Cramer was, as he did most mornings, already sitting on his porch enjoying the first of many cups of coffee while staring at the water. People draw inspiration from many sources, and Davey often found inspiration at this moment of the young day. Hiking the trails behind the cabin also helped, but this time of day was pure magic. After three cups of coffee and a bowl of cardboard-tasting fiber cereal that Jeanne made him eat, Davey would sit down at his computer and try and knock off a few pages before Jeanne rose for the day. He didn't mind letting her sleep in; she deserved it. Jeanne was planning on going to the grocery store in Newcomb at some point during the day, but he was planning on staying put and doing some stone work along the beach. The weather promised to be fine and a superb day to be by the water.

By seven thirty, the sun was already striking the water, casting reflections into the trees. It was also the time when the people began to stir. The smell of bacon could be smelled, wafting from the kitchen where Ben had begun the morning repast for the guests and employees. Josh had already had his bacon and eggs. He got a plate and sat alone at a table, not really wanting to talk with anyone. He had been up extremely late the night before. After Liza had told him her true feelings, he had drained the remaining four beers sitting on the dock next to him rapidly and needed more. The problem was that he had no access to any more. Not that he was in love with Liza, but he had felt a certain sense of attraction to her and basically assumed things were progressing positively. He had been rebuffed and he wasn't used to that, especially by the only nice-looking girl who had all her teeth within a fifty-mile radius. After his search for more beer came up empty, he seriously contemplated getting into his car to drive to the nearest store to buy some. That place would have been Mayson, and the store was probably closed at seven at night. Some cooler, saner part of his brain prevailed, and instead, he tried to walk the path around the lake but abandoned the idea after slipping off a moss-covered rock and landing square on his ass. What he eventually did was put on sneakers, shorts, and his Petzl headlight and went for a run. There was no concern for bears because none would be stupid enough to approach this young man growling through the woods as he ran to escape from some demon that was following only one step behind him. The expected quick post-run sleep was slow to come, and he actually slept very little, which made him feel particularly shitty as he ate his bacon. When he finished with breakfast, he would go rake the beach and hope that he could manage to survive the day and the inevitable sight of Liza.

For her part, Liza woke at seven thirty but lay in bed reading for a half hour. She, too, felt odd, kind of like being hit in the abdomen. She really liked Josh, but it couldn't work, and although she was confident with her decision to tell him that their blossoming relationship was over, part of her felt empty when she woke up. Liza was facing yet another day of cleaning rooms and kowtowing to the guests. Although it sounded distasteful, Liza needed a day away from Camp Wildwood and was planning on visiting her mom and brother on her day off next Wednesday.

Meredith was already awake, freshly showered and headed off for her office by eight. After the debacle in the lodge the night before, she and Michael had returned to her suite in the lodge in an oddly emotional state. Michael made himself a gin and tonic from supplies that he brought with him, and Meredith just sat and listened to him berate the uneducated masses that were overrunning the country. He began his theory on forced sterilization for anyone who could not graduate from high school. She had heard this all before and found it as crazy as ever. Now it was also boring. After a wide yawn, she explained to Michael that he could sleep on the couch on which she threw a pillow and blanket. Michael protested briefly as he headed for the sofa, but at some time in the night, he had snuck into her bed like some baleful dog. She had been too tired to kick him out and was only too happy to get up and leave him to sleep in as long as he wanted. As she walked toward the lodge, she was wondering what Pete was doing.

The Winsors made their way to breakfast at nine after the clan had showered and yelled at each other for an hour or so. A noticeable change was that Andy was not in attendance with them. The staff all agreed that Bernie was as obnoxious as ever as if the showdown the night before with Meredith's boyfriend had never happened. But it seemed to have affected Andy because he was AWOL. In fact, Andy woke early and hopped in the car for a quick drive to Old Forge where he enjoyed pancakes and peace. His plan was to return to the resort no later than noon and spend as little time around Bernie as possible. When they returned to Scranton, all would be repaired because they would spend little time in public and his hell would remain a private issue. But this vacation was becoming more torturous day by day.

Pete finally woke at nine thirty, having stayed in the bar with one of the waiters until well after one in the morning, drowning his sorrows. He knew that Michael was coming because Meredith warned him, and he had tried to prepare himself for the situation, but it was to no avail. The feelings that had assaulted him the day before were surprising and painful. Pete never let his heart stray too closely to any woman, and this sensation was odd and slightly agonizing. But Slip was strong and he wouldn't let it get him down. As he shook the cobwebs from his head, he looked out at the calm blue water engulfed in summer sunshine. It promised to be another wonderful day, and he would take advantage of it. It would only be a little over a month, and he would be back teaching overprivileged punks in his dreary classroom. Enjoy the sweet weather while you could. That was his motto of the day. Pete remembered the scuba divers. They wanted to take a look around the lake over by Davey's house. That would be a little different and exciting. *Carpe diem*!

People rose from their night slumbers and prepared for another day. The lake called, and each would go about their functions and try to enjoy the summer in their own ways. It had the potential of being an epic day.

None of them knew how epic the day would be.

19

June 10, 10:56 a.m.

"Well, what do we do?"

Michael had found her sitting behind her desk with the computer on. Meredith had escaped to her personal space with the exact intention of getting away from him. The man was twenty-eight years old and certainly had the capability of being left alone to experience the mountains by himself. But like a dog dropped off on a distant road, he had found his way to her.

"I have to spend some time working," she answered quickly, letting the lie slide off her tongue easily and without any guilt. The computer screen currently showed the CNN web page where she was trying to catch up on events outside the mountains. "It's a busy time."

Michael nodded, and instead of leaving and going outside to enjoy the resort, he turned to the walls and perused the pictures and clippings on the wall that were all her father's. He stopped in front of the aerial shot of the lake that her father had framed. The picture was impressive.

"Wow," he exclaimed with true interest. "That is crazy. It looks like a speck of blue surrounded by nothing but green. This really is a wilderness."

Meredith looked at the picture for the hundredth time, noting what Michael had just observed. From the vantage point of a few thousand feet up, the resort appeared tiny, and the woods surrounding it were deep and unspoiled. She had often been absorbed by the thoughts of what was in those trees, rarely visited by any humans. If

Bigfoot existed, the dude could certainly be living in this wilderness. She nodded in agreement to Michael but didn't say anything. He moved on and looked at other pictures of the lake and the resort depiction cabins, the beach, and the lodge from different eras spanning decades.

"This resort has been open awhile. Look at the clothes. Why did people dress like idiots in the '70s and '80s?"

"Don't know," she answered. "Disco? Jimmy Carter?"

Michael turned to her with a smile but he didn't laugh. "It's *The Brady Bunch* generation. Bad pants, bad shirts and a stupid family. That show dumbed down a generation that is today ruining America."

"*The Brady Bunch* is ruining the United States? I think that's a stretch, Michael. Where did you hear that? Rush Limbaugh?"

She expected Michael to self-righteously take a stand in favor of his opinion, but instead he had no reply and continued to look at pictures. Usually he would waste time trying to justify some stupid judgment of his that just became more ridiculous the further he debated it. Someday she was positive that he would be a successful commentator on Fox News. He wasn't getting the hint, albeit false, that she was too busy to hang with him. Her alone time was over, and she would need to become an entertainer to a person that she simply didn't want around. With a sigh, she stood and felt her tightened muscles stretch.

"Is there anything in particular you'd like to do today?"

Michael smiled. "Lie around and screw?"

Meredith put her head down like a bull and slowly shook it back and forth. She moved past Michael and wanted to get outside quickly.

"That's not going to happen, Michael."

She could hear him following her down the hallway. "Wait! I was only joking. We can take a walk or go for a swim. Hang on."

Although she wanted to escape, she did stop and turned to him. "I'm not playing your bullshit games. I run this place. I am the owner. I have daily responsibilities and need to present a positive image to the guests. They are what keep this place running, and your behavior last night jeopardized this image. To even joke about lying around inside having sex all day is in bad taste, especially since I need to do some mending after your shenanigans last night."

Part of her was thrilled to see Michael's head sag forward like a scolded dog. She knew him well enough to know that it was only an act, and he felt no shame or remorse for his behavior. This only furthered her disgust for him, and she was even more distressed knowing that, like it or not, she had to deal with him until he got in his car and headed south. Michael was here, and that meant that she needed to entertain him, and that was a burden that she didn't want. But on the positive side, she was now confident that she would never go back to him in Chapel Hill. If she had to return, she could move in with her friend Kelly.

"Let's go outside."

Michael followed her.

*****

By noon, the day had become bright, hot, and still. It was a classic muggy summer day. The temperatures in the central Adirondacks were expected to peak out near ninety degrees, which translated to mid to upper nineties farther south. The lake was a plate of glass, and the air hung over the land like a wet, soupy blanket. Many of the plans that had been laid to hike or go for a car ride were abandoned to stay by the water. The sandy beach along the water would be a popular spot. The weather guys were saying there was a chance of thunderstorms later as a cold front flirted with the area that might cool off the day just enough to make it tolerable. Even a few clouds might help provide shade from the merciless sun.

Pete sat in his chair watching the Winsor kids splashing in knee-deep water, screaming at one another. He sympathized with a couple sitting in beach chairs who were trying to read paperbacks. That pleasure was nearly impossible having to look up every ten seconds thinking the shark from *Jaws* was attacking the two overweight kids in the water. They could be great extras in a horror movie because it sounded like they were being dismembered. The Winsors were nearing the end of their stay, and he might hold a parade through the parking lot as their van pulled down the driveway. In all the years he had sat in "the chair," he had never seen such a detestable family. Bernie was sitting in a low-hanging chair on the beach under an umbrella with a bag of cheesy poofs next to her. Her ass had pushed the chair down to the sand, so the device seemed superfluous. God, she was horrible. He wished he could launch a manure grenade at her.

He tried to ignore the Winsors, but it was almost impossible. Other groups were arriving on the water, and some were taking out kayaks. It would be busy, and he hoped he wouldn't have to get out of the chair. Occupied was good because it took his mind off his personal dilemma. The thought of Meredith and guessing what she was doing with Michael was constantly in his mind. He felt the coldness of jealousy wash him, making his stomach ache. Michael was enjoying her company publicly around the resort. When he and Meredith were together, it was usually behind closed doors. That bothered him, but it was more painful to imagine the scene of the two of them together.

Pete looked back at the lodge, hoping to see Meredith but instead saw Josh walking toward the beach with a sullen look on his face. Pete was surprised because Josh was usually such an upbeat kid. Sure, it seemed that he had a surly past, but it was the present that mattered, and the kid looked somewhere off center on this fine morning. The beach had been raked when Pete had shown up to get in the chair, but Josh had not been around, which was unusual. On most mornings, he was a fixture near the beach to help guests or aid Thomas with something. Well, maybe that was it. Maybe Josh had been off helping Thomas with some other project. Still, the kid had the look of a zombie as he walked toward the water. Well, he wasn't the only one with problems.

The younger Winsor kid suddenly wailed, and Pete whipped his head around to see what the hell was going on. He was holding his face, apparently devastated because his brother had splashed water in his eyes. Bernie yelled at both her sons from the position of her strained folding chair. Pete noticed that Mr. Winsor was nowhere

THE MOON LAKE LEGEND

to be seen. That was odd because most days he was like a faithful dog following its master.

"How's it going, Slip?"

Pete looked down and saw Josh standing at the base of the life-guard chair. It was clear by a quick glance that the kid wasn't his normal self. Usually, he would be all smiles and glad to be on the beach on such a hot day. Instead, he was moping around like a high school kid who had just gotten grounded for life.

"How goes it today, Josh my friend?"

Josh kicked some sand and looked out at the water. "Another day. Just doing my job."

All right. There was something wrong with the kid, and it was time for Dr. Slip to investigate what the issue was, although it was probably too easy. When a guy became suddenly bummed out in a matter of hours, it most likely revolved around a woman, and Josh had been hunting one recently. Did she get away?

Pete looked down and would have jumped to the sand if it hadn't been for all the people he had to watch in and around the water. "Something happen last night? You look kind of down."

A gust of air pushed out of Josh's muscular chest, and he looked out toward the water again. "Bad night."

"Liza?"

The kid nodded. "She blew me off. It's over. I'm a little bummed out."

No wonder. "What did she say?"

Josh chuckled. "Basically that I was a rich kid and that she couldn't get attached to anyone. Pulled this poor girl crap on me. I just don't get it. I mean, she's the only cute, eligible girl here, and I'm..."

"Sucks," Pete said in response. He waited to see if Josh responded, and when he did, it wasn't a surprise. The request was ridiculous and wasn't going to happen.

"I could use an eighteen-pack and a few hours to drink it."

Pete decided he needed to save a person, so he slid off the chair and put a hand on Josh's shoulder. "Liza is a nice girl, Josh, but she's not that nice. I mean, she's from Mayson, and where is she going come Labor Day? You'll be in Ohio playing football. Shit, you'll be leaving here in a month, and your summer will be history. Are you going to try and hang on to her then when you have some sweet girl drop by your room after football practice? If you're just into a couple of nights of sex, then I'll tell you to stop right now. This resort is too small, and I know Meredith doesn't need drama with the staff. There's too much of it already. If Liza was into it, then I would advise you to go after it and go hard. If she's not into it, then oh well. She's not worth a slobber fest that could get you into trouble. Just smile and enjoy the mountains."

Josh was looking at his toes moving in his flip-flops, and Pete was hoping that his pep talk was working. It was hard to read the kid.

"Anyway, it might help to look at things from her point of view. She's a mountain girl. Relatively poor but smart. Probably a little jealous of the opportunities that you have. Maybe a little worried about getting involved with a guy who was leaving to never be seen again. You live in a world that she couldn't exist in. Maybe what she said makes sense, although it might be tough to take."

"Yeah," Josh muttered.

Pete realized that his words had not made an immediate change in the kid's mood, but he was sure that Josh would mull it over and come to terms. Besides, he was also somewhat convinced that Liza would buckle. He saw it all the time. One benefit he reaped from his talk with Josh was that his own strange romantic situation had been momentarily forgotten. The last twenty-four hours had been frustrating because the only time he even spoke with Meredith was a casual hello from employee to employer. Damn Michael. The guy had her undivided attention, and he was left wondering what was happening between the two of them. His greatest fear was that she was falling back for the guy, and that would put him in a funk very similar to the one Josh was now experiencing. One thing he knew was that he had to be positive and try and have as much damn fun as possible. Life was too short to be distressed all the time. Motto of the day!

"Hey," Pete said with a sudden burst of enthusiasm, "have you seen the Milakaus?" Josh shook his head and Pete continued. "I saw them after a late breakfast. Dan and Margo were running up to Lake

Placid quickly this morning but were psyched to go for a dive this afternoon. I guess they have some sort of portable sonar equipment they want to take out on the boat. They mentioned three this afternoon, and I told them you would be happy to take them out."

Josh turned and looked at him with something that looked like the birth of a smile.

"Really?" he said. "That might be cool."

Pete smiled, slapped the kid's back, and climbed back up the chair to watch the Winsor kids scream.

"Hey, Slip."

Pete looked down at Josh, who actually had a smile on his face. "Thanks."

The lifeguard made a pistol with his fingers and sent Josh on his way. He had done good, and that was all right. He leaned back for a moment and let the sun soak into his skin. It was all right, and there was nowhere better on Earth to be than Moon Lake.

*****

Jeanne was supposed to be back by early afternoon. The drive to Newcomb and the time it took her to grocery shop and walk the few stores the town boasted took a lot longer than it did to simply buy fixins for dinner at the local Wegmans in Syracuse. He knew that she got antsy when she was stuck in the cabin for too long. It was approaching the moment that he despised every summer when he took his wife on a "vacation." To Davey, being at the lake *was* a vacation, but Jeanne needed more. Last summer, they had driven to Boston and then up toward Bar Harbor in Maine. Davey felt it a waste of good lake time, but he knew that it was therapeutic for Jeanne, and therefore he needed to do it. It was a slim price to pay for an entire summer of solitude.

Davey's project du jour had actually spread into a couple of days. He had to replace a header on the deck that had begun to rot out. Using an old car jack with an old-fashioned tire iron, he lifted the deck slightly and was able to remove the punk wood. He had replaced the piece with a two-by-twelve and had completely impressed himself when his cut had fit seamlessly. However, he needed Jeanne's help to hold the piece in place while he nailed it home, so he decided to stain it before she got home.

A slight puff of breeze hit his skin, and he looked up. As quickly as it had come up, the airflow died back down. Davey wore no shirt, and his skin was soaked in sweat. It was fucking hot, and he was thankful for the shade from the forest around the house. The only sunshine stuck his patch of beach. He put down the brush he had in his hand and stepped away from his project. It was one thirty, and he was slightly worried about Jeanne's whereabouts. The odd, uneasy feeling grew when he turned to the water. The lake was like glass, and a muggy haze hung over the entire area. With no wind, he could hear the noise drifting across the water from Camp Wildass. That didn't bother him as it often did. What did get to him was the lake. Something was making his skin crawl, and that was not a pleasant sensation. He wasn't a believer in premonition or psychic phenomenon, but he knew something was askew.

His dream had set the mood. He had dreamed that he had been walking in a cemetery in his hometown—Sayre, Pennsylvania. This was a familiar place because it was the piece of land where his mother and father were interned. When he normally visited his parents' graves, it was daylight, but in this dream, it was a deep night as dark as a coal mine. Davey made his way across the grass toward the stone sarcophagus that held his parents' remains. This was especially odd because their real spot was marked by headstones in the principal cemetery. As he approached, a sensation like electricity shot through his body, and his body froze regardless of his efforts to move forward. In his dream world, he didn't have to budge because the sarcophagus slid toward him. When he forced his hand up to touch it, the entire area around him shook, and he almost fell down despite being frozen in place. Unexpectedly, the great stone slab in front of him wobbled severely and cracked. As dream-Davey watched with horror, the stone broke open, and he knew something was about to fly from the dark chasm. The quaking earth had ruptured the stone.

That was when he woke bathed in sweat with a heart beating faster than it should while a person slept. He made his way to the kitchen for a glass of water and some bright fluorescent lights. He didn't want to alarm Jeanne, so he stayed in the kitchen until he felt able to return to the bed and hopefully some quiet sleep.

Back in the current summer day, the dream became distant, but the negative effects stayed with him. He felt its darkness surround him all morning. Davey wasn't a stupid man and knew why his subconscious had dredged up such a horror show. His thoughts returned to the previous day and the visit by the kid and the divers from the resort. They had discovered that the lake was haunted. It was haunted, all right, and the house afflicted should not be disturbed. It was the story of the ancient stone. The very one that the Indians had thrown in the lake. Did he really believe that tale? Well, he sure as hell thought that the people had dumped something in the lake. Was it haunted? Did it have some mystical negative powers? He didn't think so because he was rational, and that didn't make sense. Like the Bermuda Triangle or the Winchester Mystery House. There were rational explanations for all mysteries. But was there something bad in the lake? Most definitely.

Davey knew that humans were strange creatures. They were gifted and cursed with the ability to think. For all the amazing results that have come from the human mind, just as many negatives had been created by the human imagination. Monsters, aliens, gods. For all that mankind could not explain, the brain created a solution for the puzzle no matter how ridiculous. The most interesting outcome of these solutions were often irrational fear and worship of nothing. Could the Indians have believed that some stone had bad karma because it explained some mystery that they needed an answer for? Certainly. Could that belief actually lead people to act out in a negative manner just because of the conviction that the stone was bad? Yes. Look at the crazy things that people did around the world for thousands of different religious beliefs. The word was psychosomatic. If the brain wanted to believe something, then it did, and the person went right along with it.

Davey was scared that the divers would go looking for whatever was in the lake. In deep thoughts, he imagined the existence of a methane bubble or some other gas that could do harm to animals around the shore. That was plausible, anyway. Hell, there could actually be some alien stone down there too. What the hell? Why not? Crazy but so were the existence of black holes.

He was nearly positive that they would have no success finding whatever was down there, but he knew that wherever the stone lay, it was better to leave it lying undisturbed.

He heard three quick beeps from a walkie-talkie that was stuffed in his pocket. The other device was in a waterproof box down by the parking spot. Until the communications company put up a new tower, cell phone service had been spotty, so he had bought walkie-talkies, and they still depended on them. Jeanne had returned and had paged him to come down on the Gator to get her. Good. He needed to move away from the water. He thought of the divers and hoped they would head for Champlain instead.

20

July 10, 3:36 p.m.

Dan and Margo arrived back at Camp Wildwood a little later than they planned, but it didn't matter. There was plenty of daylight, although the National Weather Service had put the Adirondacks under a severe thunderstorm watch until later in the evening. The sky was clear with no threat of violent weather, so all looked good for a dive. The lake wasn't very large, and the reality was that they would probably search in vain, but it was still exciting, nonetheless. Neither of them had actually believed that their stopover at Moon Lake would yield anything, but the discussion with Davey Cramer had sparked some interest. Besides, it was a sultry day and a dive would be enjoyable, even though the water wasn't that clear.

The resort was hopping when they pulled into the parking lot. The area in front between the lodge and the water was full of groups of guests, most on the sandy beach. The air was hot as Margo stepped out of the air-conditioned car. Their drive to Lake Placid had been longer than hoped, but the scenery from the cool cab of the SUV made the trip pleasant.

"Boy," she muttered, "it's damn hot out here."

Dan walked around the vehicle to stand next to her, looking at the lake. "Yeah, it is. Maybe we could dive without our suits."

"We'll see how cold the water is twenty feet down. I'll just be happy getting wet."

"Let's see if we can get some help carting this gear to the boat."

They walked toward the lodge and saw Thomas on the patio filling tiki lamps with citronella. Thomas seemed to be the guy at the resort to talk to if something needed to get done.

"Sure," he answered after Dan asked him for help. "I'll bring the Gator to the parking lot. Does Pete know you want to go diving?"

Margo nodded. "We mentioned it yesterday."

With that, Thomas nodded and walked toward a barn-like building across the parking lot. Margo looked at Dan, and they both smiled. It was awesome when things fell into place. They wandered to the car and waited no more than two minutes before Thomas cruised across the parking lot, kicking up dust in a green maintenance vehicle. He pulled up alongside the lowered tailgate and helped the Milakaus load their gear.

"Didn't know you needed so much stuff to dive," Thomas said. "Heavy too. Must sink like a stone."

Dan held up a belt with gray squares attached. "Actually, we're pretty buoyant in the water. We have to wear these lead weight belts to sink toward the bottom."

Thomas looked with appreciation and continued loading. Dan grabbed the black box that held the sonar. They actually had two sonar units. One was a souped-up fishing sonar that helped display objects in the water but with little clarity. The sonar considered most targets in the water fish. The second type was way more expensive and difficult to use. Known as side scan sonar, this device was able to make a much more detailed view underwater, but it was tough to use and needed a computer hookup. It was expensive and was on loan from the UNH marine biology department. Unfortunately, the resort's Boston Whaler had limited electrical capacity, so they would be using the fish sonar.

Once loaded, Thomas drove the Gator toward the dock with Margo riding in the passenger seat. Dan had to walk the distance, and that was fine, although the simple exertion in the hot sun caused him to break out in a sweat. Man, it was hot as hell. They needed to get on the water as quickly as possible. When he caught up with the Gator, Thomas was unloading their gear on the wooden dock and Margo was waiting for him near the machine.

"Thomas said we should talk with Pete the lifeguard," she proclaimed. The two walked toward the chair where Pete was sitting, looking over the water behind a pair of sunglasses.

"Pete," Dan yelled up at the lifeguard over the racket around them. Pete looked down and smiled.

"Hey, it's the Milakaus! You guys still want to go for a dive?"

Dan gave him a thumbs-up. "Definitely. Can you take us out?"

Pete shook his head. "I'll call Josh over and he can take you out. We don't have a divemaster here, which means you're pretty much on your own. I think Meredith would like you guys to sign a disclaimer."

"Really?"

"Yeah," Pete responded. "She needs to cover her ass. I'm sure everything will be cool, but she's a little paranoid about lawsuits. Can't say I blame her in our world today."

"Okay," Margo said. "I have to change, anyway."

"I'll let Meredith know, and when you guys come back from your cabin, I'll have Josh here with the papers to sign."

Margo and Dan walked away toward their cabin to put on their swimwear, and Pete grabbed his walkie-talkie. Meredith answered quickly and said she would bring the papers down immediately. Her excitement for the task lifted Pete's spirits because he realized that she wasn't happy where she was and probably most importantly unhappy with her company. He hoped she would come to the beach solo. In only a couple minutes, Meredith was at the chair, and Pete hopped down. She was alone.

"Thanks for bringing the papers down."

Meredith smiled broadly, and Pete definitely saw a twinkle in her eye. "Absolutely no problem, Slip. I was waiting for a chance to come down here all day. Unfortunately, no one drowned."

"How are things going?"

"Sucky," she answered with a smile that lit her face. "This is torture."

Pete smiled too. "How *is* Michael?"

Meredith looked at him. "Terrible. I don't know why I stayed with him so long. Last night was simply ridiculous, and I want to thank you again for diffusing the situation."

"Anything for you."

"Yeah, right," she said and punched him in the chest. "Good old Slippery Pete."

"Wish I could give you a hot kiss," he whispered slyly and got another push.

"Later. Now I have to go back to the Carolina Craze. The guy is driving me nuts. Maybe I'll have him hang out with you tonight."

Pete chuckled. "Bad idea, hon."

Meredith blew him a subtle kiss and turned to walk away. Pete couldn't wait to be alone with her again. He didn't know it, but the chances of that happening anytime soon were pretty poor.

*****

Josh pushed the throttle, and the Whaler glided out into the lake. It wasn't the easiest beginning to a cruise that he has ever had. As they were loading the equipment onto the boat, they drew the attention of just about everyone on the beach, and every single one of them wanted to go for a ride as well. Pete had come down to help them load from the dock and was left behind explaining that it was a private cruise to the horde that threw questions at him. Josh was happy to move away from the crowd and into the quiet of the lake. Except for a few kayakers, the lake was empty and extremely calm. He looked over the side at the glassy surface and could see a few feet down. Moon Lake's water wasn't dirty but was brown from minerals and microscopic plants that were in the water. The visibility today was better than he had seen it in a while, so he figured it would be a good day for the Milakaus. He drove the boat at a slow speed, and they moved toward the east and into the main part of the lake. The Milakaus were sitting in the back, looking at their gear.

"Where do you want me to go?" he asked. He knew that this was like finding a needle in a haystack and would certainly end with some stories about some fish and logs found on the bottom.

"Not sure," Dan answered. "Let's get over toward the other shore and I'll drop the sonar in. We can troll for a while and hope something interesting pops up. Then we can go in and check it out."

Josh was all right with that and gave the boat a little more gas. The speed created a breeze, which was delightful. The sun was beating on the boat that had no cover from the blazing sunshine. The heat was extreme, and Josh wished he could dive in the water, but he knew he would have to sit in the boat while the two passengers went in. He was likely to lose five pounds of water weight and probably pass out in the boat. It was hot.

When the boat got within a couple hundred feet of the south shore, Josh throttled down to idle, and the boat slowed to a drift. Dan got busy with a simple pole that had a sensor on the end. He slid it over the side of the boat and attached it to the gunwale. The wires that led from the apparatus went into a small screen that said "Lowrance" on it.

"How's that powered?" Josh asked.

"Normal car battery. We're often on boats that have limited electrical capacity. It can be hooked up to any adaptor on a boat, but we'll use the battery for now. We can cruise at a slow speed and see what we can find."

Josh nodded. "Okay. Just let me know what you want me to do."

The boat began to move forward as Josh slipped the gear into forward. The speed wasn't much more than a few miles an hour, but Dan said it was perfect. Josh had seen sonar like this before on his dad's boat. The screen showed the bottom of the lake from a side view and any undulations on the bottom. It also read out depth and surface temperature. They were moving in roughly thirty feet of water, and the surface water temperature was seventy-six degrees. An occasional fish shape popped up on the screen, indicating that something was in the water. Most of the blips were small and were most likely just what the sonar indicated…fish.

Josh reached down into the cooler under the center console and grabbed a bottle of water while wishing it was a beer. It was extremely hot on the boat, and sweat was oozing from his skin. It would be a great time to just stop the boat and dive in, but he reminded himself that he was working. As the light green shapes appeared on the screen indicating more trout, he realized it was going to be a long day.

*****

Jeanne was inside the camp putting together an apple pie with some fruit she had picked up earlier at the store. Davey could not fathom the mind-set that made a person labor near a stove on the hottest day of the summer. It was getting to the point where it was brutally oppressive and the inside of the cabin was nowhere to be. He was headed for the water with a towel and his bathing suit.

As he made his way down the gentle, scrubby slope that led to the beach, he emerged from the shade that enveloped his cabin and stepped into the direct sunlight along the beach. God, it was hot. Although he couldn't actually see it, he knew that there were people lying on beaches in the sun across the lake at Wildass. And at Lake Placid. And in the Thousand Islands. And in the Finger Lakes. The total amount of sweat being produced hourly in gallons could rival the amount of oil flowing down the Alaskan pipeline. The thought made him laugh, even though he was now adding quite a bit of his own sweat to the total. Davey threw his towel over the back of one of the two Adirondack chairs that were on the beach, and he continued on to the water without hesitating. He took four long strides into the water with his feet sinking into the mucky sand on the bottom before diving forward and outward into the lake. The water engulfed him and felt amazing, although the water was as warm as he could remember. On Memorial Day, such a dive would result in a primal scream and a hasty retreat back to the warm sun to avoid the threat of hypothermia and a cold death. Davey didn't turn and retreat but instead wallowed in the water like a hippo.

After a few minutes of soaking, Davey walked from the water and grabbed his towel. The water dripping from him was warm, and the cooling effect was going to be temporary. The heat was already settling back on his skin. It was going to be tough sleeping tonight, although the National Weather Service was calling for storms. Maybe that would cool things off. He needed to get back into the shade and allow the wet bathing suit the chance to cool him off in the shadows.

Davey heard a voice relatively close and quickly turned his head toward the water. Coming around the point that guarded the bay and his end of the lake was the white hull of the Boston Whaler from Camp Wildass. He recognized Josh at the helm and the two divers in the back hunched over some piece of equipment. A twist of uneasiness gripped his stomach, and a rush of adrenaline tingled his arteries. They were actually out there looking for it. That was insane.

"Shit," he muttered and walked quickly back to the cabin. Coming up the stairs, Davey stubbed his toe on a cement block that the wooden steps set on. "Shitballs!"

He heard Jeanne move through the cabin above him. "What is going on? Are you all right?"

Jeanne appeared on the porch above him. "I stubbed my damn toe on the stairs."

She looked at him, and a big smile spread on her face. Her hand rose to her face to cover the giggles that began to bubble from her.

"Stop it," he demanded. "It's not funny. Look at the lake."

Jeanne's head turned, and she looked through the trees at the water. "Is that the boat from the resort? What are they doing?"

"Searching."

"Searching?" she asked. "Searching for what?"

"The stone."

Her head whipped back around and regarded Davey, who was now at the top of the stairs. "The stone? The stone from that Indian legend?"

Yes," Davey answered, moving across the deck to the railing on the lake side. "The stone."

Jeanne sighed and sat down in a chair overlooking the water. "You thought they might. So what? There's nothing out there. And even if there was, the chances that they find it are extremely poor."

Davey nodded, and they both stared out over the water. The boat was moving very slowly, maybe a couple of miles an hour. It had to be baking hot on the craft, but the two divers in the stern remained stationed over what Davey deduced was some sort of radar. Jeanne was right. If there was a stone, the chances that these people stumbled over it was astronomically minute. But any disturbance of the object...

"Honey," Jeanne said, turning to him. "Relax. If it's there, they won't find it. And if they do, what will happen? Seriously. We're safe."

Davey hoped that she was right. He moved to the chair next to her and sat down to watch the boat on the lake.

*****

The first fifteen minutes had been interesting. The following fifteen had been bearable. Now the sun and heat were getting to him, and he was close to the point where he needed to tell the Milakaus that they needed to return to the resort. They were cruising slowly through the bay at the southeast end of the lake, and he could see Davey Cramer's cabin up in the trees. Man, it must be cooler up in that shade, and he wanted to be up there with a whisky on the rocks. He had been there with Liza, and a point of pain flared near his temple at the thought of her. He should be calming down and letting her go, but he couldn't. He gritted his teeth and looked at the sonar screen to take his thoughts elsewhere.

The sonar looked the same as it had a minute earlier and a minute before that. The sun was ruthless, and although he always considered himself tough, this was horrific. He was amazed that the Milakaus were intently studying the fish-finder despite the harsh conditions.

"Aren't you guys hot?" he asked.

Dan answered without taking his eyes from the screen. "It's bad, but we're used to it. It gets hot on boats in the summer. It would be nice if there was a puff of breeze, though." Dan stopped talking to Josh and pointed at the screen and spoke to Margo in a language that Josh didn't understand. It was English but a bunch of science garble that he didn't comprehend nor care about. What had he expected? Did he actually think that they would chuck the sonar in the lake and in minutes have some type of result? The lake was not Lake Superior, but it wasn't a pond either. With the unsophisticated sonar, they would have to literally stumble over the object, and that seemed unlikely with the time they had to look. But the couple seemed genuinely happy, and that was what his job entailed—keeping the guests happy.

A series of beeps erupted from the fish-finder in the back of the boat, and Josh quickly turned to the two divers. Dan and Margo had dropped their heads further, studying the image that was so hard to see.

"What's the noise about?"

Dan was holding a towel over his head in an attempt to provide more shade over the screen. "I don't know. It's…hang on."

Instinctively, Josh pulled the throttle back into the neutral position to stop the slight forward motion of the boat. All the sound around them on the water seemed muted, and all attention turned to the screen.

"Do you see it?" Margo asked with a slight edge of excitement in her voice.

Dan was intently bent over the screen. "I see…something. But it can't be. It's too…big."

Too big? What was too big? The hot, pointless afternoon had suddenly become interesting, and Josh forgot the sweat that was slipping down his back. He walked back in the boat closer to the sonar screen, and the boat shifted uncomfortably, but no one really seemed to notice.

"Is it natural?" Margo asked while she continued to stare at the image on the screen. Josh got a good glimpse and only saw a green blob. "What do you think, hon? A log? A rock outcropping?"

Josh looked at Dan and was astounded at the man's neutrality. Margo was freaking over something the sonar had detected, but he just continued to analyze the image. A silence fell over the boat that was nowhere near relaxing but instead created even more tension. Josh looked around at the perfectly calm water and the hazy air hanging over the lake. In the distance, he could hear the voices of people having fun across the lake at the resort and he looked at Davey Cramer's camp knowing that somewhere in the trees he was watching them.

"It's hard to tell," Dan finally said. "It just doesn't seem like a log or anything like that." He pointed at the screen. "That looks like a right angle. Unless there is shale at the bottom of this lake, I find it hard to believe that there is a natural rock with a right angle down there."

Josh looked at Dan and wondered what he was thinking. It wasn't more than a few seconds and Dan dropped the towel and stood upright.

"I'm not sure what it is, but I think it's worth an investigation."

Margo looked at him. "You want to dive?"

Dan nodded and moved toward a mesh bag that contained diving gear. "Why not? It's hotter than balls and we're here. Let's go check it out, make sure it's only a tree that got sucked into the lake in some storm and then say we dove this lake. And we can avoid heat stroke in the process."

"Great idea," Margo said with a broad smile. "I'd love to get into the water."

"What can I do?" Josh asked as he watched Dan and Margo begin to assemble gear that had been stowed in the few bags around the boat. He realized that they might avoid heat stroke, but he was still a prime candidate while they dove and he sat in the sun.

"Not much," Dan answered. "There isn't much wind. We'll go down and check the bottom out. Our bubbles will let you know where we are. Just stay put and we'll come back to you."

Josh sat back and observed the preparations for a dive. After close to ten minutes, Dan and Margo stood on opposite gunwales in full dive gear, although they had both decided to go sans wet suits. Dan smiled at Josh and put his regulator in his mouth with Margo following suit. They both flashed him a thumbs-up signal and pushed off. Dan and Margo were gone, falling backward into the water on either side of the Whaler with dual splashes. Josh moved to the side where Dan had gone over. He saw the silver air tank and a bunch of bubbles as Dan disappeared into the murky water.

*****

Davey observed the sudden activity on the boat and was amazed to see the two divers go into the water. They were actually diving. Did that mean that they had somehow stumbled onto something in the lake? The imagination could be a seriously awesome and terrifying force, and Davey's was running amuck. When he had first thought of buying property on Moon Lake, he had heard the rumors about it being haunted and cursed. Instead of deterring him, the reports only increased his interest in the house. It took some convincing to get Jeanne on board, but she had agreed, and they had moved in twenty-five summers earlier. It had only taken a few trips to Camp Wildwood before he developed a friendly relationship with Colin and Thomas, which a few times a summer meant drinking way too much, precipitated by some male bonding. They had been young and looking for some fun. It had been these affairs when Thomas and Colin had introduced him to the legend.

Over the years, the idea that some Indians had thrown some possessed stone into the lake had grown into some mythical tale. Yeah, Davey had spent some free time at Syracuse trying to find out as much as he could about the story. The trail was a cool one, but he had found some random but interesting stories from Mohawk lore about a blasphemy from the stars that had been thrown into deep waters. The source was a random newspaper article from a now defunct Albany company from 1897. The printed trail was not super, but the rumor mill was blazing. The mention of earthquakes made many locals shiver and talk of darkness that none wanted to experience. Many around the Moon Lake area had heard of the legend, and Colin Riley had been the leading spokesperson. That was until the autumn of 1991. After that, even Colin stopped the tales of a possessed rock in the lake. Apparently, he no longer thought it good for business.

"I bet diving in that water feels pretty good."

Davey was startled form his thoughts by Jeanne's words. He had been staring at the water while his mind drifted. "Probably better than sitting on that boat. Josh has to be frying."

"If you ask me," Jeanne said, "it's nothing but a waste of time. I honestly think Colin blew the story way out of proportion in an attempt to get more tourists to stay at his resort. The whole idea of it is just plain stupid."

Yeah, it probably was, but that didn't calm his nerves as he watched the boat on the serene water with the bubbles popping on the surface around it. If there was something down there then...

As he was about to ask Jeanne if there was a bottle of Labatt's in the refrigerator, the ground began to move.

*****

At first, Josh didn't even realize that anything was amiss. The day remained hot, and the water remained calm. He was standing by the boat's gunwale watching the bubbles rise from below. They were shifting position as Dan and Margo moved along the bottom. The water was not clear enough to see them, so the bubbles of carbon dioxide were the only indicator of their position. The two trails of escaped air were separate but never more than five feet apart until they quickly converged, creating a much more vigorously aerated surface.

It all happened so fast. There had been a sudden increase in the bubble activity as if a balloon had exploded underwater. Then there were two distinct trails again. One of the traces moved quickly away from the other. Josh looked up and felt that something was horribly wrong. That was when he noticed ripples on the water, as if rocks were being dropped into the lake. The ripples all seemed to be emanating from the boat, which was incredibly unnerving because the boat seemed to be motionless. He watched this sensation until his attention was drawn to the port side of the boat where there seemed to be something going on. Josh moved to the side and looked over at the bubbles bursting on the surface in an abundance unlike he had seen. As he stared into the water, he quickly recognized the head of a diver rushing to the surface. In one second, he saw the top of the head, and in another instant, he could see most of the body as the diver rushed to the surface. He could not tell immediately if he was seeing a male or female, but he leaned over further to give any help because he instinctively knew that something had gone terribly wrong.

It was then that the murky brown water around the diver turned black, the darkest black that Josh had ever seen. It was the complete absence of all light, and it had enveloped the entire area under the boat and around the diver. In an instant, the diver froze, only inches from the surface, and a bright white-green light burst from the blackness. It blinded him, sending him back across the deck of the boat. The moment was surreal, but Josh had the impression that the entire atmosphere around him had become the same color as the white-green light that had come from the water below.

"What the fuck?" he yelled as he fell onto the starboard gunwale. What was this shit?

The intense light faded rapidly, and Josh realized that he was partially blinded and couldn't see much around him, although somehow he knew that his situation was dire. Something was in the water, and it was not natural to the lake.

"Hey!" he heard a voice yell from behind him. "Jesus Christ! Give me a hand."

Josh turned and saw Dan trying to struggle up the stern gunwale of the boat with all his scuba gear on. Josh quickly moved to him, and with one quick yank, Dan was in the boat. He was panting and looked like he had just witnessed the World Trade Towers collapse. Dan muttered something that Josh couldn't hear.

"What? Where's Margo?"

"Go," was all Josh heard, and he didn't need a second opinion. He quickly turned the ignition key, and the engine kicked into life. Josh pushed down the throttle, and the boat lifted from the water and screamed toward Camp Wildwood. Holy shit, what was going on?

*****

The shaking at his cabin was intense for all of ten seconds before it began to mellow and then quickly died out altogether. The wooden Adirondack chair that he was sitting in swayed wildly, and he turned to see Jeanne grab the doorframe for support. As the shaking eased, Davey whipped his head toward the water and saw the boat. Josh was peering over the gunwale more out of interest than any kind of surprise or fear. He probably didn't even know the earth had just trembled while sitting on the water. As the shaking ended, Davey watched as Josh bent over further to get a better view of something in the water.

"What the hell was that, Davey?" Jeanne yelled from behind him. "That was a goddamned earthquake!"

Davey nodded, unable to reply. A fucking earthquake. God help them. He watched the boat and felt his heart sink into his icy stomach as he watched Josh react to what he saw. In what seemed only an instant, the water around the bright white Boston Whaler turned dark, almost completely black. The blackness almost appeared to be sucking the sunlight into it like a black hole. Then with a brilliant burst, an extremely vivid whitish green brightness erupted from the water and enveloped the boat. The immediate thought that burst through his mind was that this was it. The horror was finally going down.

Without thinking, he rapidly turned and looked at Jeanne, who was staring at the water with her mouth hanging open in a manner that would have been comical in any other circumstance.

"Jeanne. Jeanne. Jesus, Jeanne!"

His wife turned to him with a dull expression that bordered on disbelief and shock. He needed her to move and he needed her to move quickly.

"Wha..." was the only sound that came from her lips.

He walked up to her, grabbed her by the shoulders, and gave a quick shake. As he was doing this, he realized that the unnatural illumination that had been lighting his cabin faded to a more normal glow that now seemed weak. It was going to be bad and it was necessary for her to leave.

"Jeanne, please pay close attention to me."

His wife's eyes began to focus on him, which was a gigantic relief. "What's going on, Davey?"

"I need you to go into the bedroom and, as quickly as possible, pack a bag of clothes for one day. You are going to leave this cabin, get on the Gator, and drive down to the car. Get in the car and drive out of the mountains as swiftly as you safely can. Go to Jamesville and stay there. Stay in Syracuse. No matter how badly you might want to come back, stay there until I contact you."

She looked at him numbly for a long moment as he shook her again. "What about you?"

Davey looked at her and then toward the lake as he heard the Whaler's engine roar as Josh ripped back toward the resort.

"I need to stay here for a bit. Thomas might need my help."

"But..." Jeanne looked out at the lake. "I mean, was that what we feared? I can't believe that what we just saw was because of that damn stone."

Davey shook his head vigorously. "Honey, it doesn't matter if it was or wasn't. I'm not taking any chances with you. You need to get the hell out of here. This Christmas we can have rum drinks in Key West and debate what we just witnessed, but now, I need you to leave immediately."

To his relief, Jeanne nodded slowly and turned and walked into the cabin. Davey turned to the water and tried to figure what had just happened. The water was quiet again, although a slight breeze had begun to ripple the waters. The weather guy's predictions of storms might not come true, but he knew there would be a storm at Moon Lake unlike any ever prophesied—that is, if all the legends were true. He just needed Jeanne to leave as quickly as possible because Moon Lake had just entered unchartered waters.

21

July 10, 5:10 p.m.

Pete was having a hard time coming to grips with the chaos that had suddenly erupted around him. Although he had never before nor ever wanted to experience an earth-shattering incident like a plane crash or F5 tornado, he had all the same wondered what the brain did at the moment of such crisis. What emotions flooded the senses in the moment of terror? With the rumble of the earth and a flash of eerie light, Pete was learning just how he would respond to such an event.

Even before the earth moved, the beach had been complete mayhem with just about every guest packing the sand and splashing in the water. Even Meredith had come down in her bikini, which was pretty cool until he saw the dipstick Michael following close behind. The sweat had been pouring off him, and he required some liquid refreshment. That was the exact thought that was going through his head at the moment the earth moved. He would later remember being thirsty and jealous.

The shaking had been powerful, stronger than any he had ever felt before. Not that he was an experienced earthquake survivalist, but he had been in a couple of smaller tremors. This particular quake was rocking. The thing that was amazing was the sudden silence when the quake started. The beach had been a cacophony of screaming and yelling that almost instantly stopped as people looked around, trying to figure out what was happening and what they should do about it. And unlike a thunderous storm, the earth moving was relatively silent without thunderous downpours. One noise he heard was a squeak from his lifeguard chair as it oscillated back and forth in an alarming way. Without much thought, Pete jumped from his perch and landed on the sand, only to become one of the others staring around the resort. He looked at his chair and saw the wobbling begin to quiet. He realized that the intense shaking was relenting to almost nothing.

The moment was surreal as everyone just stood frozen in place, looking around at the quiet scene that had descended on them as quickly as the quake and surprised them. The only noise that cut the silence was a car alarm that annoyingly sounded in the parking lot near the lodge. All else seemed perfectly normal. No buildings had crumbled. No fires burned. The day was still hot. The lake was still calm and hazy with humidity. Pete was looking out over the water as chatter began among the guests as they started to realize that all was well and that they had just experienced an earthquake. It would be an event to tell the folks at home. Although the guests began to laugh and relax, a sixth sense began to crush Pete, and he knew that all was not well. Not at all. He heard a yell behind him from the direction of the lodge as the reality suddenly slipped into his head. Earthquake. The lake. The stone. Oh god, could it be?

That was when the flash of white light burst from the water over toward the other side of the lake. It was hard to pinpoint the exact spot because of the intensity, but it seemed to be from the far end. The light was nearly blinding, even from the distance he stood, and it stayed at a high intensity for at least five seconds before it began to slacken. It was as if the sun had momentarily fallen to the surface of Moon Lake and blazed like crazy. Someone had grabbed him by the shoulders and was shaking, but it was hard to turn from the spectacle on the lake. When the light faded, Pete finally turned to look into the eyes of Thomas. The look on the older man was far from any he had ever seen in the groundkeeper's eyes. Pete was looking into the face of sheer terror.

"The stone! The stone!"

Pete knew precisely what Thomas was screaming about, but it couldn't be. The whole thing was just some silly mountain legend. It was some tale to tell kids around a campfire or to scare the shit out of your girlfriend. As he observed Thomas, he recalled the location of the bright light and in an instant knew that that was the precise spot where Josh had taken the scuba divers. The coincidence did seem too wild for there not to be a correlation. The knowledge was like a sledgehammer, and his mind tried to quickly wrap around the situation.

"Do you think?" he asked the panicked Thomas. It was also becoming clear that many of the people on the beach were now staring at the two of them. Off in the lake, Pete heard the Whaler's engine quickly throttle up, and he knew that the shit was about to hit the fan.

"Pete? Pete?"

He turned and saw Meredith running and saw the light green bikini. Oh, she looked good, and he suddenly felt a necessity to protect the woman. The situation's gravity settle in, and he found that he could focus as he turned back to Thomas.

"What do we do? Is this it?"

Thomas's mouth hung open, and he looked much older than he had earlier in the day, as if during the earthquake he had been shoved into an aging machine.

"Don't know," he said as he began to nervously look around, his eyes settling on the lake. Pete knew that he had noticed the Whaler rushing back to the dock. "The last time, it was so chaotic."

"Last time?" Pete was able to ask before his attention was drawn to the lake again. Meredith was pulling on his arm and pointing at Josh in the Whaler coming in alone. Alone? That didn't add up. He had left the dock with two guests. The boat was coming in way too fast, and it was sure to make rough contact with the dock. Pete turned and ran toward the dock through a couple groups of people who were standing stock-still, staring at the developing scene in front of them.

The sound of the engine had been rising in pitch as the boat rapidly approached the dock with the future of smashing the mooring and the bow of the Whaler. He looked up and saw a look of grim determination and shock on the face of Josh. Neither of the divers were visible, and a feeling of dread struck him in the gut. Pete's feet clomped down the wooden dock, and he tried to position himself to absorb some of the impact. It did appear like Josh would pilot the boat to the side of the dock where it was normally berthed, but there was still too much speed. Josh threw the engine into reverse, but it wasn't slowing enough. Pete got down on his knees and leaned out enough to grab the boat. He grunted as he hung onto a handrail along the starboard bow and felt the power of inertia drag him down the dock, but he held tight. The rough wood was ripping into the flesh on his knees, but he clutched tightly. The boat slowed, and he realized Thomas was standing next to him.

"We got it," Thomas muttered, and Pete thought they did. Within a moment, Thomas was tying the bowline to a cleat, and Josh had jumped onto the dock with the stern line. Pete noticed that he was moving with jerky, energetic motions. Pete stood and saw the diver, Dan, lying on the deck of the boat.

"Josh?" Pete asked as the kid turned and came up to him. His eyes were wild.

He quickly looked around in a broad circle before settling on Pete. "We...we're in b-big trouble. Margo...Margo's dead. It got her. We have to move and get off the water."

"Okay, okay," Pete answered, realizing that at the moment, sane Josh had exited stage right and was not much help. Frustration made a sudden appearance as he wanted to move and accomplish something. He was about to turn from the boat, but Dan moved in the bottom of the boat, coming up to his knees and puking over the side of the hull. He turned and looked at Pete with wasted but cognizant expression.

"We need to move," Dan muttered at just a level that Pete could hear. "We need to get away from the water." Dan dropped his head and didn't seem like he was in a hurry to move.

"What happened?" Pete asked. "Where's Margo?"

"Go!" Dan spoke loudly with his head still down as if he were a drunk sitting on the deck of the boat. The guy implored Pete to leave, and yet he didn't move. What the hell was happening?

Pete looked up and turned to the beach where it seemed all the people still stood, looking at him. An exception was Josh, who had moved off the dock and was rapidly moving through the crowd and toward the buildings. He had an odd gait, somewhat like a person with cramps trying to run. Something had shocked the normal out of the kid, and Dan wasn't in much better shape. And where the hell *was* Margo? A million thoughts were speeding through his head, and he was trying to wrap his mind around just one for a moment to try and comprehend what was happening. Something made him turn around again and look at Dan. The man was back on his knees with tears pouring from his eyes. His breathing wracked his whole upper body. That was weird. Pete was watching this when the man screamed on the beach.

"Jesus Christ! What the fuck is that?"

Pete saw the man and recognized him as the gentleman from New York City who was staying in cabin 4 with his wife and kid. He was pointing out over the water, and Pete whipped around to see what he was all excited about. What he saw momentarily took the breath from his lungs, and every crazy thought he ever had rushed through his consciousness in a fraction of a second. It was pure madness. The lake looked much as it had all day—calm with some occasional ripples from a breeze with the humidity still hanging tight over the water. But there was something new, something that terrified him. Rising from the water near the far shore was an object that defied logic and basic physics. It seemed to exist only by its complete lack of color. A blackness unlike any he had ever seen before was hovering over the lake. He was convinced it looked like a boat, but then it was a tree. The shape shifted and was never anything tangible for more than a moment until it slowly coalesced into a circle. It was truly as if a portion of the air above the lake no longer existed. It had become completely empty. A hole in the atmosphere. Even the sunshine around it reflecting off the water seemed unable to escape the absolute lack of light. Looking at the apparition above the water, Pete had never been so frightened in his entire life. He was frozen, staring at it, unaware that people had begun to turn and run from the beach, a wave of noise, motion, and chaos. Then he noticed that Dan had made his way across the boat and was only a couple of feet away from him. Dan wasn't looking at the water but was holding a hand out to Pete.

"It got Margo. She's gone."

Pete looked at the man and suddenly understood. That moved him. He reached out, grabbed Dan's extended hand, and yanked him from the boat. Dan stood on the dock still in his wetsuit, and his legs wobbled for a moment before he could take a step. He moved rapidly down the dock, and Pete turned and followed him as they made their way toward the shore. Only a handful of people still stood on the beach, as most were hightailing for the lodge or hopefully their cars. He saw Meredith standing motionless, staring at him. Michael still stood by her side, gawking at the water. Why were they still there? Even Thomas was gone, and he seemed to be the only person that even had any inkling of what was going on.

"Meredith," he yelled ahead as he jumped off the dock. "Get up to the lodge."

She looked extremely confused and didn't move.

"Pete, what is it?"

Instead of answering, he grabbed her by the shoulder and pulled her off the beach. He heard a protest from Michael but didn't much care. Dan had moved ahead of them, moving quickly despite the wetsuit. Ahead, he saw bedlam as guests and employees ran into buildings, screaming and slamming doors. Car engines exploded into life in the parking lot. Confusion reigned, and Pete had no idea exactly what to do. Instinctually, he made his way toward the lodge with Meredith while the two others following. He needed to get them inside, although he wasn't sure if that would protect them from whatever had risen from the lake. Awkwardly, they made their way up the front steps and into the main room of the lodge. There were people spread throughout the great room, mostly all of them looking as if they were experiencing different levels of shock. Pete regarded them all and felt a wave of nausea wash over him. This was crazy.

*****

Sometimes odd feelings invaded her thoughts, and their suddenness surprised her. When she had been only nine years old, she had been playing in the backyard of their house in Mayson. They didn't have a sandbox or swing set, but there had been a rocky, weed-strewn pile of dirt that the kids gravitated to. Liza was alone on one particular afternoon, sitting on top of the pile just looking around her neighborhood. She had a vivid memory of watching the back of her house where her mother was hanging out laundry to dry while managing to balance a cigarette in her mouth at the same time. Really fascinating to watch. Music was drifting from the windows of the house, and Liza could hear Toby Keith's deep voice singing about a bar. It had been hot, and she wanted to be inside in the shade, but that wasn't acceptable because there was a guy lying on the couch inside. She didn't know the man. He had come home the night before with her mother and had yet to leave. Liza didn't want anything to do with him, so she sat on the pile of dirt away from the house.

Cars drove by on the road headed toward the short stretch of pavement that was downtown Mayson. Some cars pulled into the diner or general store, but most just drove on, headed for some other place to stop leaving Mayson far behind. Kitty-corner across the road, she could see her friend Kiefer helping his mother unload something from the old Ford that their family drove around. Kiefer was really just a friend out of necessity, being one of the only other kids to play with for miles. Actually, she felt kind of uneasy around him, and she hoped that he wouldn't see her sitting on the mound of dirt and decide to wander across the road to dig around. She tried to flatten herself against the dry dirt when she felt the ground begin to move.

The dirt pile shook, and rocks tumbled down the slope of the hill. The laundry that her mother hung out swayed in the air as if someone was pulling on the clothesline. The fire siren at the two bay fire station began to moan as the earth continued to shift. Liza felt a fear creep through her, knowing that this tremor was a bad one and that serious consequences would follow.

Suddenly, there was a loud crack next to her, and when she turned, her breath was sucked from her lungs. Next to her dirt pile, a fissure had opened in the ground and a red light emitted from it. Smoke and a sulfur smell filled the air next to her, and Liza felt bile rise in her throat. Oh god, what was it? She tried to stand and run, but her legs were paralyzed, and she was stuck like a bug in a spider web. Something was moving in the gaping wound that had spilt her backyard, and it was dark. So dark.

As quickly as the vision had struck her, it was gone, and she was just sitting atop the mound of dirt in her backyard. Kiefer was now walking across the street to come play with her with that goofy look on his face that she would later learn was a result of fetal alcohol syndrome. Her mother was still inside their house with her latest and scariest boyfriend. Mayson had returned to normal, but she was a sweaty mess recalling the visualization that had assaulted her. Instead of waiting for Kiefer, she slid down the backside of the mound and headed off into the woods to be alone. After an hour walk, she had mostly forgotten about the vision.

That afternoon, an earthquake rattled Mayson. It was far from the intensity of her dream, and no terrifying crack opened in her yard, but it was enough to unnerve her.

That memory burst into her head when the earth rumbled at Camp Wildwood. Liza was in the employee hallway trying to put her cleaning cart away after a long hot day in the guest rooms of the resort. Her thoughts were focused on changing into her bathing suit and taking a swim regardless of how many guests were on the beach. It was hot, and she needed to cool off. But the earth shook, and her memories took her back to that day as a kid in Mayson. The quake quickly ceased, but her mind did not stop shaking.

Her vision suddenly turned dark, and she actually shivered, although the temperature in the hallway had to be nearly one hundred degrees. Even though she had no visual access to the water, she understood that darkness had enveloped the lake and the day had turned evil. The cause of the gloom was not known, but she knew that something incredibly disturbing was the origin. Her need to hurry to the water was wiped away in an instant, and she felt a sudden and powerful urge to run to her car and drive away. Something was pushing her away from Camp Wildwood.

She shook and felt shivers of cold rack her body. The closet where she had been trying to store the cleaning cart gaped open in front of her, and the cart wobbled as her hands shook involuntarily.

The darkness of the closet seemed to yawn out at her with the threat of engulfing her whole. A scream grew in her throat, but she choked it back. Then as suddenly as the feelings assaulted her, the closet became nothing more than a simple storage space again. The heat of the hallway crushed her, and she had the odd sensation of rapidly warming after being cold. She held her hands parallel to the ground and saw that she was shaking noticeably. What had that been all about?

Liza quickly pushed the cleaning cart into the closet and stepped back after closing the door. She swiftly looked down the hallway to see if anyone had noticed her strange attack, but the passageway was completely vacant. Leaning back against the wall, she took deep breaths trying to calm her racing blood when she heard something unusual. Was that a…scream? Liza stood still, forgetting her own unsteadiness, and focused on any sound that might explain what she thought was someone shrieking. It wasn't a happy scream but one full of terror. That was odd. There was something, and yes, it did sound like screaming. Maybe the frolicking by the water had escalated to a college spring break level. Then she heard a slam, and immediately she knew that the change in the demeanor of the guests was not because of fun. What was going on?

Liza ran down the employee hallway and turned toward the main room of the lodge. The first thing she noticed was how much brighter it was than the windowless hallway where she had just had her "moment." Instantaneously, she grasped that people were rushing into the lodge and they did not appear to be enjoying the sunny afternoon. The first person she saw was a middle-aged man leaning against a couch, breathing heavily, and looking as though he had just witnessed a plane crash. Liza was looking at the man as she moved forward in the direction of the windows that panoramically exposed the lake and hills around it. What she saw was shocking. There was complete mass chaos between the lodge and the beach. The guests, who had to have numbered over one hundred, were all scrambling away from the water in every direction imaginable. Some were running for their cabins, some were headed for the parking lot, and some were making a rapid beeline right for the lodge. As she took this in, her mind was burning with the simple question: what had happened?

The double front door burst open, and Liza saw Meredith's friend Michael charge through the opening. He looked very similar to the other man who was now on the floor on his knees. They looked like they had seen hell.

"Are you all right?" she asked, but Michael wasn't hearing her. "Where's Meredith?"

Michael looked at her without seeing. "It's a nightmare." He stumbled past her, and Liza stepped out of his way. A couple more people erupted into the room, and Liza stepped to the side, trying to figure out what was going on. Then she looked out over the water and observed something that was completely illogical on a perfect hot, sunny day. Hovering over the water toward the middle of the lake was a nearly round object that was completely black. In fact, her initial thought was that it was the antithesis of light itself. What she was observing made absolutely no sense, and she considered that she was still having her vision from before. The front door was pushed so hard that it slammed against the wall, making a loud cracking noise. She turned and saw a group of four people enter the building, including one young woman wearing a bikini who was screaming.

"No! No! No!"

In just seconds, the world had turned topsy-turvy and what was normal had just flown out the window. Although it had literally been only minutes since she had finished cleaning her last room of the day with every intention of going for a swim, the new reality was radically different, and all had become distorted.

A man wearing a wetsuit appeared through the doorway, and he was quickly followed by Meredith. The sight of her calmed Liza, although it was clear that her boss was teetering on the brink of shock.

"Slip," Meredith muttered. "Where's Pete?"

Liza quickly spun around, realizing that Pete, Thomas, and Josh were all absent from the room. She looked out the window, and her gaze couldn't help but be drawn to the thing over the water. She forced herself to look down and found herself looking at a vacant beach. The day was still picture-perfect for a leisurely time cooling off by the water, but the beach was now poison. Chairs, coolers, and other beach paraphernalia were scattered across the sand and grass, left behind in people's haste to get away from the lake. That was when Liza noticed Pete, kneeling over a person that was sprawled out on the grass.

*****

He had been the last one off the beach after he pushed Meredith away from the water. It was good to see Dan trot off because Pete had no intention of carrying the man to the lodge. As he finally moved, Pete turned and glanced at the thing over the water. The object was slightly different, and he was not sure how until it dawned on him that it was larger than he had originally thought. The truth hit him with the knowledge that the thing wasn't getting bigger. It was getting closer. Like a kick in the ass, Pete increased his forward speed and looked up at the lodge, hoping that he would find sanctuary there.

There was a body in the lawn just to the left of his direct track to the lodge. Although some instinctual self-preservation impulse was driving him to continue on toward the large building, Pete knew that he had to stop and check on the guest that was now exposed on the grass. The man's back was to Pete as he came up to him, but he observed a fine layer of hair that covered the bare, rather fat shoulders. Pete immediately recognized him as a guest from Illinois who was visiting with his girlfriend and another couple. Sitting in his chair all day watching the guests, he became almost uncomfortably familiar with each person's physical features. The man's name was Ty Jamieson. He was a big fan of Miller Lite.

"Ty? Mr. Jamieson?" Pete asked as he fell onto the grass next to the prone body. He leaned over and looked at the man's face and instantly knew that he was dead. Jamieson's eyes were open and rolled back in his head. Pete put his hand in front of the man's mouth and nose and felt no air movement. He was not breathing. Although he knew it was pointless, he quickly grabbed the man's wrist and felt for a pulse that wasn't there. The shock of the moment probably caused a cardiac arrest, especially since the guy had to be fifty pounds overweight. That was the moment that Pete actually heard the voice of the thing over the water.

At first, he didn't recognize the sound, but as the screaming of the guests subsided to an eerie quiet, he heard a sound that was deep and seemed to fill the air around him. The first impression he got was that it sounded like an electrical transformer attached to a power pole. It was a deep *oommmmm* sound that penetrated his head and made him decidedly uncomfortable. Pete whipped around and looked at the thing. It was just amazing how completely black it was, especially since he was kneeling on a grassy lawn with a July sun beating down on him. Originally, the thing had appeared to assume many forms, but either he had imagined it or it had changed. Now it was almost perfectly circular. Pete could not avoid the comparison to a black hole that the Science Channel so often runs hour-long shows about. There was no circular motion inside the object like one would see in a computer-generated black hole. In fact, there was simply nothing inside it but emptiness. Pete noticed that the air around the object was wavy and unclear like quicksilver on a hot country road. He quickly thought of the legend of the stone, and a shiver raced through him. *Legend my ass*, he thought as he got up and ran for the lodge.

*****

He was thankful that Jeanne had packed up and vacated without too much fuss. The last thing he wanted was to have to worry about her during the next forty-eight hours. Was it truly a forty-eight-hour cycle? That's what the legend supposedly said. Two days. Two rotations of the planet. Davey wasn't so sure that he would make it through an entire day, let alone two.

Davey stopped walking, wiped sweat from his forehead, and looked over his shoulder. The black hole still hovered over the lake like a balloon that shunned all light. He was sure that the effect had to be created by some optical illusion, but as he made his way around the lake, it seemed that he was constantly facing the object from the same angle. When staring at it, the black hole looked two-dimensional, so he assumed that if you walked around it, it would appear flat or at least flatter. But as he walked along the lake to the west, the black hole seemed to remain exactly the same. He turned his head back to the path in front of him so that he could keep moving. *Look away*, he thought. Davey got a core sensation that staring at the black hole was a very bad thing to do.

Jeanne had left much faster than he could have hoped, probably because she understood how crucial the situation facing them was. When the black shape had risen from the lake, Davey felt an urge to just run away in the opposite direction as fast as he could. He could leave with Jeanne and return Labor Day to close the camp. But he had to stay. There was no debate. This was his lake, and he needed to make sense of what had befallen it.

The object pulsed a pure sense of everything that could be wrong in the universe. It was pure madness, and to gaze on it would lead one down the path to their lunacy. When Jeanne came out onto the porch with her bags packed, she saw the object and let out a pure, primitive scream that freaked Davey out. He realized that whatever that thing was, it didn't respond to sound, at least the sound of a woman's shriek, because it never wobbled an inch.

"Davey," she breathed, "what is that thing?"

He never responded but instead dragged his vision from the object that had grown to the size of a hot air balloon right in front of their cabin.

"Honey, you need to get on that Gator and get off this mountain."

The quickness in which she left actually surprised him. "I love you, honey." She pecked his cheek and took off for the shed where the four-wheeler was parked. He muttered goodbye and listened to the engine start and then pull away and disappear down the trail. He was left in silence with something from another star floating outside his residence. There was too much shock to realize how bizarre the scene was.

He had thrown on his hiking shoes and a light jacket before hurrying to the lake trail that would lead him to Camp Wildass. He wasn't exactly positive why he needed to move in that direction, but he went anyway, pulled by something that he couldn't fathom.

Keeping his eyes on the trail was imperative because he didn't want to trip and fall down. Lying along the lake with a broken leg would certainly be fatal under the circumstances. Plus, he wanted to be as stealthy as possible. Davey had no idea what that thing over the lake happened to be or what its function was, but he wanted to stay as unobtrusive as possible. As he slowly made his way through the trees that bordered the lake, he wondered if the black hole was aware of his presence. He seriously hoped not, but who knew.

Again, he stopped and took a gander around him. Davey had almost reached the west edge of the lake and would soon be turning north toward the resort. He looked at the sky through the trees and saw a definite darkening of the atmosphere above. Storms were building and were going to move through the mountains. The heat had been building all day. Due to the appearance of the black hole, he had forgotten the extreme weather that was suffocating the mountains. The temperature could have plummeted seventy degrees and turned to heavy snow and he might not have noticed. The black hole was sucking in his attention, and he hoped he wasn't the only one. He suddenly feared that his journey around the lake would land him at Camp Wildass where he would find a deserted resort with everyone either dead or preferably gone. If that happened, he wondered if he would muster the energy and desire to continue on alone.

This time, he refused to turn around to glance at the black hole, and instead he moved forward along the trail. He didn't need to look because he could hear the black hole behind him, sounding like a battery charger working at a high level. The normally quiet woods had been invaded by an alien sound. That was for damn sure.

The trail made the gradual turn to the north, and he slowly made his way closer to the resort. For some reason, he sensed that he was more exposed in the shadow of the black hole. If it had the ability to "see," then he was basically out in the open. In the crosshairs. Davey found himself spending more time behind trees than in the open. But he knew that he was being silly. He chuckled softly and looked ahead along the lake shore. The sandy beach and grassy lawn of the resort lay a few hundred yards away. The sun was no longer bathing the sand as thunderheads built to the west. Thunder was rumbling loudly, and it was going to rain. Davey's heart sank into his stomach when he didn't see any people hanging around the grounds.

They had all left. He was alone to face whatever that thing was hanging over the lake. Davey stopped and considered his next move. Even if he returned to his cabin, there was no vehicle there to escape in.

Then he heard the voice, and everything suddenly changed.

*****

The scene inside the lodge was a psychiatrist's dream. Any doctoral candidate could have done a seminal study at that moment on the effects of stress on human beings. There were people experiencing every level of shock, including Meredith. Pete had laid her down on one of the couches and thrown a blanket over her. Michael had disappeared into the bar and eventually disappeared. Liza sat on a chair and occasionally shot glances out the picture window toward the thing.

"How are you doing, Liza?"

She turned and saw Pete pulling a chair up to hers.

"All right, I guess," she answered without a lot of conviction.

Pete sat down. "This is some crazy shit. I wanted to make sure that you're okay."

She nodded but didn't speak. Pete settled into his chair, and the two of them looked out the window. The black thing continued to hover over the lake without any change. The only change that was evident was that the bright summer day was growing darker. Liza knew that it couldn't be later than five o'clock, so a sunset now would be premature. Thunderstorms. Perfect.

"What do you think it is?" Pete asked. Liza almost laughed out loud. How the hell was she supposed to know? She had just graduated from high school and had taken physics from a crappy teacher who was stealing paychecks from the district. Her knowledge of some basic physics and earth science was sparse, and she had definitely missed the lesson on strange, otherworldly objects that pop up from under lakes. She had also missed the one on the Lock Ness Monster, Sasquatch, and freaking Tinker Bell.

"Dunno," she answered, shaking her head. "I really have no idea."

"Well," Pete responded, sitting forward on his chair. "I hate to say this, but we seem to be the only rational people in this building. Meredith is nearing shock, which is still better than most of the guests. There's the guy lying on the floor who keeps singing 'Silent Night' and the woman who just keeps shaking her head, muttering *no* over and over. Michael the hero is in the bar drinking vodka, and there are others who are hiding upstairs. And what the hell happened to Thomas? He disappeared pretty quick."

Liza took a gander around the room and realized that Pete was correct, and she hadn't even noticed. The realization was more depressing than she would have expected because she now knew that help was going to fall on only a couple of shoulders, and one set was hers.

Pete sighed. "And what the hell happened to Josh?"

"That is weird," Liza admitted. "I thought he would be stepping up to help in any way he could."

Liza looked outside again, and if it was possible, the day had gotten even darker. She saw the body on the grass that no one had removed, or even checked on except for Pete. The girlfriend and friends that the man had been vacationing with had not gone out to check on their buddy. They were also not in the lodge. Most likely, they had run to their cabin and were holed up inside. Or perhaps they had been one of the groups of guests that had scrambled to their cars and were at that moment cruising as quickly as possible away from Moon Lake. She had gone to the window in Meredith's office and looked at the parking lot where many spaces had opened.

"Sure he's dead?"

Pete had been looking at Meredith and turned back to Liza.

"Huh? Oh, the man out there? Ty? Yeah, he's dead. Shit, he hasn't moved in the last hour, so he better be."

"How many people have left?" she asked.

Pete looked out the window. "I hope a lot. They need to get out of here. I think most have. I think we should push the remaining people here toward their cars. Maybe we should abandon ship too."

Good for them, she thought. Why wasn't she headed for her car and Mayson? The truth was that the idea hadn't crossed her mind until that moment. She worked at Camp Wildwood, and it had become home. This was where she needed to be.

"Liza," Pete said quietly. "You and I might be the only rational people left to deal with this. Try and stay cool."

She could hear the strains of "Silent Night" being sung out of key and the soft murmurings of the woman repeating *no*. Then she heard something different, and it took her a moment to realize that it was a door closing and feet moving across the wooden floor. She turned her head as did Pete, and they both saw Thomas walking across the room from the kitchen. She heard Pete sigh out loud, and she felt a touch of relief seeing the caretaker, even though he looked like he had just gotten through a bout of pneumonia.

"This is bad, Pete," Thomas said as he walked toward the two of them sitting near the windows.

Yeah, it was, she thought. Bad for sure. Liza looked back out the window, and the breath was sucked from her lungs. The black thing seemed to have moved closer and seemed incrementally more menacing. The day was much darker, and she actually heard a rumble of thunder for the first time. But what shocked her was the person on the grass in front of the cabins.

"Look!" she yelled, and unfortunately, they did.

22

July 10, 6:19 p.m.

Andy had always prided himself in being a patient man, and he certainly never imagined that he would kill his wife. Yet as the madness of the afternoon unfolded, he moved closer to that person who might act out of character.

After the previous night's fiasco in the dining hall, Andy felt himself detach from Bernie in a way that was unique in their relationship. In fact, when he woke the next morning, he deviated from his normal routine and opted to slip out the cabin door early, and he avoided the family breakfast. Family breakfast was a mainstay at the Winsor household on weekends and holidays, so he was really breaking out as he drove his car down the shadowy lane of Camp Wildwood. He decided to drive off into the mountains, hoping that some distance and time might ease his thoughts and bring him back to a rational understanding of his relationship with his wife.

As he drove west toward Old Forge, he took the time to analyze his situation with Bernie. The more he contemplated, the more doubts entered his mind. He wasn't attracted to her anymore, if he ever truly was. The sad reality was that he had originally been interested in her out of desperation, and that was a crappy reason to get married. What their relationship became was one of convenience and industry. They had children and shared a house. Andy worked and came home to a home that was frosty yet functional. In truth, he didn't mind because the stability and the kids made it all bearable. Yeah, Bernie had her bad moments that could be ugly. When those moments occurred, Andy was normally able to slide off to a special place. When he was a child, they had rented a place on the Jersey shore one summer, and that had been one of the highlights of his entire life. When Bernie acted up, he was walking the shore in front of the rental house that he had loved twenty-plus years earlier.

But this trip to the Adirondacks had been a test of his mental and emotional balance. Bernie had wanted to go to Disney again, and the thought of the tourist trap thoroughly depressed him. After a quick search on the Internet, he had found Camp Wildwood where the seclusion and forest looked soothing and insulating. It had been all that, but Bernie had been over the top, even for her. Demanding, conceited, thickheaded. She had certainly filled the criteria for all of those negative behaviors.

By ten o'clock, Andy was driving by Water Safari in Old Forge where cars were packing the parking lot on such a hot day. They had come down to the water park earlier in the week, and it had been close to torture. There was no way he was going into any of the water pools where little kids were pissing and defecating, so he sat in the shade and still sweated to the point where his head ached. The memory of the day made his stomach twist when he drove into the public parking lot near the Old Forge hardware store. Andy sat in the car for a while, quietly listening to Beethoven's Sixth Symphony. A sense of serenity had fallen over him, and eventually, he turned around and headed back toward Moon Lake. Hopefully he would be able to look at Bernie again without the new and strange feeling of rage that had recently bubbled behind his eyes.

Andy had done a decent job of tuning Bernie and the kids out as he sat in a folding chair on the edge of the sand. He had even made a rotation of standing every fifteen minutes and walking into the water to cool off. The day had become semitolerable until all hell broke loose. Like the rest of the guests, Andy and his family had turned and hightailed it away from the lake when the monstrosity appeared over the water. He wasn't sure what the heck the thing was, but his instincts knew that it was bad beyond rational belief. In only five very short but remarkable minutes, Andy had gone from relaxing by the lake in relative peace to being shut in his cabin with a couple of screaming kids and a wife that wouldn't shut up.

"Jesus Christ, Andy!" she was yelling. "What the fuck is that thing out there?"

Andy shook his head and sat down on the bed, holding his head in his hands. He didn't need to look out the big window in the front of the cabin because he knew the thing was still out there. The kids were sitting on the other bed, wrestling and screaming, seemingly unaware of the seriousness of what floated outside the cabin door.

He sighed. "I really don't know, Bernie."

"You're the computer guy. You read all those science fiction books. What is that thing?"

Andy didn't answer and instead tried to think the whole thing out, but it was not easy since there was a fire flaring in his brain. This fire was sapping all rational thought, and reality was becoming hard to grip. He looked at his wife and did not see the love of his life but a creature that disgusted him. She was like a cockroach scrambling in the tub early in the morning as he prepared to shower. At that moment, she meant nothing to him.

One of the kids fell off the bed and began screaming. Bernie didn't move but just stood staring at him with occasional flicks of her eyes out the window. Andy vaguely realized that it was getting darker outside and heard a distant rumble that had to be thunder. Perfect. A thunderstorm on top of some crazy unknown shit right from the pages of one of his science fiction books. He had listened to Bernie and wished like hell that he did know what the thing was, but it was unprecedented and defied most known laws of physics.

"Well," she breathed loudly, obviously extremely stressed out, even for her, "we need to leave immediately. I don't know what that thing is, but it has certainly ruined my vacation. I have had about enough of Camp Wildwood. Let's go, Andy."

Andy ignored her and sat on the edge of the bed and gazed out the window. It was indeed much darker than the bright sunny summer day that they had been enjoying less than an hour earlier. The thing over the lake seemed to be getting larger, and he was pretty sure that it was moving slowly in their direction. A cold shot of fear wracked his entire body caused by the vision of an entirely unknown evil. It was clear that the thing had not materialized to answer all of their dreams, and he knew that the thing was evil beyond anything that most authors of the wildest fiction could imagine.

"Andy! We need to leave. The boys should not be here."

He heard her and thought that she was probably correct, but the idea of leaving at the moment didn't thrill him. Although he feared the object totally, he had a bizarre desire to know what it was and how it functioned. There was no hurry to rush away, even though he heard other guests hurriedly exit their cabins for the parking lot.

"The other guests are leaving, and we should be too. I need to...Andy! Where the hell is my cell phone?"

He looked at her and saw the look of shock, this time caused by separation from her best friend, her smartphone. "I don't know, Bernie."

He used to affectionately call her Apple. Those days had passed on.

"Damn it, Andy! I need my fucking phone."

He believed it had happened the moment she had used the profanity. The idea popped in his head, and without a moment to analyze the plan, he spoke to his wife.

"You probably left it by the lake. We had a lot of stuff with us out there, and we vacated the area in an awful hurry when everyone else ran off."

"Goddamn," she muttered. "You're right, and my iPod's out there too. Did I hear thunder? It better not rain on them. If they get ruined, I'm gonna be super freakin' pissed off."

Bernie made a few steps toward the door and then stopped and looked at him with eyes that shone with hate and mercy. Andy knew that she wanted him to go retrieve the electronics, but that wasn't going to happen. He turned and looked out the window, delivering the clear message that he wasn't stepping out the door. The concept of what was about to go down had become apparent, and he wasn't about stop her now. His moment had arrived, and he didn't really consider the outcome.

"Fine," she ripped, directing hatred that Andy felt zoom toward him. "I'll go but when I get my stuff back, we're getting out of this hell hole."

When Bernie stepped through the door, Andy felt a wild array of feelings, including the brief desire to stop her because he knew she wouldn't be coming back. That sentiment was quickly replaced by a morbid curiosity as she walked across the grass in the fading light as the thunderstorm approached. The object over the lake remained unchanged, although Andy sensed that the thing recognized that Bernie was out there. Andy turned on the bed and watched his wife walk toward the beach.

*****

Davey was considering his crappy luck as the sky became extremely dark to the west and the bright day became dusk-like. It was bad enough that he was traversing the lake path while trying to avoid the detection of some other worldly black orb hovering over him, but now he was going to have to deal with a summer downpour complete with lightning. Death by an alien form or electrocution by lightning. Tough choice. From the sound of the thunder, he figured he had less than ten minutes until the rain began in earnest. The trick was to pick up the pace without being obvious to the black hole and without tripping and falling on his noggin.

A flash of obscenely bright light strobed across the forest and lake. The lightning was still a ways off, but it was close enough to light up the scenery. Thunder growled, and Davey stepped up his pace.

A voice yelled something from the direction of the resort, and Davey stopped and looked ahead. About two hundred yards away, a large woman was moving down the grassy lawn from the resort's cabins, looking back over her shoulder, yelling at the cabin she had apparently just left. She was too far away for him to understand her words clearly, but he could hear her tone, and Davey knew two things: the woman was pissed, and he was positive that she was the same person who made the scene in the dining room the night before. Davey watched as she yelled one last spasm of venom back at the cabin before purposefully striding off toward the beach. The woman occasionally turned her head up in the direction of the black hole but acted as if the object was nothing more than a raven sitting on a telephone wire. It was simply amazing that she marched out without any fear. The woman had to be crazy as hell.

The low electric hum that had enveloped the lake suddenly became louder. For an instant, Davey didn't notice, but the sound invaded his brain and was totality. He took an instinctual step backward and stumbled against a fallen log. Luckily, he stopped before he fell over and stood stock-still, staring in disbelief. The black hole began to pulse. The hole itself was so completely dark that the pulsing couldn't be seen, but the size of the object itself grew and shrunk in a rhythmic fashion. It didn't take Stephen Hawking to understand that something was about to go down, and there was little doubt that it would be horrible. The woman on the beach walked forward, oblivious to the change in the black hole over the lake. There was another flash of lightning, and thunder ripped through the woods, this time much closer than before. As Davey was contemplating his prospects of getting drenched by the storm, something came out of the object over the lake.

*****

"What the hell is that dumb bitch doing?" Pete muttered as they looked out the picture window at Bernie Winsor striding toward the beach. For some reason, the woman who had been a pain in all their asses seemed to be tempting fate. She was waving a steak in front of a hungry tiger. She had been psycho but not suicidal.

Liza shook her head. "I don't know, but it isn't a good idea."

Lightning flashed much closer, illuminating the grounds in an unreal white light. The flash quickly dissipated, and the roar of the thunder quickly ripped through the lodge. The glass window shivered. Bernie Winsor slowed down and looked back over her shoulder before turning and picking up her pace.

"This is going to be a big one," Thomas said coldly.

Pete was staring out the window. "Yeah. In more ways than one."

They watched as Bernie moved as fast as she could toward the sand. Liza was the one who looked at the object over the lake and gasped while unconsciously drawing away from the window. The thing was violently pulsing.

"Look," she managed to say, pointing at the lake. Pete and Thomas followed her arm and saw it too. A closer rumble of thunder echoed from the trees, and a few large drops of rain slammed onto the porch and patio in front of them. Liza heard Thomas moan as they watched something unreal happen right in front of them like some crazy horror movie. Even well after the moment, when she had time to reflect, the event seemed fuzzy and hard to remember. The object appeared to draw light into it like an actual black hole as Mother Nature began to unleash her greatest show around the lake. Suddenly, while they stared at the scene in front of them, something came out of the object and shot toward the beach. What Liza saw was not a beam like in some *Star Trek* episode but an illumination of the air between the object and Bernie Winsor. It was subtle, but a white-green pulse of air instantaneously struck Bernie. When it did, she froze in her tracks with her arms extended toward the dark sky. She actually began to glow bright white. For an instant, she had become the brightest object in view, even brighter than a lightning bolt that struck over the far hill as the storm descended. It all ended quickly and without the typical Hollywood dramatics. Bernie, in full illumination, stopped and shook as if having a seizure and then fell to the ground lifelessly. The light faded, and the darkness that filled the void was much darker than the storm warranted. Lightning flashed and the beach lit up, empty except for the chairs, blankets, and assorted beach gear that the guests had left behind in their rush to get away. Bernie Winsor's lifeless body lay among the abandoned paraphernalia. The thunder roared.

"What…," was all that Pete was able to get out of his mouth. Liza realized that she had slid backward from the window out of pure terror. Pete and Thomas sat frozen in place, and Liza hoped that no one else had seen what the three of them had just observed. It might be too much for their fragile psyches. Old "Silent Night" might actually go completely off his rocker. There was no talk and no motion from them as the storm began to drench the resort. The sound of the pounding rain could be heard through open windows and on the roof. Mercifully, the odd humming of the object was drowned out by the pouring deluge. Lightning became frequent and made it clear just how hard it was raining. With each flash, the beach was illuminated as was the body of Bernie Winsor. There were now two dead bodies sitting out there. Jesus, what was happening?

"Holy shit." Pete spoke aloud, being the first to do so. "What the freaking hell?"

Thomas moved his mouth, but no words came out. If he hadn't been forced into a state of shock before, this had likely pushed him to the teetering brink.

"I don't know," Liza answered Pete. "This is insanity."

"Pete," a voice said from behind her, and Liza turned and was surprised to see that Meredith had moved up to them. "What's going on, Pete?"

Pete turned from the window, and it was clear that he saw Meredith slide in next to Thomas. The look on his face was a mixture of fear, surprise, and determination, which was confusing and surprising all at once. Pete reached out and took Meredith's hand, and Liza could sense the compassion in their touch. The rain continued to beat down, and she realized that the electric lights inside the lodge had been turned on and were noticeable over the darkness outside.

Liza looked out the window and watched the storm that had stolen the bright summer day. A gusty wind blasted down on the lodge, and the trees around the resort were bent over by the force. The strength of the burst was powerful, and the object over the lake was temporarily forgotten. Insane. Even with something from another dimension or wherever the hell it was, good old Mother Nature still reigned supreme. The thought actually lightened her fragile mood. Then something amazing happened.

A bolt of lightning pierced the sky over the lake, shocking her by its sudden violence. Instead of crashing vertically to the lake, the bolt was sucked toward the middle of the lake and the object. In a millisecond, the bolt became entwined with the object, and the result was astounding. Through the raging storm, the circular blasphemy drew in the electrical bolt, and as quickly as the lightning dissipated, the circle began to glow and spark. Over the darkness and clouds of rain, the object's circumference blazed with an unearthly light, becoming brighter than any lightning bolt.

"Look!" Liza screamed. Pete dragged his gaze from Meredith and looked out the window. Like some malevolent star, the object blazed through the raging tempest, raging and sparking like the most powerful transformer gone wild. The storm was somehow forgotten, and the focus of the four was again drawn to the horror that had entered the scenic mountain lake only a couple of hours earlier.

"Good Lord," Thomas murmured, proclaiming what they all were thinking. Craziness had descended, and they were far from seeing peace and security return.

"My friends," Pete responded, "we are in some serious shit."

*****

Perhaps Davey finally understood what hell was. He was sitting on an old, decaying log that was literally falling apart under his ass. The rain was coming down in a torrent, and although he imagined that the downpour was showing signs of letting up, it still sucked. Regardless, the rain had soaked him straight through to his underwear, and the gusty wind seemed to blow cold air right through him. It was strange that only an hour earlier he had been sweltering, and now he was shivering. The wind was blowing with such ferocity that he worried that a tree above him might snap, crashing down and crushing him in the process. He realized how amazing it was that he was concerned with a tree fall while he had just witnessed an actual human being's horrific demise right in front of him.

The lake stretched out from the shore while raindrops pounded the water's surface. The wind whipped spray from the lake surface that only added to the moisture in the air over the lake. But the focal point that drew the eye was the black hole that had caused the woman to glow and then collapse. Davey had been close, and he could have sworn that the light had eaten at her insides, but the moment was so brief it was hard to tell. The thing had attacked her, and now it glowed like some insane, disk-like sun. Davey could hear it, even over the roar of the storm, which still included the rumbles of thunder.

"Weed eater," he muttered aloud. The black hole was making a charged sound like a weed whacker revved up. That was freaky and very unsettling because he couldn't help but debate what was going to go down next.

He needed to get to the relative safety of the lodge and hoped that Thomas was still there. As far as he knew, there wasn't much that could be done about the black hole, but it would be reassuring to be around other people, especially ones that have some experience with this insanity.

Davey looked down the trail that was now soaked with runoff. He knew the path well and wasn't worried about running into an unknown obstacle, but he knew he was in mortal danger when he moved toward the lodge. He had watched the woman from Camp Wildass approach the beach right in front of the black hole, and the rest had been horrible. The question that kept rolling through his head was how the thing recognized her and why it had attacked. Motion? Infrared? Guess it didn't matter because it knew she was there. And he was going to have to cross in nearly the same spot that the woman had walked, and that scared the shit out of him. It was pretty obvious that he didn't want to meet the same fate as that lady.

"Oh shit," he muttered as he stood from the rotten stump. The rain continued, and he figured that the screen of water in the air was most likely going to help him, acting like a shield in between his path and the black hole that was still sparking out over the lake. Lightning flashed, now a little farther to the east, and he knew the storm was passing, so if he wished to use the storm as a buffer, he decided he better get a move on. "Let's move."

Davey moved on the path, his feet squishing on the saturated ground cover. Muddy water soaked into his sneakers, but he didn't even notice since his socks were long ago sodden. Concentrating on his every step, Davey moved as quickly as he thought safe through the woods. The rain began to quickly lessen, and he felt a pang of fear push adrenaline through his veins. And then the noise from the black hole suddenly stopped, and Davey felt a fear descend on him unlike any he had ever felt before.

*****

The storm raged outside with winds that blasted from the west, coming down the hills over the lake like a wild banshee. Trees bent over in the gusts, and waves quickly formed on the water, moving toward the far shore. Over the lake, the thing was visible, even in the tempest. Pete thought it looked like some bizarre, electrified Christmas wreath. The wind was howling toward it, but the thing didn't move. It didn't even seem to wobble. It was scary, as if Mother Nature's greatest wrath had no effect on it. A hurricane wouldn't be able to budge it. It was as if the thing was taunting existence itself. Where was the fucking thing from? Pete drew his gaze away from the object and watched as runoff began to puddle and flow down the lawn toward the beach. Josh would have a lot of raking to do down there the next morning. That thought made him shake his head. Tomorrow, even if they made it that far, would anything be close to normal?

"I don't know what to say," Meredith moaned.

Thomas sighed. "This is one hell of a storm."

Lightning ripped the sky over the trees on the far side of the lake, and seconds later, a wave of thunder hit the lodge. A new gust of wind surged out of the woods as if the thunder had moved the air.

Pete couldn't talk or pull his gaze away from the scene out the window. He never thought of his own safety, although Thomas and Meredith had moved back away from the window a little. Only Liza still sat up with him, and that made him respect the girl in a new way. She had some balls. Lightning flashed again and lit up the chaotic scene outside. As he watched, the wind was rolling a lounge chair down the beach where it came to rest against his guard tower. Crazy shit.

"This is nuts, Pete," Liza said. "I mean, the storm is bad enough, but that thing just hovers out there. This is freaking scary."

He nodded as his gaze fell on Ty's body lying on the grass as it was being pelted and abused by the storm. That vision brought a bizarre stitch of reality to the insane scene. It was only an hour. One fucking hour had gone by since the gates of hell had burst open. The whole thing was surreal, and he had to take a deep breath and try to wrap his brain around the whole incident. With the suddenness of the storm, Pete had a need to turn away and find a spot away from a window to collect himself.

"We just lost power," Thomas said from deeper in the lodge. Pete hadn't noticed while staring out the window, but losing electricity in a mountain storm was far from uncommon.

"Damn," he uttered as he stood. "I need to get away for a minute."

He felt Liza's gaze on him, and it made him uncomfortable. Well, if she expected him to be the granite rock in this cluster, then she was looking toward the wrong dude. That was when the noise from the storm lessened and a greater silence followed.

"It stopped," Liza yelled. "The noise just stopped!"

Pete whirled around and looked out at the lake. The rain that had been monsoonal had slackened to a steady but lighter shower. The noise of the rain beating on the porch, patio furniture, and anything else faded as did the roar from the wind. But that was not what created the sudden silence. The thing over the lake had stopped the engine noise that had been reverberating after it had been electrified by the lightning bolt. This silence seemed to have a physical presence. For a moment, it appeared as if everything around the lake stood still, waiting to see what was about to happen next. That was when Pete noticed motion to his right on the edge of the property near the cabins. A person emerged from the trees and quickly moved across the grass, making a beeline for the lodge.

"Jesus," Pete whispered, "I think it's Davey."

Thomas stood to look out the window, and Liza leaned forward.

"Davey Cramer?" she asked.

No one answered her, but instead they moved closer to the window to see. Davey was methodically moving from the trees, looking forward at the lodge. He was far away, but Pete was sure that he detected the look of fear on the man that he knew to be so confident. Yeah, he was sure that he would be shitting bricks if he was in Davey's shoes.

"C'mon, Davey," Thomas whispered. "Take it easy and keep moving."

Pete was also wishing the resort's neighbor forward as he turned to his left to see what the object was doing. The glow that had blazed forth when the lightning had crashed into the hole was fading, and the damn thing just hovered as if waiting. It was completely impossible to perceive if it knew whether Davey was there or not. And if it did, harder still was determining its intentions. Just before the strange light had extended out toward Bernie Winsor, the circle had appeared to pulsate. Pete felt a moment of relief when he didn't notice the same phenomenon. Davey was nearly halfway across the yard, and Pete was sure that he would make it. Then Davey suddenly froze in his tracks.

"What?" Meredith uttered. "Why did he stop? Oh man, I don't want to see this."

Pete shook his head and stared at Davey. "I'm not sure what he's doing."

"He's going to be all right," Liza said flatly. "I think he just noticed the dead body."

Pete watched as Davey shook his head and began moving forward, this time at a moderate jog. Pete had no idea if this was a good thing, but the object seemed to remain in the same state of inactivity. When Davey reached the patio, Pete was pretty sure that he was going to make it safely. That was when Pete looked and noticed the strange and violent pulsations in the object followed by the electric sound. Damn.

"Jesus, Davey," Pete yelled. "Move."

Meredith had shifted to the double main doors of the lodge and was waiting for Davey. She obviously heard Pete's pleas and began to yell at Davey herself. To his credit, Davey never looked back over his shoulder, and his jog became a sprint. He was not quick, but for an older guy, he was moving. The object continued to pulse, and Pete was reminded of the moment before the light engulfed Bernie Winsor. And then the lawnmower noise revved up to a near deafening pitch. It was just as before, and Pete braced himself for more horror.

Davey stumbled up the porch steps, and his momentum carried him through the double doors and into the lodge. At the same instant, the light did materialize from the object, and instead of striking Davey, the body of Ty Jamieson began to glow with a bright light while his dead body twitched horribly. Then the light winked out, and blackness followed. An afterimage blinded Pete's vision, but he knew that the luminosity had receded into the object. At least, Davey had made it into the lodge.

"Holy shit," Davey breathed through heavily drawn breaths. "Didn't think I'd make it."

Pete was standing halfway between the window and the door where Davey now lay. He turned and looked out at the lake and saw the thing just hovering over the water, as if it was some malevolent eye staring at them. He didn't want to die in the clutches of that thing.

23

July 10, 7:05 p.m.

The manic feeling that had been gripping him like a vise was beginning to wash away, and that was all right. He knew it was all right. For months, he had been denying his urges, but this was certainly an incredibly unusual twenty-four hours, and restraint had to be thrown out the window. Restraint didn't matter anymore.

Josh was in his room, sitting on his bed, taking in normal inhalations for the first time since all hell had broken loose on the lake. The unfortunate truth was that he hadn't been all that happy since he went to bed the previous night, and nothing had helped end the mood all day. Yeah, this had certainly been an unusual day that had pushed him right to the edge. He recalled his high school US History teacher explain that the events that led to the Civil War were like straws on a camel's back. They all added up over time until the nation fractured, causing the greatest conflict in the country's history. Josh remembered that lecture as he contemplated the similar position he was now in. Straws on a camel's back. Unfortunately the camel's back was his sanity.

Sitting on the floor next to his bed was a small red cooler that he had found in the shed where Thomas kept the landscaping equipment. It had been sitting next to an ancient hedge clipper and was perfect for holding ice. Josh knew where everything that he needed was located, so it had been easy. In fact, he had been contemplating this scenario for over a week or so. It had been so effortless because he had handled the materials on most nights when he worked with Slip at the bar. When everyone was running around the grounds in

243

a state of panic, Josh had calmly walked to the lodge, filled the box with ice, grabbed a case of beer from the cooler, and snatched a pint of Jack Daniel's just for good measure. Cars had been peeling out of the parking lot, kicking up clouds of dust as he carried his booty back to the employee dorm. No one looked at him twice, even though he must have looked like a weird alcoholic automaton crossing the gravel.

Josh tipped his head back and drained the remaining half of the beer he held in his hands. He placed the empty bottle next to two others that had already fallen to the Beer Meister. He smiled. *Beer Meister.* That had been what his high school buddies had called him when they pounded brews in the basement of his father's house. The Beer Meister was back, and Josh realized that he missed him.

"Cheers!" he saluted to the room after he grabbed a new beer from the cooler, ripped off the cap, and drained nearly half of the liquid. After he swallowed, he made sure to replace the empty space in the cooler with a fresh, full bottle. The ice was probably not even cooling the bottles since he was drinking so fast, but that didn't seem to matter. He was getting drunk, and for the first time in a long while, Josh felt content.

The level to which the girl had hurt him the evening before was surprising. Few girls turned him down, and if they did, he rationalized that they had to be bitches and not worth his time, anyway. When he had come to Camp Wildwood, Josh had been in a negative state, which was certainly an understatement. After the fiasco in Florida, his life had been in a downward tailspin. But he had acclimated to the mountains and loved the woods and the lake. Still, he was a young man and enjoyed having a good time. The nights alone on the dock with a couple of beers were nice, but after a couple of weeks of solitude, Josh needed more. His party bone began to itch. The opportunity to go and get drunk wasn't really feasible, but a romance seemed probable. And Liza had slipped right into the space that needed filling. The crazy thing was that she wasn't drop-dead beautiful. Blondes with big breasts and tans tended to be his preferred date, and Liza missed on nearly all those counts. Yeah, she was cute, but Josh was amazed that he was attracted to something more than just looks. The girl was just downright cool, and he found that he needed her. During the nights on the dock, he had used all his control to keep himself from using a little force to get what he wanted. But he enjoyed his job and the mountain lake, so he behaved and hoped that time would solve the problem for him.

"Fuck her!" he shouted to the four walls that surrounded him. He had made his play on her, and to his astonishment, she had rejected his advances. That was not supposed to happen. It was not in the game plan. His design had her falling madly for him, granting total control over the situation in his hands. Liza had proven way more powerful than he had assumed. When she blew him off the night before, he had come close to stealing beer and getting drunk. His rational side held off with the hopes of salvaging the relationship with Liza and the resort. Instead, he had lain prone and awake for most of the night, tossing and turning under a sheet thrown over his body. He had gone down to work in the morning feeling exceptionally horrible, but the thought of a scuba charter on the lake had seemed positive. Yeah, right.

Another empty bottle was placed on the floor, and a fresh one was opened. Josh could feel the sweet lightness in his head and welcomed it. He was quickly getting drunk, especially since his tolerance had weakened after a couple of months of little imbibing.

"This is a pretty fucked-up situation, isn't it, Josh?"

He was slipping into his drunken routine. On many nights when he found himself drinking alone, he often carried on conversations with himself that got more animated the drunker he got. Hey, sometimes your best drinking partner was yourself, right?

"What the hell was out there? Jesus, that was fucked up."

Even through the beer anesthesia that was settling in, he wasn't ready to mentally relive the episode on the Boston Whaler out on the water. The simple thought of the lake made him shiver. He had considered climbing into his car and simply taking off like the rest of the guests, but he needed the booze badly, and that took precedence. Besides, he could always sneak away later. What cops were there in these godforsaken mountains to pull him over, anyway?

"And you're a great drunk driver, anyway."

Josh smiled and reached for the bottle of whiskey. He deftly ripped the top off and took a long sip. The liquid burned his throat, but that was all right. The heat hit his stomach, and that seemed to radiate to his head. The sensation was euphoric.

He wondered where the others were. Had they survived? Was he all alone at Camp Wildwood? He thought not, but at the moment, he was content to be solitary. He thought of Liza and he felt a different heat rise in his chest.

"Fucking bitch."

*****

They had moved away from the window and had found a table that they tried to get comfortable around. Not that the black hole was ever completely out of their minds, but there seemed to be some relief when they moved from the view out over the water. She knew that she felt better but also felt awkward to be part of this group. She was only a kid who was wasting time as a maid.

"What do we do now?" she asked, looking around at the adults spread about the table, looking like brain-dead shells of people who had been the ones running the resort only hours before. Liza was feeling kind of anxious sitting in the relative safety of the lodge but without any type of plan. These were people whom she expected to take charge. Meredith was the owner and the top of the employee hierarchy, but she simply sat at the table kneading her hands. Thomas was the older, knowledgeable handyman, who was staring at a spot on the wall that only he apparently thought interesting. Davey sat pensively in a padded lounge chair away from the table, still breathing heavily from his run across the lawn. Pete was the only person in the group whom Liza felt was still holding some sense of direction. He had pulled up a wooden chair and was sitting backward on it just away from the table, drumming his hands on the backrest. He, at least, seemed cognizant. Still, her question seemed to fall to the hardwood floor with a dull thud on the planks.

Liza decided that maybe she was too excited and should take a backseat and let the adults handle the situation. She was about to ask Pete what he thought they should do when a guy walked in the room from the guest hallway wearing shorts and a UNH T-shirt. She recognized him as the man who quickly came into the lodge wearing the wetsuit. Pete looked at him and waved him over.

"How're you doing, Dan?" Pete asked with concern. The man nodded his head without smiling and walked over and sat in a comfortable chair near the hearth. The man sighed as he sat.

"Trying to get a grip, frankly," Dan finally answered. The entrance of the new guy seemed to invigorate Pete, and he leaned forward.

"What have you been doing?"

Dan lowered his head. "Didn't know what to do. I went to the room to shower but I saw Margo's stuff all over the room and I had to leave. I changed quickly and went out back away from the lake and spent some time staring into the woods. The storm came, and I got soaked. Time slipped away, I guess."

"Dan," Pete said, "I'm so sorry."

The man nodded and didn't respond. Liza had been in the housekeeping closet when the black hole had materialized, and she intuitively knew that Dan had somehow been involved when the shit had hit the fan. Davey sat up and was paying close attention to Dan and Pete's conversation.

"You were one of the scuba divers." Davey spoke, leaning closer to Dan.

Dan nodded.

Pete spoke softly. "He was diving with his wife, Margo."

Liza looked at Dan and shifted her gaze to Davey and immediately felt respect surge for the man. He knew that the man's wife hadn't come back from the trip and decided to say nothing. Liza looked back to Dan and couldn't imagine what was going through his head. The group was silent, but Liza could feel a renewed energy that was reassuring. She felt a necessity to have some kind of plan. The idea of trying to get to her car was mounting, although she wanted to remain at Camp Wildwood and help in any way she could.

Davey had become animated, and she could see a glimmer in his eye as he leaned further forward.

"Dan," he uttered slowly, "I know this hurts right now, but we are in a pretty hairy situation. Kinda like being up the creek without the paddle, you know? We need to know what you saw."

Pete perked up. "Hey, where's Josh?"

Pete's gaze fell on Liza, and she shrunk back and shrugged. "I really have no idea. I haven't seen him since last night when I…"

"I know," Pete finished for her. "He was pretty upset."

Great, she thought. There wasn't enough to worry about right now.

Davey was nodding. "Josh was driving the boat. It would be interesting to get his perspective too."

"My guess is that he jetted when he got off the beach," she added. "He's probably halfway to Cape Cod."

Davey turned and looked at Dan again. "If you can, tell us what you saw."

Dan lifted his head and looked toward the ceiling. "Oh man, give me a second."

Liza looked away as the man who had recently witnessed his wife die tried to get his thoughts together. There was nothing that she could relate that to and frankly didn't want to know. The room was silent, and the only noise was coming from the sound of the water lapping softly on the rocks on the east side of the property. The storm had cleared, and as quickly as it had rolled in, it was gone. The day was still bright, but the sun wasn't coming back out. They would need to find candles because it was sure to get dark quickly. Liza hadn't even noticed that Pete had slipped off and returned with a glass of amber fluid, which she assumed was whiskey. Dan took the glass and sipped deeply, letting an odd grumble exit from his throat. It appeared that the liquid was going to loosen the man's memory.

"We found something on sonar," Dan said slowly as all ears listened to his words. Meredith was now in the group paying close attention with Davey, Pete, and herself. "It was pretty big and oddly shaped. It was no fish, so we decided to investigate. The visibility was pretty poor. The water was turbid with a brownish tint from minerals and plant life, I guess. I do remember the comfort of the cooler water compared to the heat on the deck of the boat. I stayed near the surface for a moment, but Margo…Margo sank toward the bottom."

Liza noticed the hitch in his voice when Dan mentioned his wife's name and felt the pang of sympathy again but intentionally pushed it aside. This was about survival for the living, and the thoughts must move forward to the future and self-preservation.

"As I descended, the light dimmed a little, but Moon Lake isn't very deep, especially over in that cove."

Davey shifted forward. "It's forty feet at the deepest spot. Maybe twenty-five or thirty where you were."

"Yeah," Dan agreed. "Twenty-five feet at the deepest. Margo and I have dived over a hundred feet deeper than that, so this wasn't a really big deal. In fact, it was kind of boring. No fish. No rock outcrops. It was just brownish water and some weeds as I floated down."

Dan stopped again and drank from the glass, seemingly savoring the whiskey this time. Medicinal. The guy deserved it.

"Margo was only a few feet in front of me, and she saw it first. She began to wave her arms at me to get me to come see what she had found. When I saw it, for some weird reason, I knew immediately what I was looking at. It might sound stupid, but I knew that we were hovering near an object from another planet. The knowledge was just flat out obvious."

"What did it look like?" Davey asked. She wondered if he was a little freaked out, especially since the thing had been sitting on the bottom of the lake only yards from his cabin.

"It's odd," Dan continued. "I was expecting something that looked like the monolith from that movie, *2001: A Space Odyssey*. I don't know. It was totally different. The thing looked more like an oversized bullet about the size of a dishwasher. For a wild moment, I thought we had found a wayward nuclear missile. It was covered with a brownish green muck that covers everything down there on the bottom. Color wasn't the giveaway, but the unnaturally smooth, round shape was. Margo was the one who did it. I guess I would have done the same thing if I had been the one closest to it, but it was her. As I watched from a few feet above, Margo reached out and began to brush some of the muck off the bullet."

Dan stopped, and his head fell into his hands. Although they all wanted to hear the climax of the memory, it was clear that Dan needed time to cope with this moment.

"Do you want to take a break?" Meredith asked, and Liza wondered what she was thinking. A break? Come on. They needed to figure out what they were dealing with. The moment was mortal.

The whiskey was gone, and Dan lifted his head. He looked pained but also had determination etched on his face.

"The muck swept away in a swirling brown cloud. She looked back at me, and although it was tough to see because of the regulator in her mouth, I saw her smile. Yeah...she smiled. I guess that's good."

"What color is it?" Davey asked, again paying the closest attention to Dan's story.

"I thought it was a deep green. If it really is extraterrestrial as the Indian legends have it, I would have expected black or silver. But the hand-sized spot that Margo cleared was a deep green. I was moving downward toward it when all hell erupted. Margo...she was...rubbing the surface of the bullet. It didn't crack. It didn't break. But in an instant, this black ooze rushed from the bullet faster than I could really see it. Margo was instantly enveloped. I kicked toward the surface out of reflex and never saw Margo again." He stopped and took a couple deep breaths. "It was so fucking dark."

No one spoke around the table. Liza found that she was imagining what it must have been like on the bottom of the lake at that moment and realized that she was shivering. A coldness had definitely fallen over the group as the reality hit home again. Liza looked around the lodge that had become their makeshift fortress and prison while the black hole reigned over the lake kingdom. She felt like a prisoner, and the light was slowly draining from the day. She knew that there was no electric light and that in an hour or so, it would be full dark with something worse than the scariest horror movie waiting outside.

"What's that? Meredith asked, cocking her ear toward the front windows of the lodge. Liza knew what it was. The small engine moan of the black hole had begun again over the lake. Pure terror rushed through her, and she felt completely exposed.

*****

Andy did not feel the expected joy that he assumed would follow the termination of his relationship with his wife. He had watched her walk toward the lake following the false trail that he had pushed her on. Yes, he had come to a point where it would either be his survival or her complete domination of their relationship. His opportunity had risen on that hot afternoon, and he had not taken a lot of time examining the aftereffects of what he assumed would happen when his wife walked toward the dreadful object over Moon Lake. When the emission had materialized and absorbed his wife, he had not felt joy but a sense of finality. Bernie was gone, and he had won.

What he had not expected after the fact was the deep feeling of guilt that began to crush him. The kids had not seen the demise of their mother, which was a godsend, but as the time elapsed and she did not return, they began to sense that something was amiss. The oldest boy, Brandon, was the first to complain about her absence. Andy was standing near the window overlooking the lake as Brandon blubbered on the bed. He resembled his mother and was at least thirty pounds overweight.

"Where did Mommy go?" the boy mumbled through tears that were rolling down his cheeks. The younger son, Dylan, was silent but shaking as he began to cry as well, perhaps simply because his older brother was. Dylan was like a smaller twin of Brandon's, only even fatter if that was possible. Andy looked at his two blubbering sons, and he contemplated the future with these fat whiners and no Bernie to deal with them. She had doted over the boys, and they were spoiled. He wasn't about to coddle his sons.

"Your mother is gone," Andy answered evenly as he turned from his boys and looked back out on the lake. It was amazing. He could barely see part of her body lying on the grass just below a contour in the lawn. It was her right foot complete with flip-flop still attached. There was still no motion from that foot. He listened to blubbering and wondered if he had made a horrible mistake.

"I want to watch TV!" Dylan moaned. Jesus. The electricity was out, and it probably wasn't coming on anytime soon. Didn't his fat-ass son understand that?

"There is no power," Andy answered as calmly as he could without losing his control. "You can't watch television."

There was a collective sob behind him. It was kind of amazing. The boys now seemed more devastated by the loss of the television than that of their mother. Ungrateful fucks. Andy looked out the window and across the water at the black hole. The storm had truly passed. The sun was trying to break through the clouds somewhere behind the resort over the hills to the west of the lake. The brighter sky only made the storm departing to the east look that much blacker. Focused right in the middle of it all was the black hole, hovering over the lake. The returning rays of the sun, the last before the night slowly settled over the mountains, struck the circular disk over the water. The edges of the hole began to rotate, and the entire object seemed to quiver. The effect was hypnotizing. At that moment, Andy realized that he had indeed made a terrible mistake sending Bernie out into the clutches of the black hole. He needed her. Only she could organize his life and take care of the children. He still loved her.

Andy Winsor walked to the screen door of the cabin and continued out onto the porch of the lakeside rental. Metal lounge chairs painted in pastel colors rested on the wood plank floors. The day's last rays of sunshine were now bathing the lake in much-needed brilliance, but Andy didn't notice. Dylan was screaming at his brother from somewhere far off. He was staring at the black disk as he stepped off the porch onto the grass.

"I'm so sorry, Bernie," he muttered as he slowly strode forward, across the grass and toward her fallen form. The disk had begun to rotate more rapidly, and a sweet music filled his ears. The last earthly image that Andy Winsor registered was a brilliant, beautiful white light.

*****

Pete was the first to the window and immediately knew that something was outside and that the black hole was focusing on it. The edges of the hole were rotating and pulsing again.

"What's out there?" Liza asked as she came up behind him with Davey close on her heels. Pete looked back and saw Dan sitting at the table, looking like a person in shock.

Pete scanned the lakefront and quickly noticed Andy Winsor leaving the front door of his cabin. The man was striding forward like a sleepwalker or a person possessed. The movement was steady and unwavering.

"Who is that guy?" Davey asked to Pete's right.

"Andy Winsor. It was his wife that got zapped while you were walking over here."

"Why?" Liza muttered softly. Pete knew that she understood what was about to happen. The sound from the black hole increased to a higher pitch, and the noise assaulted their ears. Still, Andy continued forward without slowing down. If anything, his pace had increased. The black hole was beginning to visibly glow as the last of the day's sunrays were striking it in a brilliant splash of luminosity. They were about to witness a repeat performance of what had just happened to this man's wife. Without any forewarning, a pulse of light shot from the black hole, and for an instant, Andy Winsor stopped as if suddenly frozen in place before he trembled and fell as his wife had. The light was instantly gone, and Pete was left with a strange aftereffect on his vision. After a couple of moments, the noise from the disk began to wind down slowly, and things gradually returned to status quo. Normal. Yeah, right.

"Oh no," Meredith whispered, and Pete realized for the first time that she had come to the window and witnessed the last moments of Andy Winsor as well. "This can't be happening."

As Meredith said this, she burst out into racking sobs that had probably been dammed up for the last couple of hours. He stood and went to her wondering where the magical Michael was. That guy disappeared awfully quick when the poop hit the fan. He moved next to her, and she fell into his arms, crying softly against his T-shirt. It was the most natural thing in the world, and he realized that it was most likely the first time any of the others had seen the two of them together. Liza had moved away from the window now that the show was over and was looking thoughtfully across the main room of the lodge. That girl had balls, and he was impressed. While Meredith whimpered next to him, Liza seemed determined to deal with the situation. Thomas had staggered back to the table where Dan still sat, and Davey was staring out over the lake, perhaps looking at his cabin on the far shore. This was a mess, and even worse, they seemed adrift on an unknown ocean without any idea what tactic to take.

"Did you see that?" Meredith said through her tears. "What is that thing? Is it what my father talked about from years before?"

Pete stiffened. "Your father told you about something in the lake?"

She shook her head. "No, he never said anything about something this horrible, but I think he mentioned it in his log."

"Log?"

"I found a diary of sorts in his cabinet in the office. I've read through most of it. Mostly boring administrative stuff, but there is something interesting."

Pete looked at Thomas, who was sitting with his head in his hands, and then toward Davey by the window.

"Dave?"

Davey's head slowly turned Pete's way.

"What's up, Slip?"

"We may have some reading to do."

24

July 10, 8:21 p.m.

Josh was wasted. Punked. Slammed. Faced. He had succeeded in getting plastered, and it felt good. His intake of alcohol had slowed
because he didn't want to get falling down drunk. Although that state
of intoxication sounded just fine, he wanted to stay upright in case
he decided to get some stuff done. And there was some stuff that he
wanted to deal with before he left. Every time he thought of Liza, a
growing ball of red rage grew behind his eyes. How dare she blow him
off. With every second, he felt a growing need to do something about
her disrespect, and that could only happen if he remained coherent.

And he had seen the thing over the lake. Although the alcohol
had dulled his vision, he could still tell that whatever that damn thing
from the bottom of the lake was, it was still hanging around over the
water. After he had finished his tenth beer, Josh had decided that
some fresh air was in demand. He walked out of the employee dorm
and stopped short, suddenly remembering the thing that he had seen
in the water. How could he have forgotten that shit? He had chuckled and stopped himself before turning around the lakeside corner of
the building. Slowly, he peered around the wall and looked out over
the lake. The scene that he confronted made his blood turn cold.
Although it was blurry, he could clearly see a man on the lawn as an
extremely bright radiance struck him from the water. That was obviously where the disk was. He had never seen anything like it before,
and the alien-ness of it scared the shit out of him. The light suddenly
disappeared, and the man crumpled to the ground. Although the distance was at least a hundred yards, he could tell that the body was not

complete. Part of it had been torn up and ripped out. That was some fucking crazy shit. Josh ducked back around the building with his breath suddenly coming in quick gasps. A number of thoughts raced through his head, and the most persistent one had him running to his car and getting the fuck out of the Adirondacks. Self-preservation was a strong motivator.

But he also had a deep feeling that he wasn't done at the lake. It was like the feeling he always got when he left parties before the music had stopped, especially if he wasn't with a girl. The story was unwritten, and he feared missing out on something amazing that was yet to happen.

As these thoughts were going through his head, Josh saw the guy for the first time. He had dark hair and was sitting on the steps that the employees used to enter the kitchen. The distance between them was a hundred feet across the gravel parking lot. It was getting dark, and his vision was already a little screwy, but he thought the man was Ms. Riley's live-in boyfriend. Mathew? Mickey? Josh had a hard time remembering the name, but he was fairly sure that this was the guy. He was looking at Josh and before Josh could look away, the guy stood and walked across the parking lot toward him. An urge to run swept him, but the beer and muscles took control, and he knew that even if this guy was upset for some reason, there was nothing really to fear. He was six-foot-something and less than two hundred pounds. Cake. Josh balanced his feet and stood tall as the guy approached.

"You got anything other than beer?" the man asked as he advanced. Josh noticed that the black hair that had been so perfectly combed into place was slightly disheveled and there was a look of wildness in his red tinted eyes. It wasn't what Josh was expecting, and he relaxed.

"I got some Jack in my room."

The guy nodded and looked around with his gaze settling on the woods. "I need to get my shit together. Let's have a drink."

As he spoke, the guy pulled a pint bottle of Southern Comfort from a pocket in his pants. Josh noticed that he was still wearing his bathing suit. Most of the bottle was gone, and he drained another significant amount into his mouth. Josh just watched him, unsure what to say or do.

"This is some crazy shit. Do you have a room or someplace we could go and have a couple? The darkness is kind of freaking me out."

"There's no power, anyway," Josh added with a sudden pleasure at comprehending the problem before this guy did.

"Yeah," the guy answered. "Don't you have a couple of candles or a flashlight? I'd still feel safer inside. I mean, who knows what that fucking thing over the lake is going to do in the darkness."

Josh followed the man's gaze toward the woods around the resort, and the friendly trees were indeed growing dark and creepy. What was the thing over the lake going to do when night descended? Would they even be able to see it? Again, he looked at his car, and an urge to flee hit and slipped away.

"I have a couple flashlights in my room."

Josh turned and led the way into the dorm, and he immediately noticed how dark the hallway had become. They walked on in silence, and Josh passed Liza's room. He felt an impulse to try and open the door. It was completely possible that she had returned to her room and was sitting vulnerable in the darkness. The thought slipped from his brain down through his stomach to his crotch. Despite the alcohol, Josh could feel an erection growing. That bitch. Instead, he continued on and opened his door. The room was shadowy with the only light slipping in from the fading glow on the parking lot side of the building where he had just met Meredith's man. Josh walked into the small space and looked under the narrow single bed that was in reality a glorified cot. He had brought the flashlight from home, just as he had when he was twelve and went to spend two weeks at camp Y-Millawauket, along with his sleeping bag and a sense of adventure. He figured that the flashlight might come in handy, and boy was he right on the money. He turned the large yellow twelve-volt on, and a beam of light illuminated the room. He turned a plastic gasket near the lens, and the beam broadened. Josh leaned it up on the nightstand and aimed the light at the wall. An odd, stark light filled the room. It wasn't a bright fluorescent, but it did push back most of the darkness. Josh sat back on his bed and grabbed a beer from his makeshift cooler. The other guy looked around and sat on the wooden chair that was part of the desk ensemble, the only other seat in the small room.

"These are the quarters that you've been in all summer?" the guy asked.

Josh nodded and drank from his beer. The guy had his bottle of whiskey out and was rapidly approaching completion.

"You look familiar. What's your name?"

Josh looked at the flashlight. "Josh. I work on the beach and in the bar during the evenings."

The guy nodded in recognition. "Of course. Of course, I noticed. I think I saw you last night during the fiasco in the dining room."

"Yep, I was there. And you're Ms. Riley's boyfriend."

The guy chuckled sarcastically. "Yeah. Name's Michael, and Meredith and I lived together in North Carolina. I don't think she's too happy to see me this summer, however." Michael took a long drink from his bottle, and the liquid was gone. Josh pointed to the desk and the bottle of Jack Daniel's that sat there. This guy was going to be way drunker than he was if he continued at this pace.

"Why isn't she happy that you're here?"

Michael chuckled again. "Well, my friend, we had a falling-out even before she moved up here this summer, and I believe…no, I know…that she's shacking up with someone here."

Josh looked up, interested. "Really? With who?"

Michael belched as if on cue. "The bartender, I believe."

"Slip?" Josh blurted out and laughed spastically, spilling some beer on his leg. He tried to recall any evidence to support Michael's claim, and there were thousands of times he had seen the two of them together, but everyone was with all the employees at some point or another. It was a small, close-knit group. The booze had fogged his memory, and anything seemed plausible. Slip and Meredith? "I guess I could see that."

"Oh, I see it clearly." Michael opened the bottle of Jack and took a swig. "I'm not surprised, but that doesn't make me feel any better. I was going to ask that girl to marry me. We had a house and careers. Damn it! We'd been talking about starting a family."

Michael fell silent, and Josh didn't want to speak in that moment. Besides, Michael's apparent pain reminded him a little of his own issues with Liza. The thought of her brought an immediate burning to his chest. Maybe he and Michael were some kind of brothers in pain.

Josh reached for another beer. "Women suck."

Michael laughed and held up the bottle of Jack. "You are certainly right there, Jake!"

"Josh."

"Exactly." Michael drank, and Josh thought of Meredith and Liza. Where were they?

The strangest thing about the meeting between the two men was that the black hole over the lake was never mentioned.

*****

The hallway was dark as the sun had officially fallen behind the trees and hills to the west of the lake. What remained of the natural light that filtered in through the front windows of the lodge was not able to penetrate down the inner hallway. Pete was carrying a flashlight, and the glow played peculiarly on the walls. His heart was beating rapidly, and he had to admit to a strong sense of fear clutching him with every step he took down the passage. It was crazy because he had walked this hallway hundreds, maybe thousands, of times and knew it as a safe and familiar passage. Even in a normal darkness, he would not have been spooked. But with the electricity out and the thing floating over the lake like a sick nightmare, anything could scare the crap out of a person. The evolutionary male requirement to be strong tried to force him forward, but that was barely enough to make one foot move in front of the other. The door to the office was just ahead, but it felt like a mile.

"Almost there." Pete spoke quietly to Meredith, who was clutching his hand behind him. She was not making this any easier, as she was clearly scared to the point of near paralysis. Meredith would have been left behind, but she was the only one who knew the location of her father's log. Pete honestly didn't think the log would help them at all, but Davey and Liza felt that it might shed some secret tidbit about how to deal with the black hole, so here he was with his terrified boss/girlfriend walking in the dark.

"I am so scared," she whispered, telling him something that was plainly obvious.

"I know, but we'll have the log and be back in the main room soon."

Meredith's hand tightened in his. "But that thing will still be there."

That was true, and Pete drove the knowledge from his head, just trying to move one step at a time. They reached Meredith's office, and a slight amount of daylight was still coming in the window that overlooked the parking lot. He relaxed a little as they entered the confines of her office.

"Let's get the log and hurry back," he advised, trying to get Meredith moving. To his surprise and happiness, she did just that. Meredith quickly moved through the flashlight beam that Pete had trained on the cabinet, and she opened a drawer and pulled out a couple spiral notebooks.

"Got them," she stated with a sense of accomplishment.

"Okay," Pete responded, "let's get back to the party."

With way more speed than going toward the office, the two quickly made their way back down the hallway to the main room of the lodge. As they turned the only corner in the hall, a soft glow could be seen from in front of them. Pete imagined it was candles burning on the table in the main room. He was somewhat shocked and felt a twist in his gut when they emerged and no one sat in the main room and no candles were on the table. In an instant, Pete realized that there were indeed lit candles, but the glow was emanating from the bar. The party had moved one room over, and Pete led Meredith into the lounge. Two small tables had been brought together. Candles and a kerosene lantern glowed softly in the room.

"We moved in here," Liza answered the unasked question. "We felt exposed in the windows overlooking the water."

Pete completely understood. Although he was certain that the monstrosity could not "see," it was clear that there was some way for it to understand when some prey was nearby. What that sense was would be nice information because it might really help them deal. But Pete couldn't even hazard a guess to figure out something so far from human understanding. It just needed to be understood that it had some way of knowing what was happening and that the windows were a large breach into the activity in the lodge.

The bar was indeed lit by an unsettling light being cast by flames from candles and lanterns. The effect was an unsteady glow as the flames flickered. Man, this was creepy, and he felt a chill rush his dermis. This light might be romantic in other circumstances, but this was not that at all. Pete realized that he was still clutching Meredith's hand and that he was squeezing more than she was.

"Did you get the log?" Davey asked from a chair that was pulled up to the table. There was a glass with a dark liquid in front of him, and Pete was pretty sure that it was just cola and nothing more. Davey would want to have his full faculties to deal with this problem.

Meredith held up the notebooks. "Yeah, we got them, and it was a freaky walk to my own office."

Davey stood and reached out for the notebooks, and she handed them over. Pete heard her sigh and felt her shrink beside him. He was worried about her. Shock could certainly not be ruled out at this point, and Meredith was already showing some odd signs. Pete pulled out a chair and helped Meredith into it. He fell into a chair next to her. It was a solid wooden bar chair that was sturdy but not very comfortable, especially for a long sitting. Maybe they made them uncomfortable so people would leave before they drank too much. Now that was an interesting idea. He smiled. How had his mind wandered at such a stressful moment?

It dawned on him that his future might very well be in the hands of the assembled people around the table. Liza sat to his left and she sat pensively, looking at Davey on the other side of the table. Dan the scuba diver was still with the group, which was simply amazing considering what he had been through. Davey had the notebook open on the table with his face in it, while Thomas sat next to him, gazing at nothing in particular. A one-thousand-mile stare.

"This is a very detailed log," Davey said enthusiastically. "Listen to this—'June 16, 95.37 degrees at 7:00 a.m. Clouds then sun with a high of 67. Humidity low at 36 percent.' Did he want to be a meteorologist?"

Meredith shook her head. "No."

Davey sighed. "Is there anything of interest in here? Meredith, you mentioned something before."

Meredith slowly nodded while looking at her hands that she was wringing on the table.

"I think I saw the first weird reference in September 1982."

Davey looked at the thick notebook and began to page toward the front. He must have gotten to September because he stopped and quickly read the page that was in front of him.

"Here!" he nearly yelled. "This has to be it."

Davey read the line again and then read the passage out loud.

> September 29, 1982—An earthquake. We are
> leaving NOW. Lord, help my family.

"Earthquake?" Liza muttered. "What about an earthquake? We had one today."

Her statement hung in the air over the table, much like the thing over the lake. Of course, Pete knew about the earthquakes and the correlation with the legend of Moon Lake. So did Davey and Thomas, who were both sitting with stunned looks on their faces.

"What?" Liza pleaded. "Is there some connection?"

"In a minute," Pete responded, holding his right hand in the air. "Is there anything else, Meredith?"

She was looking at the notebook. "Yes. There're a couple more entries about earthquakes. One was the first entry of 1999. There is also a very strange page in July 1993."

Davey had already found the 1999 entry and read it aloud.

> May 2, 1989—High: 54, low: 29. Cool, sunshine
> first day and it's great to be back at Wildwood.
> Snow in spots. The grounds are in good shape
> with exception of normal winter damage.
> Thomas was here cleaning up sticks and limbs

that had come down. He mentioned that there
had been an earthquake in November before the
freeze-up. He had taken snowshoes weeks later
and looked for any victims. Mostly dead deer, but
he saw a startling sight. A bear had been roused
from hibernation and had been broken and
ripped apart. Scary. I thank God the resort was
closed. Luckily, no people were around. Going to
help Thomas tomorrow and head back south on
Sunday. Plan on opening June 1.

Everyone around the table looked at Thomas, who appeared to
be in some sort of mental pain. No one spoke, and the night was quiet
with only the hissing sound of a kerosene lantern on the bar. No noise
came from the lakeside of the lodge, which was probably a good thing.
Pete thought of the Winsor kids alone in the cabin across the lawn and
wondered if they had starved to death yet. Maybe one of them had
eaten the other. There was no indication whether the black hole was
still there or not, but he was betting that they weren't out of the woods.

"What happened, Thomas?" Dan asked, leaning forward on the
table.

Thomas looked up but said nothing. Davey had already skipped
in the notebook to July 1993.

"This section is pretty bizarre. Colin seems to have lost his desire
to chronicle the local weather. In fact, he only has a couple of entries
the entire month. On the Fourth, he talks about a warm day with a
successful display of fireworks. Then there is nothing for a week until
he begins again on July 14."

July 14, 1993—Picture-perfect sunshine and
high of 82. I hope the return of the sun will clean
the resort of the darkness that has enveloped it
for the last week. This one was bad, and I'm not
sure Camp Wildwood will survive. Thomas and I
will discuss damage control, if we decide to continue on.

Pete turned and looked at Meredith, and the pain was evident in her eyes. She had most likely read this passage before, but it had to strike close to home. It also implied that her father had deceived the public to erase the history of whatever happened at the resort. There was a probability that he had knowingly put people in danger by keeping the resort open. And if she had read the passage, so had she.

Davey, Liza, and Dan were all looking at Thomas, and he was just sitting looking at his trembling hands on the table. Sitting might be a weak word for it. Squirming might be more apt.

"Thomas," Davey said slowly, "you know more than any of us here. Obviously you were directly involved. What do you know?"

Thomas rolled his shoulders and mumbled, "It don't have to be a stiff one, but I'll be needing a drink to help lubricate my mind."

Pete nodded and proceeded to the bar to make Thomas a vodka and tonic. They didn't need a drunk Thomas, but he would give him a little shot to help explain what had happened.

"What's going on?" Liza said from the table. "I mean, you guys all seem to understand something together. I feel like an outsider, and that doesn't feel very good with that thing out there."

"Me too," Dan added. He looked confused and scared.

Davey sighed. "That thing that popped out of the lake today. This isn't the first time it's happened. Dan, you probably know about the legend. That's probably why you came to this resort lost in the mountains in the first place. Although I had never witnessed it before, the rumor had always persisted about a stone cast into the lake by local Indians because it was evil. Legend held that local earthquakes 'woke up' the stone and a hideous malevolence rose from the water and killed animals that ventured too close. This phenomenon lasted for a period of time. As Dan seemed to prove today, it isn't earthquakes that trigger the stone but some type of movement near it. The earthquake appears to be caused by the stone."

Pete realized that Davey was correct, and that was something new. He threw a lime in the glass and walked around the bar to hand Thomas his drink.

"Sorry there isn't much ice 'cause it's beginning to melt."

Thomas raised the glass to his mouth and took a sip, but it was Liza who drew the attention away.

"Do you think it's still out there? And if it is, how long are we stuck here?"

Pete looked out the glass window that had such a remarkable view out over the wood deck outside the bar and the lake beyond. It was nearly pitch-black outside, and there wasn't any visibility. No tiki lamps. No festive rope lights. Just dark. During the height of the bright afternoon sun, the disk seemed to be the opposite of light. Pure darkness. Pete was pretty sure that it would be invisible at night, unless it came alive and that eerie electricity sparked around the disk as it slowly rotated.

Thomas broke the silence. "Yes, it's still out there."

25

July 10, 9:31 p.m.

The group sat staring at Thomas silently while the older man took sips from his drink and seemed to mutter to himself. Liza had never seen a grown man act this way before, but the behavior was completely understandable. Thomas held some answers that they patiently waited to hear. She certainly did because she was hoping that the new knowledge might be the key to dealing with the thing outside. It was completely eerie, and any chance she had of getting to her car for an escape to Mayson had faded when the light had dimmed in the sky. There was no way she was going outside in the dark with that thing out there. No way.

Thomas sighed deeply and shook his head. She could feel the torture coming off him, and that made her very uneasy. But the evening was pressing on toward midnight, and she needed to have a feeling of action.

"Thomas," Davey said softly, "what happened in 1993?"

Thomas looked up, and his face was emotionless. "It was bad. Very bad."

"What do you mean?" Liza asked quickly. "What was bad?"

Meredith had sat up and was now staring at her father's friend and handyman with undeterred interest. They all wanted to know but didn't want to push him. When he spoke, it was like an avalanche.

"That summer was one that I have tried my best to forget and mostly have until the earth moves. It was the stuff of nightmares.

"The year 1993 wasn't a summer that I try to remember, I'll tell ya. I was forty-three years old and married to a second wife, which

would only last a couple more summers. She would end up takin'
off on me. Probably deserved it the way I stayed around the resort
drinkin' and playin' cards every night with Colin and the others.
Guess I wasn't home more than a couple nights a week. That'll drive
a woman away, for sure. That was a buggy summer, even though we'd
had a pretty tough winter. In March, we'd had the blizzard, and the
mountains were buried in feet of snow. Hard to move around for a
week. It didn't all melt until nearly Memorial Day that year. Colin
considered delaying the opening, but spring came and the snow
melted, and we got on. The summer had been warm, and Colin
had managed to turn Wildwood into a profitable place, for sure. I
remember it like looking back at your life through a dirty window. I
lived it, but it has mostly been covered and a little foggy. Until now,
I've been glad it's been that way.

"That damn stone and the friggin' legend. When ya grow up
in these parts, up in the mountains, ya hear stories about stuff your
whole life. I'm sure Liza here knows something about that. There
were all kinds of stories kids told each other. According to most
twelve-year-olds, these hills are full of Bigfoot, UFOs, and even a few
commie spies and terrorists. I guess most places have their legends,
especially the ones passed around by school kids. But the Moon Lake
stone, that one was the most popular. You know how I figured it was
a big deal? One August night, a couple of friends of mine and I were
running around outside the house. The night was just growing dark,
and the air was thick and calm. I remember that like it was yesterday.
Those nights were so sweet. Warm and free, the way summer nights
ought to be. My daddy was out back in the sugar shack that he had
built years before with the dream of being a maple sugar producer. I
guess my daddy didn't have the willpower because the shack became
little more than a drinking spot away from my ma and his friends'
wives. They would be out there most nights drinking cans of Matt's
with the old pull tabs. Well, me and my friends snuck up on the
shack that night and sat outside a window to hear our fathers talk.
Sometimes they talked about work or the tits on the waitress over at
the Bear Path Inn. Whatever the discussion, it tended to be stories
that young boys ate up. Between belches and laughs, we learned stuff

about our daddys that we would never have imagined. It was that one particular night that we heard about the stone. The men were debating the truth of the legend, the one that we all heard. Didn't make no difference if you was twelve years old or a father of three. The stone in Moon Lake and the evil that it could unleash was a popular subject. They talked about death and darkness. And of course, they discussed whether it was real. I distinctly remember hearing Mr. Halston say that he had seen the dead animals scattered around the lake after one earthquake, and he sounded like it had scared that crap out of him. The other men had laughed at him, but I could hear the edge to the laughter, as if they wanted to make fun but couldn't. That was one of the first times I actually heard my father's voice sound nervous, and I think that scared me more than anything. Even older men than my daddy sat around scaring each other about the legend of Moon Lake. But what was really freaky was that some of these same men had seen true horror in the hills of Okinawa and Korea. How could some stupid lake scare them more than that?

"When I was seventeen, I dropped out of high school. I know now that my decision was impulsive and, frankly, plain stupid, but at the time, I didn't really see the need to know about the first amendment and what an indirect object was. I cared more about beer, chasin' girls, and runnin' around in the woods. The truth of my stupidity hit home when I turned eighteen and in no time got drafted for service in Vietnam. Yeah, that was 1968, the year the shit really hit the fan, and I found myself shipped off to Saigon then Cam Rahn Bay and the bush. Honestly, those are memories that I tend to leave stored away, and they don't make no difference to our situation here nohow. Those thirteen months in Vietnam forced me to grow up quickly, and when I returned home, I was no longer a stupid kid but a stupid adult who had personally accounted for the killing of fifteen human beings during my tour. The thoughts that I had taken other people's lives without a second thought haunted my dreams, but that's what happened, and there was no changing that. Instead, I came home with a desire to drink beer and forget the last year of my life. And of course, I had no high school diploma or course on which to set my life.

"I couldn't stay in my parents' house any longer and I needed money, so I wandered the area looking for work. I could swing a hammer without smashing my thumbs too bad, so I found myself working on construction crews. For a while, I worked over in Watertown and did some work down at Utica College. The money actually wasn't bad, and I was having fun. The rest of the country seemed to be melting down, but I just worked and drank, and that was fine with me. Let the college kids worry about politics, Cambodia, and all the other shit. I decided to take care of myself.

"The problem that I had was that I missed the mountains. Being away from home left a hole in my heart that I felt every day when I got up to go to work with a hangover. Later I'd go to bed with a new hangover waiting in the morning. Those days were hard, and I think the alcohol only numbed the pain. One night, I got very drunk in Utica and ended up in a fight with a couple of college kids. I got my ass kicked and thrown in jail to boot. That was enough. I spent the time in my cell crying. Yeah, crying because I was out of place and felt all alone. When they released me, I headed back to the 'dacks and decided to try and make a living where I grew up.

"I know that you don't want to hear me ramble on about my history at this point, but it needs to be said, I guess, to understand how I feel about this place. So to make a long, ugly story short, I met Ashley and we got married pretty quick. For me, it was awfully nice to have a place to call home, even though the house we rented was nothing more than a mountain shack. Double-wide trailer. For a while, we were in love but we were both too young to really make a marriage out of it. Thank God we didn't put a child in the middle of our problems. Time flew by as I struggled to find jobs, and Ashley and I spent less and less time together. The result was clear as a freshly shammied window. We were on our way to divorce. That was tough. I felt a failure and alone all over again. Like a leaf just drifting on the water, blown by the wind without a place to settle. My life was a mess.

"Then we came here one night. Me, my buddy Beezer, and a couple others. Camp Wildwood was a well-known place where some of the locals latched onto jobs. Those who did kinda disappeared and didn't come around anymore, so the resort had a negative image, I guess. Snobby. Crud. Go work at Wildwood and you'd no longer be one of the gang. It was kinda weird, I guess, but we knew that there was a cool bar there with some rich guests. None of us had actually ever been there, but we had heard stories. We had also been warned that the bar at Wildwood was no place for a few mountain boys to be hangin' out. The clientele was not into seeing the locals. We had enough to drink that night so that it didn't much matter to us one way or the other how others felt. We felt that we had the right to visit a bar in our neighborhood.

"Although I was plenty drunk, I still remember my first moments at Camp Wildwood. The lawns were perfectly cut, the lake lay like a silver mirror in the drawing darkness, and festive lights blazed on the patio and deck outside the lodge. It was like Christmas in the summer. As I walked up to the doors of the lodge, I felt as if I truly was at some big-time resort like ya see in the papers. Jamaica. Aruba. Hawaii. Yep, it was only Moon Lake, but it seemed magical to me. I had probably already been caught in the place's web, but I didn't know it yet. We walked into the lodge, and I was amazed by the natural wood interior and the stone fireplace. There was nothing in my neighborhood like this, and I was impressed. But what impressed me the most was Colin. The guy didn't seem put off by a few off-color locals in his bar but instead opened his arms. I liked the guy immediately. He offered me a job that night, and I laughed but knew that this was my opportunity.

"Yes, Meredith. Your father was a remarkable man. A better boss I never had. He took my losin' ass in and made me feel I had worth. Certainly there were bad times, but the times we shared up here at the resort were sweet. After a few summers, I had gained the man's trust, and he left most of the physical chores around the property to me and my workers.

"I'll tell ya…as much as I love this lake…there's times when I look out over the water and it creeps me out, ya know? Kinda like when for a split second you think you seen a ghost. Even on the most beautiful days, I could get that feeling like something just ain't right. Had it a couple of times in Nam when we'd be bushwhacking some trail in the jungle and I would get the creeps. More times than not there was a booby trap or some crud just ahead. Weird, I guess. I think most critters have a sense of danger somehow in their genes. I guess I just have some critter in me.

"That one fall 1988 that Colin referred to in his log, I remember that well. The resort was closed up. Back then, Colin always tried to push the season as late as we could. I'm pretty sure it wasn't about money but more of a pride thing. He tried to stay open until after Columbus Day that fall, and it was messy. We had a couple freezes, and the plumbing didn't like it. Then we had some cruddy weather… snow, sleet, and that damn cold rain that you can't do anything in. Only a couple of cabins were booked, so he finally pulled a plug on the season. It took us three days with old Jeremy Planter to close up the place. Raft, dock, boat all needed to come out of the lake. Pipes needed to be drained and pressurized to get any pesky pools out of the lines. Screens…well, ya all get the idea. We finished finally on a snowy Wednesday with flakes the size of quarters coming down. Ya could almost feel them hit your head they were so big. Colin handed me his flask of whiskey, which he always seemed to have handy, and we drank. He then got into his car and drove off into the snow, leaving me alone by the lake. Those moments were always hard and lonely for me. The season was over, and I was there by myself. Alone. It was too early to head for Gore Mountain where I spent my winter grooming ski hills at night. I went home instead and tried to come down after a long summer.

"The quake shook the neighborhood a week later, around Halloween. It wasn't a big one, although the rumor was that it really shook hard up near Moon Lake. I knew what that meant and steered clear of the resort for a few weeks and hoped everyone else would too. I knew that folks wandered in there on the resort property in the off season, even though it's posted and there's a chain across the road. Usually it's no big deal except when the stone wakes up. I waited a few weeks before I went back. It was just before Thanksgiving, actually. Was gonna have dinner with my sister—I was unattached at the time—and then I would head over to North Creek when they started making snow at the hill. A few weeks had passed since the quake, so

I figured it would be fine. I did find five deer. They were on this side of the lake and along the western edge. It looked as if every one of them had had their insides ate out. All that I found was a husk of what was once a prized animal. It was pretty ugly. I found the bear over on the other side near Davey's. It looked like the bear had put up a brawl because the brush had been trampled and its head…well, its head had come loose from its body. Like the others, its insides had been eaten. No wolf or bobcat was going to do that to a bear. I knew then what had happened, and the thought made me feel like I'd seen that ghost again. I looked out over the waters of the lake, at that point covered with a thin layer of early winter ice. Calm and silvery. Somethin' bad lay under that ice, and it scared me, I might admit. I went to my sister's, ate her turkey, and left for Gore, unsure if I wanted to return in the spring."

"But you did," Liza said. "Why did you come back?"

Thomas looked at her with eyes that showed strained emotion. "Because this is my home."

The words hit Liza hard. It had to be a local thing because she felt exactly the same way. That was why she hadn't jumped in her car and left with the others. She was already tied to the resort. Scary.

Davey was leaning back in his chair in deep thought. Pete stood and grabbed Thomas's glass.

"Need another?"

Thomas nodded. "I think I'll need it to get through the next part."

The group was quiet as Pete slipped off behind the bar. Liza had certainly heard stories about Moon Lake. *Don't go to the lake, or the lake monster will get you.* She had heard it all, and for a kid, it sure worked. She never considered sneaking up to the lake, even later when she realized that parents had made up the story to keep their kids from wandering off and getting drunk in the woods around the lake. She did recall one night when she was eleven or so. She asked her mother and her mother's boyfriend du jour about the Moon Lake monster. Her mother had looked at her and quietly told her to not mention it. That had been weird and created more questions than answers. But right then and there, as she sat in the Camp Wildwood

Lodge with the thing over the water, she knew why her mom had answered the way she had. It wasn't a fictional story, and the people in Mayson knew the truth.

Liza was thrust from the temporary comfort of the quiet bar when the small engine noise from the lake began again. The black hole was waking up, and who knew what dreadfulness it was about to unleash. Pete had already dashed from the bar and was looking out the window.

"Holy shit," he muttered. Davey and Dan reached the window just before Liza got there. Even before she could see the vista outside, she noticed light that strobed across the water. There was no natural light, and it looked like a fog had formed over the water. The reason that they could see anything at all was because the black hole was alive. Sparks and fingers of electricity danced in the circle immediately surrounding the hole. What they were looking at was a perfectly round arc of electricity that delineated the disk. It had become animated, and if experience had taught them anything, that meant that something was about to get zapped.

"What is it after?" Davey asked. "I don't see a thing."

"Oh no," Meredith moaned next to Liza. "It must be the Winsor kids. Those poor children sitting alone in that cabin without their parents. My heart is breaking."

Liza looked toward the cabins, expecting to see some roly-poly kid waddling toward the beach much as their parents had done. The lighting was poor and resembled the indirect light at a bizarre fireworks show. There was no one walking on the beach or the lawn.

"I don't see anything," she whispered.

"I don't see anything either," Davey agreed. "This could be an ominous trend."

As quickly as the sound had started, it stopped, and the electrical arc around the disk shut off. The lake was plunged into complete darkness and silence. Not even a breeze ruffled any leaves.

"What?" Meredith screamed. "What happened? What is going on?"

Pete moved next to her and put his arm around her shoulders. Meredith stopped yelling, which was good because Liza couldn't handle her freaking out. They didn't need that at the moment. It was Dan that spoke the same question, only more calmly.

"What just happened?"

Davey let out a breath. "It just stopped. My hope is that it didn't find what it sensed. I just hope…"

Davey fell silent, and the others all looked at him. It appeared that he thought better of finishing.

"Hope what?" Dan asked, suddenly sounding a little shrill. "Hope what, Davey?"

"Hope it's not feeling us out," Pete answered for Davey. The men looked at each other, and Liza got an uncomfortable feeling that they both understood something significant the others didn't.

"Feeling us out?" Liza asked, suddenly needing to understand as well.

Davey sighed. "It's sitting there over the lake. The real question is, why is it there? Maybe when we sit back down and let Thomas finish his story, we might learn a little more. We do know that when the disk has appeared before, it has left at some point. What determines its length of stay? Maybe it has a preset clock and has a certain amount of time it can exist at the surface. Then again, maybe it wakes up to satisfy some need. I have a disturbing feeling that the truth is within the latter."

Davey looked at Thomas, who was the only one still seated back at the table. They had all momentarily forgotten that they were in the middle of Thomas's story about the history of the legend of Moon Lake. Pete slid away from Meredith to the bar and finished making Thomas his drink while the rest made their way back to the seats that they had so recently left.

"Thomas," Davey asked, sitting back in his chair again, "is there something the black hole needs?

"I don't know," Thomas answered bluntly, grabbing the drink from Pete. "But I think it comes to the surface to feed." He continued.

"I did return to the resort the next year. Time away at Gore grooming the trails in the dark nights was weird enough. The uneasiness I felt about Moon Lake became less intense as I spent more time away. When the sun got higher in the sky and the days began to warm, I began to get excited to get back to the lake as I do every year. The idea of not returning never really crossed my mind. As I always do, I took a brief vacation to Myrtle Beach in early April and recharged my batteries. Only days after having my toes in the sand, I found myself enterin' the access road to the resort for the first time since fall.

"It was the same every spring. Rotting snow lay in drifts in the same spots. Ice still floated around the water, although some years were worse than others. The first thing I accomplished every year was simply cleaning up the debris left by the winter—branches, leaves, and the occasional unlucky critter. I would actually spend nights in my room, even though I had not hooked up the water yet. Tough when I had to take a crap, I'll tell you. That summer, 1993, had begun beautifully. The winter retreated quickly, and solid spring weather set right in during April and May. I got a lot of stuff done before Colin showed up, and we could have opened immediately. I think both of us expected having a banner year. The year would be anything but, I'll tell ya.

"It almost seemed as if the season was jinxed from the get-go. We opened a couple of weeks before Memorial Day, and it rained for right on a week. I remember sitting down by the lifeguard chair watching the water rise in the lake. It was only a couple of feet higher than normal, but out here, that's huge. The few guests we had... well, I guess they got a little cabin fever, and a couple of groups actually had a fight. Yeah, a fight here at Camp Wildwood. It was two groups of kids celebrating the end of their college year, but still, sittin' inside all day with nothing but booze to keep you interested was a bad mix. Early in June, a fire caught in one of the cabins. Nothing was damaged too seriously from a structure standpoint. Nothin' that some new boards and paint couldn't fix, but the smell of smoke was a devil to remove. Crud. I heard someone yell fire, and we all ran from dinner in the lodge and put it out right quick. Never did find out what started it, although Colin figured it was arson. Those were interesting times. Seemed there was always someone pissed off at us. Environmentalists, other businesses, jealous locals. You name it and there was some grudge. I thought someone had tossed a cigarette

275

butt where they shouldn't have, but that was just my opinion. The truth was, we had another incident that made me nervous.

"What really made me uneasy was the lake itself. There were times that summer when I was just sitting looking out over the water and that old bad feeling came up on me. Goosebumps, chills. The whole bit. Even on sunny, bright days, something always seemed... off."

"Did you ever get that feeling this summer?" Davey asked Thomas as he stared at the older man reliving a disturbing piece of his past. The question was quick and blunt. Thomas took a moment and considered it, looking at Davey the entire time.

"It's hard to say, Davey. Some days yes, I did, but I often just figured it was bad feelings left over from the summer of 1993. Most days, when I looked out at the water, it was just a beautiful piece of Mother Nature. I know that isn't what you want to hear."

Pete nodded. "No, Thomas, we need all the information we can get. I'm wondering if the stone had some kind of psychic energy or something."

"Doubt it," Davey said with a smile as he leaned back in his chair again. "It isn't logical. And Jeanne and I lived almost right over that thing for decades, and I never got the reaction Thomas did. I always thought the legend was some concocted piece of shit story that some local Indian once told that got blown out of proportion. That happens, you know. Go visit Loch Ness or Roswell."

Liza shifted in her chair as a feeling of discomfort swept her, more from the images in her head than from the actual pain in her ass. "Maybe it's because Thomas knew something was out there. The brain can do weird things."

They all looked at her, and she suddenly felt foolish for speaking out to this group, which included a college professor and a private school teacher. The good news was that they all considered her idea, but no return comments were made.

"Wait a minute." Pete quickly spoke, and all heads turned to him. "Davey, you lived here then. I mean, the next summer was my first one here because they needed a new lifeguard. But you owned your cabin for decades. You must have seen something."

Davey nodded and smiled. "Yes, I would have. The problem was that I did spend June at the cabin once the academic year at Syracuse was over, but Jeanne and I took a sabbatical, and we traveled to Italy for a vacation and some research. We didn't return until August, and classes at SU started quickly after. It seems odd but true. I was out of the country."

"What happened in July?" Meredith asked. She looked very nervous and agitated. That could certainly be justified in the current circumstances. "Thomas, could you continue."

The groundskeeper nodded and spoke again.

"July had been fine. I mean, the weather was perfect and we had great guests. From the last weekend in June through the Fourth, the resort was booked with visitors. I could tell that Colin was just thrilled with the potential profit. Things were going pretty good for him at that point. As I recall, Meredith…you were up for the Fourth weekend. Thank God you left right after, just before all hell broke loose.

"If my mind serves me right, it was the eighth of July when it happened. To answer the question I know you're gonna ask, the earth did quake. As I recall, the shaking wasn't nearly as severe as it was today, and most folks thought it was fun. The guests, they were yelling and carrying on like it was a circus. Then the center of the lake turned black, and the disk rose, just like today. I've been thinkin' about it a little. We always assumed that the stone in the lake just rumbled when it 'woke up' and that it was random. After Dan's story, I do believe that something had to disturb it. I don't know what it could have been that day. A fish? Maybe someone had snuck over to Davey's side of the lake to swim and had gone down too far. Don't know but I believe that somethin' happened. The fact was, the disk had come back, and there were guests at the lake. We were unprepared, and that's for sure. This was a first time with people, and it was horrible.

"The first few minutes were bad, real bad. The disk zapped—or whatever you call it—the first guest right away. The man was in a canoe out off the beach a piece, maybe three hundred yards. Luckily he was by himself, and I mean totally by himself. He was renting a room in the lodge all alone. If I recall, his name was Jeremy or something, and he was here 'to get away for a bit,' as he said. There was somethin' more to his story, but we never figured it out. The disk had risen from the water and almost immediately began to make that noise. I have to say that I have been haunted many times in my dreams by that sound. The circle began to spin, and the pulse of light flashed out and hit the guy in the canoe. The whole thing lasted only a couple of seconds, and the light retracted into the disk. An eerie silence fell over the water when the disk calmed down. The beach was an odd place, I'll tell ya. I honestly don't think most folks knew what the heck had happened. Most people looked over the lake like they had just watched a rocket launch or spectacular fireworks complete with oohs and ahs. There was pointing and conversation, and the canoe drifted out on the water. Jeremy was slumped over as if he could have been taking a nap. They didn't know what had happened, but I did. I had seen the deer, I had seen the bear, although there was no way of telling and I sure as crud wasn't about to go out and check that canoe. I knew what had become of the canoeist, and my thoughts turned to my survival. I quickly began to yell to get the guests off the beach. The response was quick as fear spread through the group. Like today, they ran back into the lodge and the cabins. Luckily, most stayed inside and some left.

"That day, we turned on the old public address system and made an announcement across the resort. Colin did it, actually. When I think about it, it was completely brilliant. He explained that some malfunction had occurred with an electrical cable under the lake and that everyone needed to leave immediately due to hazardous atmospheric conditions. Refunds would follow, he promised. He said it was for their own safety, of course. The effect was huge and quick. People, I could tell they were scared, began to quickly head for their cars. Lookin' back, it's amazing that they all took off as quick as they did. Within a half hour, most of the guests had vamoosed. We knew we got lucky. I remember lookin' out over the lake and seeing that thing. Just as it is today and thinkin' that that damned Indian legend was true, no matter how hard it was to believe.

"Colin and I had a powwow right in the main room of the lodge. By then, even the help had left, and we felt pretty much alone.

We discussed the legend if I recall. Settin' there in the lodge, I felt totally protected, you know. Kinda like right now, I guess. There was brief talk about what our plan was, but we decided that we had better leave, too, locking the chain over the road as we left. It was decided that in a couple days, I would scout out the lake and see if the thing was gone. Colin planned on heading up to Saranac Lake for a couple of days until I contacted him. I packed a couple things in a bag and got ready to head for my sister's. That idea wasn't pleasant, but it was certainly better than being around here.

"Colin and I left together and were in the parking lot when we saw the guy. He was jogging across the gravel toward us, waving his damn arms like a fool. From the parking lot, I couldn't see the lake, which was good. I hated to waste any more time before I left. Well, I recognized the man as a guest who had been there a couple of times before. Married with a pretty wife, although I didn't see her at first. He was stammerin' on about some couple that refused to leave and said that the thing over the lake was a UFO or something and they weren't about to miss the historic moment when contact was made. Historic moment. Crud. Damn Hollywood put crazy-ass ideas in folks' heads. It was a moment, all right, but no history needed to be written about it. Colin asked who the couple was, and I recalled a twenty-something man and woman who had been doing a lot of drinkin' and philosophizing in the bar. UFOs. They were closer to the truth than they were probably thinkin'. Colin was saying that they had to get the couple to leave and pronto when that noise revved up again. It was loud even on the far parking lot side of the lodge. We quickly ran around the side of the building and saw the disk rotating over the water. It looked like sparks were leapin' from it, and the sound was intense, louder than today even.

"The couple was standing on the dock with a damn video camera, looking right at it. I only got a brief moment to take it all in when the pulse shot out from the disk, and the couple on the dock froze and then crumpled to the dock when the glow retracted. It was over, but it wasn't. Unlike before, the noise from the thing did not wind down but intensified. Might be hard to imagine, but I could feel the hairs on my arm begin to stand up like folks say happens just before lightning strikes. It scared the crud out of me, I'll tell ya. I didn't need to watch anymore and slid back around the building into the relative protection of the parking lot. I am no hero and I'm no fool. That was a bad place to be that day, and I then knew that I was getting out regardless of what Colin wanted. Colin and the guy were right with me, and they were just as scared as I was. That was when I noticed the man's wife. She was indeed a beauty, but the look on her face hid it. Complete terror was the best description I can give. She was standing within full view of the lake but from well into the parking lot. She had seen it all and was paralyzed like a dang statue standing there. It could probably see or sense her, and the noise was still up. It was Colin who ran across the gravel and grabbed her. I thought for sure the disk would get her too. Or maybe both of them. Somehow they made it back from the parking lot, and the noise from the disk immediately began to wind down.

"I remember we all just kinda looked at each other with a dazed expression, I guess. The man just grabbed his wife and quickly headed for his car and was gone. Unlike the other guests, he had seen quite a bit and probably understood too. I hoped he would just drive home and forget about what had happened. The wife was another story. I will never forget the look on the woman's face as she sat in the passenger's seat of their car as they pulled out of the lot. It looked like she was empty. Like a shell of a person or something. I was pretty sure that the woman would never be the same again. That face would haunt me for months to come.

"Colin and I just looked at each other. We were the last ones at Camp Wildwood, at least we hoped. We didn't say much, probably because we knew what we had to do. Colin took off, and I followed shortly. I stopped at the end of the access road and drew the chain across the drive and secured it with a padlock. A 'Closed for the Season' sign still hung from the chain 'cause I hadn't taken it off in the spring. The sign swung back and forth, and I wondered if the place was indeed closed for the season. Crud, it could've read 'closed forever.' I really wasn't sure if I would ever work there again. Some serious damage had been done."

Thomas stopped speaking, and silence fell over the tavern. Somewhere Liza heard water dripping, probably from behind the bar. She looked out the window and saw nothing but blackness and wondered where the black hole was over the lake. She knew that any hope that it was gone was nothing more than wishful thinking. Of course, it was still there. Why wouldn't it be? The story that Thomas had told was intense, but it didn't really freak her out much, probably because she had just witnessed the very same thing in the flesh. As a kid, she had definitely heard the stories, and one particular rumor spread, which made perfect sense now that she knew what had really happened at Moon Lake.

"When did you come back?" Davey suddenly asked in the quiet room.

Thomas put down the highball glass that he had just taken a drink from. "I waited about five days. Truth be told, I came up to the lake from your place. I was freakin' bored at my sister's. Finally I decided to drive around Spruce Hill and came up Davey's driveway. I walked, taking it easy. I was sweatin' rocks, I'll tell ya. With every step and every foot of elevation, I expected to get a view of the lake. I finally came around that last little bend in your driveway and saw the water. The water was glass and deep blue, especially with the green trees surrounding the lake. Anyway, the disk was gone."

The group was looking at Thomas, and Liza realized that this couldn't be the end of it. Thomas had told a long, detailed story, but it did little to help them out of the current situation. It was clear the same thought was going through all their heads.

"So," Pete spoke, "that's it? I'm not sure if we learned anything new that will gain us an edge on this thing."

"Sorry."

Davey stood up and paced across the floor like the college professor that he was. "No, it's good, Thomas. Let's digest what we know. The experience in 1993 was very similar to this one, so we have a base to draw upon. The real issue that we need to examine is, what does it take to make that damn thing go away? I assume it just returned back into the lake and into that freaking stone. What we don't know from Thomas's story is, how long does it stick around? Are we stuck here for five days, or is this nightmare almost over?"

"I guess we can't answer that," Meredith piped in. Liza looked at her and saw some animation in her face. Even though she was only eighteen and the youngster of the group, Liza understood the complexities of the brain and that having a focus was a positive way to deal with a difficult situation. That was Meredith at the moment.

Dan spoke up. "Maybe we shouldn't be thinking about this in terms of time. Maybe we should be thinking about meals."

"Meals?" Meredith asked, clearly surprised. It was Davey who quickly stopped and pointed at Dan.

"Yes," Davey exclaimed. "Meals. Go ahead, Dan."

"Well," Dan began to explain with all eyes on him. "This… thing, it stays submerged in its stone under the lake for decades at a time until it's disturbed, woken up perhaps. Maybe it comes to life to feed. It rises from the water and hunts. Deer, bear, and in the summer…humans. Perhaps we need to consider the idea that when it has finished feeding, it will return back to the depths of Moon Lake."

Another moment of silence descended on the group, and Liza thought that Dan had spoken some truth. What if the thing was simply feeding? When would it be full?

Davey sighed. "That could certainly be a possibility that we need to consider. The other consideration that we have to discuss is the source of that thing and why it's here."

Pete interrupted and for the first time showed some emotion.

"This is all bullshit! We can sit here talking semantics and try and figure out what it is or why it's out there. But…shit! We are stuck here in this damn lodge with no electricity while that thing waits out there to suck the life out of us. We need to figure out what we need to do to get the fuck out of here."

Liza stared at Pete and was surprised by the outburst. The reaction was like a slap across the collective faces of entire group around the table. Of course, they could all simply leave whenever they wanted, but they stayed. Each had a reason to cling to the lodge and face down the legend. Liza was the person who seemed to have the least amount of chain holding her there.

It was Davey who quietly answered.

"Pete," he replied calmly. "I think you are one hundred percent correct. The scientific interest that I have in this disk must be considered later. Right now, we are in self-preservation mode, and our focus needs to be survival. I guess we have two realistic options. We can wait it out or find a way to make it go away."

"Or we could just leave."

All eyes turned to the source of the voice. Thomas sat looking around the group, and his hopes were clear as ice. He wanted to leave. Liza saw some credence to that thought, but she knew that Pete and Davey had no intention of leaving this story unfinished. They wanted to solve the riddle.

"How long could we stay here in the lodge?" Liza asked, aiming the question at Meredith, hoping that the others were pondering the same thoughts.

Meredith shrugged. "We have lots of food and drinks, but without electricity, it may be hard to cook it. I suppose we could set up some type of charcoal stove. Maybe out back in the parking lot."

"Running water might be tough," Thomas inserted. "We use a pump to suck water from the well out back. We do have a backup system from the lake, but that, too, uses an electric pump."

"That means we can't flush the toilet?" Liza asked with genuine concern.

Davey spoke and smiled. "If it's yellow, let it mellow. If it's brown, flush it down."

"Gross," Liza muttered. She smiled, wanly realizing that for a moment, she was more concerned with flushing a toilet than saving her life. Although it was dark outside, she was sure she could still make it to her car. For the first time since the whole thing started, she was seriously trying to remember where her car keys were. They were in the drawer of the nightstand next to her bed. She kept them there because they were useless to her all day during her rounds, and she would probably lose them in the weeds next to one of the cabins.

"Okay," Pete spoke, holding his right hand up. "I think, although maybe uncomfortably, we can manage here for a little bit. But that makes me uneasy. For example, we don't even know if the black hole is in a static state. What if it changes and begins to move? Are we really safe in here?"

Dan nodded. "If it's here to hunt, then maybe it will begin to search for prey."

"Jesus," Meredith muttered, shaking her head. "That thought never occurred to me. I mean, what if it comes looking for us?"

"Hang on, please," Davey said, breaking in. "I think it may be a jump implying that this thing had some type of intelligence or instinctual ability."

"But we don't even know what it is," Meredith added. "What if it is some wild alien life-form that we can't comprehend? Maybe it's smarter than us. Then maybe it can move and think."

Davey was shaking his head vigorously. "I'm sorry but we need to examine this rationally with our observations only. Imagination can lead us into some seriously negative corners. For now, let's assume that it will stay the way it is."

Liza noticed out the corner of her eye that Thomas was fidgeting in his seat. She turned to look at him and saw a man who appeared very uncomfortable. The others had followed her gaze, and all were now watching Thomas squirm.

"What are you hiding, Thomas?" Meredith asked.

Thomas shook his head, and Liza could tell that he was unraveling. "No one was ever supposed to know."

"Know what, Thomas?" Meredith asked, her voice rising to a hectic pitch.

Thomas looked toward the blackened window and stared out at something that only he could see. It was clear that he was uncomfortable, and that made his knowledge even more interesting. It was obvious that the man had been holding something back.

"Out with it," Davey said forcefully.

Thomas sighed. "Colin and I swore to never tell anyone, and I've kept that promise until today. I suppose Colin did too."

"What?" Meredith demanded.

"When I finally returned—this was after I walked up the road near Davey's cabin to check the lake—I came back to the main entrance of the resort. I recall that it was a beautiful summer day with beams of light breaking through the leaves of the trees in bright shafts. It was good to be back at the resort, and I was hopin' that I would find the place ready to go, if that was possible. The chain was still across the access road, and the padlock was still in place, just as it had been when I left in such a hurry. I got out of my truck to unlock the chain and didn't even notice at first. But there on the left pole that the chain attached to was a bike. Not a fancy Lance Armstrong racing bike but a simple kid's mountain bike. Walmart probably sells 'em by the dozen every spring. The bike hadn't been thrown to the side of the road but had been placed. To say that my heart skipped a beat is like sayin' that Everest is just a mountain, ya know? Anyhow, I was pretty cautious when I started driving down the lane. It was weird. I just remember it being so beautiful, more so than I could ever remember. But my mood was so dark. I had mixed feelings about hurrying to get the resort back going again but also the nagging idea of closing once and for all. Ya know, like maybe putting a nuclear bomb in the lake and being done with it.

"I came along the road to the last bend, ya know, the one where you can see the parking lot and the lodge for the first time. I got a glimpse of the lake between the lodge and the trees. The water was calm and blue, and lying in the road was a body. It wasn't no deer or bear either. This one was wearing clothes. I actually stalled my dang truck. I never do that. Slammed on the brakes without pushing in the clutch, and the bastard stalled. Jumped too. Crud, the sight of that body really shook me. I just sat there, ya know, lookin' and unable to move. I guess I was pretty scared as to what I was about to find. With hindsight, I was right to feel that way. Probably should have just started the truck back up and thrown her in reverse and gotten out for good. But of course, instead, I opened the door and stepped out.

"It was a kid. Didn't recognize him at all, but that was understandable. It was all pretty messy. The body was on its side with the legs twisted in an unnatural position. That was bad, but what the thing had done to the body was grotesque. From the throat down to the waist, the body had been ripped open, and most of the insides were gone. Blood was everywhere. There was no surgical precision, just a rippin' out. You might wonder if I puked. I think a surgeon would have upchucked after seeing what I was lookin' at. Pretty messy but I had to investigate, ya know? I was pretty horrified to realize that I was lookin' at a kid, and although there was a lot of blood, I *did* recognize the face. The kid was from Mayson. His house was only about three miles from here. Don't even want to mention his name. The fact that I knew him drove another dagger into my stomach.

"I can tell by your faces that you wonder what I did. Well, I'll say that I wandered down the road apiece to get my wits together. That wasn't like findin' a dead woodchuck on the side of the road with its legs pointin' skyward. Finally, I kinda came around and went back to investigate. It was pretty clear that the kid had been attacked right there in the road and that the thing from the lake had done it. What I came to realize was that when I looked toward the water, all I could see was a sliver of blue on the west side of the lake."

"It moved," Pete muttered weakly. "Good God, it moved."

Thomas nodded his head slowly, eyes now pointed at the floor. The realization sank in, and each person around the bar was left with their own thoughts. Liza could not imagine the black hole moving toward the resort end of the lake. She couldn't envision it hunting. That idea was completely terrorizing, and the safety of the lodge suddenly felt feeble and thin like a tent in a thunderstorm.

"What if it's moving toward us right now?" Liza said, voicing the concern that just popped into her head. "We can't even see it."

Davey nodded solemnly. "That is a serious issue. For all we know, it could be situated right outside the door waiting for us."

"Wait," Pete jumped in. "Again, we are assuming that it has some type of intelligence. It might not even know we're here."

"Insects don't have very large brains," Davey continued. "But they are excellent hunters. Animals and plants throughout the biosphere have amazing abilities to hunt and feed, and yet very few scientists would consider these creatures intelligent. They use instinct, which is much different from intelligence. Hunger is a powerful force, and the instinct to find food is strong. All the thing out there might have is the pang of hunger and the instinct to find food."

"That's scary," Liza moaned. She had just made her mind up and she needed to find an appropriate time to sneak out to her room to get her car keys. She was out.

Meredith was still looking at Thomas, who looked like he had aged twenty years. This episode was not treating him well.

"What did you do, Thomas?" Meredith asked.

Thomas kept his head down, and it was Dan who spoke.

"Do with what?"

Meredith ignored Dan's question. "What did you do? Did my father know?"

There was a slow nod as Thomas answered positively. Liza was watching Meredith, and she could see the woman cringe slightly.

"Damn it, Thomas. What did you and my dad do with the kid's body?"

Her voice echoed loudly through the bar, and Liza wondered if the black hole could hear or sense the noise. She wanted to tell Meredith to relax and shut up, but she was intensely looking at Thomas, waiting for an answer that she probably didn't want to hear.

"Thomas?!" she yelled again. The older man raised his head.

"Buried out in the woods. Colin showed up not long after, and we decided to bury him in the woods. I took his bike and dumped it into the lake. No one knows what happened to the boy except us."

"Jesus," Davey muttered. "This is crazy."

Liza could see Meredith's eyes bore holes through Thomas, and she knew in that instant that something had been lost forever. Nothing would ever be the same.

"You…my father…," Meredith stuttered, "you knew about this boy's death and never told the kid's parents. My god."

Pete moved to Meredith but stopped, perhaps realizing that Meredith was really pissed and distance might be warranted.

"Meredith," Pete spoke quietly. "Let's go out into the dining room for a minute."

Slowly, Meredith drew her stare away from Thomas and acquiesced and followed Pete into the room that would normally just be wrapping up the evening meal. That thought made Liza realize how surreal the whole thing was. Unprecedented. There was no Google search to look for advice for removing an alien black hole that devoured animals over a mountain lake. Maybe in a year, that web page might exist, if they were actually able to solve the problem.

Davey sighed, and Thomas looked defeated. With a tip of his glass, he drained the remainder of his booze and looked around. Liza figured he was hoping Pete would get him another. That wasn't happening. Thomas was done.

"Okay," Dan said, speaking up. "We know it can move and may be doing that as we sit here. Unfortunately, as I see it, we are no closer to developing a way to deal with this thing."

Davey nodded slowly. "It seems like we are still at square one, and I fear we are only sitting ducks, waiting while the wolves advance."

Liza looked at both men and felt her first true sense of dread. Both men looked like they were ready to give up.

26

July 10, 10:55 p.m.

Josh had been struck completely immobile when he saw his mother out-side the door of the employee dorm as he went out for some air. He and Michael had been sitting and drinking in his room until the air had seemed to become denser and claustrophobia began to set in. Michael had muttered about needing to take a piss, and Josh decided to walk out-side and breathe in some fresh air in the parking lot. Michael replied that he would join him when he was done, and that was okay. Michael and he had bonded over the same pain. Josh grabbed a beer can and wan-dered down the hallway and outside where he, too, relieved his bladder against the building. He leaned his head back and took in a deep breath that had the effect of invigorating his head, which had gotten kind of fuzzy back in the room. The stars were bright overhead, the thunder-storm from earlier a distant memory. He could see the reddish light of Mars, and he remembered the nights on the dock. That had been nice. Probably the best part of his summer, and he thought about going out there but remembered the disk, and his entire body shivered. The dock was off limits. Liza had spent time on the dock with him. Whore.

When he turned from the building, his mother was standing by a cedar. Even though Josh was wasted, he stumbled backward a step. It was no doubt his mother, although she was a little blurry. But what the hell. Michael had looked a little blurry back in his room through the alcohol and candlelight. The figure of his mom stood stationary with eyes that stared straight through him.

"What the fuck?" he muttered aloud, hoping the apparition would respond, but instead his mother just stood still staring at him. She was wearing khaki shorts and a blue T-shirt with writing on the left breast. She was too far away, and his vision was poor, but he knew that it was a circle with a building in the middle and the words "New Mexico Sun House." That was the name of the hospital that she had been living in for as long as Josh could remember. The times that he had visited her, she had been wearing these shirts in a rainbow of different colors.

There was no breeze, and the night was very quiet, which made his mother's lack of animation all the more noticeable. Josh thought he heard something from back near the lodge, but he wasn't sure if it had just been his imagination, which was now obviously running amuck. He was aware that his body had broken out in gooseflesh and that his heart was racing. Josh shook his head vigorously, but his mother remained when he opened his eyes.

"What do you want, Mom?" Her arm slowly rose, and her index finger pointed in the direction of the parking lot.

"Josh, please leave."

The sound entered his brain, but he was positive that her mouth never moved. Yet the message was clear as daylight. She was telling him to get in his car and take off.

"I don't want to," he heard himself say before he could even think about it. The voice that fell from his lips sounded weak and childlike. He hated it and wanted to crush the part of him that had spoken the words. Yet they were his words, and he meant them. He didn't want to leave, although every rational thought would convince a person to turn tail and take off.

The image of his mother remained the way it had appeared when he first saw it. The lines that made up the figure never moved, and he again wondered what she was doing in the grassy area near the cedar on the side of the parking lot.

"Josh, please leave. It's back and it's…so horrible." The sound entered his brain again, and this time he had no intention of dealing with it.

"No!" Josh found himself yelling, much louder than he wanted. To his amazement, the image of his mother instantaneously disappeared. Gone. Just like that. It was as if she had never been there, and if he had been sober, it would have been clear that she hadn't been.

But the drunk and simple-minded tended to see things. Wasn't that true, he thought. Why were drunk people always talking to themselves? It was obvious. They were talking to others that the sober couldn't see. He laughed deeply, standing in the parking lot where he had just seen his mother, who was really two thousand miles away sitting in a padded chair, drooling.

"What are you freaking doing?" a voice sounded from his left side. A momentary flare of rage rushed through his head at the sudden intrusion, but he was able to subdue the impulse temporarily. He turned and saw Michael walking toward him in the growing darkness. "Who were you talking to?"

"No one," Josh muttered with a twinge of humiliation and rage. "No one. Was thinkin' out loud or something."

"Thinking about what?"

Josh squinted his eyes and thought about his mother's visitation. Her warning still rang in his ears, and he knew that what she had wanted was the logical decision to make. Just get in the car and drive as far as he could with his current state of sobriety. Things had gone terribly wrong at Camp Wildwood, and all hell was to pay. But as he considered the obvious, he glanced at the lodge and saw a very weak light flickering from a window toward the front of the building. At first, it was hardly discernable, but it was there and it meant only one thing—there were people in the lodge, and he was sure that Liza was inside the structure. The fire that had died down in his chest suddenly and strongly blazed back. He knew that bitch was still on the grounds, and he thought anew of the deceit that she had played on him. That quickly, the image of his mother and her warning was washed from his mind and completely forgotten.

"I'm thinking about that bitch."

Michael looked around. "Do you really think they're still here? I mean, it looks to me like this place has become a ghost town."

Josh pointed at the window with the weak, flickering light. "Someone is in the lodge, and you know if someone is here, Meredith is. And…I just know that Liza is here. I can feel it."

Michael staggered slightly as he turned back from the lodge and faced Josh again. He was no longer holding the whiskey bottle, which had been completely drained. The darkness had settled in, and Josh could just make out his new friend's features.

"What're you planning on doing?" he slurred toward Josh through the darkness.

Josh looked at the light in the window.

"I'm going to find that bitch and do to her what I should have last night."

Michael nodded. "I'm with you, brother." He looked around. "How?"

Josh's smile could be seen even through the darkness. "I have a gun in my car."

*****

Pete and Meredith were in the dining room alone, and Davey and Dan were talking by the bar in quiet tones that she could hear but not decipher. Thomas sat in the chair by the table where he had just exposed his long-held secret. He sat stock-still and seemed nearly comatose. That poor man was shot and might never return to anything close to normal. He looked old and would be no help. Super. Liza suddenly felt very much alone and again wondered why she was hanging around the resort when any rational person would have quit a long time earlier. That was it. The final straw had crashed down in her brain, and with that, she decided that the prudent choice was to leave. She had to face facts. Her summer job had ended. There would be no more cleaning rooms. There would be no more relaxing in the woods and chilling by the lake. There would be no more weekly paycheck that she could deposit in the bank. A watershed moment had been reached, and she didn't want to drown quite yet. She needed to buck up, eat some crow, and head home to her mom's house. It didn't have to be a permanent stay but just a brief time to organize her thoughts and future. The mountains no longer played into them. Florida sounded pretty good. She had some uncle who lived down there, and that might be far enough to escape the memories of this summer.

Once the decision had been accepted, it was amazing how quickly she moved. Fluidly, she stood and walked out the archway of the bar and into the main room of the lodge. She was sure that no one even paid any attention as she slipped out. She wondered when they would even realize that she had taken off. Well, that was fine. They could stay behind and try and figure out a way to fight an evil that couldn't be fought. There was a good chance that they might not all make it to see another day. She would. It was madness, and as she moved away, relief spread through her.

The main room was unusually dark, making the bar seem well lit in the electricity-less darkness. Her forward momentum wavered slightly as she moved into the room, but her feet continued forward. There was a candle flickering on the main desk, and she remembered a flashlight that was stored below the computer that Kristen used to check guests into the resort. She moved as quickly across the room as she could in the partial light, avoiding the furniture partly by memory. With the flashlight clutched in her hand, she made her way toward the back of the lodge and the door that opened onto the parking lot. The back hallway was dark, and thousands of shadows moved as she played the flashlight from wall to wall as she slowly made her way toward the back door. She wished she could go straight for her car instead of having to go to her room. At that point, she could give two craps about her clothes, but she needed her car keys, and there were a couple of personal items that she really wanted to take with her. There was no way she was leaving some of the pictures she had brought with her behind. The hallway was freaky, and she was sure that something was waiting for her in every shadow.

She arrived at the door to the parking lot and hit the crash bar that opened the exit. The flashlight flared in her face when her hands were knocked around from the impact with the door. The door swung open. Quickly, Liza turned the beam away from her face and into the parking lot. Great, the light had ruined her night vision, and that was something that she needed as she walked out into the darkness. And it was dark. Real dark. There were stars above, but the moon was in the first quarter and wouldn't rise until much later. The beam of the flashlight created a bright patch of light, but the darkness around it appeared that much darker and gloomier. That was freaking her out. Slowly her eyes adjusted to the darkness, and she could begin to make out shapes in the dark outside the light beam.

"Great," she muttered to herself and carefully made her way down the wooden back steps of the lodge. Gravel crunched under her sneakers. That brought a swift realization to her that was like a slap. She wasn't wearing her normal flip-flops but she still had on her work sneakers. They were comfortable and perfect for a day of cleaning. Liza had cleaned her last room nearly five hours earlier, and she had yet to change. The awareness of why she was in the predicament she was in struck home, and she picked up her pace. She really needed to be headed for Mayson and right quick. As she accelerated, the flashlight began to jiggle more in her hand, and the action of the light seemed to make everything move from light to shadow. At one point, her breath caught in her throat, as she was positive that something moved in the parking lot to her right. That propelled her to a near jog as she beelined for the door to the dorm. She passed the large cedar that guarded the entrance and threw the door open.

The flashlight brightly illuminated the hallway, which was a bit of a relief. She had conjured images of a darkened hallway with ghouls lying in wait like from some Stephen King novel. With a few strong strides, Liza was unlocking the door to her dorm room. *It would be the last time*, she thought dimly. The door swung open, and the flashlight filled the space. It looked just at it had when she came in after lunch to change her sweaty work shirt. She briefly peeked over her shoulder, and the hallway behind her was pitch-black. Goosebumps leapt forth on her arms.

"Move, Liza," she mumbled.

She placed the flashlight on her dresser and began to shove clothes into the bag that she had brought with her the first day she had moved into the room. That moment had been one of the happiest that she could remember, moving off on her own for the first time in her life. Now she was hurrying home with her tail between her legs. But was that really her fault? Who on God's green earth would have imagined that that thing would pop out of the lake? After she shoved the last bra into the bag, she turned, and a pure scream of fright burst from her lungs. There was someone in the room with her. The bag dropped to the floor, and Liza couldn't move a muscle. That was until she realized that she was looking at her own reflection in the mirror across the room over her desk. The very same mirror she had brushed her hair in that morning.

"Shit." Liza bent over, picked up the bag, and grabbed a couple of things from her night table next to the single bed. In a smooth movement, she turned back and grabbed the flashlight, relief spreading over her. Okay, now she could leave, and the feeling was like waking from a particularly bad nightmare. "Let's get out of here."

The caution that she had moved with when she had left the lodge had slipped away and was replaced by a manic urge to get out of the parking lot as quickly as possible. Never closing the door behind her as she moved from the dormitory, Liza swept the flashlight across the parking lot until the glow illuminated her car. It was sitting where it had been for the last week, very close to the lodge. She had never seen the parking lot as empty as it was at that moment with only a handful of cars splattered across the space. That was good, she supposed. Most of the guests had escaped. She wondered which one was Bernie Winsor's.

Nearly trotting, she quickly closed the distance to her car like a football player running for the end zone. Her car was there. Familiar. Safe. The old beater looked like an old friend that would whisk her away from the place gone bad.

In the partial light on the edge of the flashlight beam, something moved, and in a nanosecond, she knew that this was no trick of the light. This shadow had substance. Even though her brain processed the information exceedingly quick, she was still not fast enough to react. She never made it to her car.

27

July 10, 11:51 p.m.

Two things immediately registered with her: raging power and the strong scent of alcohol. Through the confusion and terror that swept her, she felt an odd sense of relief that this was not the black hole over the lake attacking her. It was something else, and she comprehended that this might actually be more of a threat to her than that thing over the water.

"Got you, you fuckin' bitch."

The voice was slurry and obviously drunken, but she immediately recognized the owner. Josh. He hadn't left with everyone else when things had gone wrong. He had stayed, and from the early data, he had spent the last few hours drinking heavily.

"Josh?" she said shakily. "What the hell are you doing?"

He shook her hard, and her upper and lower teeth slammed together, registering a wave of pain in her jaw.

"What am I doing? What am I doing? Ha! I'm doing what I should have done weeks ago. I'm gonna teach you about respect. Yeah, respect."

Liza felt a sharp pain, worse than any she had ever experienced in her shoulder. The cause was her right arm being cranked up her back. Josh was incredibly strong, and there was no way that she was going to overpower him. That allowed her to understand the gravity of her situation. The black hole had fallen from her mind, and her only concern became the plan that Josh had for her.

"Josh…" It was all she could get out before he began to drag her toward the picnic table behind the lodge. Her mind began to weave together the likely scenario, and it terrified her. "No, Josh. Please."

"Oh yeah," he growled. "You know it, bitch. I'm finally gonna give you what you wanted but were too fucked up to ask for. Damn cocktease. You'll learn."

She was rapidly being shoved toward the picnic table. Bizarrely, images of lunches enjoyed during her break with some of the other employees crossed her mind. It was here where she had enjoyed a sandwich and yogurt that she would be raped. They always say that the majority of rapes are committed by an acquaintance. That seemed too true at the moment. But like an enraged animal, she began to fight back. This image of what was about to happen on the table was too much to accept. Uncontrolled terror was taking over, and she began to twist and squirm spastically in any attempt to break loose. The motions were useless as Josh increased his grip like a boa constrictor. Like any caught prey, Liza slowly began to stop her struggles, acknowledging the inevitable.

The flashlight was long gone, but Josh seemed to have perfect vision in the darkness. He twisted her around and gave a push. Liza felt her butt smack up against the edge of the picnic table.

"Please, Josh. No."

Josh did not respond with words but instead began to roughly fumble with the button that cinched closed her shorts. Oh no, this was going to happen, and one of her worst fears was getting realized. She began to struggle again, hitting him in the head now with free hands. Josh seemed oblivious to her attack.

"Come on," a new voice said from out of the fog that had been growing around her. "Come on, Josh. Don't do that now. What about my bitch?"

Liza suddenly realized that someone else was there, standing off to her left near the door to the lodge. The voice was familiar because of the distinguishable accent. She knew it was Meredith's friend from North Carolina. Michael.

"Not now," Josh growled, sounding more like a wild animal than human. "Later."

"No," Michael said calmly. "Now."

Liza was shocked when Josh's grip and manic movements abruptly ceased. Josh slowly backed away from her, and the tension now lay between Josh and Michael. Liza reached down to rebutton her pants but found that Josh had torn the button off. Super.

"We need to take care of our business right now. Then we can leave and do whatever we want with the girls. That will be superb, but for now, we need to take care of a couple of problems."

"Right," Josh answered, not beaten but determined. "Let's take care of business."

It was then that Liza understood the reason Josh had so willingly stopped his advances on her. In the gloom, she could see that Michael held a handgun in his hand that he was just lowering from Josh's general direction. A gun. Holy shit, was this day going to get any crazier. Josh grabbed her again and pulled her toward the back door of the lodge.

"We'll have our time later, bitch, but right now, don't forget who has the gun. Don't say a word, or I'll rip you apart."

Liza didn't respond but allowed herself to be driven back into the lodge, the very building that she had escaped from only minutes before. This was insane, and she was sure that there was no Disney ending in sight.

*****

For one of the only times that he could remember, Pete had been deserted without any answers. He had always prided himself with the ability to analyze a situation and quickly come up with a solution. Sometimes those solutions weren't the best, especially when they were arrived at through a haze of alcohol. But for the most part, he was a quick thinker on his feet. That was what made him a great teacher and coach. You had to have those skills if you wanted to survive in a classroom. But as he sat in the bar, there was no inspiration to save the day.

They had all resorted to sitting with their own thoughts, and he only imagined what each was thinking. Thomas sat motionless with a faraway look in his eyes. Pete was pretty sure that he had checked out already. Meredith was in a similar state. He had taken her away for a bit to allow her to try and come to grips with the knowledge that her father had known about this whole issue and had covered it up, including the deaths of people. It had been the boy that had really affected her. He was pretty sure that she hadn't come to grips yet, but he could only do so much for her in that instant. Davey and Dan seemed to have their shit together, although both seemed to be in the same boat as he was. Davey sat in a chair by the window, looking pensively at the table and occasionally glancing out the window into the darkness. Dan was rubbing his hands together at the table. Pete had no idea what that man was thinking. It seemed like ages since he had lost his wife, but it had been just hours.

They had briefly rehashed everything and had come up with no strategy on how to react to the black hole. Nothing made sense, and every action seemed like a death wish. The scariest idea was that the thing might eventually move and actually hunt them down. A dangerous game. Although they had no idea how it sensed its prey, Pete felt fortunate that the electricity was off because at least that dulled visual and thermal contacts. There was only one option, and it seemed that the girl had already taken it.

Liza was gone. When they realized that Liza was indeed missing, Meredith had begun to freak out again, but Pete quickly calmed her. The black hole had not revved up as it did before it killed its victims, so the good news was that Liza had probably escaped. That was their option, too, and when the realization struck that Liza had indeed vamoosed, that choice became pretty popular. But Meredith did not want to leave the resort. So he had to stay, and the others did as well. That was where they were. A silent group waiting for something terrible to happen.

"I don't hear anything." Davey spoke evenly. "I mean, usually at night, you hear a loon or a goose. There are coyotes and raccoons that make a racket from time to time. All kinds of birds. But tonight, I hear silence. Even the critters know that this is a hunker down moment. Instinct is an important lifesaving tool that the animals have. We have it, too, but we humans think too much. It throws off our natural instincts."

"What are you saying?" Dan asked.

Davey shrugged. "I don't know. Maybe we're doing exactly the right thing. Maybe we should just be hunkering down and not moving. Why do we have this mentality that we have to make it go away? That is so human. You don't see bears out there in rowboats trying to fight this thing. They wait it out. We should wait it out. Some deer or other good-sized animal will stumble into the black hole's path, and it will eat, hopefully fill up, and go back from where it came."

"But it will still be there," Meredith muttered.

"Yes," Davey replied. "But so will we, and self-preservation is another instinct that I think we should all be putting at the top of our lists at the moment."

The silence fell over the room again. Loons, raccoons, gulls, even the crickets were taking a break. There were normally all kinds of night noises, but they were all shut off. Silence. It reminded him of a cold winter day with no sounds but the wind. Hunker down. That strategy made sense and had a calming effect on him. That was the easy route to take. No action. No chances of facing the dragon toe to toe. Maybe there was little chance to be a hero, which was good because the heroes often died. Most were Hollywood fabrications, anyway. Perhaps it was best to just relax and wait this whole catastrophe out.

That was when he heard the bang from somewhere back in the lodge, and his heart jumped into his throat.

"What was that?" Dan nearly screamed, his head now up and alert. All of the group was now looking through the archway of the bar and into the main room of the lodge. The candle and battery-powered camp lights dully illuminated the room, creating more shadows than light. There was another noise, this one more like a dragging sound with an occasional thump. It was clear that something was in the building, and that just changed the game dramatically. The black hole appeared to just hover, but did they really know enough about it to be completely safe? Did it have the ability to hunt? Was there some way that a portion of the thing could break off to search for food? Anything was possible. Maybe it could take the form of Abraham Lincoln and walk into the room reciting the Gettysburg Address. If someone was to tell him at lunch that some black hole thing was going to pop out of the lake and start eviscerating people, then he would have called them crazy. Well, crazy was ruling the day. Perhaps he was about to meet President Lincoln.

"Pete?" Meredith muttered, her hands digging into his fore-arms. He looked at Davey and saw a man immobile. Davey, too, was a thinker, and he probably had just reached his conclusion to hunker down and felt safe for the first time all day. That wasn't going to work if the thing was hunting them inside the lodge and terror again reigned supreme.

Pete stood. The idea of being a hero wasn't his cause, but he did feel like he needed to protect Meredith. He would see what was making the noise, suddenly wishing he had some kind of a weapon. Absently, he grabbed the vodka bottle from the bar that he had been pouring into Thomas's glass. Not much but he felt better holding it. With tentative steps, he moved into the archway of the bar and looked into the main room of the lodge. It looked huge in the eerie light. It would be perfect for a spooky Halloween party, but this was neither the time nor the place.

"Let's move into the room," Davey said from his right. Pete realized that Davey and Dan had joined him and that Meredith was also following. There were many shadows around the edges of the room, and Pete stepped out to get a better look. His vision focused on the hallway that led to Meredith's office and the kitchen farther back. The shadows there had shapes. He was about to call out, but another voice ripped out across the room.

"Look out, Pete!"

Everything slowed down. He knew the voice was the girl's, Liza, and he knew he was in trouble. But it was too late. There was no time to react. The gunshot tore through the room.

28

July 10, 11:17 p.m.

The two bodies hit the floor at what seemed like the same instant. It was hard for Davey to tell exactly because there was a shock factor that blurred his ability to absorb the scenario. He noticed the figures lurking in the hallway about the same time that Pete had, and then he had heard Liza scream. It had to be Liza, and he wondered momentarily why she was with these shadowy forms. And who were the individuals these forms belonged to? Then two things happened in the odd twilight of the lodge almost simultaneously—one of the figures turned and punched Liza in the face, and a gunshot blasted through the space of the main room. The girl fell like a sack of wet potatoes, and there was an odd *thump* sound next to him. He heard Pete gasp with an expulsion of air, and then he collapsed to Davey's immediate left. Two people down and a bunch of people with ringing ears.

An odd stillness followed the gunshot, and no one moved, all looking around in a strange calm that belittled the moment. Davey felt his mind move in slow motion. He looked at Michael whose mouth was frozen in a gaping O. His arm holding the gun had dropped to his side, and he looked like a man who did something and didn't truly understand the consequences until it was too late. Josh stood next to him, looking down at Liza with a maniacal look in his eyes. He recalled the pleasant boy who wandered by his cabin with Liza only a week earlier and could not grasp what had changed in the guy's demeanor. He continued to turn his head and looked down at Pete. Pete's face was scrunched up in agony, and a stain of blood was blooming through his shirt over his right shoulder. The bullet had actually found its target, and Pete was wounded. Unbelievable.

"What the hell?!" Meredith suddenly screamed and knelt down next to Pete. Her cry was what stopped the feeling of slow motion for Davey, and reality crashed back around him in that instant. This was a situation that needed some immediate attention.

"Why?" Pete muttered over and over from the floor, sounding a little like Nancy Kerrigan. It was a good question, although Davey assumed most of those present knew the obvious answer. Jilted lover. Booze. A gun. Classic television drama, but instead of Michael looking satisfied with his revenge, he instead looked like he was going to puke. That was when Dan slid up and hit him over the head with the bottle.

Davey hadn't noticed Dan's movement. He hadn't even remembered that Dan was in the lodge once the chaos erupted. The whole episode couldn't have elapsed for more than thirty seconds, but it felt like a two-hour movie. Dan came in smooth and quick from Davey's right with a bottle of what looked like Captain Morgan's over his head. The blow was precise and aimed well. The bottle, which was half full of rum, made solid contact just behind the crown of Michael's skull. The sound it made was a solid crack, and Michael went down, much as Liza had only moments before. Davey again thought of instinct and realized that Dan was probably operating on that purely. Instinct would take over again quickly because as Michael collapsed to the floor, the handgun he was holding slipped from his fingers and bounced once on the hardwood floor before coming to rest only a few feet away from them. Right in the middle. There it was. A simple gun but a weapon that controlled all the power in this suddenly critical situation. Instinct was winning the race against reason, and Davey felt his muscles coiling to dive out across the floor to gain control of the firearm. It had to be done, and he was ready, even if his old muscles and bones didn't like it.

Unfortunately, his old body reacted as an old body does. It moved slowly. Before Davey could really make a movement toward the gun, Josh deftly reached down and snatched it from the floor and pointed it at Dan, who in turn comically put his hands in the air and quickly took a few steps backward as if about to be arrested. It appeared that the bad guy again had the upper hand.

"Okay," Josh muttered to all. "Everyone, calm the hell down. Liza, stand up."

The girl still looked slightly stunned, but Davey was pretty sure that she was still hugging the floor for safety sake and not because she was wounded too severely. But anyone who crushed a girl like that in the jaw was a first-class douchebag, and Davey felt an anger growing inside of him that he hadn't felt in a long time.

"Freakin' clusterfuck is what we have here. Michael?" Josh bent over slightly and used a sneaker-clad foot to poke at his fallen comrade. There was no movement. For all they knew at the moment, the blow to Michael's head may have been fatal.

"Why did he shoot Pete?" Meredith asked with a quiver in her voice. She was losing it, and Josh laughed. Davey understood that he was very drunk, and Michael was probably in a similar state, if he was still in any state.

"Why?" He chuckled. "Why? You are one dumb bitch. Seriously? Here he is, your *boyfriend*, and he comes up here to be with *you* and instead finds you all lovey-dovey with the lifeguard. Classy shit. I probably would have shot him too."

Josh raised the gun again and pointed it at Pete. Pete put his hand up in front of his face as if that would stop a .38 caliber bullet traveling faster than the speed of sound. Instead of shooting, Josh just laughed and moved the gun away, obviously enjoying the power that he had just discovered.

"You women, you just think you can fuck around with a guy's head and it's all okay. Well, it's not! Bullshit. A guy can't even look at a girl funny without being accused of horrible shit, but a woman can cheat with whoever she wants and it's all right. She can drag a guy along and then shut the fucking door right in his face!"

Josh turned and looked at Liza, and Davey didn't need a degree in relationship counseling to understand that something bad had recently gone down between the two. What a mess. It wasn't like there was some alien force outside waiting to devour them all at the moment. Now they had to deal with drunken, dismissed lovers set on revenge. Wonderful.

Liza had a small stream of blood descending from her lip. "It wasn't meant to be, Josh. We're too different."

He looked at her deeply. "'Too different.' Interesting. We are both stuck up here in the middle of nowhere. We both want each other, but we are too *different*. That's a complete load of bullshit."

Liza shrugged, and that movement did absolutely nothing to calm Josh but instead seemed to only make him angrier. Not good.

"Josh," Davey said as calmly as he possibly could. "You make some good points, and we need to discuss this. Put the gun down and let's talk this out."

Josh's smile faded quickly and was replaced by a visage of rage. "No, I will not talk. This whole thing is screwed up and over. This season is over. I'm going to be headed home but not until I get what I need."

He had a tight grip on Liza's arm and pulled her forward while the gun waved at the crew standing by the side, watching the show. The girl fought slightly, but Josh was able to effortlessly drag her across the room while everyone watched. Davey knew that something wicked was about to transpire, and instinct took over.

"Where are you taking her?" he asked, taking a step forward that made him feel more committed.

Josh stopped and looked at him. "I'm taking her outside away from you all. I'm taking her to the place where we first met and bonded. Gonna break her in. I'm going to have sex with her on that very spot, and she will enjoy it." Josh turned to Liza, and Davey could see that the girl knew exactly what he had in mind. The look was mad terror. But Davey also knew that there was a difference in her look of fear. It was not based in what Josh was planning on doing to her. It seemed that Josh was totally oblivious to what was outside hovering over the water. Leaving the relative safety of the lodge was pure suicide, and yet he was dragging her into this danger zone so he could rape her. It was insanity.

"Josh," Davey said slowly, "don't go out there."

Josh laughed. "Shut the fuck up, old man."

He yanked on Liza's arm harder and hauled her across the floor of the lodge. Davey slowly followed, feeling totally impotent.

29

July 11, 12:01 a.m.

His grip was brutally powerful, and she had no way to stop the force that drew her to the very place that had been her nightmare for the last few hours. It was clear that Josh was dragging her outside and had forgotten why being outside was bad. He had said that he wanted to take her to the place where they bonded. That could only mean one place—the dock. The dock had been where they had gone to talk. It was the focal point of their relationship. It also jutted out into the water where the black hole hovered like some horrendous, incomprehensible force. To go out there meant death. The specter of going outside into the sight of the black hole was terrifying.

"Josh," she muttered. "Don't take me outside. Let's go back to my room."

They reached the double doors that led out onto the porch and patio, and Josh actually hesitated for an instant. For a second, she thought a moment of levity crossed through the drunken haze, but it didn't take hold.

"Don't be scared," he leered at her. "You'll enjoy this."

"Let's do it in my room. It will be more comfortable."

He shook his head. "It's meant to happen on the dock."

She was about to be pulled from the safety of the lodge into the face of insanity. The whole concept of what was happening was so maddening that she felt herself getting frustrated. With a burst that she didn't know existed, she tilted her head back and let loose a primal scream of anguish.

"You're going to enjoy this, I guarantee."

Liza shook her head in vain protest. "Let's go back inside. Please!"

Josh laughed and pulled her across the deck and down the stairs to the grassy lawn. Liza stumbled down the stairs and almost fell, but the power of his grip held her up. They were on the grass, and it was wet. Her sneakers were quickly soaked, and she thought of her white shorts getting drenched. She looked out toward the lake and could see the dark water ahead with the lighter shape of the dock that stuck out into the water. That was where they were headed, and she knew that it was poison. The darkness was suffocating until it was quickly washed away.

The dark night lit up in a brilliant and stark light that made Liza step backward against Josh's vice-like grip. The suddenness of the illumination also affected Josh because his tight grip on her forearm let go and Liza was now free. She looked up, and what she saw sent a terror through her unlike any she could have ever imagined. The black hole had come alive. The circular shape was now visible and vivid as incredible bright white light glowed from the ring. It was the whitest light she had ever seen, and she needed to turn her gaze away from it. It was like staring at the sun. It was towering very close to them, right over the dock as if it had expected them to go there. To Liza, it was huge and smelled of death. The black hole had indeed moved from the far side of the lake and was now directly in front of the lodge, just waiting for its chance to devour something that moved. She was that something and she was beyond terror.

Josh was standing next to her, making an odd mumbling sound while he stared at the light. It defined a perfect circle that rotated slowly in a counterclockwise motion. Liza found that despite the incredible brilliance, she had to stare at the circle, as it was impossible to draw her gaze away. The light was so intense that she hadn't noticed the noise for a few seconds. It was loud, kind of like a motorcycle with crazy exhaust pipes. Maybe it sounded like the space shuttle *Enterprise* lifting off. This wasn't that kind of roar, but instead it reminded her of a very loud, deep-toned lawn tractor. She couldn't pin the noise down and she suddenly wondered why it mattered. It was there and it was powerful. The noise hit her and made her clothes vibrate.

"Wha…," Josh mumbled. Liza knew that he was finished and that there was no saving him. Even if she could, he was probably the last person on earth that she would try and save, anyway. Something inside her head, something instinctual that needed to survive, screamed for her to move. The paralysis that had gripped her lessened, and she felt her feet shift. There was no choice. The time to move was now, and she needed to use all her energy to get away from Josh and maybe—just maybe—the thing would leave her alone. As she moved her right foot in the direction away from Josh, the light circulating around the black hole increased in intensity. It was spinning at a frantic rate, much faster than anything that she could imagine. The effect was hypnotic, and instead of running away, Liza stopped again and stared at the force in front of her. It had caught her. This would be her end, and she found herself waiting for the moment, resigned to the termination of her consciousness.

In a flash of intense whitish green light, a beam shot out from the center of the circle. The sudden flare startled her, and she stepped backward but didn't fall. A shockwave struck her, and a crack boomed in her head. It was like standing next to a bolt of lightning, but this did not rapidly disperse. The beam hit Josh square in the chest, and his body went rigid with his arms extended stiffly to his sides. Liza watched in horror as the light entered his body and began to move inside Josh's torso. She could still hear the engine noise, along with a snappy electric sound and a gurgling that she realized came from Josh. Oh, he was done. The big, powerful football player was being eaten alive, no match for this monstrosity. Josh's body began to move like a sack with dozens of snakes in it before it crumpled and hit the ground. When she had witnessed the black hole devour Mr. and Mrs. Winsor, the light had instantaneously retracted into the black hole when the bodies hit the earth. To her horror, this didn't happen this time, and instead of retracting, the beam began to move across the grass toward her.

"Oh no," she muttered, understanding the truth. This was it, and she wondered if it was going to hurt. She thought of her mom, brother, and their crappy little house in Mayson. She thought that there should have been better memories, but that really didn't matter.

There was no attempt to run. Like a cornered prey, she waited for her end.

The beam made its way across the grass, casting a circle on the ground no more than a foot in diameter. She could hear the grass sizzle as the light crossed the lawn. She thought she now knew the thoughts of a condemned man the moment before they sent the current through the electric chair. This was the end.

*****

Davey followed the kids outside the building with incomprehensible horror. What Josh was doing was so far from sanity that it was hard to believe what he was seeing. The kid was actually walking out into the line of fire. It was suicide.

The black hole had animated, and the light had flooded the lawn with bright light. The black hole was now hovering over the lake right in front of the resort.

"It fucking moved," Davey heard someone say behind him, probably coming from Dan or Pete. That didn't much matter. The realization that the thing had moved and was now hunting them sent a shiver of cold horror through him. It appeared that it did have a conscious mind and was able to track its prey. They were in serious trouble but nothing like the trouble the girl was in now.

The sound cranked up as it had before, and the light around the hole began to buzz around in a circle. The object was much closer than before, and Davey could now actually see just how fast it moved. Faster than anything he had ever seen, and he found himself staring at it. Then the beam shot out and struck Josh in the chest. The kid was through, and it was awful. Davey watched for a moment until something made him move. He ran down the steps of the patio and watched Josh's now very lifeless body hit the grass. The beam slowly began to move toward the girl. Liza was going to be next, and that was not acceptable. He could see that she was frozen in place and was about to become a victim. Davey sprinted. Instinct now controlled his body.

In an instant that seemed like a crazy blur, Davey ran past a ridiculously bright circle of light on the ground that was only a couple of feet from Liza. Drawing some kind of adrenaline-filled strength, Davey launched himself through the air Superman-style and hit Liza near her hip.

"Move!" he yelled as he hit the ground. Pain shot up through his hip, and he let out a scream at the hurt. Probably broken, he thought vaguely. Liza had been knocked a few feet away and lay on the ground. Davey looked at her and saw her terror but didn't comprehend until it was too late. He heard a sizzling noise and looked toward the lake. The beam was almost upon him, and he couldn't move. He thought of Jeanne, and an emptiness unlike any he could have ever created in a novel gripped his heart. He hoped she would be okay. Then the brightness turned black.

*****

Pete watched Davey from the porch and was shocked by his actions.

"No! Davey, no!"

He yelled but he knew it was pointless. The beam struck his friend, and that was it. All the fear and anxiety were immediately replaced by a sadness unlike any he had ever felt before. Davey was dead, and the beam would move on and get the girl who lay on the grass next to Davey's body. His heroic actions were certainly brave but pointless because she was going to get it, anyway. So stupid. Such a waste.

The night was abruptly flung back into complete darkness. The beam had disappeared, and the black hole had once again gone dark. The horrible small engine noise also ceased, leaving a deep silence in its wake. Pete could hear Liza crying out on the grass but couldn't see her. She was alive, but he wanted to get her out of the way of the black hole as quickly as possible.

"Liza," he whispered as loudly as he felt possible, "come here. Move."

"Wait," Dan said next to him. He placed a hand on Pete's shoulder, and a bolt of pain shot through his shoulder.

"What?" Pete responded. "Jesus, we need to get her inside."

"It's moving."

Pete turned and gazed over the water. The night was dark, and it was nearly impossible to see anything, but yes, he could tell that the horror was backing away from the lodge, back out over the water. He realized he could feel the release of its pressure more than he actually could see it move away. They stood silent and still for a full minute before the end began. A brilliant white light exploded above the lake from the far side, very close to Davey's place. The entire lake was illuminated by the glow, and a weird hue covered the water, trees, and Liza standing on the grass. The black hole was now a ball of light that descended toward the water, casting an eerie reflection across the water. The light suddenly dimmed and turned greenish, and they all knew what they were witnessing. The object was returning into the lake. The water began to glow a brilliant greenish white as the brightness that had been cast on the lakeside was cut off. The light in the lake shrunk, coalescing into a smaller but still very bright patch. They watched until the light slowly blinked out, leaving the lake in complete darkness.

No one moved. There were no screams of triumph. Pete felt as if he had just run a marathon, boxed Muhammad Ali, and gone to his best friend's wake all in the last couple hours. It appeared that it was over, and all he wanted to do was leave. Liza made her way up the stairs to the porch. The dull light from inside the lodge cast shadows on the face of a girl who had gotten a glimpse of hell and returned with the memory. He wondered if she would ever be the same again. Hell, would any of them ever be the same again?

30

Two years later
June 30, 1:03 p.m.

It was a gorgeous day. They couldn't have ordered a brighter, warmer day. It was perfect. The new era of Tall Pines Resort was about to launch, and he beamed with pride and satisfaction.

Adam Tompkins stood at the end of the dock and couldn't help but marvel at the good fortune that had fallen into their lap. He and his wife, Amy, were embarking on their second career, and it was about to set sail. It was truly a dream come true.

"Pretty freaking awesome," he muttered to himself as he gazed over the glassy water.

It was awesome. The two of them loved the mountains. For Adam, it went back to his upbringing in New Hampshire where the mountains were a part of life. The influence of the hills never departed his soul, and he found himself drawn to the higher terrain. Amy had had to learn. She was from the Mohawk Valley, close to Schenectady, and grew up in a small town that was dominated by the river. They had met at Union College and had fallen hard for each other. Amy studied to become a teacher, and he had dabbled in engineering. Out of school, Amy had landed a teaching job immediately, and he had found a job as the manager of a local ski area just north of Utica. They settled into a routine that was pleasant and before long yielded a child, Lansing.

Every chance they got, they vacationed in the Adirondacks. They lived exceedingly close, so jaunts to Old Forge, Saranac Lake, and North Creek were common forays. Hiking, kayaking, and white-water rafting were part of their routine. With every trip, Adam found himself falling deeper in love with the mountains.

He chuckled out loud as he recalled the very moment when the idea first emerged between them. They had been staying at a small hotel on Long Lake, sitting by the water in Adirondack chairs, sipping from a couple of bottles of beer. The moment had been ideal, and the inspiration had just popped out between the two of them as if they had read each other's minds. They both thought it would be a wonderful idea to run a motel in the mountains. They could entertain tourists in the summer and snowmobilers in the winter. The plan fit perfectly into their present situations and seemed absurdly ideal.

Immediately Adam began searching the real estate pages on the Internet in the hopes of finding a small motel that they could buy, fix up, and earn a profit on until they retired. That was still decades away, but what an investment it was in their future. To his dismay, the number of real estate options for sale were limited, and he was about to give up when he stumbled upon a gem in the rough. There was a large piece of property that was a former resort for sale at a ludicrously low price. At first, he couldn't believe it and called the real estate agent listed on the page. Only two days later, Adam and Amy were walking the property of their dreams, and there was no question about their plan of action. The bank was accommodating at the price listed, and they put in an offer. It seemed the previous owner was living somewhere in Vermont and wanted to dispose of the property quickly. It appeared that Adam and Amy entered the scene at exactly the right time.

He heard wooden planks creak and felt his feet wobble slightly. He turned and saw Amy walking toward him down the dock with a bright smile on her face. She was happy, and that was all that mattered. As she got nearer, he could still see the white splotches on her hands and thighs from the painting she had done. All the buildings on the property had gotten a good once-over. The place looked brand-spanking-new.

"Isn't this amazing?" he asked her rhetorically. Of course, it was.

"Adam," she answered, "I am so amazingly happy."

Adam could see it and knew that she wasn't lying. She was sincerely content, and that was all he needed.

"Are we ready?"

Amy nodded. "Oh yeah."

The first guests would arrive the next day, July first. They had set the date to make sure that all would be in perfect readiness. In fact, they had waited ten months for this moment. All was in order.

She looked at him. "This will be better than it has been before."

He nodded, knowing that she was correct. It seemed that the resort had been open for nearly forty successful years before it abruptly closed down two years earlier. The realtor divulged that there had been an issue that had caused the closure. Five people had disappeared at and near the resort. All were presumed dead. It appeared that a severe thunderstorm moved through the area that fateful day, and guests recalled seeing some bizarre phenomenon over the lake that was most likely associated with the turbulent prestorm atmosphere. St. Elmo's Fire. Ball lightning. No one really pinpointed it, but the storm had been fierce and drove the guests away. No one ever found the five missing people. When Adam heard that, he took a deep breath but convinced himself that sometimes Mother Nature could be mean as hell. It was a risk that everyone took living on earth every day.

They both looked around the lake with the hills rising from the shores in all shades of green. June had been wet, and the trees and grass had benefitted, blazing in their green colors. It was truly a stunning scene. Adam turned to the shore and saw Lansing playing in the sand by the beach—the beach where he hoped guests would frolic and have a completely enjoyable time.

"Doesn't seem like a place where there are a lot of earthquakes."

Adam turned and looked at his wife.

"Stop it," he said. "It's just a bunch of people who don't like outsiders."

The only unsettling aspect of the launch of their resort was from the local populace. Adam had immediately tried to track down the previous caretaker to try and hire him but learned that he had committed suicide not long after the resort had closed. That was tragic, but the really weird thing was that no locals seemed willing to work at the resort. In fact, when he had inquired in the local town, the most common comment was not "Yes, I would love a job," but "Watch out for earthquakes." Earthquakes? Adam had quickly done some research and had learned that indeed the Adirondacks were prone to earthquakes, but most were so small they were hardly noticeable. In fact, quakes that actually caused damage were exceedingly rare and more common in Missouri! The caution seemed unwarranted.

They needed to hire workers from outside, but that had turned out to be a nonissue. People were more than willing to spend a summer at a mountain resort. It would become more attractive with the plans for a spa, in-ground pool, and Jacuzzis the following summer. The locals could continue eating woodchuck for all he cared. It was their loss.

"Mom and Dad are here," Amy said, waving toward shore. Her mother and father were going to stay in one of the cabins for the grand opening. They were pulling out the stops. Bonfires. Cookouts. Fireworks. It would be awesome. Adam and Amy hoped that her father might stay on after his retirement the next year and manage the resort while they were away. Keep it in the family.

"I love you," Amy said, and their heads leaned together for a brief but devoted kiss.

"Love you," he responded as she turned and walked back down the dock to greet her family. Lansing jumped from the sand and was now running across the lawn toward his grandparents. It was perfect, and Adam felt a tear well up in his eye. How could he have gotten so lucky?

He turned from the scene and looked out over the glassy waters of the lake. It was certainly a perfect panorama, and he understood that he was very close to heaven. Things were going his way, and nothing could derail their future. Tall Pines Resort would open the following day, and he was positive that it would be a huge success. There would be many blissful years owning part of the mountains, and he couldn't wait.

Adam smiled as a sense of security shot through his body. He grinned and gazed across the waters of Moon Lake.

About the Author

L.J. Russell grew up in Geneva, New York. A 1988 graduate of Middlebury College, L.J. experienced a number of jobs before settling into teaching after receiving a master's degree from Syracuse University. He teaches US History and has coached the varsity lacrosse team in Geneva. When he isn't teaching, he is hanging out by the water on Skaneateles Lake, often taking his boat around the lake. Nights sitting on the dock watching the water has had a dramatic impact on the direction of his writing. In the winter, he loves skiing, a sport where he spent eighteen years as a professional ski instructor.

The writing bug hit him early on as he drifted, searching for a career. Where writing has been a hobby, he has written seven books over thirty years. The idea for *The Moon Lake Legend* entered his mind and was developed through a love for the Adirondacks and after reading many H.P. Lovecraft stories. The dark woods and the secrets kept within has always intrigued him and has become the perfect setting for this story.